Book Lovers
Appreciation
Society

CECELIA AHERN completed a degree in journalism and media studies before embarking on her writing career at twenty-one years of age. Her first novel *PS, I Love You* was one of the biggest-selling debut books of 2004 and a number one bestseller. Her successive novels are *Where Rainbows End*, *If You Could See Me Now*, *A Place Called Here*, *Thanks for the Memories* and *The Gift*. She has sold close to eleven million copies worldwide and is published in over forty-five countries. *PS, I Love You*, starring Hilary Swank, is now a major motion picture. Cecelia is also the co-creator of ABC's hit comedy series *Samantha Who* starring Christine Applegate. Cecelia is twenty-seven years old and is currently completing her seventh novel.

MAEVE BINCHY published her first novel, *Light A Penny Candle*, in 1982. Since then she has written many more best-selling novels and short story collections, including *The Glass Lake*, *Whitethorn Woods* and *Circle of Friends*, which was made into a film starring Minnie Driver. Maeve has received numerous awards for her work including the Lifetime Achievement Award at the British Book Awards in 1999. She lives in Dalkey, Ireland, with her husband, writer Gordon Snell. Her latest novel is the number one bestseller, *Heart and Soul*.

MAVIS CHEEK was born and grew up in Wimbledon. She began her working life at Editions Alecto, the contemporary art publishers. After Alecto she attended Hillcroft College for Women from where she graduated in Arts. In 1979 her daughter, Bella, was born, and she began her writing career in earnest; journalism and travel writing at first, then short stories, and eventually, in 1988, her novel, *Pause Between Acts*, was published by Bodley Head and won the *She*/John Menzies First Novel Prize. Mavis Cheek is the author of thirteen novels including *Mrs Fytton's Country Life*, *Janice Gentle Gets Sexy* and, most recently, *Amenable Women*, which was described in *The Times* as 'a brilliantly funny, warm, intelligent read'. She now lives and writes in the heart of the English countryside.

ROWAN COLEMAN lives in Hertfordshire with her daughter. She wrote her first novel, *Growing up Twice*, after winning a Young Writer of the Year award in 2001, and consequently acquired both a literary agent and a publisher. In order to pursue her writing full-time, Rowan gave up her seven-year career in bookselling and publishing, and has since penned the Ruby Parker series (aimed at fame-obsessed teenage girls, it tells the many adventures of thirteen-year-old Ruby, who is famous), as well as a further seven novels for adults including *The Baby Group*, *The Accidental Mother*, *The Accidental Wife* and her latest novel, *The Accidental Family*.

BARBARA ERSKINE is the author of ten bestselling novels, including *Child of the Phoenix*, *Kingdom of Shadows* and *Lady of Hay*, which has sold over two million copies worldwide, and her books have been translated into twenty-six languages. She divides her time between north Essex and Hay-on-Wye. Her latest book is *The Warrior's Princess*.

JANE FALLON shot to fame after publication of her debut novel, *Getting Rid of Matthew*, in 2007. Jennifer Aniston's new production company, Echo Films, is to produce the film adaptation, due out in 2010, with Jennifer taking the starring role. Previously, Jane was a television producer, working on successful shows such as *This Life*, *Single* and *Teachers*, which is Channel 4's most successful drama to date. Her latest novel is *Got You Back*.

KATIE FFORDE is married and has three grown-up children. She has lived in Gloucestershire for over twenty years. Before she became a writer, she ran a narrow-boat hotel in the Midlands before going to live in Wales with her husband. Katie has written fourteen novels, including *Practically Perfect*, *Going Dutch* and her latest release, *Wedding Season*. Every story is based on her own, personal experiences and the short story in this collection was inspired by a holiday in Dominica earlier this year. Katie has several unusual hobbies and ways to keep fit; flamenco dancing is a current passion. Her favourite summer day would be walking the dogs in the Golden Valley, ending up at a local pub for lunch with friends.

ANNE FINE has written eight novels for adults, including *Raking the Ashes*, *Telling Liddy* and *Fly in the Ointment*. The most recent is her black comedy, *Our Precious Lulu*. Anne Fine has also written many prize-winning children's books, including *Flour Babies*, *The Tulip Touch* and *Goggle Eyes*. In 1993, her novel *Madame Doubtfire* was made into the hit film *Mrs Doubtfire*. Anne was Children's Laureate from 2001 to 2003, and awarded an OBE in 2003. She lives in County Durham and has two grown-up daughters. Her website is www.annefine.co.uk.

NICCI FRENCH is the husband and wife writing partnership of Nicci Gerard and Sean French. The couple live in Suffolk with their four children. Together, they have written twelve bestselling novels, including *Land of the Living*, *Killing Me Softly*, and *Until It's Over*. Their latest novel is *What to do When Someone Dies*.

PHILIPPA GREGORY is a historian and author of several international bestsellers about the Tudor period including *The Other Boleyn Girl* and a new series about the Plantagenets that begins with *The White Queen*. She is also the founder of a charity, Gardens for the Gambia, that builds wells for the primary schools of this poor African country. She lives with her family on a small farm in Yorkshire, and welcomes visitors to her website at philippagregory.com.

TESSA HADLEY's first novel was published in 2002. Her most recent work is a novel, *The Master Bedroom*, and a collection of short stories, *Sunstroke*. Tessa teaches literature and creative writing at Bath Spa University and lives in Cardiff with her partner and the youngest of her three sons.

VICTORIA HISLOP was a journalist before writing her first book, *The Island*, which became a UK bestseller. Hailed as the new *Captain Corelli's Mandolin*, it was selected by the Richard and Judy Book Club for its 2006 'Summer Reads' and earned Victoria 'Best Newcomer' at the 2007 British Book Awards. Her second novel, *The Return*, published in 2008, is set against a backdrop of the Spanish Civil War and was also a *Sunday Times* number one bestseller. She lives in Kent with her husband, Ian, and their two children, Emily and William.

WENDY HOLDEN has written nine bestselling novels. She grew up in Yorkshire and was a journalist on the *Sunday Times* and the *Mail on Sunday* before turning to full-time writing. She regularly writes features for newspapers and magazines on a range of social, topical and lifestyle subjects and is also a regular television and radio contributor. She is married with two young children and lives in Derbyshire. Her novels include *Simply Divine*, *The Wives of Bath*, *The School for Husbands*, *Filthy Rich* and, most recently, *Beautiful People*.

DOUGLAS KENNEDY was born and raised in Manhattan. He is the author of nine novels and three travel books. He has two children and divides his time between London, Paris, Berlin and Maine. His novels have been translated into twenty-one languages. In 2006 he was awarded the French decoration, the *Chevalier de l'Ordre des Arts et des Lettres*.

SOPHIE KINSELLA is the international bestselling author of the hugely popular Shopaholic series as well as the number one bestsellers *Can You Keep a Secret?*, *The Undomestic Goddess* and *Remember Me?*. Her new novel, *Twenties Girl*, was published in July 2009. She lives in London with her husband and children.

DEBORAH LAWRENSON spent much of her childhood travelling around the world with her family and living in countries such as Kuwait, China, Belgium, Luxembourg and Singapore before reading English at Cambridge. Deborah then pursued a career in journalism. Her first novel, *Hot Gossip* (a satire based on her experience working on a diary column), was published in 1994 and its sequel, *Idol Chatter*, followed in 1995. Other works include *The Moonbathers*, *The Art of Falling*, and her most recent release, *Songs of Blue and Gold*.

KATHY LETTE was born in Australia and is the author of ten novels, including the number one bestsellers *Foetal Attraction* and *Mad Cows*, which was turned into a film starring award-winning actress Anna Friel. She is now published in sixteen languages. The characters in her story 'The Wedding Anniversary' first appeared in *How to Kill Your Husband (and Other Handy Household Hints)*. Kathy lives in London with her husband, Geoffrey, and their two children. Her latest bestseller is *To Love, Honour and Betray (Till Divorce Us Do Part)*.

SARAH-KATE LYNCH worked as a journalist before writing her first novel, *Blessed Are the Cheesemakers*, in 2003. She has since written the bestsellers *By Bread Alone*, *Eating with the Angels* and *House of Joy*. She is married and based in New Zealand.

ALEXANDER MCCALL SMITH was Professor of Medical Law at the University of Edinburgh for many years. He has written over sixty books to date, but is perhaps best known for his award-winning series *The No 1 Ladies' Detective Agency*. The tenth instalment is *Tea Time for the Traditionally Built*. Alexander lives in Edinburgh with his wife, Elizabeth.

MARK MILLS' first novel *The Whaleboat House* won the 2004 Crime Writers' Association Award for Best First Novel and his second novel, *The Savage Garden*, was a number one bestseller. He is also a screenwriter and his film credits include *The Reckoning*, starring Paul Bettany. He lives in Oxford with his wife and two children. His latest book is *The Information Officer*.

SANTA MONTEFIORE has sold over two million copies of her bestsellers, which include *Meet Me Under the Ombu Tree*, *The Forget-me-not Sonata* and *The Gypsy Madonna*, and they have been translated into twenty languages. She lives in London with her husband, award-winning historian Simon Sebag Montefiore, and their two children. Her latest novel is *The Italian Matchmaker*.

ELIZABETH NOBLE published her first novel, *The Reading Group*, in 2004, and it became an international bestseller. Subsequent books include *The Tenko Club*, *Alphabet Weekends*, *The Friendship Test*, *Things I Want my Daughters to Know* and *The Girl Next Door*. Elizabeth lives in New York with her husband and two daughters.

FREYA NORTH'S first novel *Sally* was published in 1996 to great acclaim and her nine subsequent novels have all been bestsellers with *Pillow Talk* winning the Romantic Novel of the Year Award in 2008. Her tenth novel, *Secrets*, is out now. She lives in London with her family.

HAZEL OSMOND is the winner of the *woman&home* short story competition in 2008 (in association with Costa Book Awards). She is a freelance advertising copywriter and lives in Northumberland with her husband, Matt, and their two daughters, Kate and Becky.

ADELE PARKS has sold well over a million copies of her eight bestsellers, which include *Husbands*, *Playing Away*, *Young Wives' Tales* and *Tell Me Something*. Her ninth novel, *Love Lies*, was published in July 2009. She also frequently writes short stories and articles for newspapers and magazines. She lives in Guildford, Surrey, with her husband and son.

ANNA RALPH lives in Durham with her partner Daniel and daughter, Jessie. Her mother is Booker Prize-winning author Pat Barker, something that she admits initially put her off becoming a novelist herself. After leaving school at the age of sixteen (university didn't appeal to her) and working at the local Waterstone's, Anna spent a number of years in PR and journalism. In 2007, she published her first novel, *The Floating Island*, and her second, *Before I Knew Him*, followed in quick succession.

JENNY STEEL, a retired teacher, is the winner of the *woman&home* short story competition in 2007 (in association with Costa Book Awards). She lives in Bredon, Gloucestershire, with her husband Richard. They have three grown-up children and three grandchildren.

ROSIE THOMAS is the author of a number of celebrated novels, including the bestsellers *Sun at Midnight* and *Iris and Ruby*, and twice winner of the Romantic Novel of the Year Award, in 1985 and 2007. Once she was established as a writer and her children were grown up, she discovered a love of travelling and mountaineering. She lives in London. Her forthcoming novel is *Lovers and Newcomers*.

ADRIANA TRIGIANI is the author of nine bestselling books, which include the *Big Stone Gap* trilogy, *Queen of the Big Time* and *Lucia, Lucia*, which was selected by the Richard and Judy Book Club and nominated for a British Book Award. Her new novel, *Very Valentine*, is set in Greenwich Village, where Adriana lives with her husband, Tim, and daughter, Lucia. www.adrianatrigiani.com.

JOANNA TROLLOPE is the author of fifteen novels, which include the number one bestsellers *The Rector's Wife* and *Second Honeymoon*. She also writes historical novels under the pen name Caroline Harvey. Joanna was appointed OBE in the 1996 Queen's Birthday Honours List. She lives in London, and has two daughters and two stepsons. Her latest novel is the number one bestseller, *Friday Nights*.

JANE ELIZABETH VARLEY lectured in law before writing her first novel, *Wives and Lovers*. It was published in 2003 and she now writes full-time. She is married with a son and a daughter and divides her time between London and the United States. Her most recent novel is *Dearest Rivals*.

Introduction

BY GERI HALLIWELL

*T*his book is like a cosy box of chocolates, each story has its individuality and comfort. Every night I went to bed saying to myself I'll just read one story, but just like chocolate I had to indulge in one more! As a massive book lover I have to say it's an ingenious way of getting a fast fix of bite size stories for busy women who don't have the time or energy to get stuck into a massive novel.

The thing I love about short stories is that they're short, which means they have to gloriously grip you from the start, and these do. Some immediately transported me into a world of intimacy and love – there's a lot of love in this book together with a mixture of failure, success and humour.

These great stories are written by an amazing range of respected authors. Of course I have my favourites, but the standard of all the writing is incredibly high. And one of the most exciting things about them is that they are specially written for us females, us women!

It's such an inspiration that *woman&home* has been able to bring all of these tremendous tales together in one book, but what's equally exciting is the way that the book will help women affected by breast cancer.

As a patron of Breast Cancer Care I know just how vital its work is in supporting people affected by the disease. As well as providing top quality information through an amazing range of resources – all for free – the charity brings people together, giving them the chance to share experiences and support each other through what can be a truly distressing time.

Breast Cancer Care will receive £1 from every copy sold, which means it can continue to offer all of its wonderful services for free.

So by buying this book, not only are you guaranteed a good read, you know that you're helping women, men and their families touched by breast cancer.

the Book Lovers' Appreciation Society

Stories by
**CECELIA AHERN, MAEVE BINCHY,
VICTORIA HISLOP, WENDY HOLDEN,
SOPHIE KINSELLA, KATE MOSSE,
JOANNA TROLLOPE**
and many more . . .

First published in Great Britain in 2009
by Orion Books
an imprint of the Orion Publishing Group Ltd
Orion House, 5 Upper St Martin's Lane,
London, WC2H 9EA

An Hachette UK company

3 5 7 9 10 8 6 4 2

Compilation copyright © The Orion Publishing Group Ltd, 2009
For copyright of individual stories please see pg 409

All stories have previously been published in
woman&home magazine.

A CIP catalogue record for this book
is available from the British Library.

ISBN 978 1 4091 1737 7

Typeset at The Spartan Press Ltd,
Lymington, Hants

Printed in Great Britain by Clays Ltd, St Ives plc

The Orion Publishing Group's policy is to use papers
that are natural, renewable and recyclable products and
made from wood grown in sustainable forests. The logging
and manufacturing processes are expected to conform to
the environmental regulations of the country of origin.

www.orionbooks.co.uk

Contents

Mallard and May

BY CECELIA AHERN

'Ah, this is the life, isn't it, May?' Mallard sighs with satisfaction, as he makes himself comfortable along the lakeshore.

The crystal-blue water shimmers beneath the light of the sunrise, its ripples appearing like goose pimples as morning warmth touches cold. The water moves up and down as though, like Mallard, it takes a giant sigh of relaxation; breathing in and then releasing. The sun slowly rises, by far the largest buoy in the large lake. The more it peeps above the horizon, the further the orange glow seeps from the sun and spills its way, like ink, towards Mallard on the shore. His personal pathway to the sun. He knows things can't possibly get any better than this. Him and May, back in Ireland at last after a winter spent at their holiday home in South Africa.

'It's lovely, love.' May fidgets beside him, restless as always as she picks at some bread.

'You're not too cold? We could go somewhere else if you're cold.'

'No, I'm nice and warm, pet.'

'Are you tired after the flight? You look a bit tired. Maybe we should have gone straight home instead of stopping off here.'

'I am a bit tired, Mallard. It felt longer than usual. Or maybe I'm just getting old.'

'Well, it can't be that,' Mallard smiles. 'It must have been longer than usual. Why don't you go for a dip?'

'That's a good idea.' She brightens up and hops over the harsh pebbles that border the lake.

Mallard looks out to the lake and spots familiar characters bobbing nearby in the waters. He quickly follows after her. 'Actually I'll join you, May. Those French lads over there were on the flight with us. Never stopped jabbering on for a second. Do you remember them?'

'Oh, you know me, love, I was in my own world. I was just watching the view for the entire journey.'

'Well that's what I wanted to do too but it was just *bonjour* this, *oui oui* that, all the way over. And I wouldn't trust them; males such as those just come over here to ruffle a few feathers, if you know what I mean.'

'Oh, Mallard,' May laughs. 'You exaggerate too much. They look like they're a friendly bunch to me.'

'Of course they do, that's what they want you to think. For Christ's sake don't look now, May, they're looking right over at us! Ah, hello there!' he calls across to them and adds under his breath, 'They're coming over.'

'*Bonjour.*'

'Eh yeah, *bonjour* to you, too. Enjoy your flight?'

'*Oui, oui*, it was *très* pleasant. Scenery was spectacular all of the way. Let us introduce ourselves – *je m'appelle* Pierre and this is my brother, Jean-Paul.'

'Nice to meet you,' May says politely.

'This is my wife May and I'm Mallard.'

'Ah! Mallard!' He laughs.

'Yes, my parents were imaginative,' he says, feeling himself heat up.

'What a charming name,' Pierre smiles. '*Enchanté.*'

Jean-Paul doesn't say anything. Mallard eyes him suspiciously.

The four of them bob up and down rhythmically in the water. The motion is soothing and the gentle breeze of the morning sun tickles and brightens their faces, like a paintbrush on canvas.

May disappears as she dives head down into the water, and not being the best conversationalist in the world, particularly with strangers, Mallard looks around awkwardly.

'So, Mallard, are you from around here?'

'No, no, we live more inland, Carrick-on-Shannon to be precise, but thought we'd give this Lake Corrib a crack, seein' as it was such a lovely day and all, and we've heard so much about it. We always travel with a large group, from in and around the same area, but we just thought we'd go out on our own for a little while. We'll head home shortly.'

May, who's still head down, kicks the surface of the water and manages to splash the three of them.

'Eh, sorry about that. May's a keen diver.' He watches the soles of her feet, splish, splash. 'We've got a place in South Africa where we spend the winter but it's always nice to get back home, isn't it?'

'*Bien sûr. J'adore* Ireland. We come every year.'

'Is that so? Seems these days it's the other way around, with the country doing so well and all, the skies are filled with planeloads of people flying out to their holiday homes. Can't get away from the Irish at all, I find,' Mallard says seriously.

To his confusion, they both laugh and Mallard can't relax until May pops back up from the water.

'Where do you stay when you're here, Pierre?' she asks, shaking off the water from her face, sending droplets flying into Mallard's eyes.

'Every year we have spent months in Dublin city. *J'adore* Dublin. We spent most of our days in St Stephen's Green in Dublin. The weather was splendid; such a lovely park with a lake and waterfall. We have been every year, but for last year.'

Jean-Paul shoots him a warning look.

'Where did you go last year?' Mallard asks curiously, unsure of Pierre's brother.

'We stayed in Kildare last year but never again, now it harbours such sad memories for us.' Pierre's tone changes.

Jean-Paul, who has been silent for practically the entire conversation, looks away from his brother and floats ever so slightly away from them, detaching himself from the conversation.

Mallard, not good with emotions, looks to May for help. He cocks his head sideways, motioning for her to say something to the upset Pierre.

'Oh, Pierre,' May says softly, 'I do hope everything is OK.'

'*Non, mon frère, pardonnez moi*, my brother. We lost him on our last trip to Ireland.'

'Oh dear,' May says. 'How did you lose him?'

'He was shot.'

'Shot?!' she gasps. 'Sweet lord, where on earth, how on earth, who on earth would shoot him here?'

'We were exploring the area, we had never been to Kildare before. July last year. *Très* green, lots of golf courses, very pretty. But we see men with guns and they bang! bang! and Luc – he fall down.'

May gasps and moves closer to Mallard for protection.

'But surely the men were caught? And punished? I hope they were locked away for life,' Mallard says, feeling angry.

'*Non*. I'm sure these men were not, for there was nothing we could do. We had to leave him, to save ourselves. That I will never forgive myself for, but if we were to stay in the area we would be like sitting ducks. We do not know who the thugs are, where they are and how we can prove anything to anyone.'

Jean-Paul looks to him with concern and Pierre responds, '*Je vais bien*, Jean-Paul. *Merci*.'

Mallard is suspicious.

'Oh that's awful,' May sobs.

'Now, now, love.'

'What is the world coming to, at all?'

'*Oui*, the violence. So unfair, so unjust.'

'I'm surprised you'd want to return here at all,' Mallard says.

'We flew to the north of England but it was *très froid*. Perhaps we will one day return to our home country, France, but we prefer it here and Luc would have wanted us to return to this place that we journeyed to together. We travelled here from South Africa with many friends, as I'm sure you saw on our flight, and we will stay with them. *Écoutez moi*, safety in numbers, Mallard and May, remember that.'

'Yes,' Mallard says, huddling closer to his wife. 'Indeed.'

'Maybe we should go back home now, Mallard?' May asks in a quiet voice. 'Back to our friends and family.'

'Yes, my love. Perhaps we should.'

They say their goodbyes and Mallard and May watch Pierre and Jean-Paul exit the lake and make their way back to their group.

'Oh, how sad, Mallard. I don't know what I'd do if I ever lost you.'

'And I too, my love, I too.'

'You know I've wanted to thank you for not leaving me after we had the little ones . . .'

'Now, now, May,' he interrupts. 'There's no need to get into all of that. It's in the past now.'

'No, Mallard,' she turns to face him. 'I want to talk

about it, you never let me talk about it. Most of my friends and Susie just recently . . . as soon as they had the little ones, their other halves were off. I've heard of it all too often. I don't know why they felt they all had to form that little male group together,' she says angrily. Then she softens. 'But you didn't. You stayed with me and I appreciate that.'

Mallard takes in her little face, browned and soft. He smiles, 'I couldn't have left you, my love, not for a second.'

'But I am so plain and you aren't. You are . . .'

'Hush, May, why are you speaking like this? I love you. We beat all the odds, didn't we? All these years together?'

She nods, happily.

'Now, let's get back to the rest of them, shall we?'

They bob up and down in the water for a little while longer, watching the sun rising in the sky, feeling content and safe with one another and savouring the moment. Mallard nuzzles May and they smile at one another.

Shortly after the sun has pulled itself out of the water, they leave the lake, dry off and begin their journey home. After many pleasant hours spent journeying through the countryside, they reach the outskirts of their home town.

'It's very quiet around here, isn't it?' May comments to Mallard, as they make their way through the village and to the peace and quiet of their home beyond it.

'Indeed it is, I wonder if there's something going on? A gathering somewhere of some kind?'

BANG! BANG! BANG!

The loudest noise in the distance, so sudden, May lets out a scream.

'My goodness, Mallard! What on earth?!'

'Stay close, my love, stay close.' Mallard's heart slams in his chest while May whimpers beside him.

'Is it the people that Pierre was talking about?' Her voice trembles.

'It can't be, my love.' But Mallard doesn't sound so sure. 'We must make our way as quietly as possible. Find somewhere safe to hide until they have gone. Honestly, a few months out of this country and look what happens. It feels like a war zone; what on earth has happened? Hush now, we must be quiet.'

They quietly make their way through the trees, only minutes from their home, trying to make as few rustling sounds as possible. They hear the men close by and suddenly Mallard feels far too old for this situation. If he was younger, he could be faster but he and May must be still now and very, very quiet. May steps on a branch and it snaps loudly.

BANG! BANG! BANG!

He jumps. There is silence. He glimpses through the leaves, the men are nowhere in sight. He remains quiet a little longer and holds his breath, unsure if they're being tricked. When a few minutes pass, he sighs with relief.

'I think we're OK now, love. I think they've gone.'

May is silent.

His heart thuds again.

'May?' He spins around.

May is lying by his side, her eyes open staring lifelessly at the skies above.

'May,' he begins to whimper. 'Oh, my May. My sweet May. Wake up, love. Wake up.'

But he knows May won't wake, for the life in her has gone. He hears footsteps coming towards him. A hand reaches through the leaves and branches and comes down beside him. He moves away quickly. The hand grabs May and carries her upwards into the air.

'There it is,' the man says. 'That'll do nicely for tomorrow's dinner.'

'Wife will be impressed by a bit of *duck à l'orange*,' the other jokes and they make their way back out of the trees.

Mallard, broken and lost, watches from his hiding place among the reeds, as they carry his May by her legs, hanging her upside down. They make their way through the marsh, their long hunting guns resting over their shoulders.

Now there is nothing but quiet for Mallard. He sits for hours on the muddy ground, listening to the sounds of shots far off in the distance and strains his ears to hear the sound of May's call. But it doesn't come. Anger sets in as he wonders what on earth the world has become. Such sadness overcomes him as he contemplates what his world holds for him without his May.

Hunger – and friends – find him alone and trembling hours later and so, building up all the courage he possibly can, he finally leaves the safety of his hiding place and flies off towards the same sun he had watched rise that morning with May.

With each flap of his wings and with each memory of May, his heavy wings lighten as he allows his love for her to lift him. He floats higher and higher and follows his personal pathway to the sun.

Healthy Option

BY MAEVE BINCHY

*C*arol worked in 'Healthy Heart', a busy upmarket sandwich bar near the financial area. A lot of young men dropped in to pick up a smoothie filled with good fruit and vegetables, and a bran sandwich with a variety of healthy fillings. They concentrated on food that was good for you. The owner, who was called Primrose, often appeared on television.

Primrose always spoke as if her shop was a one-woman outfit. There was never any mention of Carol, who came in early and opened up the shop, spread the low-cholesterol butter substitute on the bread and prepared the fillings, which would be spread on the bran bread.

Primrose dimpled and smiled when congratulated on her efficiency and the success. At no time did she mention that once the breakfast rush was over Carol sat down in the back room and did all the accounts and kept them in order, and then she got ready for the lunchtime invasion. In the afternoon, Carol helped to dream up ideas that would create more publicity for 'Healthy Heart'. She did little recipe leaflets, which they gave out free at the sandwich bar. Sometimes people used these in magazines or even on the television, when Primrose would smile shyly and say she wasn't really all that great, these recipes came naturally to her.

Carol's friend Amy said that Carol was foolish, she allowed Primrose to walk all over her. Primrose had given Carol no credit, very little thanks and not at all an adequate amount of money. But Carol didn't agree, she liked the work, she said – she hadn't put her own money at risk renting the premises, buying the equipment.

'But you never meet anyone there, they rush in and they rush out,' Amy wailed.

Carol realised that Amy was not so much concerned about her social life generally, but about her chances of meeting The Right Man. This concern had increased ever since Amy herself had met Nick (at a friend's wedding) and become a fully paid-up member of the Couples Brigade. Now everything had to be done in pairs; late-night shopping had to be undertaken two by two or it was no use. Carol's persistently single status seemed to have begun to challenge Amy. She talked to Carol of speed dating, internet and blind dates. It was wearying, but Amy would not let up.

Carol found it very difficult to explain that, much as she would like a soul mate – who wouldn't, after all? – she was not prepared to go through this humiliating dance of getting there. Carol said she was useless at small talk, she said it was the stuff of nightmares.

'Well, do something,' Amy begged. 'You're going to grow old and grey in "Healthy Heart" and then Madam will sell the place to some tycoon and they won't want old grey people, and you'll be out on the street and wish you'd done something!' In an awful way it was true.

But what would Carol do?

Oddly enough, she got a possible idea that week.

A nice young man who collected his mango juice and ginger smoothie and his banana and date sandwich at seven o'clock every morning asked if there was anywhere he could learn healthy cooking. He would really prefer a place just for men, he said. He didn't want to look foolish in front of these dynamic, multitasking, frighteningly efficient women. Carol said she would try and find out and discussed it with Amy.

'You could teach cooking to men! What a great idea.' Amy was overjoyed.

'Yes, I suppose it would be good publicity for the sandwich shop if we had it there.' Carol was thoughtful.

'On my knees, Carol, I beg you don't do anything more for Primrose. That woman will claim it all as her idea, when it's my idea. I want you to do it for you.'

'But how? I mean, even if I were to try and do it on my own, where would I give the classes? And how would I find the pupils? How would they get in touch with me?'

Amy had it all sorted. 'You can give them your mobile phone number and you can give the classes in your own flat. We'll put up notices in the supermarket and places.'

'But my place is much too small.'

Carol was stunned to think Amy was taking this seriously.

'No, it's not. We'll tidy it up, give it a coat of paint, take away some of your worst kitsch. We can lay heavy emphasis on small groups and individual attention. They'll love that.'

Amy was so eager that Carol had hardly the heart to argue with her.

Glumly, she watched as Amy got rid of the lovely rugs and fringed pictures and little ornaments. All the magical souvenirs she had picked up in market places abroad were packed away carefully. The place looked spare and empty, and full of clear surfaces. And if Carol was honest, it looked a little dull. There was no soul in it. It was like a show house or something in an advertisement. Still, it was fairly impressive, and her kitchen was a joy to behold, gleaming and clutter-free. She would teach these men to make an easy soup, a chicken dish and zesty salad. That would be Night One. The following week she would do a red onion and tomato tart, a beef stir-fry and a cheat's apple pie.

She went with Amy and put up her advertisement in the local supermarket. And waited.

There were three replies. Perfect. Three men signed up for a course of lessons on the following Thursday. She rang them all and gave instructions on how to get to her flat.

Amy was ecstatic. For the first time ever, it would appear, her friend Carol was going to have three single men in her house. Who knew what might follow?

'We don't know that they are single,' Carol protested.

'They're single,' Amy said. 'Your mother is going to be so pleased.'

'Oh I beg you, don't tell her,' Carol pleaded. 'I can't bear to get her hopes raised yet again.'

On Thursday Carol set out all the ingredients and put on a chef's apron to look professional. As a second thought, she applied some hasty mascara and lip gloss. First to get there was Martin, a handsome gay man, next was Richard, who was an eighteen-year-old student, and finally there was Stephen, who was a brooding, serious man of about fifty.

Carol gave them all a coffee before they began. They looked a little tense and nervous, and she needed them more relaxed. Gradually, they explained why they needed lessons. Richard was going to share an apartment with other university students. The rules had said that once a week everyone had to cook a meal. He had no idea where to start.

Martin said that with today's stereotyping everyone thought all gays could cook like a dream. In his case, this was not true. He got confused and fussed, so wanted to learn confidence. Stephen said that due to circumstances beyond his control and understanding he was suddenly left alone, struggling to manage. His wife, who had gone on some kind of journey to find herself, had disappeared and taken the cookery books with her. He would survive, he explained with a hint of menace.

She got them down to chopping the vegetables for the soup. None of them had heard of stock, so she explained what it was. Carol said that at the moment they could rely on little stock cubes, but later they might learn to make their own.

'If this cube thing is OK, I think I'll stick with that rather than become adventurous,' young Richard had said. The others had nodded in agreement.

They all loved making the Mediterranean chicken. Just stick slivers of garlic in the chicken joints, cover with a jar of olives and a little box of cherry tomatoes and a little olive oil.

'It looks too simple,' said the grumpy Stephen suspiciously. When his wife had been about she made very heavy weather about putting a meal on the table. It couldn't have been as easy as this.

Carol urged them not to tell anyone how easy it was and they could judge later whether it tasted good or not. Then she got them going on the salad and by the time that was chopped and the dressing prepared, the soup was ready and the chicken bubbling nicely. She taught them to clear up as they went along, then how to set a cheerful table. By the time they sat down to eat the results of their efforts they were firm friends.

They all pronounced the food excellent and took their recipe leaflets home with them. She suggested they buy one sharp knife each before next week and also practise making a soup in the meantime. They must be adventurous and choose their own vegetables, maybe parsnip and apples. Perhaps they could invent some amazing dish between them.

She rang Amy the moment they left. 'No luck in the husband hunting but they all said the class was great and they all paid up for ten weeks. I was almost embarrassed to take their money. They helped to wash up and next week they're going to bring a bottle of wine.'

'Well, that sounds good but are you sure about the husband material?' Amy was loath to let the plot go.

'I'm sure.' Carol was firm.

'Did you tell them all about "Healthy Heart" and that pain in the face, Primrose?'

'No, I never mentioned that side of my life at all,' Carol said.

Amy was pleased. There might be some result out of all this.

The weeks went on and Carol got to know her pupils better. Richard said that his new flatmates were so impressed with the steak and kidney pie that they wanted him to make it every week. Martin said that he had made a soup for a buffet party and everyone said it was the best they had ever tasted. Stephen said that he had just made the fish pie and his ex-wife had called to collect some more of her CDs that she had left behind. To be sociable, he had offered to share his supper with her and for the first time in months they had a civil conversation and she forgot to take her CDs. And they got to know Carol too, and enquired about her social life. They had all seen Primrose on television and none of them liked her.

'Bossy boots,' said Martin.

'Very patronising,' Richard agreed.

'You'd be much better,' said Stephen.

It did wonders for her confidence.

Next time Amy started talking about meeting more of the right sort of men, Carol answered with spirit. She said she had plenty of friends. She also said she had serious thoughts about her career and that marriage could come later. A lot later if need be.

Amy was startled at the new Carol, who answered back instead of avoiding things and apologising. 'Career? What career? You work for Primrose in the health food shop?'

'True, but I might not be there forever. I've begun to think I should branch out into something more adventurous.'

On the ninth lesson, the three men said they had a favour to ask. Could they sign on for another ten sessions? They did so enjoy them and their lives were getting better in dozens of ways. They also wondered, could they invite some guests and go through the whole process of having a dinner party?

Carol was delighted. She worked out a dinner party menu and heard that there would be three guests. All men. Stephen would bring a fellow teacher from his school, Richard would bring his uncle and Martin would bring a friend from his exercise class. A straight friend, he said several times, lest there be any misunderstanding.

About an hour before the party Carol realised what they were doing. They were trying to fix her up with someone, they wanted to find her a husband. At first she had felt annoyed and insulted. They were as bad as Amy. But it was too late to do anything about it.

The three visiting men were delightful.

They 'oohed' and 'aahed' about the food and said that Carol was a natural for television. The current television cooks were only in a very poor second place to her.

Soon she began to enjoy the meal and they all planned her entry into the world of entertainment. She wondered fleetingly what Amy would think if she could see her dining with six men. In her first group of pupils she had drawn no likely husband material, but a gay man, a man who was ten years too young for her, and one who was ten years too old. Richard had his whole life to live, Stephen wanted to get back with his wife and this was all fine. The new people they had brought in might be more likely but right now they were just friends helping her in her new career. They were all saying that they would form an orderly queue to see the look on Primrose's face when she heard what her mouse-like employee was planning. Had achieved, in fact.

That was what had been lacking in Carol's life and she had never realised it – friends to give her confidence, to care about her future, to share what life threw at her.

Suddenly the whole business of grabbing a mate and marching two by two into some ark didn't seem as important as it once had. There was plenty of time, many more cookery lessons and a whole new confident career on television waiting for her out there.

A Wasp Sting

BY MAVIS CHEEK

*P*iers Patterson commuted from Croydon. Emily Hamilton commuted from Potters Bar and was rather tired of being single. Piers Patterson was in his mid-thirties, she guessed, and seemed to be just the man to change her status. Tall enough, friendly face, nice enough manner, but alas – not pushy. He worked in the accounts department and read science fiction, she was head of sales and read mostly magazines. Save for his name, he was perfect. Piers and Emily sounded like two characters in a Jane Austen novel but Emily – in her thirty-seventh year – planned to star in something a little hotter. Piers or not, he was the one. Unfortunately, he did not yet know it and seemed very far from even hazarding a guess. 'Emily,' she said very sternly, for she had read the magazines. 'Emily – you must take the initiative.'

With trepidation and a voice that became awfully high and squeaky, she rang the nearby hotel. It was a grand, imposing building on the far side of the park from their office and Emily had the distinct impression that the booking clerk guessed her dishonourable intentions. She was not, however, put off. She took a deep, deep breath and booked a double room for Friday night. The whole night. Her voice went even higher – and quavered – when she ordered a bottle of champagne for six o'clock. 'Anniversary is it?' asked the booking clerk. 'First,' said Emily, and under her breath added, 'time'. 'Aah,' he said, as if he were looking at a gurgling baby in a pram. She gave a little simper, for realism. She had never done anything like this before but, well, being single was no fun. She hoped the champagne wasn't a little over the top. But no, in all the best films and novels, like James Bond, the couple had champagne before and ate afterwards. Or she thought they did. Emily was not entirely *au fait* with ways to get laid, as some of the more racy magazines she read put it. And she was not at all sure how Piers would react either. She thought he liked her and she thought he knew that she liked him. But beyond that, he did what her mother called played his cards close to his chest. He might even be a bit too serious-minded.

She first spoke to Piers as he sat on the grass in the park opposite the office eating his lunch. He was reading. 'I like science fiction,' he said, when she finally asked, 'because it's fantasy.' There was something in the way he said fantasy that set her mind working – racing actually. It was a very long time since she had dared to have a fantasy in case of severe disappointment, but with him the idea was tantalising. That was when she decided. Being proactive, according to the various articles she read, was the way forward for modern, single women. It filled her with dread what she had to do, but she did it. She remarked that she had never seen a science fiction film. It worked. They went together to see an incomprehensible bit of boys-toys wizardry, and after that she – yes she, Emily – held his hand. He did not take it away and they kissed at the station – but no tongues. Yet.

He suggested they repeat the date, but she said she would buy him dinner instead. He smiled and cleaned his glasses with his fresh, white handkerchief, which she decided was a sign of emotion, and agreed. That was Wednesday. This was Friday. Tonight, hotel and all, was the night. She'd bought a new dress – black and strappy – which she would wear after, when they went to dinner and she thought she looked pretty reasonable really. Mature but fun. At least, that was the image she was hoping for. She kept trying to convince herself that he was bound to find her attractive, bound to.

'I'll meet you in the park after work,' she said when they shared a lift together that afternoon.

'I'll be as quick as I can,' he replied cheerfully.

Her heart, or maybe her stomach, lurched. It might be from pleasurable anticipation – it might be from the lift – but she had a feeling it was fear.

In the park, the evening sun was warm. Across the stretch of grass stood the hotel. Firm, solid and waiting. There was that lurch again. In the bag at her side was the black dress and some spicy new scent. All set. She slipped off her sandals and scrunched the grass with her toes. All was right with the world. Emily celebrated by having a two-Flake Whippy. A passing wasp, enjoying his day out but feeling in need of a little something, spied the ice-cream and descended. The owner of the ice-cream, in a mood of selfishness, refused to share. In fact, she batted her hand at the happy wasp who immediately reacted. Bat, bat, bat, she went. He was forced into rearguard action and found her naked foot and stung it. Hard.

Emily screamed. Both from pain and frustration – for her immediate thought was that this boded ill for her night of passion. It did. The toe seemed on fire and grew distinctly larger. Driven by extreme need she shoved the ice-cream cone over the throbbing toe and sat there miserably as Piers came happily across the greensward. When he saw her distress he started to run.

'What's the . . . ?' he said. His voice trailed off as he saw the upturned ice-cream cone on her big toe and the melting white and brown of its contents gently gliding over her ankle and on to the grass. He looked at her in understandable puzzlement. She did not know whether to laugh or cry, so she achieved a combination. There they were, she sitting on the grass, he kneeling – and instead of being romantic it was like a scene from *Comic Cuts*. Fantasy might be his favoured fiction, but it could hardly extend to this. 'I'm so sorry,' she wept. 'Oh, it is so ridiculous,' she laughed.

He stared at the gloopy mess on her foot. 'I've been

stung by a wasp,' she said simply. 'Right on the tip of my toe.'

And then he did a very unexpected thing. He removed the ice-cream (or what was left of it) from her foot, put his mouth over the throbbing toe and sucked. Which had a most curious effect on Emily. Hitherto she was entirely concerned with the pain. Now she could only think – Give That Wasp A Medal.

'Does that feel better?' he said, looking up and smiling, not altogether innocently. There was the faintest trace of ice-cream on his lips.

'I'm not sure,' she said. And truth to tell she was not. 'Try again.'

A little while later, and reluctantly, and only after much laughter and heart or stomach lurching, she acknowledged the toe was much improved and slipped on her sandals. He helped her up, brushed them both down and offered her his arm.

'Think you can make it to that hotel over there?' he asked.

She looked surprised to see such a place. And she supposed, thinking about it, that she could.

'We'll have a cocktail,' he said, suddenly full of confidence. 'That should sort the toe out.' He turned to her – there was that smile again – 'Unless . . . ?'

'No, no,' she said. 'A cocktail would be lovely.'

Oh well, she thought, why not? After all – the champagne could wait. Dear little things, wasps . . .

In Sunlight and in Shadow

BY ROWAN COLEMAN

'*Venice?*' Cassie had exclaimed, with some alarm, when Ellen announced her trip outside the pub on the banks of the Thames where they were meeting for a glass of wine and a catch-up. 'Ellen, are you sure?'

'Of course I am,' Ellen had said. 'I'm going on holiday, not joining an order of nuns! What's to be sure about? I'm sick of waiting for life to happen to me. I want some fun for a change.'

'I couldn't agree more,' Cassie enthused. 'I'm the one who's always trying to get you to meet people and telling everyone about my beautiful art historian friend. But, Venice?'

Ellen shrugged. 'I've always wanted to go – so why not? What is there to wait for?'

Ellen knew what Cassie's answer would be if she were brave, or perhaps cruel enough to say it out loud. 'Someone to go with.'

Three years ago the man Ellen supposed she would marry, the man she had devoted ten years of her life to had left her for another woman. Ellen was not one to make a fuss, to cry or beat her fists and tear her hair out; she was born and raised in Yorkshire. A fuss just wasn't her way; she had dealt with the loss and moved on. But some small inner part of her ceased to work and for a long time Ellen had stopped hoping or expecting. And although she didn't know what to expect in Venice, she knew she could expect something.

'It's a city for dreams,' she told Cassie as she sipped from her glass of wine and looked out over the Thames, as golden as she imagined the Grand Canal would be in the diminishing daylight.

'It's a city of lovers.' Cassie bit her lip. 'Ellen . . . I just want you to be happy.'

'Have some faith,' Ellen had told her, with a bravado that she almost felt. 'You never know, maybe I'll have a wild affair with some tall, dark and handsome stranger.'

Cassie had laughed as if the idea was preposterous, then she noticed a certain reckless glint in Ellen's eye.

'You know what?' Cassie said. 'Maybe you will.'

The Red Tower. Ellen had sat opposite the painting in the Peggy Guggenheim Collection for a long time, enjoying an unexpected moment of solitude on her last day in the city.

Venice had hardly changed in five hundred years, its vistas and views eternally the same, filled with the throng of humanity. Ellen had imagined the city empty, a dreamscape built exclusively for her so the crowds took her a little off guard. She was used to being alone in the vaults of The National Gallery spending weeks, months even, with some little known Renaissance work of art, gradually unravelling the mysteries that were woven into its canvas and secreted into its brush strokes.

And now here she was with this painting, determined to decipher it. Painted by Giorgio de Chirico in 1913 it was not her area of expertise, modern and strong; a depiction of a tower in the sunlight viewed from the darkest of shadow, it could not be a simpler image. But as soon as Ellen had seen a reproduction of the painting, it had resonated deeply with her. She felt the cool calm of the shadows, the combined fear and lure of the sunlight.

'What does it mean?' An English male voice interrupted her thoughts. Ellen became aware of someone sitting next to her on the bench, the length of his left leg a hair's-breadth from hers. It was unexpected.

'I can't decide,' she said, without turning her head. 'Whenever I look at it I don't know if the shadows are a safe hiding place or an excuse to stay hidden . . .'

'Ellen Woods,' the suddenly familiar voice said. 'You haven't changed in twenty years. Still asking all the wrong questions.'

Ellen snapped her head to look at her companion. He had black hair, eyes made bluer by his tanned complexion and a warm smile. He was dark, handsome and Ellen was fairly certain he'd qualify as tall. He wasn't, however, a stranger.

'Benjamin Parsons.' A slow smile curled her mouth. 'Ben!'

It surprised Ellen how heartened she was to see his familiar face, even if it was one she hadn't set eyes on since she was sixteen. She was even more surprised to find herself hugging him. Marginally less so than he was, she guessed by the way he stiffened momentarily before returning the embrace.

'Hello, Ellen,' he said gently, as they released each other. 'You look exactly the same.'

'Don't say that!' Ellen laughed. 'The last time you saw me I was backcombing my hair and wearing eyeliner by the ton.'

'You set my heart racing,' Ben smiled.

'Don't lie,' Ellen chided him, dimly aware of the busy gallery that still orbited them.

'Don't tell me you don't remember?' Ben asked.

Ellen's look was carefully blank.

'I kissed you under the apple tree on the last day of school. Last time I ever saw you. I felt like the opposite of prince charming, the boy with the kiss that made girls disappear.'

For a second Ellen allowed herself the memory of the sunshine warming her cheeks, dazzling her closed eyes and Ben's hand on her waist as he leaned in to kiss her.

'We moved away the next day, Dad had got a job down south,' she said with a wry smile that belied the quickening pace of her heart. 'I'd forgotten all about that kiss.'

Ben held his hand to his heart as if he'd just been dealt a fatal blow, and Ellen laughed.

'So, what are you doing in Venice?' he asked. 'It's the last place on earth I'd have thought of looking for you.'

Ellen did not let herself wonder if he had really ever thought of looking for her at all. The notion unsettled her for reasons that were entirely irrational.

'I'm an art historian,' she explained. 'I spend hours and hours with dusty paintings, finding out all about them and writing books that no one reads and I love it. And you?'

'A friend is opening a fine art gallery tonight, just off St Mark's Square. I'm an investor.'

'Ben Parsons, art dealer.' Ellen frowned. 'Doesn't seem like you.'

'It's not me,' Ben said, regretfully. 'I'm afraid I'm in property. This is something to make me feel a little bit more like a Renaissance man, I suppose.'

The two of them watched each other and Ellen supposed that it would be good for one or other of them to say something, but just then looking seemed entirely enough.

Then a slender brown arm draped over Ben's shoulder and a pretty young woman, somewhere in her early twenties, leaned over him.

'Can we go now, please,' she pleaded with a practised pout. 'I'm bored and you promised to take me shopping.'

'Jessica, I'm coming,' Ben smiled up at her. 'Two more minutes, OK?'

Ellen watched as this Jessica bent and kissed Ben on the lips, before glancing at Ellen and sighing, 'I don't know what he sees in these dusty old things.'

'Your daughter's lovely,' Ellen said dryly as she watched Jessica sway out of the gallery.

Ben burst out laughing and shook his head. 'I deserved that,' he said. 'I know she's wrong for me but she's very . . .'

'Beautiful?' Ellen joked, covering the confusion of disappointment that had suddenly crowded her chest.

'Persistent.' Ben leaned a little closer to Ellen, causing her to hold her breath.

'Come to the launch tonight.' He handed her a card that read *Luce Antica, Corte Sabionera*.

'I don't know . . .' Ellen began.

'Yes you do,' Ben said. 'You know that a gallery full of old Italian paintings is right up your street. And besides, it would be cruel to make me wait another twenty years to see those brown eyes again.'

'Stop pretending to flirt with me and I'll consider it,' Ellen said, somehow managing to hold his gaze.

'Good.' Ben stood up. 'And who says I was pretending?'

'Your trouble is your head is too easily turned.' Ellen spoke her father's favourite phrase out loud to her reflection in her hotel room mirror. She was ready to go out. But she wasn't entirely sure she was actually going to leave.

Her father was right. Fifteen minutes in the

company of Ben Parsons and her head was filled with the scent of green apples and the sensation of his palm on her waist. Of course, she hadn't told him she remembered that kiss or that she had cried for six weeks solid after her father had made them move away. Or that sometimes even now, in the first few moments of wakefulness she would find herself dreaming of one kiss, long ago. Why on earth would she? The lingering memory of a sweet-sixteen kiss had never seemed important, not until she met Ben Parsons in the Peggy Guggenheim Collection in Venice, that was.

From shadow into sunlight.

Ellen chided herself, she was utterly foolish. What man would want a thirty-six-year-old art historian with cobwebs in her hair when he could have a girl like Jessica?

Yet here she was in her best dress and her heeled shoes, the ones she hadn't had nearly enough practice walking in. And Ellen couldn't help thinking that if life was about sunshine and shadow then now was the perfect time to risk a little sunburn.

The painting was tiny, no more than an inch square, painted on a sliver of ivory with the finest of brushes. It was late sixteenth century, Ellen guessed, a portrait of an exquisite girl probably given to her betrothed or perhaps even her secret lover. Ellen was entranced by it and as soon as she had taken in the terrifyingly glamorous guests that filled the gallery, she had attached herself to the painting, as if it were an old acquaintance.

'Is it any good?' Ben asked her, appearing suddenly at her shoulder.

'Perfection,' Ellen said as she looked at him, hearing the warmth and passion in her voice a beat too late. 'The painting, I mean the painting is perfection . . .'

'Are you saying I'm not perfection?' Ben teased her.

Ellen laughed and felt blood rush to her cheeks. She was blushing.

Ben picked up her hand. 'Come with me, I want to show you something.'

He cleaved her away from the safety of the wall and led her through the clamour of guests. They emerged out of the back of the gallery on to a tiny courtyard enclosed on all sides by walls of balconies, each garlanded with red geraniums. The sun was low in the sky and Ben led her into the last remaining slither of the courtyard that was bathed in light.

'This is magical,' Ellen breathed.

'Glad you think so,' Ben said. 'Because they don't have any apple trees in Venice.'

Ellen looked at him. 'Apple trees . . . ?'

But before she could say another word she felt the pressure of Ben's palm on her waist as he pulled her to him and kissed her. As Ellen closed her eyes, the sun danced behind her lids and her body ignited at his touch. She felt his fingers in her hair and his breath in her ear as he whispered to her.

'Ellen, will you go to the cinema with me?'

'The . . . what?' Ellen laughed.

'After that kiss I was going to ask you to go out with me, but I never saw you again,' Ben told her. 'Been driving me mad all this time.'

'I'd have said no,' Ellen lied.

'I'd have kept asking,' Ben told her.

'Ben, are you out here . . . ?' Jessica's voice cut in between them and Ellen realised she was still in Ben's arms. Jessica stared at them.

'Moving on to your next conquest already?' Jessica asked. 'I was warned about you, but I didn't think you'd get bored of me this fast, especially not for her.' She sneered at Ellen. 'Enjoy it while it lasts, which by the look of you, won't be very long.'

The setting sun shuttered the last trace of warmth out of the courtyard and suddenly Ellen felt cold, old and very foolish.

'I have to go,' she said quickly.

'Ellen, please wait . . .' Ben pleaded. But Ellen had raced back inside, back into the dark, cool comforting shelter of the shadows.

It was raining in London that Wednesday lunchtime. Ellen stood on the steps of The National Gallery, letting the rain soak through her summer dress. In the days since she'd fled the heat and glare of Venice she had loved London's leaden skies all the more. Her head had been turned. She'd acted like a fool and got burnt. Her old life should have seemed comforting but somehow Ellen could not feel content to spend the rest of it having one-sided conversations with images of the long dead any more. Whatever else Ben had done to her he had set her heart beating again, even if it did ache with every pulse.

'Ellen,' Ben's voice broke into her thoughts and for a second Ellen wondered if she were daydreaming him. But no, he was really there, standing in the rain.

'Ben . . . ?'

'I brought you something,' Ben said. He held out a package wrapped in brown paper. 'It's that miniature . . . I know you loved it.'

'Ben . . .' Ellen stared at the package but did not take it. 'I can't accept that.'

'You could, I got a huge discount,' Ben said, with a hopeful smile.

'I'm not the right person for you to have your next fling with,' Ellen said with some regret. 'I'd be no good at having a fling, I'd fall in love with you and you'd be irritated and . . . I'm glad that you kissed me in Venice. But you should be looking for your next twenty-year-old.'

'Actually I'm quite annoyed you haven't fallen in love with me yet,' Ben said, taking a wary step closer to her. 'I've been in love with you since the first second I saw you again.'

Ellen looked at him again, there was truth in his eyes.

'You can't want me,' she said. 'I look like a drowned rat.'

'That's true,' Ben agreed. 'But a very kissable,

beautiful drowned rat. Come to the cinema with me, there's a matinée on at the Odeon.'

Ellen thought for a moment. 'In the gallery, you said I always asked the wrong questions. What did you mean?'

'I mean,' Ben said, taking her hand. 'You shouldn't be asking what's waiting in the sunshine, you should be taking a chance and finding out for yourself.'

'I can't come.' Ellen felt Ben's hand slip into hers and draw her closer.

'I'll keep asking,' Ben told her.

Slowly Ellen closed the last remaining inches between and kissed him.

'Good,' she whispered in his ear. 'I'll expect you tomorrow.'

After all, Ellen told herself, when there wasn't any sunshine in the sky, the trick was to make your own.

Sacred Spring

BY BARBARA ERSKINE

*S*hifting uncomfortably in her chair Sarah sighed, turning to the next test paper. The library was empty. Perhaps she could get through her marking without interruption for once.

The door opened and two figures appeared. Bother! She shouldn't have tempted providence by even thinking she could finish early. And it had to be Professor Brownley. She didn't know the other man. The professor was heading purposefully towards her table. 'I trust you're not going to be late for your class, Sarah.' As if she ever had been late in the fifteen weeks she had been a lecturer so far. She gritted her teeth and managed a smile, but inside she was seething. Why did I ever take up this career? I'd hoped I would love it, but I hate the teaching, I hate the subject, I hate you and I hate this wretched library! I have made the most terrible mistake!

As the professor sat down at the same table with his gimlet grin, she fixed her eyes on the library windows, which looked out onto a once pretty herb garden, and stifled a triumphant grin. It doesn't matter. You can't bully me, because I have found a way to escape.

Sometimes it happened at once. Sometimes it took longer. She had to concentrate. Closing her eyes against the pile of essays and the overbearing presence sitting at the end of the table, she fixed her mind on the flowerbeds with their sunlit leaves and, yes, it had worked. She had somehow imagined herself outside.

But there was a light mist of rain falling, pattering on the roses and lavender. 'This is my daydream and I want sunshine!' She bit her lip, jerked back to reality by the sudden jarring of the table as the other man sat down opposite her. A stranger. Ignore him. Concentrate. Take herself out of it. Back to the garden. And sunlight.

No sunlight. It was raining even harder and someone was standing watching her, a puzzled smile on his face. 'Where on earth did you appear from?'

She smiled. This was a far better daydream than usual. This man was tall, dark and handsome, as predicted by the fortune-teller at the local fête, who had so inexplicably failed to foretell the fact that she was about to resign from her job. Well, the stranger was not dark exactly, more mousey. And not really handsome, but nicely put together and probably not that tall either, but who cared?

'What are you staring at?' He was watching her with a quizzical smile. His eyes, she noted, were not so much the blue she had expected, more a nice kind of nondescript hazel.

'Sorry,' she murmured. 'I was thinking about a fortune-teller and how wrong she was.'

He looked even more puzzled. Then he shook his head. 'You do realise you are not supposed to be here?' He indicated some red plastic tape. It was the front line against the rapidly developing quagmire where visitors pulled up on to the grass, desperate to find parking spaces near the always full car park.

She nodded. This was the most satisfactory daydream. 'So, who are you?' She took the initiative. 'And what are you doing here?'

'I'm a county archaeologist. Tom Forbes.' He really had a most attractive smile. 'They want to extend the car park. And the garden is now closed to the public. I've come to do a survey to make sure there's nothing important here.'

'Nothing important other than flowers and trees and a small oasis of peace and beauty?'

He nodded. 'It's sad, isn't it? But people have to park somewhere, I suppose.' They were both silent for a moment.

'Will they take your word for it if you say there is something here that mustn't be buried under tarmac?' she asked suddenly.

He gave a wry smile. 'I'm afraid they would want proof.'

'So you've got to dig a trench right through it?'

'More likely, I would come and watch when they bring in the diggers.'

'So, there is no escape.' She reached out a hand to

41

the spray of pink roses and touched the petals gently, as if comforting the plant. 'There's been a place of learning here for over two thousand years,' she said dreamily. 'Did you know that?'

He seemed perplexed. 'No, I didn't. It seems unlikely. The oldest records round here are late medieval.'

She stepped away from him, staring across the flowerbeds. A shadowy figure had appeared near them. A ghostly figure. She glanced at Tom. 'Can you see him?' she whispered.

'Who?' Tom lifted an eyebrow.

Strangely, she knew who the figure was. 'He stood here once to watch the sunset across the valley.' Between them and the valley now was the college block and half the town. 'He was very wise. His scholarship and his learning were famous; he was a teacher and he was a healer and the medicinal plants he grew here and collected and the knowledge that this land was blessed brought people here from miles around. The tradition remained for generations.'

He folded his arms. 'Nice try! Except that, until ten years ago, the college was down there in the town centre and this was a sports ground.'

She shook her head as though trying to dispel the picture from her mind.

He frowned. 'Are you OK?'

'I suppose so. My own enchantment with learning is rapidly waning.'

'I see.' He laughed. 'I did wonder who you were.'

'A teacher, too. Temporarily escaped.'

'A historian?'

'No. Nothing like that. I'm an economist.'

'Sarah!'

She shivered as someone pulled at her arm. 'Sarah! Wake up! What's the matter with you?' The voice sharpened. 'Sarah! Can you hear me?'

'It's all right, Professor. I'll look after her. You needn't wait.' Someone was holding her hand. 'Can you hear me, Sarah?' The voice was calm. It was deep and soothing. She opened her eyes. The garden had gone. Instead she was staring at the stranger who had sat down at her table.

'So, there you are. Where have you been?' He smiled kindly. 'You gave the good professor a fright. He couldn't wake you.'

She glanced round. The library was empty but for themselves. 'I'm sorry. I must have been asleep.'

He nodded. He was smiling but his eyes were concerned. 'I think you were in some sort of trance, Sarah. Not something your professor understands. Can you tell me where you were?'

'I was in the garden in my dream.' She felt she owed him an explanation. 'Outside the window, there.' They had been so real, the archaeologist and the teacher from the distant past. She returned his smile wanly. 'Who are you?' Hadn't she just said that to someone else? Her head was spinning.

'David Pelham. I teach psychology.'

'Oh.' She was embarrassed. 'You probably think I'm drunk or mad. Or both!'

43

He laughed. 'Far from it. Tired and stressed maybe.'

'And late with marking these papers.' She glanced at her watch.

She returned to the library several hours later. It was a better place to work than her bed-sitter. Once she had her own flat, things would be different.

Outside, the little garden was looking tired. Someone had moved the tape and tyre tracks had carved up the grass some more. Exhausted, she closed her eyes, trying to conjure up the face of the archaeologist again, and—

'There you are!' He smiled. 'I thought you'd disappeared.'

She laughed. 'I did. I had to go back to work.'

She was reaching out to the roses when something bright caught her eye in the muddy flowerbed. She stooped and ran her fingers through the soil. It had stopped raining at last, she realised. 'What is it?' He was watching her.

'A coin.' She shrugged and passed it over to him. He scrutinised it carefully for several seconds. When he looked up his face was alight with interest. 'You know, this is incredible.' He reached into his pocket and withdrew a small magnifying lens. 'This dates from the Iron Age. Two thousand years ago, like you said.'

She stared at him incredulously.

'And someone used it to pay for their study here?'

'I doubt it! Did you put it here?' His tone sharpened.

'It's not part of some idiotic plan to trap me into opposing the university's plans?'

'No!' She was hurt and angry.

'Then how did you know it was here?'

'It caught my eye.'

'And your theory about the ancient place of learning?'

'I don't know where it came from. I just knew. And then I saw him.' She could have bitten off her tongue. She saw Tom's friendly face shuttered with suspicion. 'I pictured it,' she amended hastily. 'As it might have been. It was a guess. There's a sacred spring near here too.' She met his eyes, horrified. Why had she said that?

'Oh yes? Where exactly?' His voice was flat. Sarcastic.

She shrugged. But she knew the answer. 'Over there.' The line of houses at the edge of the college grounds was barely thirty metres away behind a high wall.

'Which one, do you know that, too?' He had followed her pointing finger with his eyes. She could feel her mouth dry. The warmth and humour between them had gone. He was mocking. 'The Edwardian mansion. There.' She pointed again.

She knew nothing about the house or its gardens. Nothing, if she were honest, about the area at all. He was walking away now towards the road. She supposed he was going to work his way round through the network of streets to find out just how stupid she was.

She wanted to follow him. To go with him. But she couldn't. She was sitting at a table in front of a pile of closed books.

She opened her eyes. Dr Pelham was sitting opposite her, studying her face. 'So, you are back with us?'

She nodded.

'Where were you this time?'

She gave a small laugh, which came out as a sob. 'Out there. In the herb garden.'

'Ah.' He glanced at the window. 'You like it there?'

She nodded.

'And you go there whenever the stress gets too much?'

'I suppose I do, yes.'

'And when you are feeling lonely and unhappy?'

She nodded.

He stared thoughtfully out of the window without speaking for several moments. 'Have you ever wondered if you are in the right job?'

She laughed. 'Often. I chose the wrong subject to study.'

'You can always change.'

'Can I? My father wanted me to be an economist.'

'And what did you want to be?'

She hesitated. Tom Forbes had guessed it at once. 'A historian.'

'Change, Sarah. We are talking about the rest of your life here. If your subject makes you so unhappy that you have to escape it like this, you have to change it. This is not your father's life. It's your own.' He stood up. 'Please think about it.' He was heading towards the door. He paused and looked back. 'Sarah, if you find yourself in the garden like that again, will you bring something back for me? Anything. Just to prove where you've been.'

It happened sooner than she'd expected. She was sitting, lost in thought. Then she was standing in the garden. Tom was waiting for her. It was growing dark and the car park behind them was almost empty.

'Did you find the spring?' She was astonished at how pleased she was to see him.

He nodded. 'I had the devil of a job. There has been so much development. The house is quite posh.' He smiled.

'It has a lovely garden,' he went on.

'And?' she prompted, as he fell silent.

'And the owner showed me her rockery. And there it was. A natural spring.' He paused. 'A very special place, apparently.'

Neither of them spoke. 'I was only guessing, you know,' she said at last.

He raised an eyebrow. 'So, guess something else for me. Assuming that now we are talking Romano-British, and that this is a site, where can I find evidence to save the garden?'

She stared round. 'Perhaps there is nothing left. I didn't see any buildings here. I just saw him, standing where you are, looking out towards the sunset. I could feel his power. His knowledge.'

There was a pause.

'What is your name?' he asked at last. 'You've never told me.'

'Sarah.'

'And where have you come from, Sarah?'

'From there.' She pointed up at the window.

He hesitated. 'You're not a ghost, are you?'

'No.' She reached out to the flowers and touched them a little anxiously, as though to reassure herself. 'No, I don't think so.' She broke off a rosebud and sniffed it. 'I promised someone I would take something back with me.'

'You're going, then?'

She nodded.

'Think about the evidence, Sarah. We need anything you can find—'

But she had gone.

She saw Dr Pelham the next morning. Reaching into her briefcase, she pulled out the rosebud. It had wilted. He took it and stared at it and then raised his eyes to meet hers. 'How long have you been able to do this?' He sat down opposite her again.

She shrugged. 'It never happened before I came here. It's scary. I'm really out there, aren't I?'

He nodded.

'And I'm still here too?'

He nodded again.

'These things don't happen in the scientific world, do they?'

He smiled. 'Maybe they do.'

'Will I always be able to do it?'

It was his turn to shrug. 'I suspect your stress and unhappiness has caused some kind of psychological dislocation. Who knows how long it will last?'

She thought about it. 'Is it true they are threatening to turn it into a car park?' she asked suddenly.

He nodded.

'And they have applied for planning permission?'

'I believe so.'

'So that is real. I met the archaeological surveyor down there.' She felt herself blushing under his thoughtful gaze. Was Tom real, or part of the dream? Was the ancient stranger part of the dream, too?

'I'm not dead, am I? Or mad?'

He laughed. 'No.'

'Tom thought perhaps I was a ghost.'

'You don't have to be dead to be a ghost. So that part might be true.' He smiled gently. 'We'll talk about it one day, but not now, alas. I'm flying to the States tomorrow for a lecture tour.'

She felt bereft.

That evening she rang the county archaeological service. No Tom Forbes worked there.

To her amazement the professor agreed she could resign her lectureship at the end of term and transfer to another department. He would even help her try and sort out some sort of grant to do a second degree, but it was months before she returned. This time she was happy. She walked out to the garden and stood staring round. Someone had fenced off the edge of the car park and the grass was no longer muddy. There was a bench now to sit on. Slowly she sat down.

'Sarah?'

Tom had appeared behind her. 'Where have you been? They wouldn't tell me anything.'

She moved up, so he could sit beside her. 'I rang the council and they said they'd never heard of you,' she said.

They stared at each other and suddenly they were both laughing. 'Was either of us really here before?' she asked. 'Why hadn't they heard of you?'

'Because I work for the university, not the council.'

'This university?' It had never occurred to her. 'So you are real?'

'Do you want to pinch me to prove it?' He stood up. 'I want to show you something.'

He drove her to Well House. 'I've got to know the owners quite well and they said I could bring you to see it.'

'So you knew you'd find me one day?'

He nodded. They walked slowly across the lawns towards the rockery. There, nestling among the rocks, was a small, dark pool of clear water. 'There you are,' he said. 'A natural spring. It's in the records. It's been regarded as sacred for hundreds of years, perhaps thousands. This was a centre for learning and magic.'

She found she was smiling. 'So my ghostly teacher probably did exist?'

'Oh, yes. I think he existed. Wait till you hear the

best part of this story. The land on which the college is built once belonged to this house. When it was sold they put a covenant on the use of part of it. A small area of garden which can never be built on.'

She couldn't contain her glee.

'Our garden?'

He nodded. 'There's no record of why it's so special, but we know, don't we?'

'So it's safe?'

'The university has been reminded. It has been suggested that the garden is used as a place of rest and tranquillity for students. Hence the bench.'

She turned to look towards the wall that hid the college building from sight. A figure was standing there, watching them. She could see him clearly this time, his strong features, his coiled bracelets and the carved staff on which he leaned.

'Tom?' Sarah whispered.

'I can see him.'

After a few seconds the figure smiled and nodded his head. Then he was gone.

'Do you know what I think?' Tom murmured as they stared at the wall. 'I think he conjured us out of the mist to save his garden.'

'Powerful magic,' she said softly.

'Powerful indeed.'

'Did you give that coin to the museum?'

'Not yet. Why?'

'I think we should throw it into the spring as an offering.'

He looked shocked. Then he smiled. 'To ask its blessing, to seal our friendship and to ensure that we come back?'

'Something like that, yes.' She smiled.

Somewhere in the past the old man nodded. If they had listened they would have heard him chuckle . . .

People Like Us

BY JANE FALLON

*I*t was everything they had ever dreamed of. White-washed walls against the azure blue of the sea, sprawling gardens lush with oranges and succulents, cheerful geraniums in pots on the three terraces; a marble pool that seemed to hover dangerously out over the cliff's edge, giving the illusion that you could swim straight out into the sea below; an open-faced summer house complete with its own kitchen.

Space enough for both their extended families to come and stay without them all tripping over each other. Katherine squeezed Mark's hand and felt a wave of excitement as he squeezed back.

The house was right in the centre of the area they had selected as the place where they would like to start their new life. A ten-minute walk down to the beach but with all the amenities a pretty Spanish village had to offer. There was a cobbled square with a café, a bar and a general store. Every Wednesday and Saturday, so Maria, the estate agent told them, there was a produce market that attracted people from all the surrounding farms. There was the promise of enough life around them to keep them from getting bored, but all the peace and solitude they could ever wish for. It was perfect and what's more they could afford it. OK, so it was right at the top of their price range, it might be a bit of a squeeze, but it was, most definitely, possible.

By the time the tour had ended – which had taken considerably longer than they had anticipated, the house and grounds being so much larger than anything else they had seen – Katherine had already mentally moved in. She was imagining the farewell party they would have back in Croydon, the tears her parents would shed as they waved them off, the delight on the boys' faces when they saw their new home. She had got as far as to picture her sons, tanned and healthy, speaking fluent Spanish and living the safe, outdoor carefree life she had always wanted for them, when Mark said something that brought her daydreams to an abrupt end.

'It's beautiful,' she heard him telling the agent. 'But, I don't think it's right for us.'

'What?' Katherine said, putting a hand out as if to stop him saying anything else. 'It's perfect.'

'People like us don't live in houses like this,' Mark said, shrugging her off. 'This is a rock star's house.'

Katherine wondered for a second whether she'd heard him correctly. 'We can afford it, that makes it a house for people like us. Mark, this is better than we ever even dared to hope for.'

'I just can't see us living here, that's all. I think we should look for something more . . .'

She interrupted him before he could finish. 'More what? More beautiful? I don't think that exists.'

'I was going to say "more us".'

Katherine pushed her hair back from her face, trying to take in what she was hearing. She looked at Mark, who turned away as if to indicate that the subject was closed.

'Excuse me,' Katherine said to no one in particular. 'I'm going to go back to the car, I don't feel well.'

'Let's keep looking,' she heard Mark say to the property agent as she moved off. 'I think we should look at smaller places, maybe.'

Katherine walked through the fragrant gardens to get to the front of the house where their car was parked. Once there, she couldn't face the thought of the journey back to the villa, the three of them sitting in silence, or worse still, Mark babbling on, trying to justify his decision.

She thought about starting to walk back, but she knew it was miles and besides, she didn't think she would be able to find her way. She sat down heavily on a low wall next to the car, dreading the moment the others would appear from behind the house.

'Let's just not talk about it,' she said as soon as she saw Mark approaching the car.

'Don't be ridiculous, Kat,' he said. 'Maria says there are plenty more places we can look at.'

'I mean it. Don't,' Katherine said, pointedly getting into the back seat so that Maria would have no choice but to ride up front with Mark.

On the journey back she stared out of the window at the beautiful countryside and tried to get her head round what had happened to them. Mark's refusal to consider the house had bothered her for two reasons. Firstly, of course, because she wanted to live there – she could see the two of them growing old there, surrounded by their children and then their grandchildren and some day maybe even their great-grandchildren.

But secondly, more importantly, his remarks had upset her because she didn't know when 'people like us' had started to mean dull people, people with no style, people who didn't deserve to live a glamorous life. People who had long since ceased to find themselves exciting, so why would they view each other in that way? People who were comfortable, safe and, she suspected, boring.

She knew that her relationship with Mark had grown a little tired lately, a little routine, maybe. It was inevitable once you had children, she knew that. There were more important things to worry about than drinking cocktails and trying to find your G-spot. But, try as she might, she couldn't put her finger on the point when they stopped being Katherine and Mark, and instead became 'Mummy' and 'Daddy'.

'Mummy'll kiss it better,' Mark would say when one of the boys cut his finger. Or: 'Ask Mummy to help you,' when one of them presented him with their homework. Understandable. He was hardly going to refer to her as Katherine. But then, once, 'Are you ready, Mummy?' directly to her when the boys weren't even in the room. And then again, a few days later, 'White wine, Mummy?' on one of the increasingly rare occasions when they had ventured out for dinner with two of their friends. Worse, two of their still blissfully child-free friends who were in the first flush of romance and could hardly keep their hands off each other. The friends had laughed – pityingly, Katherine had thought – and one of them had said, 'God, don't tell me you call each other Mummy and Daddy now?' and Katherine had said, 'No! Of course not. As if,' and had shot Mark a look that said: 'Will you please shut up.'

Maybe Mark was right, she thought now, looking out of the window at the mountains. Maybe rock stars didn't call each other Mummy and Daddy once they'd had kids. Maybe they were too busy being fabulous and living in a house like the one she and Mark had just rejected.

She felt a rush of guilt. So many of her friends would have given anything for a husband who relished fatherhood as much as Mark did. He was kind and considerate, he didn't spend his evenings down the pub with the lads or comatose in front of the television. It was just that he wasn't very . . . exciting.

The dream had been all hers, she knew that. She had visualised sunshine and large glasses of wine and lazy days by their own pool, interspersed with making the odd bed or cooking a couple of portions of bacon and egg for their guests' breakfasts. Maybe it had even been a subconscious attempt to put back some romance and glamour into their non-rock star lives.

Mark had been hesitant at first, unsure of change, but she had soon convinced him of the benefits for their two boys. They would be able to live an enviable life, afforded a freedom both Katherine and Mark would have been loath to grant them at home. The whole family had been diligently learning Spanish. They had done their research on the best areas in which to run a b. & b., and had read books about the perils of the hotel trade. It made perfect practical sense, but Katherine had also harboured dreams of a new start, a romantic vision of the four of them laughing and working and playing together. A picture-postcard family living a life other people could only dream of. Maybe not.

When they reached the rented villa they were calling home for the duration of their week-long house-hunting trip, they said goodbye to Maria, agreeing to meet up the following day to see some more properties that were, as Mark put it, 'more suitable'. Katherine looked at him critically as he walked up the steps ahead of her – striped polo shirt, too-short shorts, which made him look as if he was on his way to play football. In 1972. Open sandals revealing hairy toes. An identikit forty-year-old father who had long since stopped worrying about what he looked like.

'I'll put the kettle on,' Mark said when they had let themselves in. Katherine bit her lip to stop herself snapping at him. She didn't know why the whole thing was making her so angry, but she knew it wasn't really the house so much, lovely though it was – it was the implication behind what he had said. His apparent acceptance that the passion, the . . . well, the sex . . . had gone from their relationship.

'The reason rock stars have big houses is because they can afford them,' she said, trying, and failing, to sound calm. 'And we can afford that house.'

'It came out wrong. I just meant it wasn't practical for a b. & b. Too big. That's all.'

Katherine turned on her heels. 'That's not what you said, though. You said people like us didn't live in houses like that. Whatever people like us are.'

She walked out before he could respond, and headed upstairs to the cool dark of the bedroom. How could he have said that to her? No wonder all the sparkle had gone out of their relationship, if that was the way he felt.

She moved across to the bed and, as she did so, she caught sight of someone she didn't recognise in the mirror. A woman. Denim A-line skirt cut at just the right mid-calf length to make the wearer's legs look their most dumpy. Two inches shorter would be ideal. Even six inches longer would at least have had some kind of boho-chic appeal. Baggy T-shirt, one that was printed with the name of a popular holiday resort and that was designed to be as shapeless as possible. Comfortable pumps. A mousy bob, tired eyes, no make-up. Katherine stopped dead and stared at her reflection.

'Oh my God,' she said to the room. No wonder Mark thought they weren't glamorous enough for that house. He was right.

She dug around in her luggage for her nail scissors and hacked away at her skirt until she was able to pull a two-inch strip of material from right round the bottom. She tried it on; it skimmed her knees perfectly. She picked at the rough edges trying to make it look as if the distressed look was intentional. Then she swapped her oversize T-shirt for a strappy vest and her pumps for the only pair of heels she had brought with her for special evenings out.

She tied her hair back in a high ponytail, found the few sad bits of make-up she possessed and applied them, and stepped back to admire the effect. OK, so she wasn't exactly catwalk material, but she looked younger. She looked like she hadn't given up completely.

When she got downstairs Mark was intently chopping chillies for a marinade. He looked at her like he knew she was angry with him, but he didn't quite know why.

'You look nice,' he said, and she felt terrible that she had made him feel so uneasy.

'I look like what I am. A forty-year-old mother of two,' she said miserably.

Mark walked over and put his arm round her. 'A beautiful forty-year-old mother of two. In a skirt with a very strange hem-line,' he said. 'And what's wrong with that?'

Katherine knew he wanted her to smile, to show him that everything was all right, but she couldn't quite make herself. 'I don't feel beautiful,' she said. 'I don't feel like me. In fact, I don't know who I am. I'm just "people like us", middle-aged, dull and . . . frumpy.'

'You're none of those things,' Mark said. 'Listen, if you want to live in that house we can live in that house. It's just . . . well, I thought the point of this move was for a better life. If we turn that place into a b. & b. we'd be cleaning all day. It'd be a full-time job just keeping the garden in shape. Either that or we'd have to take on people to help us and then we'd have to work even harder to pay them. I don't want you to have to work that hard. That's one of the things we're trying to get away from, isn't it?'

Katherine nodded. 'I guess so.'

'A rock star could live there with a staff of ten and not even think about it. We'd have to work twice as hard as we already do just to keep afloat. That's the only difference. Well, that and a few million in the bank.'

'And the groupies,' Katherine said, managing a smile at last. 'Don't forget them.'

'Oh, I could attract groupies. I just choose not to,' he said, smiling, and this time Katherine laughed. Mark could always make her laugh in the end. That was one of the things that had first attracted her to him, had first made him stand out from the crowd. It was something their friends envied, she knew, that easy jokey way they had with each other no matter what was going on in their lives.

'My point is,' he continued, 'that what I said wasn't meant to be a judgement on you . . . on us. OK, so we're ordinary people with ordinary lives. So what? We love each other . . . don't we?' he added nervously, looking at her, and she nodded. 'We have a great family, we're about to move to a beautiful country and work for ourselves and have this whole amazing new life. So we can't live in a house a rock star would live in, but I don't want to. I want to live somewhere we can afford with you and the boys, and be able to have enough time off to go and sit on the beach together. And that's enough, isn't it?'

Katherine looked at him. He was so sincere. 'Yes,' she said and she realised as she was saying it that she meant it. 'It is.'

The Holiday of a Marriage

BY KATIE FFORDE

*W*hen did I realise my marriage had died? Was it when I stopped being excited when I heard my husband's car pull up in the drive? Or when he only ever took me out to dinner because our daughter had phoned him at work to remind him it was my birthday? Hard to tell really, I just knew it had.

It's much easier in retrospect, to look back and ask yourself when was the last time you sat in bed together, drinking tea and reading your books, or went for a walk on a Sunday afternoon, and held hands, or ambled round Waitrose, discussing what to have for dinner. When you realise it's been months, if not years, since you've done any of them, it's best to be realistic and accept it's over.

Edward and I weren't half-killing each other, but we weren't communicating either. We weren't fighting because we weren't talking beyond the basics. The children had left home and he spent more and more time at work. The bad thing was, I didn't mind that much. I had my own part-time job and was happy to fill the time left over with hobbies. I went to auctions, car-boot and jumble sales, buying bits and pieces, doing them up, and selling them to local shops and at car-boot sales. I didn't make much money but it satisfied me, and I enjoyed the people it brought me in touch with.

It annoyed me to have to stop messing about with paints, glazes and varnishes to cook him supper, something I'd once loved doing. Now, I was buying all the 'instant and cheating' cookery books and frozen mashed potato in industrial quantities. All that 'fresh and local' thing seemed a waste of time when he just ate, watched the news, read the newspaper, fell asleep in his chair and then went to bed, without seeming to notice that I stayed up much later than he did.

Currently I was painting a little can, which, when I'd finished with it, would sport an auricula against a pale grey background. I knew just the shop to take it to. The owner's brother sometimes took a turn minding it and he was rather attractive in a laid-back, actorish kind of way. I took the fact that I was even thinking about other men as a sign that things had reached the point of no return. I'd always despised women who played away but now the idea of an affair with a man who really noticed you seemed lovely. I wouldn't do anything about it until I was no longer married though. My marriage vows were still important.

To my credit, I did my best with Edward, but he was so scratchy and irritable. And when the children came round with their partners they noticed he was often quite short. 'What's up with Dad?' my daughter would say. 'He shouldn't speak to you like that. I wouldn't put up with it.'

Somehow I couldn't explain that after being married so long it was hard to talk about your relationship, especially if you hadn't ever made a habit of it, and we hadn't. I didn't think he'd mind us splitting up, really, apart from the upheaval. Emotionally, I thought he'd be fine with it.

But when would I tell him? We'd have to talk about our relationship then. I couldn't just leave a note saying 'It's over.' Edward may have stopped being a good husband but he deserved a proper explanation.

Of course I kept putting it off. I poured all my energy and frustration into restoring things. Had I had an analyst, they probably would have said I was restoring bric-à-brac because I couldn't restore my marriage. Whatever. But for some reason I didn't want him to have any reason to complain about me. I wanted right on my side. I was also aware that, for an older man, he was quite attractive. He had all his own hair and drove a nice car. I knew someone would snap him up the moment I'd let him go.

Then, just when I was forcing myself to think about Christmas, in late November, he told me he'd arranged a holiday for just afterwards.

'We haven't been away for ages,' he said. 'I thought it was time I took you somewhere special.'

Well I'd been thinking that too, for years, but I hadn't mentioned it. I probably should have mentioned it, because now, it was a bit too late. But when he described what he'd planned, I really wanted to go!

'We'll set off from London City Airport,' he began. 'I know how you hate big air terminals, and fly to Paris. From there we'll go to Guadeloupe, just for a night. And then take the fast ferry to Dominica. Oh, and we'll go business class,' he added.

I absolved him of knowing I was planning to leave him – he just wasn't that sensitive. But if he had known, and had wanted to stop me going, this was the way to do it. I had always longed to go to Dominica, a small, mostly undiscovered island in the Caribbean that was called The Nature Isle. I loved long walks, following trails and that feeling of history I imagined an island like that would give me. And I had always wanted to travel business class. Edward did a lot, with his work, but on family holidays there were too many of us and we always went the cheapest way possible. We didn't go anywhere very far away, either. So this would be the holiday of a lifetime. Or, the holiday of a marriage.

I justified my rather mercenary decision to go on the holiday by telling myself it wasn't fair to Edward not to. He wouldn't want to go without me and he deserved a holiday. He'd been working incredibly hard. Also, I was bound to be able to find just the right time to tell him. His mobile phone wouldn't ring, a meal wouldn't need cooking and there wouldn't be a property programme I was desperate to watch on television. (I adored property programmes, especially those ones when people went to a whole new location; maybe this was another sign I wanted to move on?)

The journey went like clockwork, from the taxi to the airport, via the transfer in Paris that involved a little gentle shopping, to the arrival in the warm exoticism of a Caribbean night. It was perfect. Even the little hotel we stayed in had an unexpected charm. It had only ever been somewhere to sleep before catching the ferry in the morning, but I loved it. In spite of wanting to leave my husband, I was having a good time!

I had decided to wait until we'd recovered from our (rather wonderful) flight, exotic stopover and ferry ride before mentioning being unhappy in our marriage. This meant at least three days of enjoying Dominica, the elegant hotel, the stunning views and the luxurious bedroom before my announcement would spoil it.

Sex had become very infrequent recently – not surprising, really. We were both getting older and Edward worked long hours. The magic had definitely gone out of it for me, and I quite often pretended to be asleep if I thought he might want it. Not that I needed to often, actually.

But that first night, when he moved across the big, white bed and took me in his arms I found something about the scent of ylang-ylang wafting in from the garden, the sounds of the tree frogs and crickets, and, it can't be overlooked, the very good rum punches we'd drunk before dinner, put me in the mood. There's definitely something to be said about a change of scene, good-quality sheets and the knowledge that you don't have to get up early in the morning. It was the best sex we'd had for ages. Edward didn't exactly say that, but he did say how wonderful it had been. I had to agree. It made me a bit sad, actually.

Still, one fabulous night wasn't enough to make me change my mind. I was still determined to ask for my freedom, I just had to pick a time.

At the second wonderful hotel, right on the edge of a cliff, where the sunsets were almost too spectacular, we met a delightful honeymoon couple. She was feeling just a bit lonely as you can do on honeymoon, if you don't know your husband well. I was happy to have some female company and the men were both glad to find someone who wanted to go scuba diving. We drank a lot of rum as a foursome, sitting under stars like halogen lamps, breathing in air as soft and warm and perfumed as expensive bath oil, and it was arranged. The boys would leave early and scuba dive, and we women would have breakfast together, lie around the pool and maybe find a craft shop for some gentle shopping later.

We were drinking coffee by the pool, still summoning up the energy to put proper clothes on and go shopping when Julia sighed deeply.

'Are you exhausted? Honeymoons can be tiring.' I thought back to ours – making love several times, night and morning, and it had been lovely, but a bit strenuous.

'No, it's not that. I'm just looking forward to the

time when we've been married a bit longer, like you and Edward.'

A flash of guilt stung me. I hadn't told Edward yet, but I hadn't changed my mind. Had Julia been able to guess something? 'What do you mean?'

'Nothing really, it's just you seem so easy with each other. Nick and I still have so much to find out. And Edward adores you!'

'Does he?' This was a bit of a surprise.

'Oh yes. I saw him look at you the other night. It's obvious the sun shines out of you.'

'Oh.' I didn't know what to say, really. I thought Julia must be so loved-up herself she was seeing things. But it was rather sweet. Maybe Edward would be more upset than I thought he would be.

'Yes. You'd dropped your hat and were picking it up and he smiled at you with so much love. You didn't see because of your hat but it made my heart clench.'

Remorse flooded over me. He still loved me! And I had been planning to leave him. How could I have done? Maybe when I'd been feeling neglected he had been loving me all the time. All those little digs he seemed to make probably meant something quite different. How confusing!

I made a big point of being as nice as possible when he and young Nick came back from scuba diving. I got some massage oil from reception and gave him a massage. I was hoping for a bit of 'afternoon delight' but he fell fast asleep. Still, there was always tonight.

As I tiptoed round the bedroom, tidying up, I

thought what a lucky escape I'd had. I'd been planning to leave a good and faithful man for reasons that now seemed ridiculous. Thank goodness I hadn't said anything.

A couple of days later, when we'd had a long day following a trail to the most fantastic viewpoint, and had come back to the hotel, he said, 'There's something I need to talk to you about.'

Panic punched me in the solar plexus as I realised what he wanted to say. It seemed so obvious suddenly – he was going to leave me – that was why he'd taken me to this beautiful place, given me such a lovely holiday because he was going to leave me for a younger woman. It all made perfect sense – the late evenings at the office hadn't meant he'd been working, he'd been with Her. His reduced sex drive was because he was getting it elsewhere. I felt such a fool and so sad. Julia must have imagined the smile she'd intercepted. She was young and on her honeymoon; she would think things like that.

I licked my lips. 'Well, what do you want to say?'

'Not here. I want the right spot. We'll both have a shower and change then go to that spot in the garden overlooking the sea where we can watch for the parrots.'

I even thought, as the water poured over my head, that he'd chosen that spot so that if I kicked up a fuss he could shove me over the edge and say I'd slipped. I felt truly ghastly, and wondered if I should leave a note in the bedroom, just in case.

He was definitely edgy as I followed him down the narrow path. This wasn't a pleasant stroll he was taking me on, it was a journey. He had news and I knew what it was.

'Darling,' he began.

That was a little bit encouraging. If he'd called me Anna there'd have been bad news, definitely.

'I don't quite know how to say this . . .'

'I bet you don't,' I said, terrified that I was going to cry. Would that make him push me off the edge and into the sea? It looked quite appealing, actually, very blue and beautiful. But there were a lot of trees to hit on the way down, and rocks at the bottom.

He frowned. 'Sit down.'

I sat, fighting tears. We'd been married for nearly thirty years. Maybe if he was going to leave me I could fling myself down on to those rocks. Then I pulled myself together. That was just silly.

He took my hand. 'Darling – um – you may have noticed that I've been working very long hours lately.'

'Yes,' I snapped, hanging on to my dignity as well as I could.

'It's been for a reason.'

I nodded. The words 'I bet it has' didn't qualify as dignified.

'I've been trying – oh, this is so difficult!'

'Just spit it out,' I said. 'It's going to be hard however

you dress it up.' By now I was thinking about the journey home, with us not speaking. I bit my lip.

'OK. I want to take early retirement. I want us to move to the country. I want to be a potter!'

They say shock does funny things to you, and they're right. I couldn't take it in. 'What?' It came out as a whisper.

'Oh, I knew you'd find it hard. I'm fed up with working in the oil business. I want to spend more time with you! In the country. Can you bear the idea?'

'You mean, all those extra hours . . .'

'I was doing as many hours, as many deals as I could, so my final salary and my pension will be as good as it can be.'

'Oh.'

'So how do you feel about selling up and starting a new life somewhere else?'

It was hard to put my whirling thoughts into words. He'd never be a perfect husband but I wasn't a perfect wife. What I did know is that I didn't want to stop being one, imperfect or not. Eventually, I managed to say, 'I've always loved those property programmes when they up sticks and move to the country. Now we can do it in real life!'

Then, I'm almost ashamed to relate, he kissed me. And we were late for dinner.

The Only Snag

BY ANNE FINE

Sarah and David Arbuthnot had to wait nearly a full eight months to get into their lovely new house. It seemed the problem was with the drainage at that end of the estate. ('Never mind,' David kept soothing impatient Sarah. 'Better that they get all that sorted than we end up flooded.')

She wasn't comforted, but did her best to spend the time usefully choosing furniture and fabrics. As soon as each window went in, Sarah was there on site, checking and measuring before she made the curtains. 'We've practically got a whole spare house in here,' said David as he inched past the new table top up-ended in the flat that they'd been forced to rent till 'River View' was finished. But it did mean that almost within a few hours of the removal men finally leaving, the house looked perfect.

'Fantastic job!' said David. 'Well done you!'

She gazed around her. Yes, it had all come right. So now it was on to the next thing. 'About the garden . . .'

They had discussed it several times, of course. And all the months they'd been waiting, Sarah had been collecting photographs of other people's gardens, some out of magazines and some she had taken herself. More than once she had been startled when home owners appeared in their upstairs windows: 'Excuse me? May I help you?' and Sarah had blushed as she explained that she, too, was moving to a house that had a garden of just the same shape and with just the same sort of slope. She'd just been passing, and the way they'd laid out their garden was so lovely. So did they mind awfully . . . ?

Of course, once they understood, they never minded at all. Indeed, they were usually flattered, instantly inviting her through the gate in order to show her round and tell her where they'd bought the snake-bark willow, or why they'd decided to put the lavender bed on this side rather than that. So it was really rather tiresome to have to start with something as dull as the lawn. Nonetheless, David set to with the seeding. (They had considered turf, but, frankly, money was quite tight by then and Tom the builder, probably realising that he had pushed their patience well beyond the limit, had made a point of spending his last day clearing and smoothing the ground round the house till it was almost perfect.)

'Pity about the manhole,' David said.

Once he had mentioned it, she couldn't bear it. There it was, mercifully to the side, just at the top of the slope. But it was still where she had hoped to have the smoothest line of grass. 'Give it a go,' urged David.

'Perhaps when the grass grows thicker, we won't even notice it.'

Of course they did.

First, Sarah painted it green to match the grass. That looked ridiculous. That very afternoon she had to go back to the hardware shop to buy some paint remover.

'I'm going to plant something beside it,' she told David. 'To draw the eye away.' They settled on buddleia. She was impatient so they spent a bit more than he expected getting one that was already established. Sarah quite often found herself stepping across on her way to, or back from, her car in order to pull the buddleia's branches so they would drape over the manhole. The problem, it turned out, was that the eye was first drawn to the pretty bush, and then, inevitably, down to that tiresome metal circle set in the lawn.

'I know,' said Sarah. 'Let's build a little rockery in front of it.'

'Brilliant!' said David. It took Sarah an age to find the sort of stones she wanted, and after that they had to toil for hours till she was satisfied with their arrangement.

'This isn't working. Either I'll see the manhole every time I walk to the car, or I'll be staring at it through the kitchen window.'

'What about setting the rockery all around it?'

She lost her cool. 'Oh, yes? And get a circle of mirror cut to lay on top of it to pretend it's a pond?'

He just kept packing earth around the rocks, noticing that once again her impatience, fighting with frugality, had won hands down and she'd splashed out on larger plants. The rockery lasted through the winter, but only because Sarah was in the habit of drawing the curtains at dusk, so didn't spend very much time looking at it.

By spring, the idea of the mirror circle had burgeoned into something far more fanciful. 'This is what we'll do. We'll buy one of those water features – a little fountain – and lay the pool bit right on top of the manhole.'

'But what if someone needs to get into the drain?'

'We'll get a special sort of water tray made – one we can slide to the side.'

'That won't be cheap.'

It wasn't. And it didn't work. It just looked tacky. After a few weeks, Sarah had had enough of trying to pretend that it was acceptable, and had gone back to her garden design books. It seemed to David she'd become obsessed. Even when things went badly for her at work, she had begun to interrupt her very own grumbling with things like, 'Hey! Suppose we . . . ? No. That won't work.' The day his own firm's long-term rivals astonishingly slid into receivership, she broke into his account of how the news flew round the warehouse to say to him, 'I know! What about looking for a sundial with a big, round base?'

He sighed. 'That bird table looked bad enough.'

She gnawed a hangnail. 'You're right. If that damn bird table looked so horrible, so will a sundial.'

She was so sunk in gloom she didn't hear the rest of

what he told her. Just as she didn't notice the state of the rest of the garden. Everywhere out of the sightline of the manhole had been neglected. The verges were unclipped. The ceanothus was already out of hand. The little steps down to the back gate still lay bare on both sides.

Just as she didn't notice him.

Next morning, almost before the two of them were up, Tom, their old builder, arrived. 'What ho!'

'Problem?' asked David, knotting his dressing-gown round him.

'You tell me,' Tom said cheerfully. 'I'm here for snagging.'

'Snagging?'

'You know,' said Tom. 'Normal procedure. It was all in the papers that you signed. We leave the house to settle, then we come round to fix any problems that arise. Snagging, we call it.'

'Oh, right.'

He waited while they had a little think. The plumbing all worked perfectly. The windows didn't stick. None of the doors had swollen. David made Tom a cup of tea while Sarah wandered round the house, looking for anything she might regret not mentioning as snags.

She came back, defeated.

Tom looked delighted. 'Right, then? All tickety-boo?'

'Tickety-boo,' agreed Sarah, almost regretfully.

Tom gazed out of the window. 'You've done a good job here. Garden looks nice.'

Perhaps because he had as good as invited them to make complaints, Sarah came out with it. 'Apart from that manhole.'

Tom squinted up the garden. 'What manhole?'

'That one up there.'

'Where?'

'There!' She pointed irritably. 'It's been driving us mad.'

'Oh, really? Sorry about that.' He didn't sound as if he were the least bit bothered. In fact, he made so little of her grievance that, as he was leaving, she made a childish face at him behind his back.

Together, Sarah and David watched as, instead of making for the gate as they expected, Tom strolled up the garden slope. Together they watched as he bent down to inspect the manhole they'd complained about. They watched, astonished, as he slid his skilled, strong fingers under its edge, braced his wide shoulders to prise the heavy metal circle upright, then rolled it back towards them down the side of the lawn as if it weighed no more than a child's hoop.

'Sorry about that!' he called back over his shoulder as he kept up with the manhole as it rolled, somewhat unsteadily, out the gate. 'The only snag is that we keep forgetting to count them!'

Straight and True Like
the Lilies of the Field

BY NICCI FRENCH

The first question is always what to wear. I knew that we would all have been asking ourselves that from the moment the invitation arrived, going through our wardrobes in our minds, mentally trying on this red dress, that low-cut shirt, that pair of boots, for size. Hair up or down? Lips red or pink? Jewellery loud or discreet? Glamour or flamboyance? Of course, the question is really not what to wear but who to be. Even more so in my case. Who do I want them to see when I walk through that door after twenty years? I thought about buying something for the occasion, but you can always tell when an outfit's new, and you don't want to seem to be making too much of an effort. The trick is to look good, but casually so.

Grey cashmere cardigan, so light it feels like a cobweb against my skin, tight charcoal-grey trousers that make me look thinner, my favourite shoes with a small heel, hair (cut and highlighted last week) scooped up in a messy bun, small silver studs in my ears, a plain silver necklace that Robbie had given me on our wedding anniversary. I stood in front of the mirror, turned to one side and then the other, smiled at myself over my shoulder, faced myself full on and nodded. I would do. Stupid to care so much. Stupid to feel that it mattered. Stupid to feel my heart racing faster than normal and my mouth dry in anticipation.

Everything was smaller than I remembered. The door was just an ordinary door; the corridors didn't stretch endlessly on; the cloakroom was just a cloakroom after all, although its smell of pine and stale sweat rolled back the years – shorts and Aertex shirt and goose pimples on a chilly, damp February morning. The hall, when I reached it, was half the size I'd pictured it, and less darkly lit. It buzzed with voices and the chink of glasses, the peals of laughter. I had deliberately arrived late and it looked as though most of us were already here: the class of '88, and I could see women falling on each other with whoops of delight, hugging each other tearfully, or holding on to each other's arms and examining each other in hilarious amazement. I stood at the entrance, trying to make out the people I remembered, then took a determined breath and stepped into the room. It felt like going out on to a stage but it was an anti-climactic entrance, because nobody noticed me at first and I didn't know how to penetrate the tight huddles of friends reunited.

'Whoops! Sorry.'

A large woman with a yellow jacket and hair like a bronze helmet had backed into me. White wine slopped over the rim of her glass.

'Don't worry.' I narrowed my eyes to make out the face behind the face. 'Judith Fairweather,' I said.

'That's right.' She gave a girlish laugh and waved her left hand with its thick gold band on her fourth finger. 'Fairweather as was, Glover as is. Isn't this odd? I've just seen Mrs Butcher! She looks exactly the same; I'm still terrified of her and I still don't know how to conjugate "*être*". I'm sure I recognise you, but I don't quite . . . Sorry.'

'Sally,' I said. 'Sally Martin.'

'Sally! Of course!' She clapped me heartily on the back. I could tell she still didn't remember me, but was making a gallant effort to pretend. 'Of course. Well, I'm off to the loo myself – do you remember how they used to have that stiff toilet paper that scratched your bottom? See you.'

I made my way towards the table of drinks and took a glass of sparkling water and a handful of peanuts, which I fed into my mouth one by one, then walked over to a large group and inserted myself.

'Hello,' I said. 'This is all very strange, isn't it?'

Everyone looked at me expectantly, their faces ready to light up in smiles of recognition. And I looked at them. Helen, who used to be so thin, with her double chin now and frown marks creasing her brow; Gail, once so curvy, looking scrawnily immaculate in her black suit; Fi, who used to refuse to eat her school dinners and would have to sit all day over cold, greying rice pudding; Jane Jones, who had been the school's champion runner but who didn't look as though she ran much now; Jemma of the brown plaits who was now ash blonde; Lily the giggler, and Pauline, the group leader, the one we all wanted to please . . . I saw them as they were now and I saw them as they used to be.

'Hi! Yes, isn't it. You're . . . ?'

'Sally.'

'Sally! Sally – I can't quite remember your last name.'

'Sally Martin.'

'Were you in Mrs Elliot's class too?'

'Yes.'

'I can still remember the register,' said Helen. 'Anna Astley, Julia Atwood, Caroline Bawdsley, Jemma Brown, Yvette Brown, Emma Burns . . . Oh what came next?'

'Sarah Cairn, Cindy Chester, Gail Craig . . .'

'Chloe Davenport, Bella David.'

'Bella David!' I interrupted, laughter spluttering out of me. 'What an unfortunate name! Do you all remember Bella?'

'You mean, Fat Bella?' Gail gave a shout of mirth. 'God, how could I forget? I had to sit next to her in Chemistry. Do you remember, Pauline?'

'Remember?'

Pauline thrust out her stomach, puckered up her face, and said in a whine: ' "I don't know why you all have to be so cruel. You should think about how it would feel if it was you." That Bella?'

Everyone giggled.

'She smelt funny.'

'Yeah, you used to hold your nose when she walked past.'

'Did I? How awful – I don't remember that.'

'And she was always trying to join in.'

Pauline grinned at us. For a moment she looked so like the dimpled teenager I used to know that I couldn't breathe properly; memory plays such tricks. 'Do you remember how she invited us all to her birthday party – how old would we have been?'

'Sixteen?'

'And we all said we'd go and none of us did; we went to the cinema instead.'

'So we did. That's the kind of things I'd ground my kids for doing now.'

'But you never know what your kids get up to at school, do you? Best not to find out either.'

'Her mum was really odd too. She walked with a stick and her hip kind of swivelled.'

'I remember us all imitating that once,' Fi said. 'It didn't even occur to me that she would mind. It just seemed funny. How terrible is that?'

'She didn't mind,' said Pauline. 'It went over her head.'

'She was always trying to please you, Pauline. I think she thought that if you liked her, we all would.'

'I guess she so badly wanted to belong,' I said. 'But that's one of the awful lessons that life teaches, isn't it? That the more you care, the worse it gets. How do you teach someone not to care though?'

'I remember that practical joke you played on her, Pauline.'

'Which one?'

'Where you got your brother to ring her up and we all listened while he pretended to be that weird boy she quite liked, inviting her out.'

'Oh God, yes! She waited for hours outside the school the next day.'

'And then the following morning you repeated the phone conversation to her word for word. Her face went all mottled. I thought she was going to explode or something.'

'Does anyone know what happened to her?' asked Fi.

'She killed herself,' I said.

'What?' said Fi. 'Really?'

I looked around at the startled faces.

'That gave you a shock,' I said with a laugh. 'No, it's not true. I haven't a clue what happened to her.'

'I heard she dropped out of college,' said Jemma.

'Didn't she have a breakdown?' said Jane.

'That's right. Actually, I think she was in a psychiatric ward for ages. My mum knew someone who knew her mum.'

'I wonder if she's all right now.'

'I'm getting hungry,' said Pauline. 'Shall we get food? As long as it's not shepherd's pie followed by rhubarb and custard.'

That set off another lot of shrieked memories about

crumble and awful peas, and the cabbage that was cooked for too long, and shoving in the lunch queue.

As the evening progressed, the noise got more and more raucous. These thirty-eight-year-old wives and mothers and doctors and lawyers and horse riders and bridge players and skiers and lunchers and shoppers turned back into the giggling schoolgirls they had once been, or thought they had been or wished they had been. Tania McDougall, who had been a quiet girl who sat at the front of the class and played the bassoon, was talking loudly about boyfriends and parties and wild escapades.

Sometimes it was the other way round. Sue Robertson, the first person in the class to lose her virginity (aged about fourteen and three-quarters), or at least the first to publicly announce it (the news was passed around in awed whispers during a Monday morning assembly), was now a matronly figure, showing photographs of her three children, each at a different boarding school.

Girls from the current sixth form were moving around the room with platters of little sandwiches and pastries and miniature pizzas. I thought they looked a little dismayed, as if they had caught a glimpse of their future. I struck up conversation with one of them, a girl called Courteney, who was slim and beautiful, captain of the hockey team, grade eight at piano and violin, and was planning to study medicine at Edinburgh. I told her that the school had clearly come up a bit since we had been there.

'As you can tell,' I said, gesturing at the room, in one corner of which Francesca Nichol and Lucy Turner were holding on to each other and attempting to sing the school song. They only got as far as the first line, which they repeated several times in increasingly loud voices, 'Straight and true as the lilies of the field,' they warbled. I grimaced at the words. Straight and true.

'Over there,' I said, turning back to Courteney. 'Out of the door on the other side of the kitchens, is where we used to go and smoke at lunchtimes, at the top of the steps. It was a perfect position because you couldn't be seen either from above or below.'

'We still do,' said Courteney, laughing. 'Now it's the one place where you can't be seen by the security cameras.'

'Security cameras?' I said. 'That's something new.'

'There were some break-ins,' said Courteney. 'Some computers were stolen.'

'When I was here, the staff were more worried about boys getting in.'

'The boys are already here,' said Courteney. 'We have a joint sixth form.'

'That takes some of the fun out of it,' I said, but Courteney didn't look convinced.

'The funny thing is,' said Charlotte Nugent, lurching towards us and slurring her words slightly, 'is that all these girls – I still think of them as girls – I know them so well and I feel so close to them and I share so many memories with them and . . . I'll have another one of those.' She took a glass of white wine from a passing tray and replaced it with her empty one. 'You want one?'

'I'm on water,' I said.

'What was I saying?'

'You were saying how well you remember these girls.'

'That's right. Now admittedly, there were some ups and downs. I mean, for example, Claire Porter over there stole my boyfriend, Luke Morgan, literally from under my nose. Girls can be such bitches. But nevertheless, I can't believe I haven't kept in touch with these people. I mean, literally, I feel closer to these girls than most of my current friends, even my husband, for God's sake. I know that it's stupid the way people talk about being at school as the happiest days of their life, but now that I'm here it feels true in a way. It's as if everything just means more in a way. I'm going to start crying on your shoulder in a moment.' She looked at me. 'I'm really sorry but who are you again?'

I bumped into Pauline on her way back from collecting a drink.

'Fancy a ciggie outside?' I said. 'Back of the kitchen?'

'I shouldn't really,' she said. 'I've half given up.'

'Remember that PE teacher everyone fancied, Mr Ransom, who used to catch people there and lecture them about harming their chests?'

Pauline laughed.

'I can't resist it,' she said. 'Just the one.'

It was completely dark outside. We could only find

our way to the top of the steps with the aid of the little torch I had in my bag.

'That's useful,' she said.

'Christmas present,' I said.

I lit two cigarettes and gave her one. She took a drag.

'Funny evening,' she said. 'It feels as if no time has passed at all. We're all the same.'

'I've been thinking about that girl,' I said. 'The one who got picked on?'

'You mean Fat Bella?' Pauline said.

'I was feeling bad about it,' I said.

'Don't,' said Pauline. 'It was just part of the rough and tumble.'

'But for her,' I said. 'It must have been awful.'

Pauline laughed. 'She did us all a service. Useless as she was. Looking back, maybe we were lucky to have poor old Bella to kick around. It brought us all together.'

'But don't you feel bad? You were the one everyone looked up to. You could have stopped it.'

'It wasn't such a big deal. She probably enjoyed it, in her own protozoan sort of way.'

'You don't understand,' I said. 'I'm wanting you to say that you regret it, that you're sorry it happened.'

'But I'm not,' said Pauline. 'I don't regret any of it. What's your problem? Why can't you just enjoy the party?'

I stubbed my cigarette out very carefully on the wall

and then placed the butt not on the ground but into my bag.

It was a beautiful morning. You could see right across the Heath. The crocuses and the daffodils were out, so we had breakfast in the garden. I sat drinking freshly squeezed orange juice enjoying the view. Robbie sat stubbornly with his back to it, reading the newspaper.

'When are you due in court?' I asked, tipping my face towards the sun and closing my eyes.

'Ten thirty,' he said. 'I'm starting the summing up.' He looked over the newspaper. 'What are you up to?'

'Meetings,' I said vaguely. 'Tasks. Oh, but I wish I could sit here till evening, doing nothing. It's lovely. We've made it through the winter.'

'I tell you what,' he said. 'Why don't we meet after work and . . . Bloody hell!'

'What?'

'Wait.'

I took a sip of coffee.

'What is it?' I said. 'Did Arsenal lose? Has Kate Moss retired?'

'That school reunion of yours.'

'I didn't go in the end.'

'Someone died there.'

'What?'

'You can read it for yourself: "Mother, thirty-eight, dies in fall at school reunion."'

'What happened?'

'Pretty obvious, isn't it? "High-spirited celebrations."'

"Uninhibited." A comment from the local police chief about women and alcohol.'

'Who was it? Does it say?'

'Hang on. Here we are: Pauline Whistler. Do you remember her, Bella?'

'Remember her? Yes. I remember.'

The Last Word

BY NICCI FRENCH

When I came into the kitchen, Tom was sitting at the table reading the newspaper and eating breakfast, looking mellow, utterly chilled. In the meantime, I was already agitated, my head buzzing with things to do, and I hadn't even left for work yet. That's the thing. Tom and I are married and we live in the same flat and yet we seem to exist in different time zones. If I'm on London time, Tom is in somewhere like Athens, somewhere Mediterranean and easy-going and about two hours later than me.

And we're from different generations. I dress like a grown-up, in suits and polished shoes. I have to because I go to an office and help people buy houses and make wills. Tom is the same age as me, but he dresses like a student. He is a consultant, which means he hangs around the flat. He wears a dressing-gown for hours until he pulls on some jeans and a T-shirt.

We eat differently as well. Breakfast for me is a cup of coffee. If I have time, I have a second cup of coffee. Tom says that breakfast is the most important meal of the day. He makes himself porridge with water, squeezes orange juice for himself. He takes several kinds of vitamin pills as well. I could see them on the table next to the orange juice in an irritating little line.

Tom spends most of the day in the flat, but he reads the newspaper from beginning to end and follows the news on the web during the day. I don't have time to find out what's happening in the world as I spend my time out in it, working.

I looked around the kitchen. The used oranges were scattered around the juicer. By the time I returned in the evening they would be sour and fermented. The saucepan Tom had used for the porridge was next to the stove. There at least was one thing I could do before I left. I took it to the sink and started scrubbing it viciously.

'I was leaving it to soak,' said Tom, the first words he had spoken to me today.

'No you weren't.'

'I was going to. After you had gone.'

I finished cleaning out the pan with a ferocious final scrub from the washing-up brush, then dumped it on the side of the sink with a clatter.

'You're making a point,' he said.

'Am I?'

'Go on then,' he said. 'Say what it is you want to say.'

'I wasn't making a point,' I said. 'But the point I would have been making, had I been making a point, would have been that you always say you're leaving something to soak, but then you never wash it up. It just sits in the sink. But now it's been done and so it won't be there all hard and crusty when I come back in the evening.'

'I never wash it up?'

'I wash it up later.'

'If you waited, then I'd wash it up, once it had soaked enough.'

Tom closed the newspaper with steady, deliberate calmness. Then one by one he swallowed the pills with a gulp of freshly squeezed orange juice. Omega 3. Gulp. Vitamin E. Gulp. Glucosamine. Gulp. He smiled at me.

'I just want to know,' he said. 'Are we having our argument again?'

'Which argument?'

'There are various ones, but I think this is the one where you tell me how much more work you do around the house than I do.'

'Tom, Tom, please stop this.'

'Amy, Amy, please, I don't want to.'

'I really have to go and get ready for work.'

'Meaning I don't?'

'I didn't. But you don't, do you?'

He pulled the cord of his dressing-gown tighter and planted his elbows firmly on the kitchen table between us.

'Meaning that what I do isn't really work. Meaning that you're the busy career woman and you do the housework. While I'm at home, unemployed in all but name and at a loose end, don't you? That's what you think.'

'I don't. And I don't want to have this conversation.'

'Who makes the bed in the mornings?'

'That's just shaking the duvet.'

He put his hand to his chin and looked thoughtful, like a caricature of thoughtfulness.

'Oh, sorry, Amy, I forgot the first rule of the household. When you do something around the flat it's important and hard work, but when I do it, it's not worth mentioning.'

Anger itched inside me; I let myself give in to it: 'Anyway, you make the bed because you're the one who gets out of it last. As a general rule.'

'No one orders you to get up early.'

'For goodness sake, Tom, I have to get up to go to work, remember?'

'As you keep on reminding me.' Tom's tone became sarcastic. 'I suppose that means it doesn't count. It doesn't matter what I actually do, does it? You think you're the tidy one and I'm the slob.'

'I didn't say that.'

'Whereas actually, it's the other way round. Leaving things all over the place. Slippers on the stairs. Coats on chairs.'

He leaned over and pulled at my jacket; it slipped on to the floor and coins spilled out of its pocket, rolling across the tiles.

'I was going to wear that today. That's why it's on the chair, or was.'

'You can't admit you're wrong, can you?'

'It wasn't me who brought all this up. But now we're

talking about it, well then. I vacuum the carpets. I wash the clothes. I put things away. I come home late, and I'm tired, but it's still me who clears up the mess, cleans out the fridge . . .'

'You clean out the fridge? And I suppose you think you do all the cooking?'

'Not all of it.'

'Roast chicken and garlic bread.'

'What?'

He held up a hand, counting off his fingers.

'Spaghetti carbonara. Cod with mashed potato. Bacon omelettes. Liver with onions.'

'Why are you listing meals?'

I looked at him. He hadn't shaved for a couple of days; his eyes glittered in his stubbly, frowning face, under his thick brows. He seemed amused by all this in a way I didn't understand. It didn't seem amusing to me in any way at all.

'Do you know what I sometimes wish for? Do you want to hear? I sometimes hope there's a God. Do you know why?'

I bent down and picked up my jacket from the floor and some of the coins from the lino. I pulled the jacket on. I really didn't know what to say or where to begin.

'I've hoped that there's a God so that he could come down and appear in this kitchen and say, "Tom, you're right and Amy, you're wrong."'

'I think he's got more important things to do.'

'But there isn't a God. Or at least he hasn't appeared, so I've taken matters into my own hands.'

'Can we just stop this, Tom? This is just demeaning.'

'No, it's not. It's the truth. We need to face up to the truth and the truth will set us free. Wait here, I'll show you. Don't you dare move.'

He jumped to his feet and dashed from the kitchen. If, a year or two previously, he had told me to wait while he got something, I would have expected him to return with a present: a jacket or two tickets to Paris. Now there was just a sickly, ominous feeling like a hole opening up at my feet.

For a few moments I willed myself to get up but instead just gazed at the space where he had been sitting, a little headache ticking above my left eye. Gradually the rage subsided, leaving in its place a dull hopelessness and shame. When he returned, he was carrying something I couldn't see. A sort of folder. I tried to change the tone.

'We're both tired,' I said. 'It's a difficult time. So for my part, I'm sorry if I . . .'

'If? Which means you're not.'

I took a deep breath. 'I'm sorry that I got angry like that. It was wrong.'

'All right, Amy. I accept your apology,' he said. I felt the rage hot inside my chest.

'Now it's your turn,' I said.

He sat next to me and laid a yellow folder down and beside it an exercise book. He flicked it open.

'Yesterday: March 16th.'

He thumbed over a page of the book.

'Put out the compost. Turned off lights that had

been left on in spite of previous discussion about saving energy.'

'What is this?'

'Wiped smeary mirror in bathroom. Replaced empty lavatory roll with full one again.'

'This is a joke. Right?'

'Cooked for the third time this week.'

His voice was getting louder; I looked at his mouth opening and shutting, opening and shutting. It was hard to think clearly. I looked at his bare feet on the tiles (that had apparently been washed on March 15th) and saw that there was hair on the toes.

'Lasagne. Tried to ignore the loud chewing sounds she made.'

'This isn't funny,' I said.

'You get offended when I point it out. Collected petrol receipts for tax form. Went through itemised phone bill. There are numbers on there, by the way, that need explaining, but we'll come to that later.'

I stood up. 'I've got to leave.'

'March 13th, went to the supermarket. £107.53. Had to put back the cheese biscuits and the vodka. Went to the dry-cleaner's to collect her dress. Swept the yard. You are not to leave the room until I've finished. Sex: let's see. March 12th, for nine minutes only, and then before that, hmm. March 4th. Eight days' gap. You said you had your period. That's rather a long period, isn't it? And anyway, you also said you had a period, let's check, yes, three weeks before that. You think I'm stupid? I check the bins, you know. I look at the bathroom shelves.'

'Can I see it?'

'Sure.' He handed it to me.

I flicked through the fat exercise book. I saw page after page of dates and times and observations and grudges and sour observations, all in his neat, square handwriting. There were exclamation marks and underlinings and even a table tabulating the time spent on housework in December and January. When this is over, I thought, I will walk straight out of the door into the warm spring day and I won't come back. Not today and not tomorrow and not ever again.

I looked at some of the entries. Emptying the dishwasher, mending a bike puncture, washing a baking tray. A failure on my part to thank him. Later in the book there was a section tabulating some of my failures: an apple core by the side of the bed, hair in the bath, a low-cut top I'd worn while going out with friends.

'What's in the file?' I asked. I was filled with a sudden heavy foreboding, as if the sun had gone behind a dark cloud and we were in the chilly darkness.

'Why don't you look?' he said.

I flipped the file open. There were print-outs of digital photographs. They all showed areas of the flat.

'What are these?'

'Isn't it obvious?' he said with a happy smile. 'Look. Here's before, here's after. After I've cleared up. And look at the time and date on the image. Here's the cupboard the way you left it. And there it is after I'd spent the day taking everything out and then sorting it out. That's the bookshelf in the bedroom after I'd fixed it. You didn't even notice that, did you? And there are dozens of them. Look.'

As he flicked through them, it looked like a photographic exhibition of our life.

'There it is, in black and white and colour.'

He closed the file and laid it down and then slowly and implacably raised his eyes and met mine. 'So what do we do now?'

When the alarm went, I could hardly believe it. I looked at the clock and groaned. Six forty-five. I heard the heavy breathing of Tom next to me. It took more than an alarm clock to wake him in the morning and more than me shaking him gently. I sighed and leaned over him to kiss him on the cheek, breathing in his thick morning smell. His hair needed cutting; there were creases on his cheek from the pillow. Still asleep, he muttered something and turned on his side, putting his forearm over his eyes. I resisted the temptation to shake him, to force him to get up with me, or at least to show him I was getting up first.

It took an immense effort to pull myself out of the bed. I showered in hot water and then cold water and then hot water to wake myself up. I pulled on a dressing-gown and went downstairs. I had arrived back late after a long and rather stressful day at the office, so I hadn't really taken in the full devastation. It was almost comic; not quite. A couple of Tom's friends had come round. They'd ordered an Indian takeaway and watched whatever it is they watch. The living room and kitchen looked as if there had been a student party followed by a police raid followed by a riot.

I put the kettle on for coffee and started to clear up. It wasn't quite as bad as it looked. Almost the worst thing was that someone had drunkenly got the two bins mixed and had tipped the Indian leftovers into the recycling bin and I had to empty it and rearrange it. As for the rest of it, it just took a couple of bin bags and a quick run around with the vacuum cleaner and a mop, where a beer bottle had tipped over and been left. The smell of beer and stale cigarettes wasn't pleasant at seven in the morning and I had to open two windows and breathe the fierce cold air.

I looked around the living room with a feeling of virtue. It would need a proper scrub and wipe down when I got back from work, but it would do for the moment. I made myself a pot of coffee and sat at the kitchen table. This was my peaceful part of the day. After this it would be work and phones ringing and e-mails and meetings.

'Hi, babe,' said Tom, walking into the room, rubbing his eyes. 'I thought you were going to bring coffee up. That's what you said.'

On a good day, I rather liked the way Tom looked in the morning. He had pulled on a pair of jeans and a striped shirt that was only half done up. His hair was disordered, his jaw line softened by a couple of days of stubble. It felt like I was the serious grown-up one going off to work and he was the mad artist staying at home. But this wasn't a particularly good day.

'I thought you'd like to sleep in.'

'The vacuum cleaner woke me up; you were making an awful racket.'

'So sorry about that,' I said, a touch sarcastically. He looked around, frowning, but then just gave a shrug and poured himself a cup of coffee, sitting down at the table and stretching his arms above his head.

'Never mind,' he said.

'It was an awful mess.' Damn. I hadn't been going to say that.

'What was?'

'Downstairs. It was almost impressively chaotic.'

'You could have left it for me,' he said.

'Yeah, right.'

'So then, that's OK.'

'As long as you had a good time,' I said.

His face turned serious.

'I don't like it when people are sarcastic,' he said. 'But I'll answer you as if you were asking a real question. I needed to see them. You know, because of everything. I've known them for years. They understand what I've been through.'

I made myself overlook the greasy remains of the takeaway, the sleazy DVDs that had been scattered around the television.

'I'm sorry,' I said. 'But is this – not this, me – is it all too much for you?'

He shook his head slowly.

'No,' he said, taking my hand in his. I tried not to wince as he squeezed my fingers together.

'Because, Tom, if it is . . .'

'Judy,' he murmured. 'Judy.'

We stared at each other. I saw my face reflected in both his eyes and I shivered because I suddenly felt that a ghost was in the room with us: another woman with a different face. For one eerie moment, I felt that she was looking back at me out of Tom's eyes and a tremor of fear passed through me.

'It's hard to know that I'm with you now because of such a tragic accident,' I said slowly. 'In this flat, too. I saw the picture of this flat in newspapers, with headlines about a tragic accident, before I ever crossed the threshold. I saw a picture of you, too – you with Amy. The tragic couple.'

'You're my future, Judy,' he said. 'But Amy was my past; she always will be.'

'All I want is to look after you,' I said. 'To look after you and make you better.'

Suddenly I remembered I was still in my dressing-gown. I was going to be late. I stood up and gave him a kiss.

'I've got to dash,' I said. 'Did you pick up my suit from the dry-cleaner's?'

'No,' he said.

'Oh,' I said.

He looked at me sharply, his features hardening so

that for a moment he was a stranger. 'Is that a problem?'

'No, not really,' I said. 'It's just that I've got this important presentation. I told you about it. You said . . . oh, never mind.'

'I'm sure there's something you can wear.'

I didn't speak. I was desperately trying to think of something. There was the old green jacket. That might do.

'I've got to go,' I said. 'Huge day. Is that all right?' He nodded mutely. 'I'll try and stop off at the shops on the way back. Do you want me to get anything?'

Tom thought for a moment and then pulled a small, black exercise book from his pocket.

'I've made a list,' he said.

Cold Calling

BY PHILIPPA GREGORY

*H*e answered the phone on the second ring, hoping that it might be someone who would entertain him; or at least silence the nagging voices in his head.

'Hi, this is Raefe.'

'Hello,' the determinedly friendly voice started. 'I wonder if I might take a moment of your time to talk about luxury holidays. Have you booked your holiday yet?'

He usually got rid of cold callers at once; but her voice was so pleasant: warm and with the slightest roll of the Rs, like an Irish regional accent, that he answered: 'No, I haven't. Not yet. What sort of destinations do you offer?'

'Oh, we do everything,' she said enthusiastically. 'Anything you can imagine: cruises, honeymoons, special occasions, safaris, city breaks. What sort of thing do you like to do on holiday?'

'Actually, this is a good moment for me that you called. I was thinking about booking my honeymoon.'

'Oh, how lovely,' she said. 'I hope you'll be very happy. When are you getting married?'

'Not till next year, in May.'

'May is a lovely time to go abroad. What sort of trip did you have in mind?'

'I don't know,' he said. 'Could you suggest something? I've no idea really. I'm a climber,' he said. 'So usually I go to the mountains.'

He heard the catch in her throat. 'Mountains,' she repeated, as if she were thirsty for the cold water of the streams. 'D'you know, I've never in my life been to the mountains.'

'You must have!'

'No really. I never have. I only went to the country once on a school trip. And then it was a farm and desperately flat. And now . . . now I suppose I'll never go anywhere.'

'There is something about the mountains, you don't have to be a climber to feel it. The air is so clear that it makes everything you see bright and sharp. And the higher you go there are fewer and fewer people until when you get to up high, at the top . . .' he broke off.

'What?' she sounded quite entranced. 'What is it like at the very top?'

'Oh, it was a long time ago, I try not to think . . .'

'No tell me, please. I want to know. I want to know so much. When you get to the very top of the mountains, what's it like?'

'It's like heaven,' he said quietly. 'I used to feel that I had climbed right out of this world and into another, as if only angels could breathe that cold clean air and I could look down to the valleys below and see the beauty of the world as it is and feel just . . .'

'Just?' she prompted.

'Just joy.'

He heard her sigh. 'Joy. Right?'

'Yes.' He had never spoken to anyone of this before. It was ironic that after having dozens of counsellors asking him to open up to them and to say what he was feeling that he should speak for the first time to a stranger, a disembodied voice from a call centre. 'What's your name?' he asked.

'Maria,' she said, 'but I'm not supposed to tell you my name. We're not supposed to make personal calls.'

'This isn't a personal call, you're selling me my honeymoon, aren't you?'

'Yes,' she said. 'Well, I hope I am.'

'Oh, you are,' he said. 'Where are you calling from, are you even in the UK?'

'Yes,' she said, but her voice had changed. 'Outside Lincoln, actually.'

'What's the weather like?' From his own window he could see the small garden, with the new path carefully sloping down to the small fish-pond; where, it was hoped, he would sit on sunny days. 'It's cold here. I'm not going out.'

'I can't see anything. The windows are way too high. Anyway. Who cares? We should be talking about your holiday.'

'OK. What mountain destinations do you offer?'

'I don't have a mountains section on my sheet,' she said. He could hear her rustling papers. 'Where are the mountains? Alps?'

'I'd like the Alps,' he said dreamily. 'In May, the spring flowers will be coming out and the snow-caps will be melting off the peaks. The streams will be pouring down the hills and the trees will be coming into leaf. The trails will be slippery and the rocks will be wet . . . but the smell of the water and the greenness – oh yes. That would be wonderful.'

'I could check out honeymoon destination hotels,' she said. 'I have a list of them, all right.'

'Oh yes, the honeymoon,' he said as if he had forgotten. 'You see, I always used to stay in mountain refuges. You can trek from one to another, over the very top of the peaks.'

'Not for a honeymoon,' she said firmly. 'If I was getting married I'd want a lovely hotel and a honeymoon suite. They give you free champagne, you know, and put flowers in the room and everything. I'd want that.'

'Would you?' he asked, amused. 'And a special table at dinner and the band playing "Congratulations" and all that sort of thing?'

She gave a little sigh of longing. 'I'd have done almost anything for a honeymoon like that.'

He laughed. 'I shouldn't think you'd have to do almost anything. Just meet the right man, fall in love and do it.'

He was certain he heard a thickness in her voice, as if she were distressed.

'It's not that easy,' she said. 'You would think it would be, you would think it ought to be, but some people, now and then, some people just get it wrong. And then everything goes wrong for them.'

'Do they?'

'Yes,' she said. He was certain now that he could hear tears below her speech. 'Yes. Sometimes, you know, you can get it so wrong. You even wake up in the morning and wonder how you could have got it all so very wrong.'

'I made a mistake,' he acknowledged to her. 'I made one small mistake. But oh – I was sorry after.' He could almost see his climbing boot standing, safely enough, on the ledge of rock and then, the moment of miscalculation and the bouncing sickening fall to the limit of the rope, the scream of the rope coming away as it failed and then a long, plunging, unending drop in which he had plenty of time to know that he would die for certain. Then the moment that he hit the ground, backwards on a rock. He had lain still for a moment and then as he realised he was alive, he also knew that everything had changed.

'What was it?' she asked. 'Your mistake?'

'I fell, climbing,' he said shortly.

'Were you badly hurt?'

He flexed his hands. 'No, more frightened than hurt,' he said. 'I was lucky. But I had never been afraid before. So what was your mistake?'

'I married the wrong man,' she said lightly as if it hardly mattered. 'A bad one. A really bad one. I won't be having a lovely honeymoon, like yours, that's for sure.' She broke off and he heard someone whisper to her, urgently.

'I can't talk any more,' she said. 'Supervisor's coming my way.' In a quite different voice she said: 'Would you prefer France, Italy or Switzerland?'

'France,' he said at once. 'The French Alps.'

'And for how long?' she asked. He could hear her tapping into a computer as she ran through the questions on her sheet.

'Say a fortnight,' he said. 'Is your supervisor there now?'

'Exactly,' she said crisply.

'OK, so can you call me back when she's gone?'

'I can do that,' she said brightly. 'I'll give you a reference number and call you tomorrow with prices.'

He wrote down the number that she dictated. 'Has she gone? Can you talk now?'

'No, sir.'

'It's like a prison!' he exclaimed.

'Yes,' she said. 'Exactly.'

'But you will call me tomorrow?' He was surprised by the urgency of his desire to talk to her.

'Yes,' she said, her voice suddenly low and intimate. 'I promise.' Then she said clearly: 'Leave it with me. Have a nice day.'

She thought of him as she ate her dinner in the canteen, which rang with the clatter of trays and knives and forks and loud voices. She wondered about the girl he was going to marry and if she knew that to marry a man who could feel joy at being in the mountains, who could revel in his own strength and courage and yet not use it to bully others, was a privilege. She did not think of her own marriage, of the husband who had abused her until she could see only one way to escape him. She never thought of him now. He was dead to her and she would never bring him back to life, not even in her thoughts.

That night, on the little narrow bed listening to the sluggish, regular snores of Alice, she thought of him walking from one mountain refuge to another, over the very tops of the peaks, with the streams flowing down to the valley below. When she fell asleep she was smiling.

'Hi, this is Raefe.'

'This is Maria, from the—'

'Hey, I was so hoping it would be you. I'm so glad you called me.'

'I've been thinking of you.'

'Have you?'

'Yes,' she corrected herself. 'Well, thinking of your honeymoon.'

'Oh yes, my honeymoon. But I wondered if we could talk about another destination. I was thinking of the UK.'

'Wouldn't she want to go abroad?' she asked.

He laughed out loud at the disappointment in her voice. 'Is that what you would like?'

'I'd so like to fly somewhere, you know, get on a plane and when you get off you are somewhere completely different. And it would be like being in a film, going up the steps of a plane.'

'Where would you go?'

'Oh God, I'd go anywhere. Anywhere.'

He heard at once the note in her voice which told him that she was, like him, somehow trapped. 'Why don't you go?' he asked quietly.

'Oh, I couldn't leave my . . .'

'Your?'

'I couldn't leave my son,' she said. 'I have a wonderful little boy. Just four years old. I bath him and put him to bed every night of his life. I couldn't leave him. I couldn't go away.'

'Don't you work shifts?'

'Yes,' she said. 'Course I do. This place is open night and day.'

'Then how can you see him every night?'

For a moment she was silent, as if puzzled how to answer him. 'Sometimes I bath him in the morning,' she said. 'Anyway, we're not allowed to have personal conversations.'

'I know you're not,' he said. 'But sometimes I get so lonely and it's crazy really, because I could talk to any one of a dozen people. But they don't know how I feel. And I can't tell them. I guess I don't want to talk to them, not to my friends, actually especially not to my friends. And then I feel lonely. Stupid, isn't it?'

'I can't talk to anyone anyway,' she said. 'And I don't

want to. There's nothing I can say about what happened . . .'

'Your mistake?' he asked.

'My mistake,' she confirmed. 'I did it and now I just have to live with the consequences.'

'Could you talk to me about it?'

'I'd rather not,' she said. 'It wasn't a good thing. And if you knew – well, then you might not want to talk to me at all.'

He hesitated. 'I don't know. I can't imagine that you could have done something so bad that I wouldn't even talk to you. I like . . .'

'You like?'

'I like the sound of your voice.'

He could feel, even down the phone, that she was smiling. 'I like the sound of yours,' she said very softly. 'I like it when you talk about the mountains. I'd rather you told me about the mountains than we talked about me. I've been wanting to call you all day, just to hear you talk about them. Will you tell me about somewhere that you've climbed?'

'Shall we go there together? Like an imaginary journey?'

'Yes,' she said. 'Oh yes, yes. Let's.'

'We are in Scotland,' he said, 'and this is one of the most extraordinary places in the world. We are going to climb the Old Man of Hoy, a stack standing alone in the sea.'

He could hear her sigh.

'The sea is below you and you climb in cracks and

crevices in the rock. The air is salty; when you lick your lips you can taste the spray from the sea. The gulls fly all around and when you come over a ledge you are face to face with a couple of puffins, and it's noisy – not like climbing in the mountains – with the cries of the fulmar. And when you get into a rhythm of climbing and you can hear the waves breaking on the cliff beneath you, it's like you and the sea and the gulls are moving together, as if you are all part of the same thing and there is no separate you – just the sea and the rock and the climb.'

She was silent for a moment. Then: 'Thank you,' she said, as if he had given her a gift.

He did not say glibly: 'For what?' because he knew. He too had been there once more, as high as the seagulls, without fear, like them.

He paused for a moment. 'You know, anyone can learn to climb. There are climbing walls at most sports halls and good climbing teachers. If you have good arms and legs you can be a climber. You could go high.'

'I suppose so.'

'Will you call me tomorrow?' he asked. 'Same time?'

'Yes,' she said.

He held the phone to his ear until he heard the click as she disconnected.

'Hi, is that Maria?'

'Yes, how did you know?'

'Because I wait for you to call me. I look forward to

it. I woke early this morning, hoping you wouldn't forget.'

'I wouldn't forget, but I can't call you again. They log the calls here, if I don't make a sale I can't keep calling.'

'Can you call me after work?'

'I can't.'

'Can I call you?'

He heard her sigh. 'No. I can call you, but I have to get . . . er . . . permission.'

'Why? What d'you mean?'

'You know, I've been thinking about you,' she suddenly said. 'It wasn't true. You're not going on honeymoon, are you?'

He did not hesitate. 'No. I don't even have a girlfriend.'

'Why did you say so?'

'I wanted to talk to you.'

There was silence as the two of them absorbed this.

'You don't have a four-year-old boy that you bath every night, do you?' he asked in return.

'He's in care,' she said quietly. 'I think about bathing him every night, every night at seven. But they took him away from me.'

'Why did they?' he almost whispered. 'Was that the mistake?'

'The mistake was his father,' she said. 'I got into my car to drive away from him, I was going to hide and never see him again. I had my boy in his little carry-cot in the back. But my husband came out after us and he stood in front of the car and threw a mallet at the windscreen. It smashed it, but I could still see enough. I put my foot down. I drove straight at him.'

'Did you kill him?' He was appalled.

'Yes,' she said simply. 'And I wasn't sorry then and I'm not sorry now. I'm in for twelve years and I've only done one. I'll not see my son outside of a visiting room till he is sixteen and I will never see you. I suppose you won't want to call me now and I don't blame you. But I liked talking about the mountains. Thank you for that. I am sorry if you think I cheated you out of the stories. I'll keep them in my mind, you know. I'll think about them. Even if I can never go there. I'll think about them.'

'But it's the same for me,' he said, driven to honesty by the bleakness in her voice. 'When I fell, I wasn't OK as I told you. I broke my back. I'll never climb again. I'll never walk again. I'm stuck in my house and they have rebuilt my garden path, so there are no steps. Just a little slope down to the fish-pond for my wheelchair. I really hate that. I can't tell you how much I hate it. And I liked talking about mountains to you. I had tried to put them out of my mind, but now I can think about them again. Even if I can never go there, just like you. I'll think about them.'

She was absolutely quiet for a moment and then she said, 'I have to go. The supervisor is watching.'

'Will you call me? Will you get permission to call me?'

'Yes, I will,' she said softly. 'If you want me to.'

'I do,' he said. 'It can be like you're my girl.'

'Funny sort of girl,' she said bitterly.

'Funny sort of guy,' he returned. 'Will you call me?'

'Yes, Raefe,' she said. 'Will you try out that path in the garden?'

'OK.' He thought of the smooth and carefully graded path as a new challenge to a man who had loved the mountains. 'OK. I will. I'll tell you about it when you call, Maria,' he said. 'My girl.'

When he put down the phone, he was smiling.

The Widow's House

BY TESSA HADLEY

*T*his is not a ghost story. That sounds like an old trick, a signal to reassure readers that a ghost story is exactly what they're going to get. But really, this is not a ghost story; even though it takes place in the dead days between Christmas and New Year, when the supernatural is as traditional as turkey. More traditional than turkey.

Janni Lanaghan is clever and sceptical. She lives in Cardiff and is writing a PhD thesis on cultural constructions of Welsh identity between 1900 and 1985; she has promised herself that these empty days before New Year will be dedicated to pushing on with it. She doesn't work at the big IKEA desk bought specially for the purpose, but on a silly, rickety little table in the living room where she can only just fit her iBook, because the seriousness of the big desk in the study terrifies her and she has a superstition that her best thoughts always come in flight, provisionally. All the books she is using have to be spread around her, open face down, on the floor. For a couple of days she has the house to herself. Her partner Chris, an engineer in a hydraulics company, is visiting his family in Aberdare. Her twelve-year-old daughter Nell is staying with her dad (who is not Chris) in Brighton. Their absences gather pointedly in the hushed and concentrated space, willing Janni to get on. The thesis really is very good, original and intelligent (her supervisor says so), but Janni has a problem completing things. And in the meantime, like all postgraduate students, she's taken on much too much hourly-paid teaching at her university in order to help pay the bills, which makes it harder than ever to imagine finishing.

At six thirty in the evening of the first day she lifts her head, waking from a dream of thought, and looks around at the room under its snow of papers as if she's seeing it for the first time. Suddenly, her legs are cramped where she's been sitting on them and her back aches from hunching over the keyboard. When she writes she always works intently, contortedly, hugging her knees to her chin or tucking them under her; Nell says she 'scrungles up' (Nell is daintier and more poised). All day Janni has only paused once in her work, to fill a cafetière with strong coffee, which anyway she then forgot to drink. But at the edge of her absorption she has had a warming awareness of release ahead – she is going out in the evening, she has been asked to a dinner party with friends. When she saves her file now finally on to her USB key and closes her iBook, the sensation is satisfying: accomplishment and anticipation balanced perfectly. She runs a deep foam-bath and sorts out clothes to wear, imagining

Nell's advice. Janni isn't enthusiastic about her looks, but tonight before she dashes out (late, inevitably) she casts a wary eye over her reflection. Young still (thirty-five), lanky, awkward, blondish; not too bad. She sprays the perfume she usually forgets about and then bangs the front door behind her in exhilaration – no babysitter tonight to hurry home for. It's a twenty-minute walk up through the park to the lake. Chris has the car. She is looking forward to drinking. And talking. For all the clamour of words inside her head, she feels the day's silence wrapped around her like a skin.

Janni loves Chris: 'like bread,' she thinks to herself, although she hasn't ever put it like that to him, in case he doesn't understand what a good thing bread is. But she quite likes socialising without him. When he's with her, the big handsome mass of him weighs on her mufflingly and she intuits his criticisms of the company before he's even felt them. He's steady and decent and wary of pretension. Halfway down her first big glass of red, tonight Janni feels entirely at ease, entirely herself, among these friends. Richard is a good cook: the food is vegetarian, spicy (Janni had forgotten to eat while she was writing). He is a lecturer in her department at the university, his partner Tanwen works for the Assembly. Paul and Hannah are musicians, they have a son in Nell's year at Cardiff High. Also there's a woman Janni has met before at Richard and Tanwen's parties: Mara, who had a husband sick with something, perhaps leukaemia, and then the husband died (but he must have died a year ago now at least). At the last party Janni was shy of talking to Mara, not knowing how to speak about what had happened to her, or how not to speak about it; this evening it seems obvious that the thing is not to fuss. Mara is laughing and gossiping just like everybody else and flirting mildly too with Paul, who is earnest and small and drawn to women; he has a perfect boy's head like an angel in a painting. Of course Mara is gossiping and flirting. All that kind of stuff doesn't stop just because somebody's died. Mara's only Janni's age, or perhaps a bit older. She's small, with precise, neat movements, straight, dark hair, a lot of kohl around her eyes and a ruby stud in her nose. She's wearing a silky dress splotched with big red poppies and she says unexpected things in a calm voice, turning a silver bangle on her wrist.

For some reason they all talk about knitting. Hannah is teaching herself to knit. Richard remembers itchy knitted balaclavas he was forced to wear to school in winter. Janni tells them about the striped baby rompers for Nell, still half-finished on her needles in a cupboard.

'Have another baby,' says Mara. 'So as not to waste the striped rompers.'

Janni is startled; her new friend has divined a wish she's hardly acknowledged to herself. Once, in passing, Mara mentions her dead husband Luke; she bought him an Aran jumper on an Irish holiday. For Janni it's as if the easily flowing stream of their conversation snags on a rock sticking up dark and hard into it – the flow backs up for a moment in little purling waves of awareness and then slides past and onwards, recovering itself. By the time Tanwen serves out home-made Christmas pudding ice-cream, they are arguing about *Big Brother*. Paul and Hannah don't let their son watch it. Janni says she lets Nell watch it but knows she shouldn't. Nell is fanatical, Janni and Chris aren't allowed to talk to her while it's on; sitting straight-backed in her chair, she devotes to it an unsmiling religious attention.

'She's watching to find out what life is like,' says Mara.

'That's what I'm afraid of.'

'Such genius television,' says Richard.

'It's so banal,' says Paul.

'Sublimely banal. I wish I'd thought of it.'

'I wish you'd thought of it,' says Tanwen, meaning money.

'I adore it,' says Mara. 'I'm hooked. Who does Nell want to win this time?'

Paul smiles at Mara with intensity, shifts on his chair so that they're leaning slightly together. 'But you're watching it with irony.'

She seems to wonder, tucking in her chin. 'Am I? If I was I didn't notice.'

'Isn't it exploitative?' asks Hannah severely. 'It's a form of torture, depriving them of privacy. No place they can go where they're not watched.'

Janni waves her hands definitively. 'But what's truly awful is that under ultimate surveillance, seeing right into their most private, private moments, there are no secrets. That's the awfulness. Nothing was waiting to be revealed. The nothing is more shaming than if there was a something.'

At this point she goes upstairs to the bathroom. She has been enjoying herself, she has been voluble and lively; she has a flash of vivid consciousness of her own noisy personality because of its cessation in the solitude of the bathroom, like catching a reflection unexpectedly out of the corner of an eye. Richard and Tanwen's bathroom is big and luxurious but rather ugly, she thinks: thickly carpeted in green, with a bath sunk into a kind of raised platform and one of those power shower units in a glassed-in cubicle. There's no chaos of silly bath products crowding all the surfaces as there is in her bathroom at home. Richard and Tanwen don't have children (or rather, he does, by a previous relationship, but they don't live with him). Janni has drunk several glasses of wine. She's perfectly steady on her feet and capable of knowing what she's doing; but her mind, spinning out of engagement, experiences its own vertigo, a sickening drag. As she holds her wrists under the cold water tap turned on hard, her mood in a convulsion reverses itself. She knows this sensation, it's happened to her before, just at this same point in a sociable evening.

She wishes suddenly that she hadn't come out, that she'd preserved intact the honour of her day's hard labours. She particularly hates the idea of herself spouting on with what seems to her now fake ingenuousness about privacy and secrets. If she really set such a high value on privacy and secrets, then wouldn't she have kept quiet about them? Also, she's haunted somewhere at the back of her mind by the absence of Mara's husband, Luke. She knows it is none of her business to dwell on him, because she never even set eyes on him when he was alive. But it frightens her that anyone might be so lightly dropped behind the living, might be so completely vanished and forgotten, so that all the clothes he wore and all the books he liked and the things he said began to belong to the stale past and not to matter any more.

When Janni goes downstairs again she can't properly recover her pleasure in the evening, although she goes on laughing and arguing. Her stomach feels tight and bloated. They transfer into the front room to have coffee and Richard puts music on the hi-fi; he likes jazz although nobody else does. It's characteristic of Janni that even though she isn't enjoying herself any longer, she doesn't make a move to go home; she can't help trying to press out more pleasure from the stale end of the occasion, hoping it still has revelations in store. The conversation resolves into a trickle of reminiscences of teenage Saturday jobs. Richard was supposed to deliver the local free newspaper and dumped them all in a disused garage, which then caught fire and burnt (he never confessed this to his family). Hannah cleaned the dormitories in a boys' public school. Even when it's midnight and Hannah and Paul get up to leave, Janni hovers indecisively in the flurry of farewells and exclamations. 'Oh, it's snowing! Come and look! It's snowing outside!' They pile out of the front door into the sleeping street, hugging bare arms or wrapping scarves, to look up at where snowflakes are swarming in the cones of light under the streetlamps; so weightless they hardly seem to be falling, only drifting dizzily. Snow is settling on the cars and the hedges in the gardens. They don't get much snow in Cardiff and when it comes it only usually lasts a day or so.

Only Mara and Janni are left now; Tanwen would obviously like to get on with the clearing up, although Richard is finding more music he wants to play for them. Janni fetches her coat.

'It will be lovely walking in the snow,' she says.

Mara offers to give her a lift home. 'You can't walk in this.'

'I could. Don't you think it would be lovely?'

'They'd find your frozen body in the morning,' Richard says gloomily. 'Buried in a deep drift, a last message scribbled on a cigarette paper clasped in your tiny hand.'

'It's hardly even settling on the road. My hands are huge and I don't smoke.'

'But what would your last message be?'

'Don't be silly. I'll give her a lift home.'

Alone with Mara in her tiny car, Janni feels as alertly wide awake as if she hadn't drunk anything. Mara changes gear with crisp precision. They float down the hill through streets made simplified and childlike in the falling snow; the bleached city sprawls below them, innocently open, patched with black. It turns out that Mara lives only five minutes' walk from Janni's house. 'Come in and have a nightcap,' Mara suggests. 'I don't want to go to bed yet.'

Although it's in a terraced row, Mara's house has the air inside of a neat cottage. She lights a gas fire in the front room and draws long velvet curtains. Snug chairs and a sofa are piled with pretty cushions; every surface is arranged with interesting things, collections of shells and pebbles, a brass ship's compass, coloured Moroccan glasses painted with gold, an assortment of old metal type from a printer's shop. Janni is smitten with longing, comparing it with her home, where the chairs are only piled with washing and unsorted mail.

When Mara goes to make tea, Janni takes the opportunity to look around for photographs of Luke; but there aren't any photographs. There's a collection of tiny mirrors in all sorts of frames and some quirky odd prints and pictures – a field of blowing grass, a cat curled up, a dervish smoking under a tree; nothing that offers any clue to Mara's history.

Even the books – the usual contemporary novels, a few popular science titles – don't give anything away, unless the ones on mountaineering belonged to Luke. Janni means to ask Mara about him directly – isn't there every sign that Mara has chosen her for a friend and isn't this just the right hour for confidences? But when Mara comes back with the tea and whisky Janni is suddenly shy and in fact Luke's name only comes up once or twice in their conversation, accidentally. The single malt comes from Luke's father; a client sends it to him every Christmas and he passes it on because he doesn't drink whisky. Mara moved to Cardiff because Luke got a job in administration at Welsh National Opera (where Mara still works). He's absolutely gone from this house, Janni thinks. She's tidied him away. He's hardly left a trace.

Mostly Mara makes Janni talk about herself. Little and plump and pliant, she curls up in her chair with her feet tucked neatly under her, reminding Janni of the cat in the drawing on the wall. She hasn't smoked all evening, but when Janni assures her that she doesn't mind, she rolls herself a tiny cigarette in liquorice paper. She's a good listener, warm and amused. Janni talks to her about Nell's father, dangerous and unstable, and about Chris, whose kindness can be exasperating.

'I ought to be going,' Janni says eventually, reluctantly. 'What's the weather like outside? It'll be funny going back to an empty house.'

'Why don't you stay? The bed in the spare room's made up. It makes no difference to me.'

Undressing in the strange room, Janni feels exhausted, finished. She puts on the faded ironed pyjamas Mara has laid out for her. This bedroom at the front of the house is emptier and plainer than all the other rooms she's seen: there's just the double bed, a chest of drawers, a Turkish rug on the sanded boards and the same thick velvet curtains as downstairs. The feather duvet is a heavy winter weight, there's a blanket folded across the bottom of the bed in case she needs it; she closes her eyes and sinks away almost instantly, down and down amidst the white linen, into a profound soft sleep.

Then she's jolted suddenly, so that she sits up abruptly against the pillows, shocked and awake. She stares around at the room in the dim snow-light; it hasn't changed, but she feels as if something has happened, momentous but invisible, like an explosion sounded below the pitch of human hearing. Partly it's just a recognition of the obvious, that's come to her in those moments of unconsciousness; it's obvious, to begin with, that this front bedroom would have been where Luke and Mara slept, that Mara must have moved herself after his death into the smaller crowded room at the back of the house. And then, of course, these are Luke's pyjamas Janni is wearing; if they were Mara's they wouldn't have been so roomy on her. The trouser legs are too long, the ends of the sleeves hang down over her hands. But it's more than just those things. Sometimes when Janni is with Chris's family in Aberdare, he and his mother chat together in Welsh – that's how this feels, as if something quite plain and possible is just out of her reach, behind the muffling wall of her incomprehension. She had been afraid that Luke was forgotten; but this bed with its clean, white linen is a sea of sorrow, saturated with the absence of the dead man. No wonder Mara fled to the back room. Janni feels as if, when she fell into the bottom of her sleep, he was waiting there.

This is all that happens to Janni. She sleeps again eventually and in the morning she hardly remembers her dreams. Months later Mara shows her an album of photographs of Luke, and Janni has an odd feeling that she recognises him: blond, broad, cheerful, dark-stubbled, a trick of light on his glasses. That's all. She might easily have seen him anyway, on the street, in the time when he was still alive.

It really isn't a supernatural story.

The Warmest Christmas Ever

BY VICTORIA HISLOP

*B*ack in October, Jennifer had gone to seasonal fairs to find the exact shade of ribbon that she had envisaged for displaying this year's cards. It was the palest Tiffany aqua, to pick up the cool tones of her newly painted hallway. The entire house was now beautifully decked out for Christmas and this year her theme had been inspired by some images of Nova Scotia that she had seen in a magazine.

Jennifer, or 'Jen' as she signed herself, always had her cards written and posted by the first week of the month and it was a source of irritation that other people did not do the same. If cards were going to be incorporated into her bunting-inspired display then it was severely inconvenient to have them arriving after the middle of December. Everything had to be in place by the 15th at the very latest.

For her, the whole season was about efficiency as much as creativity.

Computerisation had streamlined the card-sending operation beautifully and now, at the push of the button, she could watch a satisfying concertina of address labels emerging from her printer, certain that the list would be up-to-date. When last year's cards had come down on January 6th, she had made a note of those which came from newly acquired friends and, before neatly boxing them, had updated her records to ensure that they would receive a card later that year.

December was the most frantic month of the year. All the others were a holiday by comparison, except of course the last fortnight of November which was when she did the Christmas shopping. She aimed to purchase (and ideally to wrap) all her presents before the first window of the advent calendar was opened.

By mid-December her perfect vision of Christmas was beginning to take shape. A twenty-foot, symmetrical, non-dropping tree stood in the hallway adorned with clear glass icicles and perfectly positioned white (non-flashing) lights. At its foot was a neat pile of presents in foil wrapping with silver ribbon and labels. Philip, her husband, and their teenage boys had carried the tree into the house, but that was where their involvement with the aesthetics ended. George, eighteen, and Henry, sixteen, hardly noticed the wreath nailed to the front door, let alone appreciated the fact that the clementines that adorned it were fresh and replaced every three days by their mother. They certainly did not listen to her appeal to avoid slamming the front door, which badly disturbed her perfect waxy fruits.

The penultimate week before Christmas went by following a pattern of events that was as fixed as the date of Christmas itself. There were the drinks parties at other people's houses and when all of those had come to an end it was time for Jennifer and Philip's own 'At Home'.

One of the advantages of holding a drinks party this close to Christmas was that she could be assured of upstaging all the other hostesses. Her party was the finale. This year her flaming, bite-size Christmas puddings left her guests literally speechless as their teeth closed in on the moist fruits that had been marinaded for five days in armagnac. The neighbourhood was literally agog, not just with the excellence of the food and the decor, but with the flawlessness of the hostess in her long velvet dress and matching manicure.

One year she had employed the boys and some of their friends as waiters. This had seemed a fashionable thing to do and a way of having her children present whilst giving them a function. It had been a disaster. Wine had been slopped over party frocks, canapés had slid to the floor from carelessly carried trays and guests had gone home with the wrong coats.

'Never again,' she had vowed.

This year it was back to the usual girls from 'Creative Catering, Professional Parties'. Jennifer would be able to relax. There would be no spillages with these trained waitresses who had a sixth sense for a half-empty glass that needed refilling and a discreet way of gliding about the room with her elegant platters of food.

Her party was a triumph, even though she hardly

had a moment to speak to her guests and by the end of it her feet were blistered from patrolling between the kitchen and the drawing room as she anxiously policed the flow of food and champagne. Meanwhile, she glimpsed Philip having the time of his life, smiling and laughing as he entertained his friends with City anecdotes. 'Why,' she asked herself, 'does he never bother to dress up for parties?' His old cords and checked shirt were somehow too homely for a host in her opinion, but when she looked about her most of the men were similarly attired while some of their wives were almost irritatingly overdressed. There was the odd bow tie, but generally the men had dressed 'down', while their wives had dressed 'up'. The chilled Moët almost ran out as guests quenched their thirsts, sweltering in the over-heated house.

At five o'clock on Christmas Eve, the whole family, including two reluctant teenagers, trooped out to church. When carols had been sung, they drank the obligatory mulled wine by the lych-gate and Jennifer was mildly annoyed that strong winds and a light drizzle messed up her newly streaked blonde hair. They had sung 'In the Bleak Mid Winter', but the landscape it described seemed remote. Far from being hard as iron, the moist earth allowed an early glimpse of daffodil tips.

Back home, a log fire glowed in the hearth and above it the perfectly aligned Christmas cards flapped, disturbed by the gusts that came down the chimney.

Bows of the tree twitched, loose ends of gift ribbon flickered almost imperceptibly.

That night Jennifer lay in bed, tossing and turning, going through lists of lists of lists in her head (juliennes of carrots, purée of parsnips, braised red cabbage, Brussels, chestnut stuffing, cranberry stuffing, sausages wrapped in bacon, brandy and Cointreau butter, malt whiskey cream, mince pies, star-shaped shortbread for morning coffee), hoping that nothing had been omitted from her preparations.

The parents-in-law were scheduled to arrive at eleven in the morning along with Philip's sister and her husband (both teachers), three girls (only the eldest not in hand-me-downs) and their rescue dog, a mongrel called Bonny. They were never given the chance to return the lavish hospitality that was heaped upon them.

Christmas was Jennifer's 'thing' and there was an unspoken understanding, even if it was mildly resented, that Philip and Jennifer would not budge from their elegant, mock-Georgian home during the festive season. Everyone had to go to 'The Pines' if they wished to be together.

And each year, the hostess had to exceed expectations. Or at least that was what she aimed for. This year's big surprise was the bird. Or rather, the birds. For the first time, she would be producing a pigeon within a pheasant within a goose within a turkey. Many times she had pictured the perfect cross-sections of meat, each layer a different, but complementary colour. It would be magnificent and she glowed in anticipation of her mother-in-law's exclamation of surprise.

It was not only thoughts of the big lunch and worries over whether she had made enough Christmas crackers that kept her awake. A wind had begun to howl around the house. Doors banged, rafters creaked. While the rest of the family slept soundly (the boys were now far too old to be lying in wait for Father Christmas), Jennifer had to wait until five before she finally fell into a fitful doze.

Only a few hours later, as the light began to peep through the narrow slit between thick brocade curtains, she woke with a start and threw back the duvet. It was nearly eight o'clock and she had intended to be up at seven. The alarm had failed to go off.

In spite of the intense preparations that had gone on for so many weeks, her first thought was for all the things that remained to be done.

She stumbled, eyes half-shut, on to the landing and flicked the light switch. 'Damn,' she thought, 'of all days for a bulb to go.' Almost tripping over the silk sash of her dressing-gown in her haste to get downstairs, she discovered that none of the lights were working in the hallway either.

By the time she reached the kitchen, she knew that something was not quite as it should be. Without the hum of the fridge, there was a deathly silence and the absence of the familiar glow of the boiler light confirmed her worst fears. The entire house appeared to have fused.

'Philip!' she screamed out. 'Philip! Help! Help!'

He was woken from a deep sleep by her cries. In his somnolent state he pictured her wrestling with a violent intruder. He had read earlier that week that the early hours of Christmas morning were a popular time for burglaries, given that beneath the average tree nestled several thousands of pounds of mint-condition electrical goods. He took the stairs two at a time and found Jennifer safe, alone and brandishing the large torch from under the sink.

'The electrics . . .' she gasped. 'Something has gone wrong with the electrics.'

Philip's efforts in the fuse cupboard were fruitless and soon they discovered why. It transpired that the violent storm of the previous night had brought down a major power line and there was a widespread cut. When they braved the lashing rain and went out into the road they could see that every house in the village was in darkness. A recorded message from the regional electricity board was not encouraging. Power would be resumed 'in due course'. A forty-minute wait on the line to speak to an operator only revealed worse news. There was little chance of the fault being corrected until after the Christmas break.

For Jennifer, news that the end of the world was nigh could not have been more devastating. At least for that, her mother-in-law would probably stay away. Philip's efforts to calm her down did not go down well.

'You just don't understand,' she shrieked at him. 'This is not like any other day! It's not just any other meal!'

'Mum, Dad does realise that,' interceded George, anxious that his long-suffering father shouldn't take the blame.

'We'll find some way round this,' bumbled Philip.

The two boys and their father stood, while Jennifer sat at the kitchen table, her head in her hands.

Philip had opened the back door and now stood on the terrace looking down the garden. The sun had broken through the clouds. He glanced back at Jennifer.

'I've had an idea,' he said. 'Come out and help me, boys.'

Barefoot, still in their pyjamas, they dutifully followed him across the soggy lawn. Jennifer stood at the window and watched them. It was a sweet sight. The three of them looked like sleepwalkers.

For ten minutes they disappeared and while they were gone she went upstairs to get dressed, not in the new dress she had bought for the day. It seemed pointless now. When she came downstairs again, she saw that the barbecue had been wheeled on to the terrace and further down the garden a bonfire was being built with dry wood from the log store. Philip returned to the kitchen, smiling, his hands black, pyjama trousers soaked to the knee. He went to the fridge, took out a bottle, popped the cork and clumsily filled two glasses, allowing their froth to spume on to the work surface. 'Let's have a look at that bird,' he said, taking a slurp.

'Birds . . .' said Jennifer.

'Oh yes, birds,' replied Philip.

Jennifer went to the fridge and removed the magnificent creation, placing it lovingly on the granite work top.

'This is what I propose,' he said. 'That we slice into this thing, marinade it in something or other and barbecue it in strips.'

'Strips . . .'

This was a man who had no idea how to switch on the oven, but could do wonders with charcoal.

Jennifer took a long gulp of her champagne and felt it spread through her veins. She could feel her control of the situation slipping away. For the first time she could remember, she felt herself letting go of the reins. The sun shone on her back. It was like spring and she felt a sudden and unexpected surge of warmth for her husband. She watched as Philip clumsily hacked the precious meat into chunks and dropped them into a spicy marinade of his own recipe. The boys came in from the garden, marking the pristine floor with trails of mud. They set about wrapping two dozen potatoes individually in foil and buried them in the bonfire. By now Philip had rigged up an old metal ladder over the bonfire and the Christmas pudding began its long steaming process.

The family arrived on the dot of eleven. The mother-in-law, usually so nervous around Jennifer, seemed visibly to relax when she saw that her daughter-in-law was less tense than usual. The others were perfectly at home with the chaos and Philip's sister enjoyed the change to the formality of the usual routine.

'What can I do to help?' she asked, rolling up her sleeves, an offer she would never have dared to make in the past.

The champagne bottle sat on the table in front of Jennifer and her sons went to and fro. It was warm enough to sit in the garden and drinks were carried outside. The dog chased the girls round and round. Though he did not know it, on a normal Christmas Day he would have been left sitting in the car.

As the light began to fade, Philip declared that the meat was cooked. They all sat snugly under rugs at the garden table. Every scrap of the succulent turkey, goose, pheasant and pigeon was devoured and by seven o'clock, a row of empty bottles stood in a line along the table, some of them holding candles and others now emptied of wine. A blanket of warmth wrapped itself around them. There had never been a Christmas lunch quite like it. It was beyond perfection. Jennifer sat close to her husband, licked her fingers and smiled.

Oxbridge Blues

BY WENDY HOLDEN

'We've got to motivate her,' John said to me, frowning. 'She's never going to get anywhere like this.'

I laid my silver fork down in the dark and glossy wine sauce, raised my cut-glass goblet of Domaine de Vieux and looked defeatedly at my husband. He hadn't even commented on the *coq au vin* I had made, using a new recipe that had taken rather longer than I imagined. This had involved simmering for hours on top of the stove first before baking the dish in the oven for a final richening of the flavours. It never ceased to amaze me, the work these traditional peasant dishes took. Traditional peasants, I always thought, must have had a lot of time on their hands.

John swigged his wine impatiently and levered some of the casserole into his mouth. His expression didn't even change; he was obviously not tasting it. The suspicion that tinned stewing steak would have done just as well closed depressingly in. 'I mean, we've sent our daughter to the best schools money can buy,' my husband pointed out heatedly. 'And now she's coming up to her A-levels, she's slacking. She can't afford to take her foot off the accelerator now. Not if she wants to go to Oxford or Cambridge.'

I nodded. I usually did when John got steamed up. He was usually right anyway and when he wasn't it was rarely worth saying so.

'Listen to her,' John thundered, stabbing an angry finger up towards the dining-room ceiling. 'She said she didn't want to eat with us because she was revising. But she's not. She's just lolling about, listening to music. As per bloody usual.' He pierced a carrot in disgust.

'Calm down,' I said soothingly. It was, of course, hardly surprising that John was het up. He was a successful financier with an office in London, which meant not only long and arduous days at the office but long and arduous commutes home at night. We lived in a pretty red-brick Victorian former rectory in the Vale of Beauvoir, which was lovely for me and handy for Jasmine's nearby private school, but anything but relaxing for John. On top of this, he had now to bear the sight of his daughter, as he saw it, poised to throw away all the educational advantages he had purchased for her with the sweat of his brow over so many years. It was easy to see why he was angry.

'I'll clear up,' I added comfortingly. 'You go and sit down with the newspaper and I'll bring you some coffee and some of the lovely fudge I made today.'

'I've read the newspaper,' John snapped. 'I've read it on the train. Every bit, even the Court Circular.'

'Telly, then.'

John shuffled off, grumbling. I, meanwhile, cleared the table musing on Cambridge and the plan that Jasmine should go there. I'd gone there myself, studied English and left with all sorts of ideas of taking the world of journalism by storm.

But then, in my first year as a magazine assistant, I had gone to a dinner party and met my knight in shining armour, John, who also happened to be a red-hot financial superbrain. Before I knew it, my urge to work had melted away and I was ensconced in a life of moneyed leisure. From which I'd never emerged. OK, so I did the school run (in the brand-new, shiny, four-wheel drive we kept besides a family car, a sports car and a little shopping runabout for me). I also did most of the cooking – I had taken several Cordon Bleu courses (although we got caterers in for anything big). But otherwise I rarely had to lift a finger. We had cleaners, car valets, window cleaners and gardeners. Even though I'd taken garden-design courses, too. And when Jasmine was younger, we'd had a nanny as well.

As John started to doze in front of *Gordon's Kitchen Nightmares*, I slipped quietly upstairs and knocked on the door of my daughter's bedroom. Bedroom suite, I should say; besides a large room to sleep in, Jasmine's part of the house had its own bathroom and a large study complete with state-of-the-art computer, plasma-screen television, sound system and every other gadget known to woman.

'Come in,' someone shouted sulkily over the noise, and I entered to see, just as John had predicted, Jasmine sprawled on the bed. She was reading the 'Society' section of the *Guardian*, her long feet in black tights banging the wall in time to the music. 'Can you turn that racket down?' I mouthed, pointing at the sound system.

Jasmine turned it down a fraction and regarded me stonily from between long, black hanks of hair.

I sat down on the very edge of the bed. 'Come on, darling. Daddy's worried you aren't revising. You know how much he wants you to go to Cambridge.'

Between the strands of black hair, the green eyes flashed. 'Oh, come off it, Mother,' Jasmine snapped. 'What's the point of me going to Cambridge? You went, and look at you. You're a housewife. You don't even work.'

'Darling, I don't have time to work,' I smiled at her. Not without reason; my schedule was intense, frankly. What with regular pedicures, manicures, waxings, bleachings and facials, plus trips to see my gym instructor as well as organising everyone who did the actual work in the house, I barely had a moment to myself.

Jasmine stared at me stonily. 'Whatever. I'm not interested in bloody Cambridge, OK?'

'Well, what are you interested in?' I challenged. It was increasingly hard to tell.

To my surprise, she waved the *Guardian* at me. 'Kids. I'm thinking of working with kids. Training to be a social worker.'

I tried to stop my eyes from bulging. Her father would hit the roof if he heard this. John had not paid out hundreds of thousands in private-school fees for our daughter to go and work for the local council. It was nowhere near aspirational enough.

'Darling, you're overwrought,' I said hastily. 'All that, erm, revising. I'll bring you a cup of tea and some nice biscuits. I baked them today. They're . . .'

'I don't want any biscuits,' Jasmine hurled at me, her dark hair whirling furiously around her head.

'I've been thinking,' John announced the next evening, as he took off his Burberry mac in the hall and dumped his briefcase on the polished wooden oak floor. 'About Jasmine.'

'Oh?' I said carefully, lowering the bone-china tureen of Billy-Bi mussel soup – John's favourite, which I'd made as a special treat from the Cordon Bleu recipe – on to the silver mat on the antique dining table.

'How to motivate her,' John announced, striding in to the dining room. 'Let's take her down to Cambridge for a weekend. Show her your old college and all that. Everything she'll be missing if she fails to get in.'

I pulled out my hand-carved and polished oak chair and sat down, carefully not raising my eyes to his. I felt immediate gut resistance to the idea, not only because of the pressure it was putting on Jasmine, but because of what it meant to me, too. It was over two decades since I last walked through the gateway of King's College, and I knew, without actually having admitted it before, that I'd stayed away for a reason.

As the years had gone by, I'd seen many of my university peers go on to achieve; some great, others at least interesting, things. I'd followed some of their progress in the newspapers and always felt guilty about what had happened to me. Or, rather, not happened to me. I hadn't needed Jasmine's outburst to be guiltily aware that I had given up an entire education just to be a housewife, albeit a very upmarket one with antique furniture, membership of two top spas and the services of a personal shopper.

But I could tell by the way John threw himself down, shook out his pressed linen napkin and whirled it on over his pin-striped trousers that the decision had already been made. We were going to Cambridge and that was that.

A couple of weekends later the three of us mooched around the market square in Cambridge, where Jasmine displayed the day's first flicker of interest as she examined a stall with bags on, and I absorbed with some surprise that the racks of second-hand clothes stalls I remembered, selling enormous worn overcoats, West German army surplus, ancient tailcoats and white linen jackets to impecunious students, were now all gone. Presumably they had all been bought up, at last.

I recalled some of the sequined 1960s minidresses I had bought for a song – literally as well as metaphorically. I had sung backing vocals in a student band; something about which I had almost forgotten. I stood in the market square and remembered what fun it had been and how I could never imagine having that sort of confidence now. I looked down at my sensible, expensive, camel tie-belted coat and pricey, low-heeled boots. Had that carefree singer really been me?

'Here's King's College,' John said with reverence as we approached the world-famous entrance. John was a red-brick university man himself, a comprehensive boy who'd done well at Leeds, and I suspected his determination that Jasmine enter these hallowed halls was at least partly to do with the fact he never had. But just as we three were about to enter them now, the small wooden door within the big wooden gate opened to let out two floppy-haired youths talking loudly in distinctively Sloaney voices. I watched a wave of disgust cross Jasmine's face.

Inside the college court, I felt old memories

overwhelm me. There was the entrance to the bar, where I'd sat so often with friends I now hadn't seen for years. There was the stunning chapel, where I'd first heard real choral music. We walked through the archway and down to the river. Here were the punts – the flat-bottomed boats propelled along by a pole – where I'd spent many a summer afternoon with various boyfriends, some more serious than others, none of whom had been remotely like John. Those college boys had treated me as an equal in brains and ambition, not as a glorified servant who occasionally and increasingly unwillingly provided sexual favours. As I looked down at the dancing waters I felt resentment ball in my throat and push upwards. Resentment at myself as much as John; I'd allowed him to do this to me, after all.

'God, what prats,' Jasmine observed, of a punt full of students popping champagne corks and shouting.

'I was a prat like that once,' I smilingly reminded her. I did not add that I had never felt the prat then that I felt I was now, trapped in a life of unchallenging and utterly unrewarding leisure and married to a domestic despot. John's home was his castle and I was a prisoner in it. How had it happened? I was going to have a career, earn my own money, have a life, be a writer, a journalist, an editor, well, something. What had happened to all that? Most of the people I had sat and planned it with had done it – I saw their names in the newspapers all the time. So why hadn't I?

Finally, we passed the white neo-classical façade of the Senate House, where I had sat all my university exams. Immediately the tense atmosphere of that ornate interior, the narrow desks in rows on the black and white marble floor, flooded back to me. As did the brilliant sunshine of the day I had got my results, a first-class degree. I remembered jumping around on the bright green grass, delirious with happiness, champagne foaming everywhere. It had seemed the beginning of the rest of my life, not the end of it, as it had subsequently proved to be.

I stared glumly at the Senate House's carved façade. Something was stirring within me, and it wasn't, for once, the urge to buy a PowerPlate machine, try a new spa or see my personal shopper to decide on this season's capsule look. It was something long buried, that could no longer be kept down.

'Look,' Jasmine said from the back of the car on the way home. Her tone was defiant but conciliatory. 'Thanks for taking me. It was nice to see Cambridge – don't get me wrong, Mum, it's a lovely place. But I don't want to go there. I can't say it's my idea of fun.'

A heavy silence fell in which all that could be heard was the smooth, expensive motor of our smooth, expensive car eating up the miles of motorway beneath us. I could feel John beside me, straining with the effort not to erupt in screams of frustration. 'And what, may I ask,' he managed at length in muffled, yet still acid tones, 'is your idea of fun?'

I closed my eyes and waited.

'I want to work with kids,' Jasmine answered immediately. 'I want to be a social worker.' While I could guess at the pain this could cause my husband, the fearlessness with which she answered made me admire my daughter. If only I'd had the courage of my convictions.

'I see,' said John. He cleared his throat. 'And what does Mummy think of that?' He slid me a sidelong, expectant glance from the wheel.

Jasmine waited. She was radiating insouciance from the back seat, but I sensed her nerves. 'I think that's fine,' I said slowly. 'I think, in fact, that it's absolutely admirable.'

There was a gasp of joy from behind me. There was a rattle of silver bracelets and a pair of slender arms flung themselves round my neck. 'Mum!' gasped Jasmine. 'Dad!' she shrieked a second later as John narrowly avoided crashing into the back of a pantechnicon.

His eyes were on the road, but they were furious. 'So much for her expensive education,' he spat.

I shrugged. 'Calm down. On the contrary, the better educated she is the better off we all are. The social services need good people, and I'm sure Jasmine will be brilliant.'

He could not resist looking at me then. 'What's happened to you?' he demanded, outraged. 'You were as keen on her going to Cambridge as I was. She's missing a great opportunity.'

I smoothed my expensive highlights. 'But even the

best opportunity's only as good as you make it,' I answered, tapping the newspaper on my lap containing the names of two of my college contemporaries. One was an editor on the newspaper, another a senior publisher who had been mentioned in the media section. I was planning to get in touch with both of them with a view to unearthing some long-buried projects.

'However late you leave it,' I added, smiling.

The Christmas Ring

BY DOUGLAS KENNEDY

$\mathcal{M}$y ex-husband had his extravagant moments. When we first were going out he thought nothing of whisking me off for a long weekend to Mustique, or arranging two tickets on the Concorde to Paris, when that supersonic option still existed. And upon deciding that we would marry, he marched me, on Christmas Eve 2002, to a private jeweller on West 46th Street (no store-bought ring for my corporate-raider husband) and plonked down seventy-eight thousand dollars for a multi-diamond ring, which somehow managed to look refined and ostentatious at the same time. I knew the price because Todd told me the price – he always told me the price of everything – and because two years after our marriage (when things were starting to go very wrong between us), I had it reappraised. The jeweller (another Diamond District operator) actually called two colleagues over to marvel at the cut and refinement of the diamonds, and the value of the carats.

'If I was you I'd have it reinsured for one hundred and fifty thousand,' the jeweller said. 'But if you want to sell it right now, I'll give you one hundred and thirty, no questions asked.' I made the mistake of mentioning this conversation to my husband over dinner at some Michelin-starred place that evening (we were always eating out – even though we spent over one hundred thousand on a bespoke kitchen in our Tribeca loft).

'The ring's actually doubled in price?' he said, sounding shocked. 'Let me see it . . .'

'I'm not taking it off. In fact I'm never taking it off. It's my running-away money.'

'Yeah, right,' Todd said with a sour laugh. 'As if you needed the money.'

He had a point. Though I wasn't pulling down his million-nine per annum, I was making somewhere in the high six figures. Because, like Todd, I too was a corporate stain – a lawyer, specialising in mergers and acquisitions – and, as my husband was fond of telling everyone, someone who was even more hard-nosed than he was.

'Anne is the ultimate pragmatist,' he once informed a group of our friends, much to my considerable chagrin and rage. But the bastard did have a point. I'm a litigator, he's a litigator. And litigators are not known for their romantic sensibilities. Only Todd didn't see himself that way. He was a killer in the courtroom who fancied himself something of an aesthete; an opera fanatic who could sing entire arias from Verdi's *Don Carlos* when there was a willing audience of anyone he wanted to impress. Suddenly this legal eviscerator showed to the world that, behind the Darwinistic façade, he had soul. Whereas I . . . I was the legal technician with a heart made of reinforced concrete.

'Anne can never find the poetry lurking behind life's essential complexities.'

Or, at least, that's the story he put around when he filed for divorce six months ago. We mediated ourselves into a negotiated settlement (I got the apartment; he got the weekend house in Litchfield), and everyone in our little legal and social circle commented on how predictably controlled I was in the face of Todd running off with a rather well-known soprano just three weeks after the divorce was finalised. When I say 'running off' I mean 'marrying' . . . in a big-deal wedding in Milan where the bitch was singing Mimi at La Scala. I had to dodge a lot of commiserating looks from professional colleagues, all of which were under-scored by the question: 'How the hell could you – the pit bull of litigators, the relentless inquisitor who could probably even find the dirt on the Pope – not have sussed that your husband had been carrying on a full-blown affair for over two years?'

Maybe it's because I simply can't find the poetry lurking behind life's essential complexities.

Of course I maintained a steely dignity in the face of all this. Whenever someone offered commiserations or made a comment about the tackiness of Todd's post-divorce rush to the altar, I'd bat it away with a comment like: 'You are looking at a happily divorced woman.' Or I'd resort to irony: 'In private Todd was always a diva . . . so I'm not surprised he simply had to marry one.'

And in private . . . in private, I was falling apart. As in losing three kilos a week without even trying. And then suffering six nights of insomnia – my entire nervous system suddenly becoming so overloaded that, in the middle of a negotiation over some merger and acquisition, I excused myself and locked myself in the Ladies and balled my eyes out . . . all the submerged grief suddenly coming out in a ferocious wave.

Afterwards I remade my face and told myself that the poison had been vented . . . or some such jive. I went back in and closed the deal. I headed home and drank six glasses of a very good Graves and once again could not render myself unconscious. When I stepped on the scales the next morning to discover that another kilo had slipped away, I phoned my doctor and begged for an emergency appointment.

'Have you ever thought you might be depressed?' he asked me after running a battery of tests on me.

'I don't do depressed.'

'Well, you're doing it now.'

He gave me some mild antidepressives that would help me sleep, and counselled me to take some time off and stop thinking that I could just equate divorce to a far-too-painful pair of shoes I had insisted on wearing for years, but now could simply kick off and pretend I never owned.

Terrible metaphor, Doc. But I did start taking the

pills. They did no damn good. Correction: they did knock me out for three or four hours. But then I'd jolt awake around 2 a.m. – and the despair and sadness would descend again, and I would find myself in the middle of an extended self-accusatory fugue, in which I wondered out loud how the hell I could have let such a fantastic man like Todd go . . . how my relentless drive, my inability to decompress and 'realise that life is not all surface achievement' (as Todd once so trenchantly put it), had finally driven him away.

So I was now functioning on three hours of sleep – and kept shedding kilos . . . the great shitty irony of this situation being: you are the shape you once so craved . . . and you are now completely alone.

Just how alone I was hit home as Christmas approached. My parents – retired realtors from New Jersey, now happily ensconced in a perma air-conditioned retirement villa on a golf course in Arizona – had announced that they would be on a Caribbean cruise over the holidays. Meanwhile my two closest college friends – Mimi (a journalist on *Time*) and Amanda (a mutual fund manager) – were both heading out of town to do family stuff, leaving yours truly alone in the city.

Then there was the phone call from Todd. It came late on the afternoon of December 21st – and when I saw his name flash up on my cellphone I hesitated for a moment before answering it.

'To what do I owe this honour?' I asked. We made small talk for a few minutes, during which time I learned that Todd was flying to Switzerland on Christmas morning (he was tied up in a last-minute big takeover thing) to join his beloved for a week of skiing in Davos (*bien sûr*). And then – in true Todd style – he cut right to the chase.

'That ring I gave you . . .'

'What about it?'

'You didn't have it revalued recently?'

'As a matter of fact I did. And its value keeps heading north. One-eighty-five.'

'Lucky you,' he said.

'Yeah, lucky me.'

'You want to sell it?'

'What?'

'You heard my question: do you want to sell it?'

'To whom?'

'To me.'

'But . . . why?'

'Because . . . I'd like to buy the ring back from you.'

'And why the hell would you want to do that?'

'I have my reasons.'

'As in: her.'

'I want that ring.'

'Why?'

I knew the answer to that question. Because though he easily parted with all the material stuff of our divorce – signing over to me the three million dollar loft without hesitation – the ring was personal. He had to have the ring back to fully break with me. Or, at least, that was my snap analysis of the situation . . .

based on the knowledge that Todd was someone who always played to win and had to have things go his way.

'I have my reasons,' he said.

'I'm sure you do. But I'm not selling.'

'I'll give you one-ninety for it.'

'No dice.'

'One-ninety-five.'

'Happy Holidays, Todd.' And I hung up.

He called back the next day.

'Be reasonable,' he said.

'Why are you so bent on winning this ring?'

'Because I want it.'

'Call your Mr Pupkin on West 46th Street and let him sell you another.'

'Yours is the ring I want.'

'And I want an explanation.'

'First law of negotiation: explanations are always an extraneous element.'

'What a gem of an insight. No wonder they pay you all that money, Todd.'

'And you can go have sex with yourself while you're at it.'

'Second law of negotiation: never offend the individual from whom you want something.'

'Two hundred and five.'

'You really are desperate. Trouble in paradise with Miss Big Voice?'

Now it was his turn to hang up.

I thought that was the end of it, as a full day went by without hearing from him again. As there was more than enough despair in my life right now, I was relieved – as his calls simply added to the gift basket of despair that was this year's Christmas. But – as I kept telling myself – it was only one damn day . . . and with a ferocious amount of work on right now (there was a big anti-trust case I would be taking to court in early January), I decided that I would ignore the tinsel and the fake snow and the compulsive consumerism and the boozy bonhomie and would simply pretend that Christmas was elsewhere.

So I worked all day on the 24th. And somewhere around four that afternoon, Todd phoned me again and said: 'Two hundred and twenty thousand – final offer.'

'You are desperate.'

'I just want the ring.'

'No . . . she's the one who wants the ring. Isn't that what this is really all about?'

'First rule of negotiation: explanations . . .'

'. . . are extraneous. But I don't want an explanation, just a confession. You're doing this because she knows about my ring and – for a whole bevy of psychosexual reasons – wants it.'

A long pause from Todd. Then: 'If I say "yes", will you sell it to me?'

'If you say "yes", then I will sell it to you . . . for two hundred and fifty thousand dollars.'

'Deal.'

'So say it . . .'

'Yes, she wants the ring because my ex-wife owns it.'

'How pathetic.'

'You are entitled to your opinion.'

'And you are a quarter of a million dollars lighter.'

'I need the ring tonight.'

'Nine p.m. in the bar of the St Regis. Bring your cheque book.' Now it was my turn to hang up.

After this conversation I didn't feel triumph – even though I had beaten the bastard at his own game and was about to receive a surprise Christmas bonus. No, the one overwhelming emotion that hit me was an immense, desperate sadness. I had money – so much damn money – and nothing else.

Still there was work to finish up – and if there was one thing I was good at, it was legal work. So I pushed on until eight thirty, at which time I packed up my briefcase and pressed the security code to unlock the firm's front door. I was the last person here on this Christmas Eve night.

I took the elevator down to the lobby. It too was deserted, bar the security guard on duty at the front desk. I must have passed this man dozens of times – as I was always working late and he was always the night man. But this was the first time ever I properly looked at him. He was an African in his early forties – with a face that was prematurely lined and world-weary; someone, I sensed, who had seen far too many terrible things at far too young an age.

'You shouldn't be working tonight,' he said as I was leaving.

'Nor should you,' I said.

'I need the money. Do you need the money too?' That stopped me in my tracks. I blinked and felt tears.

'No,' I said, 'I don't need the money. But I need the work.' He nodded. He understood.

'Where are you from?' I asked.

'Somalia.'

'Been in the States long?'

'Five years.'

'Family?'

'A wife, three children. But they are still in Mogadishu.'

'Why haven't they joined you here?'

'Can't bring them over. Not enough money.'

'What do you make here a year?'

'Maybe eighteen thousand.'

A third of what I made per month. A quarter of what my ex-husband made per month. The world was absurd.

'Is this your only job?' I asked. He laughed a tired, sardonic laugh.

'Do you know anyone who lives in New York on that sort of money? No, I drive a cab six days a week. Noon until eight. Then I work here all night from ten to six.'

'When do you sleep?'

'I get four hours every morning Monday to Saturday. I catch up on Sundays.'

'How much money would you need to get them to the States?' I asked.

'Why are you asking me this?'

'I'm just interested.'

'There are all sorts of problems. We ran up a lot of debt in Mogadishu. Fifteen, twenty thousand dollars – and we borrowed from local money-lenders, so the debt is endless. And then there are the legal costs of the visas, and I would need to find us a big apartment here, and how can I do that on what I earn? So . . . it's hopeless.'

Pause. It might have lasted no more than five seconds – but in that five seconds I suddenly knew what I was about to do . . .

'What's your name?' I asked.

'Gheddi.'

'Gheddi,' I said, trying it out. 'Interesting name.'

'It actually means "traveller" . . .'

'Well, that makes sense. I'm Anne McGregor, by the way. And here's what I'd like to suggest . . .'

Gheddi heard me out – his astonishment increasing by the moment. I must have spoken for five straight minutes, telling him about my divorce, the job I hated, the way I couldn't sleep right now . . . everything about my high-powered, over-pampered little life, and how my ex-husband was now pressing me into . . .

When I reached the end of this rant – and told him my proposal – he said: 'But I've only met you a few minutes ago . . . and I still don't understand why you are doing this . . .'

My response was a simple one: ''Tis the season . . .'

'But . . . what do you want from this?' he asked.

'I want nothing . . .'

'Absolutely nothing?'

'That's right.'

'I don't know what to say. Life does not work this way.'

'It does tonight. But listen . . . you really need to leave now for the St Regis. Remember: it's a Mr Todd Michaelis. He'll be in the Martini bar. And I'll have phoned and briefed him before you arrive. Jump in a cab, tell the driver to wait for you – and you should be there and back within fifteen minutes. Meanwhile I'll hold the fort here.'

'I could get into big trouble if my bosses found out . . .'

'Would that really matter now?'

He smiled. 'You have a point. Thank you, Miss Anne. I am . . . overwhelmed.'

'Don't be. But here . . .' I said, slipping off the ring and handing it to him, 'you'd better hurry.'

'I'll be back.'

'I know that.'

As soon as he was out the door I phoned Todd. 'Change of plan,' I said, and I then informed him that a Mr Gheddi Kokundea would be arriving any moment with the ring, and that the cheque for a quarter of a million dollars should be made out in his name.

Todd did not take this news well. 'Are you insane?' he asked.

'It's my money and I can do what I want with it.'

'You're a fool.'

'You're entitled to your opinion.'

A pause. I could hear him fuming. 'I don't get it,' he finally said. 'I mean, why?'

I could have said so much at this point – especially about a subject that I had been dodging for years, but which I now knew was unavoidable: my own terrible ongoing sense of emptiness amid all this plenty. But I knew that whatever explanation I put forward would have no impact on my ex-husband.

'Aren't you the one who said that, in a negotiation, explanations are always an extraneous element?'

'Come on,' he said, 'don't elude the question. Why?'

I thought about this for a moment.

'Maybe because, for the first time in my life, I've found a little poetry lurking behind life's essential complexities.'

Then I added two words – the final two words, as it turned out, we ever spoke to each other . . . because, after handing over the cheque to Gheddi, Todd never contacted me again.

And what were these two profound words that ended all conversation between us?

'Merry Christmas.'

Valentine's Day Blues

BY SOPHIE KINSELLA

I've been tense all day. Which is ridiculous. What's the big deal? So it's Valentine's Day.

So the whole world has gone crazy with padded cards and teddy bears and novelty underwear. So the reception desk was like a forest of plastic-swathed red roses this morning. So my colleague Barbara received a bottle of champagne at lunchtime from a 'mystery admirer' (her husband of twelve years, Keith) and paraded it around as though she'd won an Oscar.

There's no reason why any of it should affect me at all. First, because Rob and I have been broken up for over two months now. And secondly, because we never used to do any of this slushy stuff anyway. He was always too busy setting up one of his dodgy deals to remember Valentine's Day. Or birthdays. Or Christmas. Not really a festive, special day, 'Let me bring you a cup of tea in bed' type, Rob. More like 'Can you lend me fifty quid, my shirts need picking up, see you later, love'.

When we first got together, of course, I couldn't see any of that. All I saw was the cheeky smile, the twinkling blue eyes, the designer jeans, the cocky, charming air. He behaves as though he has the keys to the world, Rob does. For a while you can get suckered into thinking you do, too.

Truth is, he doesn't have the keys to anything, except a clapped-out Ford Mondeo. And the flat of his bit on the side, Naomi. Not that she's his bit on the side any more. She's the girlfriend now, the real deal. I saw them in Tesco, pushing a trolley together, him letting her boss him about in that flirty way he does. Larking about with a pair of melons. Pinching her thigh as they turned into the frozen food aisle.

I hope they'll be very happy.

That's a lie. I hope . . .

I don't know what I hope. I wouldn't want him back, that's for sure. When I was at my sister's the weekend after we split up, huddled under the spare-room duvet, she came up with a slice of home-made cake and made me sit up and eat it. Then she said, very gently, 'But he didn't make you happy, did he, Kate?'

Talk about the pressures on the modern-day woman. We have to hold down a job and exfoliate and know what Pilates is, and find a man. Now it turns out the man has to make us happy too?

Chloe never liked him, either. She was tactful about it – but I could see it in her face every time she came back from college and found him still on the scene. My daughter's a wise girl. I called her earlier and she was getting ready for some Valentine student bash. I hope she doesn't get her heart broken . . .

She won't. She's got her head screwed on properly. Not like her mum.

Anyway, to work. If the rest of the world wants to go crazy because it's February 14th, let them. My evening plans are to sit here in the deserted office, catching up with all the odd little bits of filing I need to do. Then home, a glass of wine and a nice pizza from Waitrose. (I don't go to Tesco any more. No particular reason.)

'Kate?'

I look up. It's Neil, who works opposite me. He's standing at the corner of our open-plan office, with about ten thousand pink 'I love you' helium balloons clutched in his hand.

I exaggerate. Maybe twenty.

'Hi, Neil.' I glance up, then resume typing.

'Are you staying long?' He clears his throat. 'The thing is, I'm meeting Ally here. It's kind of . . . a Valentine's surprise.'

'Here?' I look around our drab office, with its blue carpet and old, metallic blinds and strip lighting.

'That's the surprise.' He's getting all pink and flustered now. 'I'm going to transform the place. Balloons, streamers, music, champagne . . . Only she'll be here by eight . . .'

'You want me to go?' I finish my e-mail and send it with a sharp click. 'I've work to do.'

'I thought . . .' He rubs his nose. 'It's Valentine's.'

He assumed the office would be empty. Of course he did. Who sits working late on Valentine's Day?

'I forgot,' he adds lamely. 'I forgot about you and Rob.'

For a moment I consider saving face. Inventing plans for tonight, a new man, dinner at a posh restaurant overlooking the river.

'It's fine.' I close down my computer and push back my chair. 'I'll go. Have fun.'

It's fine. I'll have that gourmet feta and red onion pizza I've been saving for tonight. Open a bottle of wine. Maybe some garlic bread on the side.

The flat's freezing as I open the door, which is strange. Normally the heating would have kicked in by now. Still. It's pretty efficient, it should warm up soon. I whack up the thermostat, get out my pizza and slide it into the oven.

Five minutes later I know something's wrong. The flat is still arctic. The cheese on top of my pizza is still solid.

We live in a mansion block with pretty good maintenance – but when I call the porter's mobile, it's engaged. My next-door neighbour Mrs Blackett doesn't appear to be in. In frustration, I poke my head out of the front door of my flat to see Caroline, who lives above me, tripping down the stairs, wearing a red satin dress covered in love hearts.

'Hi, Kate!' She does a twirl. 'What do you think? I'm going to a Valentine's Ball! Are you going out for Valentine's?'

'No,' I say shortly. 'Is your flat freezing?'

'Isn't it awful?' She nods. 'The porter says they're working on it, but it'll be another hour before everything's back on.' Her mobile trills and she lifts it to her ear.

'Hi, honey! Yes, I'm just coming. See you, Kate. Give my love to Chloe.' She disappears down the staircase and I heave a sigh.

A freezing flat and a frozen pizza. I'll have to have a sandwich instead.

I'm halfway through cutting the first slice of bread when my hand stops. It's too cold for a sandwich. And I was so looking forward to my pizza. What I'll do is, I'll pop out and get a takeaway one. I'll bring it back and dig out my old electric heater. Lose myself in a good book. It's no Valentine's Ball – but it'll do.

My local pizza restaurant is decked out in love heart bunting and a red banner screams 'Special Valentine Menu!!!'. As I enter, my heart sinks. I should never have come here.

The place is stuffed with Valentine's couples. Each table has a red rose on it and some diners are perusing pink heart-shaped menus. At one table, a violinist is serenading an embarrassed-looking woman while her husband records the moment on his phone. At another, a couple are feeding each other spoonfuls of a giant ice-cream sundae. The whole sight makes me want to heave.

'Have an Amore!' A fresh-faced waitress with blonde curls pushes a glass of pink liquid into my hand. 'It's our special Valentine's cocktail!' she beams. 'Do you have a reservation?'

'No,' I say. 'I'm just here to get a takeaway pizza.'

'For two?' she asks, getting out her order pad. 'Because tonight we have a special offer. If you buy a Pizza of Love to share . . .'

'I don't want a Pizza of Love, thanks. Just a regular pizza.'

'It's very good,' she persists. 'It has fresh tomatoes and olives shaped into a love heart.'

Can't she get the message?

'I don't want a Pizza of Love, all right?' I snap. 'Or a pink drink.' I thrust it back at her. 'Some of us don't believe in Valentine's Day. I'd like a Napolitana and garlic bread. Thank you.'

'Fine,' says the waitress after a pause. 'Fine.' She dumps the drink on the counter and scribbles down the order. Then she looks up, clearly unable to keep quiet. 'It's only a bit of fun. It doesn't do any harm.'

'It's not fun,' I retort, unable to prevent a bitter tone stealing into my voice. 'It's cynical consumerism! The whole thing's become ridiculous. Cards and flowers and presents and special evenings out . . .' I spread my arms around. 'You're only laying on all this fuss to make money.'

'No we're not!' She opens her eyes wide. 'It's to make people happy! It's for romance!'

'Romance?' I lift my eyes to heaven. 'I'm more likely to believe in Father Christmas than romance!'

She opens her mouth to reply — then, as another

couple enter the restaurant, obviously decides it's not worth pursuing it.

'One Napolitana and a garlic bread,' she says, reverting to a businesslike manner. 'It'll be about twenty minutes, if you'd like to wait in the seating area.'

'Thanks.'

I slump down on a seat in the waiting area and morosely examine my nails.

Believing in romance has done nothing for me. The next time I go for a man, I'm going to be hard-headed about it, like my best mate Fiona from school. The minute she reached London, aged twenty-one, she went into action like some kind of steely headhunter. She drew up a tick list and targeted only suitable candidates. Didn't waste her time with losers or dreamers or charmers. A couple of them turned out to be no-hopers but she got there in the end. She's been married to Gavin for sixteen years now. Two kids. He commutes from Kent.

Whereas I did what? Got pregnant before I'd even worked out the tube map. Stephen was a nice guy, but we barely knew each other. It was never going to be happy families. He moved to France when Chloe was three – and that was pretty much it.

I mean, I wouldn't have changed anything. Chloe's the best thing that ever happened to me. But she's eighteen now. Grown-up and leading her own life.

Which leaves me. Sitting on my own, not getting any younger. On impulse I get out my diary and a Biro and turn to the back page.

Tick list, I write firmly.

1. Solvent. 2. Professional. 3. Reliable.

A man in an ancient leather jacket has just come into the pizza place. He's in his forties, unshaven and wearing Armani jeans, which reminds me:

4. No jeans.

This guy's jeans are different though. Shabby and soft-looking. Rob used to get me to iron the creases into his, vain sod.

The waitress is trying to press a pink cocktail on the guy, but I don't think he's even noticed her. He's on his mobile phone, thrusting a hand through his dishevelled brown hair.

'It's a great feeling,' he's saying. 'I just hope . . . Well, anyway. I'll send it round tomorrow. Bye, Michael.' As he puts his phone away his eyes are glowing and I find myself wondering what he's talking about.

'Hi.' His eyes focus on the waitress. 'I'd like a takeaway pizza, please. A Margarita with anchovies.'

'Have an Amore!' She hands him the pink drink and he looks at it, nonplussed. 'Would you like our Pizza of Love? Tomatoes and olives shaped into a love heart . . .'

'A love heart?' He looks bewildered.

'For Valentine's Day?'

His crumpled brow clears.

'Valentine's Day. Of course.' He looks around the place as though spotting all the balloons and bunting for the first time. 'Forgive me, I'm a little preoccupied.'

'If you buy a Pizza of Love to share . . .'

'Not to share.' He cuts her off with a rueful smile. 'It's just me, I'm afraid. What's on it, again?'

'Tomatoes and olives.'

'Sounds delicious.' He smiles at her. 'I'll have one.' He sits down next to me and we exchange brief smiles, just as his phone rings. He glances at the display, winces, then answers.

'Hi, Mum. Yup, finished. Sending it off to the publishers tomorrow.' The glow has appeared on his face again. 'Yeah, I'm pretty pleased with it. Just getting a pizza to celebrate.' There's a pause, and he sighs. 'Mum, I don't see Amanda any more. You know that.' There's another pause. 'I know it's Valentine's Day.'

I can't help a tiny smile – then quickly look away as he glances up. Come on, Kate. Stop earwigging on a stranger's phone call. Back to the tick list.

5. Employed.

No more entrepreneurs, thank you. No more get-rich-quick schemes, no more signing away my savings. Thank God I had the sense to keep back what I did, or Rob would have had it all. I want someone safe. Someone steady.

6. Staid. 7. Ugly.

Not too ugly, obviously. But I don't need to be with a Greek god. In my opinion the really good-looking ones are just trouble. There's my list. And I'm going to stick with it.

'I've no idea what's wrong. I need to find a good

local garage. I'll ask around.' The guy's voice cuts into my thoughts. 'OK, well have a good evening. See you soon, Mum.' He puts his phone away and leans back, contemplating his socks. They're nice socks, blue and red striped, poking out of his battered brown shoes.

'Excuse me?' I venture. 'I couldn't help overhearing. Do you need a garage?'

'Yes!' The man turns, eagerly. 'Do you know one?'

'Morrisons, in Gardam Street. I've been going to them for years.'

'Morrisons. Thanks. Could I borrow your pen?'

He takes the Biro and scribbles 'Morrisons' on his hand, then sticks the pen behind his ear in an automatic gesture.

'Er . . . my pen?'

'Your pen!' He claps a hand to his ear. 'I'm so sorry.' He hands it over and I can't help smiling. I'm about to speak – but his phone rings again and he raises his eyebrows at me. 'I do apologise. I've been a hermit these last few months. All my friends have clearly got word that I'm back in circulation . . .' He lifts the phone to his ear, his face lit up. 'Hi, Philip. Yes, it's true. I've finished the book. It's a grand feeling.'

I look at him anew. He's written a book. That's pretty impressive.

He glances at me, sensing my gaze on him, and I quickly look away. The blonde waitress catches my eye and, misunderstanding, comes over.

'Your pizza will only be about another five minutes. OK?'

'Great,' I nod. 'Thanks.' I survey my tick list again, pen poised over the page. But for some reason I've lost my impetus.

I wonder what his book's about.

The man's finished his call now and we're both sitting there in silence. The violinist is serenading a nearby table, his stomach jiggling as he plays. He looks ridiculous – and as I glance at the guy, I see he's amused too.

'So you've written a book?' I say before I can stop myself. 'That's amazing.' I'm worried he's going to be offended – but his face breaks into a smile.

'It feels pretty phenomenal.' He nods. 'It's my first, so just to get to the end . . .'

'A novel?'

'No, a biography. Of someone called Dorothy Wordsworth. She was . . .'

'Wordsworth's sister.' I nod. 'She wrote herself too, didn't she?'

The man is staring at me.

'You're the first person I've ever told, who actually knew who Dorothy Wordsworth was. Most people say "Oh, his wife?" '

'I like poetry.' I feel embarrassed under his gaze. 'I studied English at college. I'll look out for the book.'

'Do!' He nods. 'So where did you . . .' He trails away as two waiters walk past me, carrying pizzas decorated with lurid red tomato love hearts. 'Is that what I've ordered?' He looks alarmed. 'It's a bit full-on, isn't it?'

'I think so.' I can't help a smile.

'One Napolitana, one garlic bread.' The waitress appears in front of me, holding a pizza box. 'That'll be eight pounds. Sorry to keep you waiting.'

I hand over a tenner and take the warm pizza box.

'I'll just get your change . . .' The waitress disappears, and the guy smiles at me.

'Well . . . nice to meet you. My name's Oliver, by the way,' he adds. 'Oliver Bridge.'

'I'm Kate.'

'Kate.' We shake hands awkwardly over my pizza box.

'Here you are.' The waitress hands me my change. 'See you again, have a nice evening.'

'Thanks.' I pocket my change, leaving a quid for a tip. But I don't stand up.

This place is warm. I'm having a nice conversation. It beats the bleakness of my cold, empty kitchen.

And . . . I like this guy. I like his vague, self-deprecating manner. His scruffy brown hair. His bright striped socks.

'I just wondered.' The words spill out before I can stop them. 'If you don't have any plans this evening, maybe . . . if you felt like some company . . . we could . . . share a table . . .'

Oliver's face lights up. 'I'd love some company. There's a table free over there. We could nab that.'

'I just thought, it beats going back to an empty flat,' I add awkwardly. 'That's all.'

'Quite right.' He nods and beams at the waitress, who's approaching with another pizza box. 'I'm so sorry, there's been a change of plan. Could we have these to stay?'

'To stay?' She looks from face to face as though suspecting a joke.

'We've decided to eat together,' he explains, and drains his pink cocktail.

'Also, I'd like another one of these, and so would my friend here.'

'You'd like an Amore?' She's staring at me incredulously. 'You?'

'Um . . . yes please,' I mumble, shamefaced. 'Thanks.'

'. . . total psycho . . .' I can hear her muttering as she walks off.

'So!' Oliver offers his arm in a gallant gesture. 'Shall we?'

As I stand up, my diary falls to the floor and as I pick it up I glimpse my tick list.

Solvent. Professional. What a load of meaningless tosh. I don't know what I was thinking, really. Already, I'm putting together a new list in my mind.

1. Smiles. 2. Writing book. 3. Wants to eat pizza on Valentine's night with me.

That'll do, for starters.

Across the Bay

BY DEBORAH LAWRENSON

Gradually the mountains appeared across the bay. Lost in a mother-of-pearl haze until late afternoon, they came into focus as the day cooled. By early evening the high ridges were solid, rust red across a wind-wrinkled sea.

'I once rode a moped across those mountains, all the way to Sitia,' said Leonie. She and her daughter Emily were sipping drinks, sitting on wide sofas in one of the resort hotel's rather stylish bars. This one was like a stone boat moored at the end of a long jetty. Emily did not respond.

'An old-fashioned moped, the kind that leaked oil constantly and had punctures. When Melissa's broke down right up in the mountains, an old man offered to lend her a replacement – he went off and came back with a donkey!'

In the Greek landscape, the immense blue of the light and seas and sky was a world of possibility, of myth and magic . . . and of freedom. Perhaps it was still there, just as she remembered from that summer when she was nineteen.

Emily – at seventeen, both coltish and knowing – unfolded her long legs and stood up, generating considerable eye-overtime from the barman and waiter.

'Marta and I are going into town later,' yawned Emily.

'Who's Marta?'

'The Dutch girl I was snorkelling with this afternoon. There was an octopus, we were all watching it. It was, like, rippling sideways over the rocks on the bottom.'

'Into Elounda?' persisted Leonie.

Emily gave her a pitying look. 'There's nothing there. We're going to check out the clubs in Ag Nik.'

'I see . . .'

'It's OK, there's a bus to get there, and we'll get a cab back.'

'The thing is . . .' began Leonie, then stopped herself. The thing was, she knew exactly, first-hand, what girls Emily's age got up to in clubs in Agios Nikolaos. 'Perhaps we could all go in together, have dinner, and then—'

'Mum!'

With Emily and Marta off to town, she strolled out on a jetty lit by hurricane lamps. The night air was so soft it was like wearing warmed silk.

Was it a mad idea, to come back to Crete after so many years? She didn't know quite what had made her choose to return. And if a journey was the purest form of introspection (she had read that somewhere), then what was she thinking when she booked this week in the sun?

Her first holiday since the divorce.

This place, on the western horn of the Mirabello Bay, was gorgeous. But (and here Leonie had been struggling to put her finger on exactly what was wrong) it didn't seem like Greece, just a kind of staged version of it, with its smart restaurant pretending to be a waterside taverna, and its manicured beaches edged with hibiscus, and rooms like tiny whitewashed fishermen's cottages.

Across the wide blue bay was the real thing.

A large, noisy party of Russians took over the main beach the next morning. Interesting that it was the Russians who were in the most expensive villas in the complex, with their own infinity pools; the men in their odd beach outfits, one in an astonishing mustard-print shorts and shirt set, all elbows and grabbing at breakfast, and intense mobile phone conversations on the sand. Their violently peroxided women stood waist-deep in the sea, talking, never swimming.

While Emily slept through it all, Leonie borrowed her snorkel and slipped away to the sea world of sunlit blues and greens.

'I met a lovely Greek guy, when I was here,' Leonie told her over lunch under a linen shade. Before I became invisible, she didn't say.

Emily narrowed her eyes.

'His name was Georgios.'

A sigh from her daughter indicated a depth of irritation rarely experienced outside a full-scale Embarrassing Parent Appearance. 'Don't tell me, he was a waiter. God, they're persistent.'

'No, he was a student – at the University of Trieste. He was back home in Sitia for the summer. He was helping a friend run a disco, that's where I met him.'

'What, like at a club?'

'The Disco Minotauros.'

'You are joking . . .'

'I'm not, actually. You know, Ems, I was your age once.'

Emily gave a wince. Yeah, right, it implied.

So here I am, old and boring, thought Leonie, waistline expanding, bottom spreading with every mouthful of taramasalata, trying desperately to hold on to the scraps and tatters of my previous certainties as they flap and fly. My world is shrinking, tipping away from the sun, melting into the brown of parched hillsides and support hosiery.

Emily stared at a line of teenagers moving in a pack around the rocks to the far beach, where they would flop like seals, according to their custom.

'I thought I might hire a car, go along the coast a bit,' said Leonie. 'Do you want to come or are you happy here?'

Emily was barely listening, straining at the leash to join her new-found friends. A blonde girl had bounded up to the group and was making the boys laugh. One grabbed her by the waist and swung her around. 'No, you're all right . . .' said Emily. 'I'm going to stay here. You're just going for the afternoon, right?'

Well, of course just for the afternoon, thought Leonie as her daughter ran off. Some of us have responsibilities. Although a lot fewer now, she reminded herself. She was practically young, free and single again. Well, free and single, anyway.

The hire car, a tiny silver Seat, had a ferocious clutch. Leonie lurched several times as she manoeuvred out of the hotel car park. She had a map open on the passenger seat but doubted she would need it. The route she wanted to take was a simple one: into Agios Nikolaos and east to Sitia, taking the high mountain road. If she, Melissa and Clare had managed it all those years ago on three patched-up mopeds, it should be a piece of cake in a car.

Agios Nikolaos was larger than in her memory. Then, they had stayed in a room for three near a street with a tree growing right out into the road at a drunken angle. Was that still there? At a roundabout, the dual carriageway to Sitia was clearly signposted, but where was the old route, with its crumbly red soil and rocks, and perilous drops down to the famous old 'wine-dark' sea?

Leonie concentrated hard. Lorries and buses ground across her. Cars buzzed far too close.

Sitia 70 km. It seemed she had no option but to take the chance this was the road.

Passing the outskirts of the town it all began to look

more hopeful. The colour of the exposed earth and dust was right. So were the scrubby bushes fighting for survival on the bald hills. She took the first exit towards the coast.

That summer they had stopped at a beach along here somewhere, leaving the mopeds to drip while they ran into the turquoise sea.

A sign read Pahia Ammos. The name had no resonance, but there was something about the pale grey sand and the stones under the tamarisk trees, the dark blue of the water and the brown-mauve hills in the distance, that seemed familiar. She drew up and parked.

She swam there for old times' sake, immersing herself completely in the water, then floating with her eyes on the great hills massed on the horizon round the bay where she had started. Finally she emerged, conscious of her dimpling thighs, her hair sea-encrusted and coarse under her hand. She ordered a coffee at a beach taverna and let the breeze tighten her skin and dry a lacy patch of salt on her sarong.

Did everyone else wonder about other lives they might have had? Was that what this was all about? And was that why men left their wives – the fear of missing out, of having only one story? Her best friend Melissa was the first one to go through it, years ago now, but others had inexorably followed. Men casting off wives and children and smart new kitchens in extensions like there was no tomorrow.

No one was safe. Her staid neighbour, Sarah, had been sure of her husband, Stephen, right up until last week when – out of the blue – he upped and went after twenty years. There were women everywhere, finding themselves right back where they started.

Back in the car, Leonie followed the road which hugged the coast. To her left, the deep indigo sea; ahead, Sitia.

Was that what she was really intending to do – drive to Sitia?

She wouldn't have time to get all the way there and back before the evening. And anyway – she tried to reason with herself – was it the place she wanted to see again, or the person she used to be? She thought of Georgios. The nights on the beach at Sitia, days baking in the sun. His gentleness and soft, golden skin, the mop of curly hair and naughty grin. His dirty toes in open leather sandals, she reminded herself.

He wouldn't do now, of course. It was just curiosity, being here that was bringing it all back. Where was he now? What had become of him? She hoped he was happy.

The road was climbing, becoming steeper. Heat was coming in gusts, defeating the car's air-conditioning system. Sweat started to trickle between her back and the seat. When she dared to look, Elounda was far below her. She could see Spinalonga, the island, clearly by its side. This was definitely the right route. She felt a tingle of excitement. When she could, she would pull in and get out to see the spectacular view properly.

Round the next bend, she had to brake sharply. The car in front had stopped, blocking the road, and a man had got out. He made a signal by which she understood that she should stop, too. Cautiously, and seeing that she had no other option, she obeyed, feeling for her bag and her mobile as she cut the engine, and opened the window.

'What is it?' she asked nervously, in English. Was this the kind of situation all women feared, a set-up to make her get out of the car to be robbed, or worse? To think it had been Emily she had been worried about, not herself.

The man walked round to her window. 'The road, he is gone.' He was in his forties, like her, with dark, curly hair flecked with silver and a round stomach. He didn't look menacing but you never knew.

'What do you mean, gone?' asked Leonie. The heat of the metal window frame scorched her arm as she turned towards him. Cicadas were sawing up a throbbing beat.

He pulled a face, then spread his hands to show the difficulty of explaining in English. 'See it,' he said.

She would have told Emily not to get out of the car, always to think about personal safety – the world was not how it was when she was young, but there was a kind quality about the Cretan's smile that made her willing to take the chance now.

He led her round to the front of his car and pointed.

A garish tumble of orange rocks, concrete and tarmac had taken half the road – more than half the road – with it. The road ended in a crater.

'It's a landslip!' she cried.

'This no good now.'

'No . . . I can see that.'

'You want I show you . . . how to go other road?'

She felt the breeze catch her skirt, smelt the thyme growing on the scrub. Could it invoke some magic, to find some ghosts down there by Sitia's harbour and long shingle beach – or did they not exist in the hard, bright sapphire of the present?

Here she was, on this crumbling road, this dangerous ledge above the blue, blue bay that had once carried three friends on an adventure. How much had changed since then?

'OK,' she said at last. 'I mean, yes – please.'

'Where you going?'

She hesitated, then looked him straight in the eye. 'Sitia.'

He looked surprised but then smiled. 'I take you.'

Sun-dazed, Leonie nodded. The man guided her as she made the tricky three-point turn then led her back the way she'd come.

A sharp left into the hills took them on to a rutted, hard-baked orange path, which tossed the car like a boat on stormy waves. She assumed it led to the new main road. Ahead, the man was bobbing smoothly over all obstacles. It was all she could do to keep up with him.

She changed down another gear, but the engine protested rudely. One more massive jolt and it was all over for the Seat. She tried again but the brutish clutch refused to engage.

Leonie switched off the engine and sighed.

'I'm fated not to get to Sitia,' she told the man when he came back to find out what was wrong.

His name was Sophocles, unlikely as that seemed. Gallantly, he had called a breakdown service and driven her back to Agios Nikolaos. They were sitting overlooking a deep-water lake linked to the harbour by a narrow bridge. In early evening, shops were open and the tavernas were busy.

'It's just as I remember it!' she enthused over a glass of wine. She was enjoying herself now. 'We ate swordfish at that little place there, and then went dancing . . . !'

Sophocles laughed with her, then was serious. 'Would you like have dinner with me?'

He waited patiently, a hint of sadness in his eyes.

This is what Georgios probably looks like now, she thought. A portly Greek gentleman who is kind to strangers. Someone with a past and children now, just like me.

There was a long pause during which time seemed to expand with possibilities and then contract.

'I think I really should get back,' she said.

*

At the hotel complex, Emily was nowhere to be seen. Feeling oddly happy, Leonie settled back on a comfortable wicker chair in the bar on the water and contemplated the red mountains. It was impossible to work out where exactly the landslip had occurred. The road was invisible.

After a while her eyes drifted away from the seascape to the smooth almost-Greece of the hotel's waterside. She watched a lovely long-limbed girl on the beach walkway. She was on the jetty before Leonie realised it was Emily.

Close-up she was unmistakably tear-stained. 'Where the hell have you been?' she cried. 'Don't you think I might have been worried?'

'I'm sorry, I had quite a – Ems, what's wrong, sweetheart?' asked Leonie, reaching out to her daughter.

'Nothing . . . everything.'

Leonie drew her into a hug.

'They've gone off without me,' she sniffed. 'Marta and this other girl who's butted in, and the boys didn't seem to care if I was there or not, and last night I thought Jens really liked me . . .'

Leonie stroked her back but said nothing.

She wouldn't have been seventeen again for anything.

The Wedding Anniversary

BY KATHY LETTE

*T*he secret bedroom fantasy of every mother is . . . sleep. This is what Cassie thought to herself as she slid between the crisp hotel sheets, careful not to wake the snoring lump beside her. She tested the pillows approvingly and then snuggled down with obvious relish. For a tenth wedding anniversary, Cassie's parents had given them a gift-wrapped night in a London hotel, complete with the heroic offer to babysit their three rambunctious grandchildren.

Cassie had been vaguely dreading some kind of dutiful celebratory sex, but the red wine had taken its soporific effect on her husband and all that lay ahead of her was the deep, deep peace of an uninterrupted night's sleep, with the added bonus of a luxurious lie in. What with the sandwich making, egg frying and lost-sports-kit locating, it seemed to Cassie that the Dunkirk evacuation would be easier to organise than a working mother getting her kids up and out of the house in the morning. After the evening chaos of meal cooking, homework helping and housework completing, it was no wonder she was always too tired for sex.

A wave of contentment washed over her. On the cusp of sleep, she sighed with satisfaction and then gently pecked her husband good night on the ear.

This was her mistake. What she'd forgotten was that husbands invariably interpret the smallest act of affection as foreplay. She saw the hand before she felt it, creeping stealthily over from the other side of the bed. It clamped on to her breast. Cassie's eyes opened wide in terror. Oh no, she thought. Not The Hand! It was the stuff of horror movies. Every woman's worst nightmare. Men make horror movies about The Blob or The Alien or The Thing. What terrorised her husband were Wolfman, the Zombie, Dracula, Frankenstein. What terrorises women, Cassie realised, well, weary mothers that is, is The Hand. The Hand groping over the sheets for you, uninvited. The Hand – that most predictable of matrimonial gestures, signalling that conjugal rights are being requested despite your bone-achingly deep state of exhaustion. You shrink from it. No! No! I'm a sleep-deprived mother! You feign premature death, pneumonia, catatonia . . .

Yes, that was it! Cassie decided to pretend to be asleep . . . But, undeterred, he moved in for a kiss, running his tongue around her upper molars, once, twice, around and around until the titillation became so intense she was tempted to flick on the telly to watch the darts final. She wondered how many wives felt the same way? Her girlfriends often joked over cappuccinos how their favourite position is the 'doggy position', 'where he begs . . . and I just roll over and play dead'. But did they really mean it? Cassie felt sure that a worn-out wife would do everything to discourage her husband, bar stretching razor wire around her bed and setting bait traps. While men want the tumbling in the hay to recommence six weeks after childbirth, mothers want to tie up the sheaves and put them in the barn.

Cassie snorted with tedium, a noise Rory evidently mistook for a groan of passion as he then began twanging this and tweaking that. Craving sleep even more desperately now, she found herself contemplating the most effective sex-stalling technique she'd ever devised. But it would have to be used sparingly, so as not to induce heart failure. Just when hubby was snuggling up and she felt the prod in her back, why not mention, casually, that the tax department had rung earlier in the day and wanted to audit his accounts? Not only would he lose the inclination for sex, he'd also lose the desire for sleep, which meant she wouldn't have to put up with his snoring either!

Cassie sucked in air in alarm. What had happened to her, she wondered? She wasn't just faking orgasms, she was flunking them. On those official forms, after it says 'Sex', she'd have to start writing 'NOT IF I CAN POSSIBLY HELP IT.'

But if only Rory's every move weren't so mechanical. And if only it included a little cuddling and nuzzling. When was the last time he'd hugged her when she wasn't horizontal, she conjectured? Rory never asks me my favourite position either, which is, by the way, deputy head teacher, she quipped to herself. A promotion she'd never achieve if she didn't get some shut-eye! If only he'd quit fumbling and just get on with it, she sighed inwardly. Why it is that men can assemble a hand-held rocket grenade launcher from the internet and yet they can't find . . . Oh wait. Yes. He'd found it. Houston we have lift off . . . !

Cassie was just starting to surrender to the feeling of pleasure spreading warmly through her, when she suddenly cut short her own excitement. God knows she didn't want to encourage the man. That would delay sleep even further! Cassie laughed to herself, but her laugh caught in her throat as the shrill squawk of the fire alarm shattered the air. A tongue of smoke curled under the door to taste them. Rory leapt out of bed, alert, his eyes on high beam. 'Bloody hell! There's a fire.'

Cassie felt a jolt in her abdomen as her body stiffened to meet the blow. All she could hear was her own stark, jerky breathing. But before she could panic, Rory was back at her side, swaddling her with wet bathrobe and towels. With a feverish grip, he propelled her towards the door. 'Take a deep breath.' Arms wrapped tight around her, he then bundled her out into the hall. The smoke made her eyes stream and her throat seize up. Death, Cassie realised, gasping, really is a breathtaking experience. With the sonar accuracy of a bat, Rory located the fire exit. Shielding her body with his own, he shouldered open the door. As they descended the stairs and the fug of fumes lifted, Cassie was bewildered to find herself still alive. It had all happened so quickly. She patted her body to make sure she still had everything she'd started out with. 'Hold on to me,' came Rory's steady mantra. 'Stay calm.' 'Breathe slowly.'

Other guests flooded on to the stairway from each landing until they were a river of terry towelling. She didn't know if the tears plopping off the end of her nose were from the smoke or pure terror.

By the time they reached Level Three, firemen were hurtling upwards past them, firing salvos of water. When the lava flow of bleary-eyed guests oozed into the hotel foyer, the night manager greeted them with a brittle smile and assurances that the small blaze, started by some candles in a guest's bedroom, was under control. For the next hour the whole hotel seemed to hold its breath in a tourniqueted silence. The atmosphere was lachrymose with smoke haze. Rory scooped her up and held her ashen face close to his chest. He navigated his way to a lounge chair and placed her gingerly upon it. Through the slits of burning eyes, she gazed at the other guests. A woman Cassie vaguely recognised from the telly was sobbing uncontrollably in between piercing utterances of 'Do you know who I am?' She was wearing little more than a pint of baby oil and a tight-lipped smile. Cassie took in the celebrity's black lace underwear and satin mules. All the women, Cassie now noticed, were revealing silks and satins beneath their gowns. She glanced down with embarrassment at her saggy, baggy flannelette nightie and airline bed-socks and thought how flannelette pyjamas are the sexual equivalent of World War Two soldiers laying minefields across the entrance to their tunnels.

Wasn't it ironic, Cassie mused, clutching the damp robe around her, how having loads of sex before marriage had made her feel dirty and cheap; but after marriage, not having loads of sex was making her feel dirty and cheap. In the early days they'd been at it like rabbits. Was this marital myxomatosis her doing? Perhaps she should try harder? Don a filmy gown? Get a prescription for She-agra? Make the first move? After all, one good turn . . . gets most of the blankets, she admitted, realistically. But exactly when had this slow drip sexual ennui set in? Cassie ruminated. When had sex become more dutiful than enthusiastic? With a sickening heart, she remembered that she and Rory used to do something that involved a fair bit of nestling and stroking – but she couldn't remember what exactly. She could recall that she liked it though. What happened to those sex-surfeited days we once had, Cassie pondered? Those days where we dinged furniture, took headboard divots out of the wall, broke beds, destroyed mattresses and ran up chiropractic bills?

'Cass?' At the sound of his voice she felt a dolorous tug at her heart-strings. Her husband leaned over her as if she were a lost kitten. 'Darling?'

'I'm OK,' she said with counterfeit calm. And looking up at his concerned face, she suddenly remembered why she'd married him. His love had always covered her, like treacle. A fondness spilled and rippled over his face, even now, after all these years. She loved the way his whole being was lit up by that ready smile, a smile that rendered him instantly likeable. It complemented the insouciant way he cocked his elbow on to the window ledge of his car while whistling a tune. He was her rock. Her lighthouse. His attention might be blinking and intermittent, but there was still warmth and illumination. Rory gently tugged her to her feet and cuddled her close. It dawned on her that he was hugging her when she wasn't horizontal.

A high-pitched screech, loud enough to set off car alarms in, say, Nova Scotia, alerted the fatigued throng to the fact that the minor televisual celebrity had lost her temper with the hotel manager, who'd been enquiring if she had a penchant for lighted candles in her room. Beet-faced, she was making finger gestures at him that couldn't quite be misinterpreted as the Vulcan sign for Live Long and Prosper. Her boyfriend, who was sporting a pointillist portrait of a naked Pamela Anderson on one bicep and Marilyn Monroe on the other, narrowed his small, close-set eyes at the manager. Cassie thought that they were eyes that screamed 'maximum security prison'. He looked so much like a hardened criminal, Cassie couldn't believe that the hotel security hadn't sent off the CCTV footage to the police the moment he'd checked in. When the Neanderthal threw a punch in the hapless hotel man's direction, Rory moved in quickly to defend him.

'Steady on.' Cassie heard Rory's calm, even voice.

She was just about to try to defuse the situation with a quip along the lines of the fact that holidaying in a top hotel shouldn't really mourn more early deaths than space travel, stunt-doubling and bull-fighting, when she saw the knife. She felt a spidery crawl of horror up her spine as the huge, angry man jabbed the blade in her husband's direction. The interesting thing about looking at a knife aimed at your husband's groin is how small the tip of the blade is and yet what a huge hole it would make in any future reproductive plans. Rory darted expertly away from each thrust. He was backing towards the lobby doors, drawing the man and his knife as far as possible from the crowd.

Cassie's face distorted into a mask of horror and a silent scream warped her mouth. When she pictured her husband on their wedding anniversary it was not with a tag on his toe. She was so sick with anxiety that she didn't hear the heavy click of the fire exit door behind her. But she knew her husband's antagonist had been overrun and disarmed by the barrage of big and burly firemen, because her heart had started to beat again.

As the crowd praised and back-slapped Rory for his bravery, Cassie found herself basking in the glow of his glory. 'Don't ever play the hero again,' she warned, trying to keep the tremor out of her voice. 'But meanwhile, I'm writing to Downing Street about sending you in for a halo fitting.'

After the police had arrived and pressed charges and

the offending couple had been taken into custody, the fire chief conferred monosyllabically with the night manager. A curt nod indicated that the anxious, exhausted guests could now return to their rooms.

Upgraded to a suite some time later, Cassie squeezed Rory's hand and snuggled into his shoulder.

'You were fantastic,' she told him. 'Amazing. And do you know how I'm going to reward you?' Half an hour later they were cosily ensconced beneath the duvet, fingers sticky, mouths wet. They could talk about their sex life and his need to help more with the housework later. Right now, companionable, comforting love was warming her with emotion. 'You're hitting my E spot,' she told her husband, playfully. And that's when Cassie realised that there's only one thing it's imperative a couple be able to share in bed – breakfast.

Chocolate v. Husband

BY SARAH-KATE LYNCH

'You've let yourself go.' These were the words that kept ringing in my ears long after Henry walked out on me.

Of course, 'I've met someone else,' was the real clincher, coming as it did so hard on the heels of 'It hasn't been right between us for a while, Caroline, you must know that.'

Well, as it happens, I hadn't known that. We'd been married eight years, had good jobs, a lovely house, nice cars, lavish holidays, we never argued. I thought we were happy.

But after Henry dropped his bombshell that awful night I realised that it probably hadn't been right between us for approximately the same amount of time that it had been right between him and a blonde real estate agent from Chiswick. Her name was Imogen, she was tiny and only at the very, very, very beginning of her thirties.

'She understands me,' Henry had said, looking at me encouragingly as though hoping I might find it in myself to be thrilled for him. 'She wants to grow the way I do.'

'He's just such a bastard,' my girlfriend Nell soothed me over a bottle of our favourite Sauvignon Blanc a week after Henry had decamped for Chiswick. 'Let yourself go? You're in the catering business. What does he expect?'

For reasons of this not being what I wanted to hear, I started to cry.

'This is not about you, Caroline,' my much more tactful friend Esther assured soothingly. 'It's about men being spineless, childish, pathetic and selfish and they really shouldn't be allowed to live or breathe, at the very least in England but preferably the world.'

This was more like it, so I stopped crying and reached for a glass of wine.

'Maybe you could try WeightWatchers again,' Nell offered helpfully. 'Or give Jenny Craig another bash.'

Yes, or the Atkins Diet, I thought to myself, putting the wine glass back down again to weep. Or the skipping rope. Or the running shoes. Or the seaweed wrap at the beauty spa in Hammersmith that was supposed to suck out five pounds of ugly fat, but instead gave me a rash on my bottom that lasted a month.

After they'd gone I stripped off all my clothes and stood in front of the full-length mirror in the bathroom.

'You have let yourself go,' I told my reflection sadly. I had piled on the pounds since I was married – doesn't everyone? – but deep down I hadn't thought it really mattered. How wrong could I have been.

I grabbed at a roll of flesh around my middle then turned side on and saw how much my boobs had drooped, how my bum wobbled. To add insult to injury, as I twisted to get a better look at the damage, there it was: another chin.

I sat on the edge of the bath, wondering if there were any razors anywhere, so I could kill myself right then and there. But I'd been waxing for years, even my armpits, and anyway, I felt bad but rather amazingly, to my own surprise, not that bad.

Realising this, I stood up and took a defiant stance. I had great hair, everyone said so, and I flicked it over my shoulders, which I pulled back while simultaneously sucking in my stomach.

There I was! The girl who married Henry Simpson. She was still in me!

I would lose the weight, I decided then and there (still sucking in my stomach). I would get a grip on myself and I would get Henry back. I could do it, I knew I could. If I worked longer and harder than I ever had before, I really could do it.

The next day I went to work and told my assistant that I wanted her to have a more hands-on role with the catering. She could be the one to lick the aioli off the spoon and 'test' the marinated feta fourteen times to see if it was right and I would concentrate on marketing and new business.

After work, positively humming with inspiration, I

put on my running shoes and took off around the block at a spirited walk. Ten minutes later I thought I was going to collapse, so I dropped in on Nell who lives not far from me.

'Oh hurrah,' she cried when she answered the door. 'I was just looking at a fresh bottle of Pinot Gris wondering if it was too sad to drink it on my own. And now here you are!'

'Count me out,' I said, still sweating profusely. 'I am on a mission.'

'A mission to what?' she asked.

'To get thin and get my husband back,' I answered, flopping into a chair.

Nell, still single after more than two decades of ever hopeful dating, clasped her hands in front of her chin, eyes shining. 'You'll do it, Caro,' she said. 'I know you will. And you and Henry will be happy little lovebirds all over again.'

Considerably cheered by that notion, I walked briskly towards home, stopping in at the corner shop.

'Hey there, how's my favourite customer?' drawled Zak, the tall, dark son of the short, fat store owner.

Zak was ridiculously handsome and knew it, as did the ever-changing collection of lovestruck blondes usually installed at the counter whenever he worked. They slouched there all but drooling over the news-papers as they took in his chocolate-coloured skin, his big, brown eyes, his broad, broad shoulders.

'Where's Mr Hassani?' I asked, nervously. The truth was, I had once had a rather unladylike dream about

Zak involving the two of us and a Black Forest gâteau and ever since then I had found him rather hard to deal with, preferring his divine but deeply unsexy father.

'Retired, Mrs S,' Zak answered with a wink. 'You have to come to me for your chocolate fix now, yeah? KitKat?' he asked, reaching for one.

I shook my head.

'Violet Crumble?'

'Just a bottle of water, thanks, Zak. And a news-paper.'

'We have a new frozen cheesecake, you know. Chocolate flavoured.'

I stood my ground, shook my head again and Zak took my change but seemed most put out, brushing away his current blonde as she leaned in to kiss him.

The next day, I walked for a full half hour, the day after that thirty-five minutes. My hips ached and I sweated indelicately, but still I had never felt more determined in my whole life.

'Curly Wurly?' Zak asked, when I dropped in to get my bottle of water.

'Cadbury's Creme Egg?' No, thank you. 'Are you sure, Mrs S?'

Within a fortnight, I could handle walking for one hour at a respectable pace and by the end of the month, I was doing five-minute intervals at what could almost pass for a run if you were from Mars and didn't really know what one was.

'Nell tells me you're trying to get Henry back,' Esther said curtly over the phone one night as I sat down to my Lean Cuisine meal of not very much with even less on the side. 'Is that why I haven't heard from you lately?'

I had not told Esther about my repatriating Henry plan for fear of getting a lecture on how he didn't deserve me.

'He doesn't deserve you!' she exploded.

Esther had married twice, both times to City bankers who had left her for their secretaries. She had two lovely sons, but they were strictly the only males she could abide.

'There are worse things than being on your own, Caroline,' she said. 'And Henry is one of them.'

Well, what did she know?

I avoided her but kept working at my new regime and just nine weeks after Henry left me, I stood on the scales and watched the needle hover at my long lost wedding weight of nine stone two. It hadn't really even been that hard. A bit of a re-structure at work, an hour or so of daily exercise, no wine, a lot of Lean Cuisine and a small amount of hard fought battle with Zak at the corner shop.

'No Yorkie, Mrs S? No Twix? No Mint Aero?' He had actually jumped up from his stool the last time I had gone into the shop. 'Dark chocolate Bounty bar? My dad says they're your favourite.'

Upon reaching nine stone a couple of weeks later, I felt ready to meet Henry. He'd only seen me once since he left, when he'd come to pick up his Vietnamese cookbooks and I'd been a wreck, bursting out of a too-tight silk blouse and crying uncontrollably.

Now, I wanted to stun him with the new, thin, calm me, but before I could work out how to orchestrate this, he turned up on my doorstep. I was just about to head off on a run and was wearing shorts that I knew did great things for my newly toned legs and a sports bra that worked wonders on my droop.

'Can I come in?' he asked, pushing gently past me and going to sit at the kitchen table. 'Please forgive me, Caro, but I really need to talk to you.'

My heart was beating furiously inside my sports bra. He looked so lovely, so familiar. Although older than I remembered, perhaps. And his longer hair didn't really suit him.

'Of course, Henry,' I said calmly, leaning against the kitchen bench, so he could see how thin I was. 'What is it?'

'It's Imogen,' he replied.

My sports bra stopped beating. 'Oh no,' I whispered, tears welling up in my eyes. 'You're not getting married?' But Henry shook his head. 'Is she pregnant?' We had decided not to have children, so it would have killed me if he'd had a change of heart with her.

'No, no, it's nothing like that,' he said. 'It's just that, well, I think I might have made a mistake.'

'A mistake?'

'She has this stupid little dog!' Henry cried and lifted the leg of his trousers which were clearly freshly stained and had a series of little rips near the hem. 'It keeps peeing on me and then when I try to kick it away the bloody thing bites me. Imogen says it's my fault, but honestly I'm not doing a thing to provoke it.'

'That's the mistake?'

'Her flat, Caro!' Henry cried. 'It's so bloody tidy you can't put a coffee cup down on the table before she's collected it up, washed it, dried it and put it away. And there's never any food. She doesn't cook! And she doesn't like my Banh Pho Bo. She says it tastes like mud.'

'I still don't understand, Henry,' I said, as softly as I could. 'What has this got to do with me?'

'Well, darling, I want to come home,' he said plainly. 'I want to come back here.' He looked around the kitchen, with a week's supply of coffee cups up-ended on the draining board and then he turned beseechingly to me.

I opened my mouth to scream with joy, but strangely no sound came out. Here he was, the husband I had made myself the old me for, begging to come back, which was just what I had been doing all this for, but there was only one slight problem. He hadn't actually mentioned me in any of this. Hadn't he left me because I had let myself go? And here I was all taut and terrific and, erm, he hadn't even noticed. After all my hard work and agony, could he not see me? Was he not really looking?

'I was just on my way out for a run.' I was dazed, to say the least.

'Yes, of course,' Henry said. 'This must have come

as such a shock. I've behaved awfully, I know that, darling, and I'll make it up to you, I promise I will, but you're right, you need to think it over. You go. I'll be here. Waiting.'

I slipped out the door and for the next hour I pounded the pavements, my head spinning. What about all that business of my not understanding him? Not growing? What about being alone for the rest of my life? What about spending it with him? With each long stride I became more confused. This was what I wanted, wasn't it?

I stopped at the corner shop, exhausted, and setting my face into a tight scowl, I approached Zak.

'No!' I said aggressively before he could even open his mouth. 'No Snickers, no Walnut Whips, no Yorkie bars, no Picnics, no Mint Cakes, no Rolos.' My shoulders were hunched, my fists were clenched at my sides, my feet wide apart in warrior stance. 'No Smarties, no Caramels, no Minstrels and definitely no chocolate cheesecakes!'

Zak looked at me steadily. Then he took a deep breath, opened the door behind the counter into the mysterious back office and thrust his blonde of the day through it.

'You are so hot, Mrs S,' he breathed. 'Fancy going out with me?'

This quite knocked the wind out of my sails. The corner shop stud was asking me out?

'I am forty-one years old, Zak,' I eventually stuttered. 'I am probably almost very nearly old enough to be your mother. I have cellulite. I have corns. I am only two months out of a failed marriage which, with any luck, perhaps, maybe, I don't know, I should be able to salvage.'

Zak shrugged. 'If you just let yourself go a bit, you'd be perfect, if you ask me. What about it, Mrs S?'

If I just let myself go a bit? For a moment, I quivered with rage. Wasn't it letting myself go that had got me into trouble in the first place? Yet almost as soon as the quivering started, it stopped, the rage abandoned me. Here was a young, virile, drop-dead-gorgeous man telling me I wasn't let go of enough. How could that be? Who was to say? Suddenly, it was all too much. There was simply nothing for it but to burst into tears. Not the silent, cute sort either but great, big, noisy ones.

One potential customer scurried out of the shop before buying anything, another moved obliviously in behind me to form a queue.

Zak, clearly not used to such a violent response to his proposals, backed away and opened the office door letting the blonde out.

She stared at me sulkily as I continued my undignified sobbing.

'Well, don't just stand there,' she instructed Zak, picking up a *Hello* magazine. 'Get her some chocolate.'

Zak snapped into action and handed me a KitKat.

Watching his biceps flex and the muscles in his torso ripple beneath his tight white T-shirt certainly slowed down my tears.

But as I snapped open the KitKat wrapper with an expert hand I suddenly knew with a clarity that some-times only dairy milk and wafers can bring that I did not want to go out with a ladies' man half my age and I did not want to spend the rest of my life with Henry.

I gave half the KitKat to the blonde, thanked Zak from the bottom of my heart, then headed out of the shop in the direction of Nell's house. I needed my girlfriends and a glass of crisp, white wine.

I was letting myself go again, but in a good way.

Men Don't Wear Pink

BY ALEXANDER McCALL SMITH

*I*t was generally agreed by all right-thinking people –
which meant that both Mma Ramotswe and Mma
Makutsi were of one mind on the issue – that it was
best for men not to get involved in women's business.
Of course every rule has its exceptions, and the exception here was that if a woman asked a man to get
involved in some decision or scheme, then that would
be all right – up to a point. The difficulty, though, was
that once you invited a man to get involved, then he
would tend to exceed his authority and take over. And
that, as everybody knew, could lead to problems.

One might have expected that a rule of this nature
would work both ways. Curiously enough, thought
Mma Ramotswe, this was not the case, and just as
everybody agreed that men should keep out of women's
affairs, so too did they agree – with equal vigour – that
there were few items of men's business that were not
more efficiently dealt with by a woman. Banks, for
example, would be much better run, according to Mma
Makutsi, if women were in charge. There was a bank in
Gaborone that had recently appointed a woman

manager and which had promptly won a newspaper award for best business of the year.

'There you are, Mma Ramotswe,' said Mma Makutsi, cutting out the report from the newspaper and passing it across to her employer. 'You see this. That bank run by that lady has been chosen as No 1 business of the year. That is very good.'

Mma Ramotswe read the news report. 'Yes, that is interesting news, Mma. I have been in that bank and I could tell that it was well run. It was very clean, for a start. No paper lying round.'

Mma Makutsi nodded. 'That is because that lady knows how to keep a house clean,' she said. 'Men are very untidy, Mma. Look at those apprentices out there. Mr J.L.B. Matekoni is always having to tell them to pick things up. All the time. They have never learned.'

Mma Ramotswe nodded. Mma Makutsi was a bit harsh on the apprentices, she felt. And there were some very neat men, but then again there were many rather messy ones. Perhaps the truth lay where it was so often to be found – somewhere in between.

She looked at the picture in the news report. The bank manager in question, a tall woman in a rather smart business suit, was shaking hands with the editor of the newspaper, also a woman. It was a picture that said a great deal about how things were changing in Botswana as women assumed their rightful place in the economy. She felt pride in this; this was happening all over the world – in enlightened countries – and it seemed that Botswana was leading the way.

The whole subject of men, of course, was a difficult one, and there were some tea breaks at the No 1 Ladies' Detective Agency when a good half hour was devoted entirely to the subject. Such conversations sometimes dealt with the affairs of their wider families – the engagement of a remote female cousin, for instance, might require careful consideration and analysis of the merits, or otherwise, of the new fiancé – or they might touch on something said or done by the men in their own lives. These were Mma Ramotswe's husband, Mr J.L.B. Matekoni, a kind and patient man about whom there would seldom be any complaint, and Mma Makutsi's fiancé, Mr Phuti Radiphuti, the proprietor of the Double Comfort Furniture Store and a man of many merits and strengths behind his rather shy exterior and occasional stammer.

It was something done by Phuti Radiphuti, in fact, that illustrated in a rather dramatic way the rule that men should not try to get involved in women's business. And it all started when Mma Makutsi arrived for work one morning in a rather startling red dress.

As a general rule, Mma Makutsi would arrive at work twenty minutes or so before Mma Ramotswe herself. That was because Mma Ramotswe had the two foster children to get off to school as well as having to make Mr J.L.B. Matekoni's sandwich lunch. Mma Makutsi, by contrast, lived alone in a small house that required very little upkeep and she had nobody to get out in the morning except herself.

That morning, when she was the first to arrive at the office, Mma Ramotswe wondered whether there might be some problem with the minibus that Mma Makutsi caught at her road end. These buses were generally very reliable, but, like all mortal machines, broke down from time to time under the sheer burden imposed upon them. If that had happened, then it could be another half hour or so before Mma Makutsi turned up.

It was only ten minutes or so, and when Mma Makutsi arrived Mma Ramotswe was still sipping on the cup of red-bush tea she had prepared for herself. At first the older woman said nothing when her assistant came in the door, but she soon recovered.

'Good morning, Mma Makutsi,' she said. 'I hope that you did not have to walk in to work today. It is already very hot and . . .' As she spoke, Mma Ramotswe's gaze moved over her assistant's garb. It was a most peculiar dress. It was . . . well, it was difficult to describe. Rather like a tent? A tent that had collapsed in the wind? And that red? It was not a colour that one normally saw in a dress – or in anything really, except, perhaps, overripe tomatoes.

In general, Mma Makutsi had reasonable dress sense, thought Mma Ramotswe, even if you would not exactly describe her as fashionable, and there was always the question of those rather intimidating glasses that she wore. She could not help that, of course, but Mma Ramotswe wondered whether the glasses had to be quite so large. Would it not have been possible to see quite as much of the world as one needed to see – through smaller, more focused glasses?

Mma Ramotswe took another sip of tea to cover her surprise. She was a polite woman, and it would not do to show astonishment over the outfit of another woman, even a dress of this sort.

'I have boiled the kettle,' she said. 'The water is hot. You might like a cup of tea after your walk, Mma.'

Mma Makutsi crossed the room to her desk and put down her handbag. 'I am sorry I am late today, Mma Ramotswe,' she said. 'I do not like being late in to work. But I was driven in today by Phuti, and he was held up at his aunt's place. That is why.'

Mma Ramotswe nodded. 'It doesn't matter, Mma,' she said. 'You are always early and so it doesn't matter if you are sometimes late. I would only complain if you were always late – and you are not. So I am not complaining.'

As she spoke, Mma Ramotswe's eye remained fixed to the new dress. Was there some special occasion that Mma Makutsi was going to today? She had not said anything about that, and yet surely she would never wear a dress like that unless something was happening? And even then, what sort of occasion would prompt one to put on something like that?

Mma Makutsi moved over to the shelf at the side of the room where they kept the kettle. As she ladled tea into the teapot that was kept specially for her, the door that led from the office of the agency into Mr J.L.B. Matekoni's garage next door opened. Charlie, the older apprentice, looked in.

'Is there any tea?' he asked. 'The boss is working on a very difficult gearbox and he . . .' His voice trailed off as he caught sight of Mma Makutsi's dress.

'I am making tea,' said Mma Makutsi, adding, 'And why are you staring at me like that? Don't you know that it's rude to stare?'

Charlie smiled. 'And it's rude to wear things that make other people stare,' he said quickly. 'Like that thing you're wearing, Mma.'

Mma Makutsi spun round. 'Have you never seen an expensive dress, Charlie? Maybe not. Maybe you think that everybody wears any old thing. Maybe you don't know anything about fashion.'

Mma Ramotswe gave the young man a discouraging glance. 'Tell Mr J.L.B. Matekoni that I will bring his tea through to him when it is ready,' she said. 'We have work to do in here.'

Charlie gave a final exaggerated glance in Mma Makutsi's direction and left.

'He is a very cheeky young man,' said Mma Makutsi.

'All young men are a bit like that,' said Mma Ramotswe soothingly. 'And there is nothing wrong with your dress, Mma. It is a very fine dress. It . . .' She stopped. It was difficult to think what one might say about a dress like that.

Mma Makutsi sat down. 'Oh, Mma. I know. I

know. This dress is a present from Phuti. He bought it himself.'

This explanation made everything clear, and much easier.

'Phuti bought it himself?' asked Mma Ramotswe.

Mma Makutsi nodded. 'I do not know why he suddenly decided to do it,' she said. 'Dresses are very personal, aren't they, Mma? And why would a man want to do something like that? Dresses are ladies' business, Mma – even in these modern days. They are not for men to get involved in.' She paused, smoothing out the folds of the garish fabric. 'Can you imagine Mr J.L.B. Matekoni getting it into his head to buy you a dress, Mma?'

Mma Ramotswe thought for a moment. Her husband was a kind man who often bought her little presents, but she could not picture him ever doing anything like that. She shook her head.

'There you are,' said Mma Makutsi. 'Mr J.L.B. Matekoni would never do something like that. But Phuti went off and bought this . . . this outfit from one of those women who sell dresses in front of the President Hotel. He was very proud of it.'

'Oh dear,' said Mma Ramotswe.

'Yes,' went on Mma Makutsi. 'He brought it round last night and said that he would come and take me into work this morning. He asked me to wear the dress.'

'This is a very difficult situation,' said Mma Ramotswe.

Mma Makutsi nodded. 'I do not see what I can do, Mma,' she said. 'I had to wear the dress this morning. And he was so pleased with it he asked me to wear it tonight when we go to the cinema. I think he is very proud of having bought it.'

Mma Ramotswe shook her head. 'This is very awkward, Mma,' she said. 'And the more you tell me, the more awkward it becomes.'

Mma Makutsi needed no reminding of the delicacy of the situation. 'Phuti is very easily upset,' she went on. 'I cannot tell him that I do not like it. I just cannot.'

Mma Ramotswe agreed. It was one thing to upset a husband, who was safely in the bag, so to speak; it was quite another to upset a fiancé. She thought hard. No situation was so difficult as to be without a solution, and this one, surely, was no exception. Phuti was no doubt trying to show that he was one of these new men that one read about. These were men who took an interest in clothes and matters of that sort; who helped their wives in the kitchen; who were ready to speak about their emotions. Well, that was all very well – it was a very useful thing for a man to help in the kitchen, and a well-trained man could make a very good cook – but there had to be limits, and the choosing of dresses was surely one of them. If Phuti could only be taught – in the gentlest possible way – that clothes were very personal and that even a new man should refrain from involvement in such matters . . .

Mma Ramotswe had been staring down into her teacup while she thought. Now she looked up brightly.

'I have had an idea, Mma,' she announced. 'I think it is a very good idea.' She rose from her desk and crossed the room to the door that led into the garage.

'Charlie!' she called.

The apprentice appeared. 'Is the boss's tea ready, Mma?'

Mma Ramotswe drew the young man into the office. 'Charlie,' she began, 'I have a little errand for you. You can take my van to do it.' She knew that Charlie liked driving, even as modest a vehicle as her tiny white van.

'I will do it, Mma,' said Charlie. 'What do you want?'

'I want you to go to the shops,' said Mma Ramotswe. 'You must know the best shop for men's clothes. Very smart clothes.'

Charlie beamed with pleasure. 'I am No 1 when it comes to fashion,' he said, glancing dubiously at Mma Makutsi's dress. 'That is what all the girls say. I am the man.'

'Good,' said Mma Ramotswe. 'So please will you go and see if you can find me a pink shirt. A man's size – quite big. About the size of Mr Radiphuti.'

Charlie wrinkled his nose. 'A pink shirt, Mma?'

Mma Ramotswe nodded. 'That is right, Charlie. A pink shirt. Very bright pink.'

'But men . . .' Charlie began.

'See if you can do it, Charlie,' Mma Ramotswe insisted. 'Regard it as a challenge.'

A few hours later, Charlie returned bearing a large,

rather fancy shopping bag. 'I have found one,' he said. 'I had to go all over the place. But I have found you a pink shirt.'

After the young man had handed over the bag and gone back into the garage, Mma Ramotswe glanced at the neatly folded shirt and winced. 'Now, Mma Makutsi,' she said. 'Here is what you must do. You're seeing Phuti this evening, aren't you?'

Mma Makutsi nodded.

'Then you must give him this present,' said Mma Ramotswe. 'Tell him that you wanted something that he could wear when you wore your new dress.'

Mma Makutsi smiled. 'You are a very clever woman, Mma Ramotswe,' she said. 'That is widely known, you know.'

The next morning, when Mma Ramotswe came into work, Mma Makutsi was sitting at her desk. She was once again dressed in one of her normal dresses – and how well it suited her, thought Mma Ramotswe.

'Did it work, Mma?' she asked.

Mma Makutsi nodded. 'It worked perfectly, Mma. And I do not think that Phuti will want me to wear that new dress very often.'

'And do you think he learned a lesson?' asked Mma Ramotswe.

Again, Mma Makutsi nodded.

'Good,' said Mma Ramotswe. 'Men are very good at many things. But there are some things they still need to learn. And they learn quickly, you know, Mma –

provided that you teach them in a . . . gentle way, shall
we say.'

'We shall,' said Mma Makutsi.

Bred in the Bone

BY MARK MILLS

*O*nly later did she realise why she had worn the shoes. There were any number of pairs to choose from – shoes were her vice, her guilty secret – but she had opted for the brown ones with the buckle and the low, square heel. Sturdy and well-made.

Safe.

She had wanted to feel safe, that much was clear to her now. It was hardly surprising. Who in her situation wouldn't have reached for some crutch, albeit unconsciously, with which to steady themselves?

She glanced over at Adam, slumped and silent at the steering wheel, somehow smaller, more shrunken than she had ever seen him before, as if drained of vital fluids. Under normal circumstances, he would have been railing against the other drivers, pointing out their deficiencies or drawing her attention to his own prowess. He was particularly proud of his 'lane selection' when approaching traffic lights and roundabouts, shaving useless seconds off their journey time.

But there was none of that now, no stabbing at the pedals, no wrestling with the wheel, no obscene gestures or mumbled curses. In fact, he seemed oblivious to the building swell of evening traffic, staring straight ahead with flat, dead eyes.

'Say something.'

He didn't turn. 'What do you want me to say, Kath? Our son is going to die.'

'We're all going to die.'

She regretted the words even as they left her mouth.

'He's seven years old for Christ's sake! He deserves a longer life.'

It was a moment before she said, 'I'm sorry.'

'You're sorry, I'm sorry, we're all sorry. Tell me something I don't know.'

And she almost did, right there and then, taking him at his word. Fear checked her voice – fear that once she had spoken, life as she knew it would be over. There would be no going back, no shutting the lid on Pandora's Box. No more lazy Christmases at his parents' farmhouse in the Black Mountains, no more weekend breaks on the Norfolk coast, no more games of baseball on the beach, no more crabbing off the jetty, no more . . .

She wrestled her thoughts back to some kind of reality, seeking comfort in the present. Not that their current predicament offered any solace. The consultant at the hospital had been very clear on that fact.

'The test results are in and I'm afraid they're not good.'

Three people seated around a desk in a dismal little box of an office tucked away at the back of the oncology department, its walls devoid of ornament, of distraction – almost as if the room had been expressly designed for the dispensing of cold, stark truths. Their third meeting in as many weeks and almost four months since Ben's breathlessness had been ascribed by a bevy of experts to leukaemia. Four truly terrible months, fraught and sleepless. And now this: the final, cruel verdict.

'There's not enough of a match with either of you, or your daughter, to make a bone marrow transplant viable.'

Viable? What sort of word was that to use when handing down a death sentence on a child? It had rankled at the time. Little more than an hour later, it still did.

They were stuck in stationary traffic now, Adam uncharacteristically resigned to the inevitable. Kath turned and peered through the window at the pavement, the first office workers wending their way home. At a break in the weary hordes, she caught sight of herself in the plate-glass frontage of a charity shop and found herself asking: What did I do to get here? What did we do?

Nothing exceptional. Adam had been a second-year Archaeology and Anthropology student at Corpus Christi; she had been attending a secretarial college. 'Arch and Anth' – a subject for thickos and/or slackers, or so the other students liked to say. And everyone knew that the 'seccies' were all on the hunt for a husband. Well, she hadn't been. And she had proved it in the first few months, wilfully wrecking her reputation while catching up on life. Strangely, it was exactly this that had drawn Adam to her – her destructiveness – or so he later claimed, some time down the line, when they were officially an item.

Back then, she had seen it as a gift, his ability to understand, to relate, to sympathise with others. Now, she saw it as a curse, his anthropological training to blame. How could he hope to place himself in the world when he viewed all mankind at one remove? He could never allow himself to become just another member of the tribe, subject to his own rigorous scrutiny.

He had abandoned an initial flirtation with journalism in favour of 'doing' rather than 'saying', resulting in a year of fieldwork in Borneo (during which time they both slept with other people, although he still vociferously denied it). Then, after their marriage, it was a job at an NGO, before being poached by another NGO. And then came the damning proclamation of the role played by NGOs in the developing world, which might or might not have had something to do with a junior being promoted above him. Carbon offset was his new thing.

Not an easy career path – principles inversely proportional to the size of the wage packet – which could hardly be said of most of their friends. Freddy, for example. Freddy was hopelessly, shamelessly ambitious, with little or no conscience to keep him in check. Not so very different to the Freddy she had first met in Adam's college rooms in Cambridge that sticky June day, recounting the lurid details of his recent conquest of a Sidney Sussex lesbian. Freddy, disarmingly laconic and self-effacing. Freddy, who knew what he wanted then went and got it: the job in the City, the house in Holland Park, the foreign wife with the long legs (carefully selected to drive the height of his male progeny well over the six feet he himself had failed to achieve). Totally shameless, yet utterly compelling. He and Adam had remained fast friends, the best of friends, despite their differing paths. It was Freddy who had spoken with such unexpected emotion at their wedding, Freddy who had driven them home from St Thomas's when Clara was born. And it was Freddy who had seized on her throwaway comment, effectively changing their lives.

One simple line uttered in passing, in jest, over dinner one night: 'The hatchback of Notre Dame.'

It was rare to see Freddy agitated.

'Citroën will kill for that,' he said. 'Or Renault. They'll certainly pay for it. It's a whole bloody ad campaign, TV, posters, the works. I can see it already – a lovesick Quasimodo in a Clio.'

Some people talked, others acted. Freddy raped his contacts for the name and number of the creative director of Goad, Maddox and Shaw, an aggressive young advertising agency looking to steal the Renault account from one of the old guard. A meeting was formally arranged. Kath was issued with strict instructions on how to play it. Confidence was the key, according to Freddy. If she didn't believe she was sitting on a gold mine, then neither would they.

She must have done something right. Men in suits were summoned to the office to hear her deliver her pitch for a second time, and there was an offer on the table before she even left the building: trainee copywriter with a generous starting salary which more than covered the cost of full-time child care for little Clara. Even back then, she was wise enough to know that they weren't buying her, they were buying the idea, but she soon discovered she had a gift for the game, for the kind of pithy wordplay that appealed to clients. Paired off with Max, an experienced art director, they rose rapidly through the ranks, the hot new team at the hot new agency. The industry award for the Renault campaign helped.

To begin with, Adam had observed her meteoric ascent with a strange mix of pride and bewilderment. Then the jealousy kicked in, fuelled by his own languishing career. The sudden reversal of their roles became the predominant, exhausting theme of their lives.

They were over it now. He was over it – at peace with the pleasing change in circumstances afforded by her success: the new house, the new car, the private schools for the children.

And then Ben had grown strangely breathless while running for a ball in Battersea Park . . .

Leukaemia. Cancer of the blood. A drop of poison in his genetic cocktail. Or maybe it was punishment, some kind of retribution for one small lapse on her part.

As she pushed these thoughts from her, Adam spoke. 'What do we tell him?'

'Not the truth.'

'Kath, we can't pretend it's all OK.'

But it might be, she thought, it just might be.

She was suddenly awed by the power of her secret – the power over life and death that she held in the palm of her hand. Her secret, although she now shared it with another, with a stranger in a white coat.

The consultant had shown admirable discretion in his handling of the matter, the awkward choreography required, summoning her back into his office alone on some creaking pretext.

'I'm not sure how to say this, Mrs Ellis . . .'

'Yes . . . ?'

'Your husband put himself forward for the bone marrow tests.'

'Yes.'

'Excuse me, but I'm curious why he would do that.'

'Do what?'

'Put himself forward . . . when he's not the biological father.'

With Kath unable to bring herself to reply, the doctor was obliged to break the ensuing silence. 'It's more common than you might think.'

She glared at him. 'Is it?'

'Do you know who the biological father is?'

No, she didn't. Not for sure. Not till now. Although there had been times when she had suspected.

'I mean, that's to say,' the doctor persevered nervously, 'do you know how to locate him?'

'Yes,' she replied.

'There's a good chance of a viable match.'

That word again. And that look in his eyes: genuine sympathy for her plight, yet coupled with a clear sense of what he felt her duty to be.

'Thank you, doctor,' she had said, stiff and formal, terminating the conversation.

One lapse eight years back – a fleeting encounter, an aberration, a mistake. Not that she hadn't enjoyed it at the time. She had; there was no denying it. She still toyed with the memory from time to time, relishing it. Her first business trip abroad, a chance for the hot new team at the hot new agency to meet their Paris-based cousins. They called it synergy. She called it a welcome break from the pressures of home life, tensions with Adam then running at an all-time high, the hunter-gatherer fighting his corner, refusing to concede defeat. No, three days in Paris with Max had been a very welcome prospect.

She sometimes wondered if he had planned it, contrived it. She had even come close to asking him, but had somehow never mustered the required courage.

'Kath, it's Freddy.'

'Freddy?'

'Where are you staying?'

'The . . . I can't remember, something French, near the Place des Vosges.'

'I'm at the Georges V.'

'You're here? In Paris?'

'Business, like you.'

Like her. Two equals travelling the world for the greater good of the free market economy. That's how he had made it sound. And that's the message he had driven home to her over dinner in some Art Nouveau brasserie. Fine food, friendship and flattery: a heady mix, helped along by a bottle of vintage Krug to celebrate the dramatic turnaround in her life. It was the first of three bottles they drank that night.

As far as she knew, Freddy's banking activities had never taken him to Paris, before or since. Or maybe she was doing him a disservice. More than ever, she wanted to believe that she wasn't to blame, that he had forced her into a corner, that he had travelled to Paris with the express purpose of exacting his dues, of calling in the debt she undoubtedly owed him, exploiting her vulnerability, fully aware of the problems back home with Adam.

But it hadn't been like that. They had simply got drunk, then they had gone back to his palatial room in his fancy hotel and they had made love, wild and unruly. And when she had sensed him reaching his peak, she had asked him to pull out of her, and he had done so – just in time, or so she had assumed.

Ben. Little Ben. Fast on his feet. A natural leader of the pack. Even then, apparently. Sweet, beautiful little

Ben. It didn't matter who he belonged to. Wasn't that the point? Could Adam possibly love him any less, even knowing the truth? Little Ben didn't belong to anyone – he was already his own person – and he was going to die soon if she didn't act.

Kath glanced down at her shoes – brown, buckled, safe. Then she raised her head abruptly and said, 'Adam, pull over.'

'What?'

'Pull over. Stop the car. There's something I have to tell you.'

The Magic of Italy

BY SANTA MONTEFIORE

'*D*id you remember my wash bag?' asked Robert, without taking his eyes off his novel. 'And my sunglasses?'

'Yes,' Polly replied, her stomach lurching as she considered the possibility that she might have left them on the chest of drawers in the hotel room.

'Good,' he said, satisfied. 'I'd hate to have to buy another pair. I hope the hotel in Incantellaria is a damn sight better than the one in Naples.'

'I'm sure it will be,' she said reassuringly, her gut twisting again at the thought of his sunglasses now on the face of one of the Italian chambermaids. She bit the skin around her thumbnail. When Robert was in a mood, he pulled her down with him like a helpless crustacean stuck to an anchor. Something small would undoubtedly lift him up again, like the flirtatious glances of a pretty girl, but she would remain for the best part of the day grounded on rock.

'It's very warm for October, isn't it?' she said, changing the subject. He didn't reply.

She looked out of the train to the misty Italian

237

countryside whizzing past her window. The air vibrated in the sunshine, the cypress trees grew dark and heavy and the odd cluster of pretty houses released brown-faced children like swarming bees from a hive, running to wave at the passing strangers on their way to the glamorous Amalfi coast. A couple on a moped buzzed up a dusty track, the girl's brown legs slim and toned as her white skirt billowed out behind her and Polly felt a sharp stab of envy. The south of Italy was carefree, warm and succulent, like a glowing peach in the sunshine, yet the knot in her stomach denied her even the smallest pleasure from its taste. This was meant to be a holiday, yet, so far, she had done little but rise and fall to the undulating landscape of Robert's moods.

She watched him read. Slouched in his seat, his blue shirt tucked into jeans, one leg carelessly tossed over the other, revealing old school socks in pink and blue and the silver glint of the buckle on the belt she had bought him last Christmas. He was handsome, with shiny dark hair and indigo eyes framed by indecently long eyelashes, and intrinsically arrogant, as if he took it for granted that he was better than everyone else.

When they had first met, five years before, his insouciance had excited her. She had been flattered that a man well-known for finding most people intolerable, had desired her. She had dressed for him, grown her hair for him, organised his life for him like a good assistant without realising that the mould she was shaping would set like clay. Her world revolved around him and from the outside they appeared the perfect couple, but she only shone with his reflected light. She wasn't sure who she was any more and, worse, what she would be without him.

Polly didn't want to dwell on the times she had considered leaving Robert. They were too many and too painful to contemplate. After all, they were in the most romantic country in the world and if it wasn't for his foul mood, she felt certain that after so many years together, he would surely propose. He was forty-one, she was thirty-six; he was her last chance, the final stop, the end of the line. She had put all her eggs into his basket. If he didn't propose, she feared time would run out and she'd never have children.

At last the train stopped in Sorrento and they disembarked. The travel agent had arranged for someone to pick them up at the station and take them to Incantellaria by boat, explaining that the best way to see the town was from the sea. 'It is the most enchanting place. *Incanto* means charm in Italian. You will see that it is no coincidence that it carries the name.' Robert had cared only that the hotel was comfortable. 'Well, it's not the Pelicano, but it is cosy,' she'd said. 'Let's just say it has a certain rustic charm.'

'I don't want rustic charm,' Robert had complained, contemplating the lack of digital television and room service.

'I insist you try it, if only for a couple of days. Then you can travel further down the coast to Portofino and spend the last leg of your trip in unabashed luxury,' said the travel agent. Robert had agreed. Polly had had no opinion. Whatever made Robert happy would make her happy too.

To Polly's relief, there was a man with 'Mr Judd' written on a card waiting for them in the sunshine. He nodded in recognition and Robert shook his hand, impressed that everything was going according to plan in a country where nothing usually did. The man gesticulated that they follow, his grey hair catching the breeze and floating up like goose down. '*Io mi chiamo* Lorenzo,' he said. 'Lo-ren-zo.'

'Jolly good, Lorenzo,' said Robert, putting his arm around Polly's waist and tossing her a smile. 'Let's hope he can navigate his way to Incantellaria.'

'Incantellaria,' Lorenzo repeated, the only word he had understood, and grinned, revealing a broken front tooth.

'All right, darling?' Robert asked her, as if checking she wasn't still smarting from his bad temper. 'Not long now.' She ignored his comment, after all she wasn't the one who complained of delays and lost luggage but hurried dutifully after him, smoothing his train like an anxious bridesmaid.

They climbed into Lorenzo's dusty car. A Madonna statue suspended from the mirror swung violently as Lorenzo set off down the narrow streets to the quay. Polly gazed out of the window where a couple of old widows dressed in black sat chatting in a shady doorway and a group of small children in grubby shorts kicked a pile of orange leaves. A pretty waitress flirted with a group of old men in caps and waistcoats playing cards at a table beneath a tree. Something stirred inside Polly – a longing to be part of this languid life where people had time for each other and for themselves. 'Isn't it charmingly quaint?' she said to Robert.

He chewed his cheek. 'You sound like the travel agent. You should write the brochure.' She should have known better than to share the moment with him when he hadn't eaten. Robert was never his best on an empty stomach.

Down at the quay, Lorenzo took them to a small motor boat where a handsome young Italian sat waiting for them. His skin was tanned the colour of toffee and his eyes were a sparkling green. When he saw them he smiled, the lines around his mouth and eyes growing long and deep. 'Ciao, Lorenzo,' he greeted his friend, slapping him on the back affectionately. They shared a joke, then the young man, whose name was Fabio, settled his eyes on Polly. 'Is this your first time in Incantellaria?' His accent was attractive but it was his gaze, the shameless way he looked at her in front of her boyfriend, that caused her stomach to flip over.

'Yes,' she replied, turning to Robert.

'I'd like to get there before sunset,' said Robert, an edge of sarcasm to his voice.

Fabio shrugged laconically. 'I'll get you there in time for lunch,' he said, taking their bag and hauling it into the boat.

'Is this thing safe?' said Robert, stepping in behind Fabio.

'You can swim, can't you?' said Fabio, turning to help Polly. She took his hand and they caught each other's eyes. She felt the colour rise to her cheeks and looked away.

'Jackass,' muttered Robert under his breath as Polly sat beside him. 'Don't think I didn't notice the way he looked at you.'

'You should be flattered,' she replied, hiding a smile.

'Maybe, but you shouldn't. They flirt like that with everyone.'

'Thank you, darling. How sweet.' She folded her arms and decided to ignore him. He'd be better once he'd had something to eat.

Fabio motored the boat out of the peaceful cove and into the open sea. Steep cliffs rose up black and sheer, the rocks sharp and unforgiving. Polly felt a wave of apprehension. Where in the world was Incantellaria? What if Robert didn't like it? What if the hotel wasn't to his taste? She began to bite the skin around her thumbnail again. Fabio watched her, intrigued. He ran his eyes up her long legs, admired her smooth, pale skin and the slimness of her ankles. She had a small waist and the low *décolletage* of her dress hinted at full, plump breasts. Her wavy blonde hair was blown off her face as the wind tossed it about playfully. He couldn't see her eyes, hidden behind large sunglasses, but he imagined they were blue. She didn't look happy.

He glanced at the man he assumed to be her husband, sitting silently by her side, his mouth turned down in an angry pout, and decided he was wholly undeserving of such a sweet-looking woman. Sensing him watching her, Polly pulled her cardigan tightly around her. The wind had an icy edge to it.

Suddenly the rocks fell away and the boat rattled around the corner where Incantellaria was revealed to them like glittering jewels in a secret chest. Polly caught her breath. The bay was lined with white houses whose grey tiled roofs caught the sun and sparkled. Pale blue shutters framed wide-open windows where black iron balconies were decorated with pots of bright red geraniums. The tower of a church rose up behind them and beyond were green hills thick with pine trees. The air was at once infused with rosemary and thyme and up on the crest of the hill, she could see an old look-out tower, like a blind old man relieved of responsibility, mulling over old memories. 'It's beautiful,' she sighed, her spirits rising independently of Robert's.

'There had better be something good to eat,' said Robert. 'I'm starving.'

'I am very proud of Incantellaria,' Fabio shouted over the wind. 'It is the jewel of the Amalfi coast.'

'Have you lived here long?' Polly asked.

He smiled and Polly's stomach flipped over again. 'All my life,' he said, and Polly was sure there was magic in that smile. Robert bristled – for him that smile meant nothing but trouble.

They disembarked. Robert first, leaving Polly to follow. Fabio once again took her hand and helped her step on to the quay. 'Your husband is not a gentleman,' he said under his breath. Polly looked into his eyes and saw his concern beneath the twinkle of humour.

'He's not my husband,' she replied, then caught her breath, appalled that she had felt it necessary to correct him.

Fabio raised his eyebrows. 'You must be staying at La Luce,' he said.

'How do you know?' she asked.

'Because that is the only hotel. You will like it. Your boyfriend?' he shrugged. 'I'm not so sure.' Polly smiled, turning her attention to Robert who was striding up the quay towards the houses, having left the bag for Fabio. He bent down and picked it up.

'I'm sorry,' she said. 'It's very heavy.'

'For you I'd carry double.'

'I bet you say that to all the girls.'

'Then you would lose your bet.' He grinned at her and began to walk slowly up the quay.

'Now, where is this place?' said Robert.

'Come, I'll show you,' said Fabio, walking on past Robert. 'It's not far.'

They followed him up a narrow paved street and into a square, dominated by a pretty white church. Robert saw the sign above the door and screwed up his nose.

'Is this it?' he asked. 'It's not what I expected.'

'It's adorable,' said Polly, clapping her hands together with glee. 'I bet we'll have a room with a sea view.'

Robert looked at his watch. 'I hope there's

something to eat.' Fabio caught Polly's eye and shrugged again. Robert's ill humour seemed to amuse him. Polly was embarrassed; somehow in London, Robert didn't seem so bad. Here, in this quiet, quaint Italian town, he was uncomfortably out of place.

Polly was right – they had a pretty white room with wide doors leading out on to a small wrought-iron balcony with a view over the roof-tops to the sparkling sea beyond. She leaned on the balcony and gazed down into the square below. Her mind drifted to Fabio. She wondered where he had gone and whether she would see him again. Suddenly, she felt infected by the carefree air of Incantellaria. The breeze picked up the skirt of her dress and it rustled about her legs. She swept her hand through her hair and closed her eyes to the sun on her face. She imagined she lived here, in the tranquillity of this enchanting little place, so far from all that was familiar to her. She could live another life, start again, be someone totally different. Her dream was swiftly cut short by Robert complaining that he couldn't find his sunglasses. Once again her stomach plummeted with anxiety. She'd obviously left them behind.

'How could you?' Robert snapped. 'I can't trust you to do a bloody thing! All I asked was that you packed my bag. Well, I can see I'll have to relieve you of that responsibility.'

'Let's get something to eat,' she suggested. 'We can buy another pair.'

'They don't make them like that any more!'

'They're only glasses,' she said bravely.

'Wrong. They're my only glasses!'

They sat outside on the terrace, choosing a table in the shade so that Robert didn't have to squint. Polly enjoyed the serenity of the place, for once able to detach herself from Robert's bad mood. They barely spoke. Robert drank a glass of wine and ate a vast plate of spaghetti after which he sat back sleepily. He took her hand. 'Let's go upstairs and have a siesta.' He grinned at her, but his grin held little charm.

'I'm going to explore,' she replied, getting up. 'I'll see you later.' Robert watched her leave in amazement. She had never refused him.

Polly skipped down the street among fallen leaves that swirled in the wind, feeling a new sense of freedom. She wandered up the sea front, taking pleasure from the children playing there. A couple of old men in caps stood chatting, moving their hands vigorously as Italians do. A restaurant spilled out on to the pavement, full of people relaxing and smoking over glasses of wine. An old woman in black presided over the clients, moving slowly from table to table like a grand vessel. A pretty dark-haired waitress flirted with a table of handsome young men. Her laughter rose above the chatter and Polly was envious of her place there.

Polly began to walk down the beach. The sea surged up the sand that was littered with pretty white shells. 'May I?' She turned to see Fabio walking behind her.

'Hello,' she said, surprised.

'You are alone?'

'Of course.' She thought of Robert sleeping and felt a sense of relief.

'This is the most romantic place in the world. You should be sharing it with the man you love.'

That phrase 'with the man you love', would change everything. She looked at Fabio with mounting excitement. So far from home and surrounded by such natural beauty, she realised then that she no longer loved Robert. He had become a habit she had believed to be love. Never had she imagined she could walk away. Tough times had just made her struggle harder to make their relationship work, as if she believed there was no alternative. Fabio was handsome and charming. He clearly desired her, which made her feel good. She felt the luxurious stirring of independence long forgotten and continued to walk with a spring in her step.

They sat on the rocks, watching the setting sun turn the water to copper and talked about their lives until Robert receded into the back of her mind, almost gone entirely.

She returned to the hotel, the sensation of Fabio taking her hand as they walked back up the beach still fresh upon her skin. She felt light-headed, as if a door had opened wide where there hadn't been one before. Robert had slept. He was in a good mood. He was affectionate, but Polly was now detached like a little boat floating away on the sea. As if sensing the shift, Robert proposed over dinner. He took her hand, looked deep into her eyes, apologised for his ill humour and promised to behave better in the future. Polly hesitated before she replied – wasn't this what she had always wanted? 'Yes,' she said and her voice sounded very far away. He reached across the table and kissed her, but he no longer felt familiar. Her thoughts turned to the beach and Fabio and the now dissolving sense of freedom she had so enjoyed.

That night they made love, but Polly was just going through the motions and felt little pleasure. It was then that she realised how little Robert knew her, how little she had allowed him to know. While he slept she stood on the balcony, gazing out to sea, imagining what her life might be like if she stayed in Incantellaria.

Robert decided he didn't like the hotel or the town. 'I want to take you to the most expensive hotel in Portofino,' he told her. 'My future wife deserves the best.' But as they climbed back into Fabio's boat, Polly had made up her mind. She didn't expect to ride off into the sunset or to live happily ever after, but she knew that if she didn't take this chance, the door might close on her forever. She glanced at Robert and felt little for him but compassion. There is nothing deader than dead love. Fabio's face was solemn. He barely looked at her. A door had opened in his future too, but he could sense it slowly closing, shutting out the light of opportunity.

At Sorrento, Robert disembarked. Fabio lifted the suitcase out of the boat – it felt lighter than before. Polly remained seated. Robert turned. 'Come on, darling,' he said.

'I'm not coming,' Polly replied steadily. Robert frowned. Fabio stared at her in disbelief. 'I'm staying in Incantellaria.'

'You're what . . . ?' Robert's face flushed with fury. How dare she humiliate him in public!

'I cannot marry you. I'm sorry. Take me back,' she said to Fabio. The Italian's smile was wide and infectious. Polly felt the fizz of bubbles in her stomach and the exhilarating feeling of finding herself at last. As the boat motored away, Robert was reduced to an angry little figure on the shore, diminished in power and importance.

'To Incantellaria,' said Fabio. Polly stood beside him and let him put his hand around her waist and draw her close.

'To my future,' she replied. 'Whatever that may be.'

A New Start

BY JANE MOORE

*P*eering in to Joe's room, a feeling of melancholy swept over me. For years, I had been nagging him to keep it tidy, joking that I'd need a donkey to get from one side to the other. Now it was eerily empty, the majority of his 'stuff' packed in a rental van and on its way to Leeds, where he was starting university in a few days' time.

I picked up a dog-eared old tennis ball from the centre of the room and lobbed it into the wastepaper bin, noting the various carpet stains from over the years . . . a rite of passage from Ribena to Carlsberg. His once-precious drum kit, a sixteenth-birthday present he'd driven us mad for, was still in the corner of the room, caked in dust and draped with equally unwanted clothes.

So this is what empty-nest syndrome feels like, I thought, perching on the edge of his bed and staring wistfully at the wall mirror framed by dog-eared photos of Joe and his school friends. It was different from when his two older brothers had left home, because my youngest was still around, making me feel wanted.

This felt more final somehow, even though he'd promised to come home most weekends, accompanied by a large bag of washing. But I knew the routine because I'd been here before . . . lots of visits in the early months then, once the university social life kicked in, we'd see him at Christmas and sporadically through the summer, when he popped in *en route* to the latest festival or some French campsite.

This, I mused, was my parenting swan-song, the day I no longer held the full, day-to-day responsibility for any of my children, becoming more of an occasional consultant in all their lives. Or at least that's how it felt.

Sighing heavily, I attempted a small smile to snap myself out of it. My boys were healthy and spirited, what more could a mother ask for? And after all, this was the start of a new chapter I had so often fantasised about, where instead of the children and their 'me, me, me' time, it was finally going to be our time for my husband Stuart and me – less passionate or spontaneous than the early, child-free years perhaps, but, hopefully, nonetheless enjoyable.

The mere thought of the gloriously time-rich, selfish years I was about to embark upon had sustained me through the more mundane, sometimes troubled times of our marriage, when I had almost lost myself under the piles of washing, the turgidity of morning traffic jams on the school run, the endless demands of my children. There were days when the combination of my work as a law firm receptionist, dealing with angry litigants and tearful divorcées, and running a home had run me ragged, spinning more plates than an end-of-pier magician.

I would catch a glimpse of those Nile cruises, advertised in the back of Sunday supplements, and picture us, sailing into the glorious sunset, hand in hand like the smiling couple featured in the photograph. OK, they were probably models who didn't even know each other, but they were selling an escapist dream and I bought it. My mind would race with images of us strolling round villages rich in culture, taking in the atmosphere, drinking chilled wine at our leisure without three moody teenagers muttering that it was 'so boooo-ring'.

Then, when we returned home, we'd finally build that gazebo we'd always talked about, the one we never got round to buying because what precious spare time we had was always swallowed up by our sons' school football and rugby matches or being their taxi service day and night. The plan was that I would read (and actually finish) a novel there, sheltered from the midday heat, while Stuart perused the newspaper or attempted the crossword.

And then, in a few years' time, if any of our sons managed to stay with the same girlfriend for more than five minutes, there might be grandchildren we'd adore and indulge before handing them back, fractious and tearful at the end of the day, grateful that the exhausting, early years of parenting were behind us.

That was my fantasy, my expectation, if you like. After all, that's the deal, isn't it? The payback for the years of selflessness. I walked downstairs and prepared a celebratory dinner for the start of our brave new world together.

'I've met someone else,' Stuart said matter-of-factly after chewing the last mouthful of a particularly tender rump steak I'd cooked to perfection.

'Someone else?' I parroted, genuinely bewildered.

It may seem naive, but the full implication of his statement didn't hit me at first. Why would it? After all, this was the man I'd been with for twenty-three years, the husband with whom I'd respectively enjoyed and endured the typical 'ups and downs' of married life, the father of my three children, for God's sake. I trusted him. This wasn't supposed to happen. We were about to start enjoying more time together . . . weren't we?

'It's Lisa,' he added, the clatter of his cutlery hitting the plate accentuating the new emptiness of our house.

Lisa. Now there was flesh and bones added to the 'someone else', in the slim yet suspiciously pneumatic shape of his thirty-year-old secretary. Yes, my husband was cheating on me with a living, breathing cliché.

'What are you saying?' The familiar prickle of fear was creeping across my forearms and my head started to spin. I gripped the edge of the table, fearful that if I let go, I might keel over.

'I'm saying . . .' He paused, letting out an almost imperceptible sigh . . . 'that I'm leaving you.' He at least had the grace to look sheepish.

I ran to the kitchen sink and retched, my forehead turning instantly clammy as my pulse began to race, my heart thumping against my chest. I knew I was in the grip of a panic attack because I'd experienced one before, when our first-born, Oliver, then six, had started to choke on a small chicken bone and I'd stood by, paralysed with fear while Stuart fought to extract it. I'd felt completely helpless and out of control, just as I did now.

The next half an hour was a blur, but I remember him leading me back to the table, putting his arm around my shoulders and telling me it was for the best, that our marriage hadn't been right for years and this was going to prove a new start for the both of us. That, ultimately, I would end up thanking him for his honesty.

I looked at him in disbelief, the injustice of his words stabbing me back to my senses.

'What are you talking about? You've never mentioned being unhappy before.'

'I know,' he mumbled, scraping his foot back and forth across the lines of floor tiles. 'I decided it was better for all concerned if I waited until the last of the children had left home.'

'Which was precisely twenty-four hours ago.' I tapped my watch and stared at him incredulously. Then another thought struck me with the ferocity of a punch straight to the breastbone. 'You waited? How long have you and she . . .' I couldn't bring myself to say it.

He looked distinctly uncomfortable. 'That's not important.'

'It's important to me,' I wailed. 'How long?'

'Four years.'

My breath caught in my throat. Four cheating, duplicitous years when he'd been leaving her bed to come home to mine 'for the sake of the children'.

'We never meant to hurt you.'

We. Such a small but reassuring word when it includes you in its equation, yet so chillingly devastating when the sum of its parts are suddenly your husband and another woman. If I had felt unsettled when Joe had left home earlier today, now I felt bone-chillingly terrified and lonely.

'Well you have,' I mumbled miserably, my head tipped towards the floor in despair. 'Devastatingly so.'

I looked up at him, uncertain who this man was any more. Stuart could be accused of many things during our time together, but an adulterer? It had never even crossed my mind. Now, looking at him with the same objectivity as one usually views a stranger, I saw someone smaller, weaker, pathetic even. Someone I could no longer bear to look at.

'Just get out,' I spat.

ONE YEAR LATER

Well, I finally went on the Nile cruise I'd always dreamed about, and we enjoyed the sunsets, local villages and chilled wine sipped at our leisure. OK, so my dear friend Nina and I didn't hold hands at any time, but to be honest, her companionship was just what I needed. We gossiped and laughed our way through the two-week holiday, reminiscing about our shared good times as young girls about town, pre-marriage, children or responsibility. We talked about serious matters too . . . Nina's memories of the dear husband she'd lost to cancer just two years earlier at the terrifyingly young age of forty-two, and my slow recovery from Stuart's humiliating betrayal.

After a couple of glasses of wine one night, Nina had started to look apprehensive, dipping her toe in the muddy waters of my marriage by sharing a few tentative observations. When I encouraged her, she opened up more, finally admitting that she'd never thought Stuart was good enough for me.

'You're such a sparky, fun woman,' she enthused. 'And he diminished you somehow. There were two of you – the carefree Amanda of old that I still saw when we were alone, and the more subdued, world-weary Amanda you always seemed to be around him.'

She'd apologised the next morning, mortified that she'd gone too far. But I was grateful to her for voicing and confirming what I'd been mulling over in my mind for the past few months.

In the immediate weeks after Stuart had left, I'd suffered immense pain, fearing I might go mad with grief. But eventually, as time passed and everyone's attention diverted from me and back to the normal stresses of their own lives, I finally had space to reflect on what I'd actually lost. I realised that the initial pain had been a cocktail of humiliation, concern for the children and fear of loneliness. In hindsight, it had little or nothing to do with the loss of Stuart, more the companionship I'd imagined he'd bring me in old age.

Nina was right – I'd been going through the marital motions for years, pushing any misgivings to the back of my mind, assuming that once our lives were less busy we'd suddenly rediscover each other again, realise what made us fall in love all those years ago. But the reality, I now knew, was that the frenetic whirl of bringing up children, of being parents locked in a mutual aim, had been the glue holding us together. Once they'd left home, we'd fragmented.

I'm still only forty-five and perhaps one day I'll meet someone new and start again. But I'm in no hurry. As I write this, I'm sitting in the shade of my new gazebo, built with the help of my eldest son. At first, the thought of sitting alone in silence scared me, but now I love the tranquillity of it. Without the day-to-day issues of the children to discuss, what would Stuart and I have said to each other anyway? When I think about it, we'd run out of conversation years ago, just coexisting under the same roof.

I still see him, of course I do. Our children may be grown up, but they would still be devastated if we were hostile to each other, so every so often we have a family get-together, perhaps a Sunday lunch, where the boys and I share our news and laugh at new jokes and Stuart sits staring mournfully at me, like an old bloodhound waiting to be thrown a biscuit.

With depressing inevitability, he and Lisa split up just three months after he arrived at her minimalist flat with his battered old suitcases. It seems she'd been hooked on the subterfuge of it all, getting a sexual kick from the deceit. Once she'd won her 'prize' she rapidly lost interest, berating him for being 'set in his ways' and 'curmudgeonly'. Suddenly, the man she'd thought mature and wise, seemed old and predictable.

I know all this because he told me, shortly before he begged me to take him back. It had been a terrible mistake, he said, a midlife crisis of the worst kind. He could see it now, he said, the places we'd go, the fun we'd have.

I won't deny I was faintly tempted, wondering whether remorse might galvanise him in to becoming the man who'd so entranced me when I was twenty-one that I married him within a year. But then I realised he was still the same man, that it was me who had changed over the ensuing years. I'd outgrown him, simple as that.

I also remembered the cold manner in which he'd delivered his bombshell, how it must have been meticulously planned by the two of them, how his allegiance for four long years had clearly been to her rather than me, his loyal wife who deserved better. The trust was gone and so was my inclination to even try and make the marriage work.

So I said no, that in a way he'd done me a favour, just as he'd claimed the day he left. I told him that the time I'd spent on my own had made me realise that I hadn't just lost my sense of self under the daily burden of keeping a job, running a house and bringing up three children, I'd also lost it via marriage to a man who clearly took me for granted, who had grown bored of me, but stayed for the sake of the children.

He cried, something he hadn't done since his father had died ten years ago. But I knew he wasn't crying for the loss of me, just as I now know that I hadn't been crying all those weeks for the loss of him. It was loneliness we both feared, that's all. So I reassured him that, like me, he too would grow to love his own company and find immense pleasure in solitude, that he'd soon learn companionship is always there when you want it, either in your children, friends, or, yes, even your ex-wife or husband.

Then I gave him a reassuring hug and ushered him out of the front door.

The Blind Spot

BY KATE MOSSE

*A*n afternoon in early December in a pretty market town in Sussex. The smell of bonfires, damp earth, the unmistakable signs of winter creeping across the windowsill. A plain modern flat, all straight lines and angles, glass and 1960s railings overlooking the mortal remains of the old flint Roman walls.

It's dusk, still just light outside, that time *entre chien et loup*. The sharp colours of another sunny, chill afternoon are fading now. The narrow street below is empty.

From September to July, the streets in the city centre are criss-crossed morning and teatime with children in their green sweatshirts, sky-blue sweatshirts, their red blazers and navy-blue blazers, purple and grey caps, as pupils from the many different local schools walk to learn, then back again at 3.30 p.m. During the summer holidays, the narrow streets are instead filled with tourists come for the traditional English holiday of countryside and seaside, and blustery summer storms. But there are few restaurants at this end of town, the schoolchildren have already gone home and the theatre is dark until *Peter Pan* opens next week. There's nobody about. She closes her eyes, prickling with bitterness. The story of a boy who never grew up. Appropriate.

Laura lies on her back on her sitting-room floor, knees drawn up, arms flung out wide on the carpet as if to claim the space. Her black curls are tinged with grey at the temples. In her right hand is a key, small and brass, a replica of something old rather than an original. To her left is a thick-bottomed tumbler of untouched whisky. On the table behind her, a pack of tarot cards.

She has a decision to make, a decision too long avoided. For weeks now, she's not been able to shake the feeling that she is in limbo, waiting for something to happen. Her waking hours and sleepless nights are filled with vivid dreams. The memories of every reading she has ever had, of the person she was once and might be again, shift, slide and merge together as ghostly snapshots of the future and past.

The cards have kept her company all of her adult life. From the first time, a gangly and giggling teenager in the 1970s, sitting in a brightly painted room in London, with the smell of incense mixing with curry from the restaurant below, to her adult self reading for others, the story of the decades of her life played out in the pictures on the cards. The tombs and churches, the pillars of the Temple and the throne of the High Priestess, the Tower rent by lightning, the promise of the treasure suit, the images are as familiar to her as the lines on her face.

And yet now, when she is most in need of guidance, she has lost her courage. Or maybe it is fear that stays her hand. Fear of what might be revealed. For although the cards show possibilities only, suggest choices and interpretations, Laura knows that she will be unable to resist the darkest reading. She is too lonely. And, alone, she is capable of seeing significance where there is none – in the colour of the sky, the flight of a flock of birds, in the turn of a card.

Laura gets up. The flat is small and functional, serviceable, perfect for one. There's no concession to the season. No Christmas decorations, no tinsel or stars or gaudy greetings cards. There is no tree. Only the prints and framed paintings contradict the atmosphere intended by the bland inoffensive walls. Everything else is new. But there are bookshelves everywhere, words and thoughts and ideas on every surface. The usual novels, a healthy library of detective stories and thrillers, fighting for space among the dominance of books about the tarot, ghost stories and divination.

On the dining table in the corner of the room is also a chessboard, brought back from Cairo by the boyfriend who would become her husband. Its mother-of-pearl inlay now chipped around the edges. On the patchwork of diamonds and crosses the frosted, wooden pieces sit patiently in rows, rarely touched.

On the mantelpiece above the imitation gas fire is

the small, brown, wooden box where she keeps her cards, wrapped in black silk. She has several sets, but this tarot pack is her favourite, given to her by her husband on their fifth wedding anniversary. Next to it are two, thin, single-stem glasses, with incense sticks in them.

Laura loves the feel and smoothness and the sense of holding history and myth in her hands. Some say the game comes from China, India or Persia. Others that it's from Ancient Egypt and found its way into Europe with gypsies; that the word 'tarot' derives from an Ancient Egyptian word – *ta-rosh*, meaning 'the Royal Way'. Others, that it is a corruption of the name Thoth, the ancient Egyptian god of magic. There are twenty-two cards in the major arcana, which depict different stages in a person's development, numbered in Roman numerals from I to XXI. The Fool – the child in us, the liberated soul, the wise traveller – has no number assigned to it. He is free, unfettered by pessimism or worldly concerns.

The fifty-six cards of the minor arcana are more like standard playing cards. Divided into suits – wands, swords, pentacles and cups – they expand themes from the major arcana and indicate possible future events. Only the presence of a Page, as well as a Knight, changes the balance of the Court cards.

Laura doesn't think it matters, this lack of certainty about where the first cards came from. All history is narrative, different stories for different times. What matters is the end of the journey, not the beginning.

She lifts the box down and carries it over to the table, then lights two candles and sets them at the corners, as if to mark out the space. She fills a glass bowl with water, scented with pale pink rose petals, and fills a smaller white china bowl with salt, and places them on the table. Finally, she unwraps a bloodstone, to aid clairvoyance, from its covering, and places it between the candles. The flames shimmer, sending thin shadows dancing across the plain black and white cloth she bought in a market in Mexico.

Laura takes the pack from the box and places the cards face down. Then she begins to separate the cards, sliding them over one another against the fabric of the cloth until the whole surface of the table looks like a patchwork quilt of blue and silver stars. When she is sure that the cards have been shuffled thoroughly, she stacks them and places the pack in front of her and sits down on her old wicker chair. When she sold the family home, she got rid of almost every stick of furniture that symbolised their life together. Only not this chair. She hadn't been able to bring herself to part from it.

She needs only four cards for this reading, the Blind Spot. It is a reading for self-awareness and self-perception, not for seeking a specific answer to a particular question. Each card can be interpreted in several ways, depending both on the order in which they are drawn and the way the card is facing, upright or reversed. Her bookcase is filled with books of explanation and history and technique, old battered paperbacks bought for ten pence in a local second-hand shop next to brightly coloured tarot handbooks from America, the spines cracked and broken.

Different stories for different times.

Laura closes her eyes, lets her head drop and takes a few deep breaths until she feels ready. When she opens them, the room seems changed. Shimmering, expectant, as if it, too, is holding its breath. She is no longer aware of the occasional sounds spiralling up from the street below, the slamming of a car door or a human voice. There is nothing but the flickering candlelight, herself, the Querent, and the quartet of cards.

Laura draws the first card and places it face down at the top left-hand corner of a square. This card indicates clear identity, the ways in which we perceive ourselves in the same manner as others also perceive us. Laura places the second diagonally to the first, in the bottom right-hand corner. This card is the Great Unknown, the unconscious processes that are effective without her, or others, being aware of them. The third, she places beside it, beneath Card One, making the shape of the capital letter 'L'. This card shows the shadow that is hidden, the sides of ourselves that are known to us, but that we try to hide from the eyes of others. Finally, the fourth, which reveals forms of behaviour that others perceive in us, but that we ourselves do not recognise. The Blind Spot.

She turns over the first card. The fierce, authoritative gaze of the Hierophant, Card V, looks up at her. Laura narrows her eyes. The number five, the number of mental inspiration, creative thought and intellectual synthesis, is also that of enlightenment and initiation. Also known as the Pope or High Priest, it stands for the world of belief and the deep trust that stems from a conviction or faith. It indicates, too, the need for order and awareness. Laura smooths her fingers over the red-robed figure, over the grand pillars beside the throne and his triple crown, over the images of supplicants at the Hierophant's feet, as if the colour and shapes will absorb through her fingertips in to her skin. It is a card of morality, a card of ethics and steadfastness, or significant decisions seriously taken.

Is this how she is seen by others? How she sees herself? She thinks of the letter lying on the table beside her bed, half accusation, half entreaty, and thinks it is. The edges are crumpled, the paper creased from too much reading between the lines. It is how he sees her, that's true. Steadfast. Immovable.

She draws the second card, a Queen in profile – before a pale blue sky with low white clouds – sitting on an ornate, carved throne. On her head she wears a golden crown. Around both wrists are bracelets of golden thread and her cloak, rich and luxuriant, held at the throat by a silver butterfly brooch, is a deep blue. In her right hand, she holds a long, silver sword. Her left arm is raised, in welcome or in authority. The Queen of Swords denoting intelligence and a complex personality, someone who is self-reliant, swift to act and skilled at balancing opposing factions and ideas. This card represents the 'Great Unknown'. Laura frowns. Does its appearance here indicate a period of awakening? That she should acknowledge the need to act?

She draws again. Again, the suit is Swords, the three. A red heart pierced by three silver blades, set against a stormy sky. Grey clouds, grey light, rain as sharp as needles. Her heart skips a beat. The shadow that is hidden, the pain she knows is there, but that she tries to shield from others. Laura knows this card. More than anything, it denotes a decision that is made in opposition of feelings. It is a card of disappointment in love, of injury and insult.

Laura blinks back the tears that have come into her eyes.

To all her friends, the rest of her family even, it appears she has coped remarkably well. And she works so hard at appearing OK, in control, that they believe her when she tells them she is all right.

But she isn't. And she will never be all right.

She stares at the spread, suddenly sickened by the feelings that have been loosened inside her. For a moment, Laura imagines herself ripping the cloth from the table in an act of violent liberation. She can almost hear the sound of glass splintering, the candles snuffed out in a pool of rose-scented water, the bloodstone snagging the threads of the carpet, the satisfaction of the Queen cast down.

Her heart is thumping. The sound of blood hammering is loud in her ears. She takes a deep breath. It is only the thought of the letter – written, she noticed, on her birthday – still waiting to be answered, that keeps her sitting in her chair.

Laura reaches out, for a moment, just resting her hand on the pile of cards, as if for support. She is reluctant to finish. This card, above all others, shows what others perceive of us, but which we cannot see for ourselves. About ourselves.

She draws the final card and places it in the empty space.

The square is now complete.

Laura looks down. Catches her breath, a pause. Then emotion sweeps through her, relief or surprise or happiness, she cannot yet tell, only that in the instant everything begins to change.

It is the Ace of Cups, one of the most joyous of all cards, the luckiest, celebrating the mystery of love in all its forms. Lilies lie upon the water and from a golden goblet above, held by a white hand in the clouds, four streams flow down. A dove, of peace or divinity, hovers above. It is clear. That there is still a chance of reconciliation, although the desire for it is buried very deep in her. It is clear that two broken hearts will never make her whole again.

Laura stands up, feeling a weight has been lifted from her shoulders. She notices, for the first time, that the flat is bare. She smiles, half-remembered words from a children's story come into her mind, 'Always winter, but never Christmas.' Quickly, with determination now, she puts the cards back in the box on the mantelpiece, puts back in its place all her paraphernalia, the tools by which she uncovered the decision she had already taken. She pours the water down the sink, leaving the faintest scent of roses in the kitchen. The whisky too. She doesn't need it now.

With the letter in her hand, she opens the slatted wooden shutters that give on to her tiny balcony. The frosted December air sneaks in and curls round her bare feet, like a cat. The grey flint of the Roman walls glints, sharply, in the orange glow from the street-lamps. The dusk sky is a dark blue, just tipping to black, the colour of the back of the cards. Soon, there will be stars.

She returns to the table, this time with a pen and piece of paper before her, and thinks about how to start such a letter, long overdue, to a son, long estranged. A son who took a car without asking, who thought he stood above the law, who caused the crash that had ended his father's life. A son Laura vowed she would never forgive.

Now she understands that if she does not forgive, then she cannot go on.

Laura picks up her pen and begins to write, the metal nib scratching softly on the paper. At her shoulder, she feels the presence of the wife she once was and the mother she can be again, returning at last to keep her company. Later, she will go out and buy decorations. A string of white lights, a tree to fill the aching corners of the tiny flat with the smell of pine and remembrances, gold and silver trinkets. Baubles of hope and celebration and the possibility of beginning again.

In the wooden box, swathed once more in folds of black silk, the Kings and Queens, the Hierophant and the Empress sleep until the next story, a different ending.

Thirteen Days With John C

BY JOJO MOYES

She had almost walked straight past it. For the last hundred yards, Miranda had been walking with a kind of absent-minded determination, half wondering what to cook that night. She had run out of potatoes.

It was not as if she was diverted by much on this route any more. Every night after she returned home from work, while Frank sat glued to yet another 'unmissable' football match (Croatia v. some African country tonight), she would put on her trainers and walk three-quarters of a mile along the footpath that ran alongside the common. It stopped her niggling at Frank, while showing him that she did have a life without him. When he looked up from the television, that is.

So she had almost ignored the distant ringing sound, subconsciously filing it with the car horns, the sirens, the other background noises of the city. But when it sounded shrilly, close by, she had glanced behind her, and realising there was nobody else around, she had slowed and followed the sound down to the bushes.

And there it was, half hidden in the long grass – a mobile phone.

Miranda Lewis stood and looked down the empty path in front of her, then picked it up; the same model as her own. In the second it took her to register this, the ringing stopped. She was debating whether to leave it somewhere more visible when a chiming chord announced the arrival of a text message. It was from 'John C'.

She glanced around her, feeling oddly furtive. Then she reasoned – it could be the owner, asking the finder to return it and, after a brief hesitation, she opened it:

'Where U darling?' it read. 'It's been 2 days!!!' Miranda stared at it, then tucked it into her pocket and began to walk.

Miranda, her best friend Sherry liked to remind her, was once a bit of a fox. If anyone else had emphasised the 'once' bit quite as much, Miranda might have been offended, but as Sherry added, twenty years ago, boys had actually genuflected at her feet. Her daughter Andrea smirked when Sherry said this, as if the idea of her mother being remotely attractive to anyone was hilarious. But Sherry went on and on about it because Sherry was outraged by Frank's lack of appreciation.

Every time Sherry joined her on the walk, she would list Frank's faults, comparing him with her Richard. Richard got sad if Sherry left a room. Richard organised 'us' time every Friday for the two of them. Richard left love notes on her pillow. That's because you never had kids, you earn more than he does and Richard had an unsuccessful hair weave, Miranda thought, although she never said it.

But this last eighteen months, she had begun to hear Sherry's views with more receptive ears. Because Frank had begun to irritate her. The way he snored. The way he always had to be reminded to empty the kitchen bin, even when it was visibly overflowing. The way he said plaintively, 'There's no milk!' as if the milk fairy had not been, even though she worked just as many hours as he did. The way his hand would snake across her on a Saturday night, as routine as his washing of the car, but with possibly less affection.

Miranda knew she was lucky to have a marriage that had lasted twenty-one years. She believed there was very little in life that could not be solved by a brisk walk and a dose of fresh air. She had walked a mile and a half every day for the last nine months.

Back in the kitchen, a mug of tea beside her, she had, after the briefest struggle with her conscience, opened the message again.

'Where U darling? It's been 2 days!!!'

Its awful punctuation and abbreviation were somehow offset by the desperation within. She wondered whether to call John C and explain what had happened, but there was something in the intimacy of the message that made it feel like an intrusion.

The owner's phone numbers, she thought. I'll scroll through. But there was nothing in the list of names. No clue except for John C. It all felt odd. I don't want to call him, she thought, suddenly. She felt unbalanced, as if someone had intruded into her safe little house, her haven. She would hand the phone in at the police station, she decided, then she registered another icon: Diary. And there it was: tomorrow's date, with 'Call travel agent.' Below: 'Hair, Alistair Devonshire 2 p.m.'

The hairdresser had been easy to find; the name had sounded familiar and as she looked it up in the directory she realised she must have passed it many times. A discreet salon, off the high street. She would ask the receptionist to ask their two o'clock booking if she'd lost a phone.

Two things happened that made Miranda falter in her resolve. The first was the fact that, seated on the bus in traffic, she had really very little to do except look at the stored pictures. And there he was, a smiling, dark-haired man, grinning into a mug, his eyes lifted in some intimate moment: John C. She glanced at more messages. Just to see if there were any clues, of course. Nearly all were from him.

'Sorry could not call last night. W in foul mood, think looking for clues. Thought of you all night.'

'Can see you in your dress, my Scarlet Woman. The way it moves against yr skin.'

'Can you get away Thurs? Have told W am at conference. Dreaming of my lips on your skin.' And then a couple more that made Miranda Lewis, a woman who believed there was little in life that could surprise her, thrust the phone into her bag and pray that no one else could see the flaming of her cheeks.

She was standing in the reception area, already regretting her decision to come, when the woman approached her.

'Do you have an appointment?' she said. Her hair, a sleek aubergine colour, stuck up in unlikely tufts.

'No,' said Miranda. 'Er . . . Do you happen to have someone coming in at two o'clock?'

'You're in luck. She cancelled. Kevin can fit you in.' She turned away. 'I'll just get you a gown.'

Miranda was left seated, staring at her own reflection in the mirror; a slightly stunned-looking woman with the beginnings of a double chin and mousy hair that she hadn't had time to tidy since climbing off the bus. 'Hello.' Miranda started as a young man appeared behind her. 'What can I do for you? Just a trim?'

'Oh. Um. Actually, this has been a bit of a mistake. I only meant to . . .'

At that moment her phone rang and with a muffled apology she rummaged in her bag to get it. She pressed text message and jumped slightly. The phone she had pulled out was not hers.

'Been thinking about last time. You make my blood sing.'

'All right now? I've got to be honest, sweetheart. That's not the best style for you.' He picked up a limp lock of hair.

'Really.' Miranda stared at the message, meant for the very person sitting in this chair. You make my blood sing.

277

'You want to go with something else? Shall we freshen up your look a bit?'

Miranda hesitated. 'Yes,' she said, looking up at the woman in the mirror.

To her knowledge, she had never made Frank's blood sing. He did occasionally tell her she looked nice, but it always felt like something he felt he should say than something he really meant.

'Shall we go mad, then?' Kevin said, comb raised.

Miranda thought of her daughter, yawning audibly whenever Sherry went on about their teenaged double dates. She thought of Frank, failing to even look up from the television when she returned home from work. 'Hi, babe,' he would say, holding up a hand in greeting. A hand. As if she were a dog.

'I tell you what,' said Miranda. 'Whatever your two o'clock appointment was going to have, I'll have.'

Kevin raised an eyebrow. 'Ohh . . . Good choice,' he said, seemingly reappraising her. 'This is going to be fun.'

She had not run the footpath that night. She had sat in the kitchen and re-read the messages and then jumped guiltily and glanced towards the living room when the next text arrived. Her heart gave a little lurch when she saw the name. She hesitated, then opened it. 'Am worried about U. Too long now. Can bear it (just!) if you don't want to do this, but need to know U R OK. XXX'

She stared at the message, hearing its loving concern, its attempt at humour. Then she gazed up at her reflection, at the new, shorter cut with the reddish tint that Kevin had pronounced his best work all week.

Perhaps it was the fact that she didn't look like herself. Perhaps it was because she hated to see anyone suffer, and John C was clearly suffering. Perhaps it was because she had drunk several glasses of wine. But, her fingers trembling slightly, she typed a reply.

'Am ok,' she typed. 'Just difficult to talk right now.' Then she added: 'X'. She pressed the send button, then sat, her heart thumping, barely breathing until the return message came.

'Thank God. Meet me soon, Scarlet Woman. Am blue without you. X' A little cheesy, but it made her laugh.

After that first evening, it became easier to respond. John C would text her several times a day and she would reply. Sometimes at work, she would find herself thinking about what she would say and her colleagues would remark upon her sudden blush, or her distractedness and make knowing remarks. She would smile and not disabuse them. Why would she, when John C's next text would arrive not half an hour later, professing his passion, his desperation to see her?

Once she had deliberately left one visible on her desk, knowing that Clare Trevelyan would not be able to stop herself from reading it – or passing on its contents in the smoking room. Good, she thought. Let them wonder. She liked the idea that she could surprise people occasionally. Let them think she was an object of passion.

If, occasionally, it occurred to her that what she was doing was wrong, she buried the thought. It was just a bit of make-believe. John C was happy. Frank was happy. The other woman would probably contact him some other way and then it would stop. She tried not to think about how much she would miss it, picturing herself doing the things he remembered them doing together.

It was almost two weeks when she realised she could no longer put him off. She'd told him that there was a problem with her phone, that she was waiting for a new one, and suggested that until then they only spoke by text. But his messages had become insistent:

'Why not Tues? May not have another chance till next week.'

'The Old Gentlemen. A drink at lunchtime. Please!'

'What U trying to do to me?'

It wasn't just that. John C had begun to consume her life. Sherry looked at her suspiciously and remarked how good she looked, how Frank must finally be doing something right, in a way that suggested she thought this unlikely. But John C's messages created an intimacy she had never felt with any other man. They shared the same sense of humour, were able to express even in abbreviated form the most complex and naked of emotions. Unable to tell him the truth, she told him her hopes and secret wishes, her dreams of travel to South America.

'I'll take U there. I miss yr voice, Scarlet Woman,' he told her.

'I hear yrs in my dreams,' she replied, and blushed at her own audacity.

Finally, she had sent him a message. 'The Old Gentlemen. Thursday. 8 p.m.'

She wasn't sure why she had done it. Part of her, the old Miranda, knew that this couldn't continue. That it was a temporary madness. And then there was new Miranda, who while she might never be able to admit this to herself, had started to think of John C as her John. Miranda might not be the phone's original owner, but John C would have to admit that there had been a connection. That the woman he had spent the last thirteen days talking to was someone who stirred him, who made him laugh, who scrambled his thoughts. If nothing else, he had to acknowledge that. Because his messages had changed her, they had made her feel alive again.

Thursday evening found her fussing over her make-up like a teenager on her first date. 'Where are you off to?' said Frank, looking up from the television. He seemed a little taken aback, even though she was wearing a long coat. 'You look nice.' He scrambled up from the sofa. 'I meant to tell you. I like your hair.'

'Oh, that,' she said, blushing slightly. 'Drink with Sherry.'

'Wear your blue dress,' John C had said. She had bought one specially; low in front with a kick skirt.

'Have fun,' he said. He turned back to the television, shifting slightly on the sofa as he lifted the remote.

Miranda's confidence briefly evaporated at the pub. She had nearly turned back twice on the way there and still could not work out what to say if she saw anyone she knew. Plus the pub was not the kind of place where they dressed up, she had realised too late, so she kept her coat on. But then half a glass in, she changed her mind and shrugged it off. John C's lover would not feel self-conscious drinking alone in a blue dress.

At one point a man came up and offered her a drink. She had started, and then, realising it was not him, had declined. 'I'm waiting for someone,' she said, and enjoyed his regretful look as he walked away.

He was almost fifteen minutes late when she picked up her phone. She would text him. She was just starting her message when she looked up to find a woman standing at her table.

'Hello, Scarlet,' she said.

Miranda blinked at her. A youngish, blonde woman, wearing a wool coat. She looked tired, but her eyes were feverish, intense.

'I'm sorry?' she said.

'It's you, isn't it? Scarlet Woman? Gosh, I thought you'd be younger.' There was a sneer in her voice. Miranda put down her phone.

'Oh, I'm sorry. I should have introduced myself. I'm Wendy. Wendy Christian. John's wife?' Miranda's heart stalled.

'You did know he had one, right?' The woman held

up a matching mobile phone. 'He mentioned me enough times, I see. Oh no,' her voice lifted theatrically. 'Of course you didn't realise it wasn't him you've been talking to these last two days. I took his phone. It's me. It was all me.'

'Oh God,' Miranda said quietly. 'Look, there's been—'

'—a mistake? You bet there has. This woman has been sleeping with my husband,' she announced to the pub in a ringing, slightly tremulous voice. 'Now she has decided that this might have been a mistake.' She leaned forward over the table. 'Actually, Scarlet, or whatever you call yourself, it's been my mistake, marrying a man who thinks that having a wife and two small children doesn't mean he can't keep screwing around.'

Miranda felt the silence of the pub, the collective eyes burning into her. Wendy Christian took in her stricken expression. 'You poor fool. Did you think you were the first? Well, Scarlet, you're actually number four. And that's just the ones I know about.'

Miranda's vision had become strangely blurry. She kept waiting for the normal sounds of the pub to resume around her, but the silence, oppressive now, continued. Finally she grabbed her coat and bag and ran past the woman to the door, her cheeks burning, her head down against the accusing stares.

The last thing she heard as the door swung behind her was the sound of a phone ringing.

'That you, babe?' Frank raised a hand as he heard

her pass by the doorway of the living room. Miranda was suddenly grateful for the irresistible draw of the television. Her ears rang with the accusations of that embittered wife. Her hands were still trembling.

'You're back early.'

She took a deep breath, staring at the back of his head over the sofa.

'I decided,' she said, slowly. 'That I didn't really want to go out.'

He glanced behind him. 'Richard will be pleased. He doesn't like Sherry going out, does he? Thinks someone's going to steal her away from him.'

Miranda stood very still.

'Do you?'

'Do I what?'

'Worry that someone will steal me away?' She felt electrified, as if whatever he said would have far greater implications than he knew.

He turned to face her and smiled. 'Course. You were a fox, remember?'

'Were?'

'Come here,' he said. 'Come and give me a cuddle. It's the last five minutes of Uruguay v. Cameroon.'

Miranda felt the warmth of his hand on hers and relaxed. 'Two minutes,' she said. 'There's something I have to do first.'

In the kitchen, she reached for the mobile phone. Her fingers, this time, were assured.

'Dear John C,' she wrote. 'A ring on the finger is worth two on the phone. You'd do well to learn this.'

She paused, then added: 'Foxy'. She sent this, then turned off the phone, stuffing it deep into the kitchen bin. Then she walked back into the living room, back to where her husband was waiting.

The Mother of the Bride

BY ELIZABETH NOBLE

On the morning of Fleur's 'destination' wedding, a beautiful May morning with a gentle breeze and a cobalt sky, the bride-to-be and her three bridesmaids were booked into the spa of the five-star hotel where the wedding party were all staying. The perma-tanned, perma-smiley wedding co-ordinator the hotel provided for 'all its brides' would meet her there to 'go over arrangements' while she and her best friends were massaged, exfoliated and painted.

Fleur's mother Claire had been invited to join them, of course, but she didn't like the spa. She didn't find it at all relaxing, lolling around in a cotton robe without the benefit of Lycra and underwire. It seemed indulgent, and it was so expensive . . . Fleur had seemed a little miffed. She had been calling Claire 'the mother of the bride', instead of just Mum, for several months now, as though it was a title she had been awarded. It seemed to Claire that Fleur considered attendance at the spa one of the mother of the bride's 'duties', along with dressing in a colour that blended well with the rest of the bridal party, which would, of course, look much better in the photographs.

Claire disliked the photographer, Clive. He had a receding hairline, and a ponytail, which was probably grounds alone, but she didn't like the way he took in her whole self in a sweeping glance whenever he looked at her, either, and called her 'mum'. He was going to be taking 'reportage-style' photographs, apparently. That meant he would be in the spa right now. Taking photographs of the girls, giggling and drinking pink champagne, in their robes. Later he would photograph them getting dressed. Fleur had confided to her mother a desire to be photographed in just her underwear and her veil. Just for Mike, she said.

It seemed a shame not to include the dress. 'The dress' (that had a title too, somehow) was the most stunning, extravagant garment Claire had ever seen. Strapless, tight-fitting to the waist, from where it cascaded to the floor in a shimmer of chiffon, it had seed pearls and Swarovski crystals hand-sewn on to it, so that it threw rainbows and sparkles when she walked – or more, it seemed, floated – in it. She almost doubted her connection to the exquisite creature wearing it. It didn't seem possible that this was her daughter.

Shoes, impossibly high, with matching embroidery, from the same small boutique near Madame Tussauds. Lily of the valley, imported, refrigerated, and tied with a satin ribbon. New underwear from Fenwick on Bond Street. A small tiara from Liberty . . . This wedding had been in the planning stage for nine months, but in Fleur's head, it seemed, her whole life.

Claire, eschewing the spa, had eaten breakfast, late, on her balcony, watching the pool area below come to life. It was half term, and the hotel was full. Fathers commandeered sunloungers and mothers blew up armbands, issuing commands from the sides of their mouths as they exhaled fiercely. Everyone slathered themselves and each other in sunscreen. People were so much more careful now.

It had been a beautiful morning when Claire had married Fleur's father, too. June, not May, and warm, rather than hot, but with the same blue sky. 1974. More than thirty years ago. Claire had shared the narrow bed of her childhood, on her last night as a single woman, with one of her bridesmaids, her six-year-old niece Katharine, who had fidgeted and pulled at the covers. In the morning, Claire had swept the yard that ran along the front of her parents' terraced house, connecting their home to the neighbours she had known all her life. The postman had handed her the small pile of letters and bills. 'Beautiful morning,' he'd said, squinting against the bright sunshine. 'I'm getting married today!' she had replied, beaming back at him excitedly. 'Good luck to you then, girl,' he'd smiled. It had seemed a strange thing to say to her. She hadn't thought she needed luck. She hadn't thought she'd needed anything, except Simon.

She hadn't gone to the spa that morning – no such thing, of course – but she'd had her hair set at the place on the corner where her mum had been going forever and where they'd known her since she was a child. They'd gone together, she and 'the mother of the bride' – who wore lilac, by the way, which did not match either the bridesmaids, the bouquet or the groom's tie . . . They'd had some champagne. The Saturday girl had painted her fingernails for her, she'd remembered, looking at the 'menu of services' Fleur had handed her while she was trying to persuade her to join them. Peach, to go with the roses in her bouquet.

Thirty people had travelled to Cyprus to be with Fleur and Mike on their wedding day, and to have a short holiday in the sun. They'd had big stag and hen parties, his in Brighton, with go-karts and a pub crawl, and hers in London, with a West End show and tea in a posh hotel that served cakes shaped like little designer handbags. They wanted the wedding itself to be small and intimate, they said. 'Just people we know we want to celebrate our silver wedding with,' Fleur joked. She was so animated. She hadn't stopped beaming since they'd got there, and she fell delightedly on every new arrival like a puppy.

There hadn't been many more people at Claire's. Maybe forty-five or fifty. Simon had had lots of aunts, dour and wearing unflattering hats. You didn't seem to know so many people in 1974, somehow. You couldn't have afforded to feed a lot more than that, even with just a reception in the pub, and a cake chosen from the brochure at the bakers in town. Her parents had never had much money, and she and Simon were saving for a house of their own. But a wedding still attracted a crowd in those days. It was an event. People waited in the churchyard for a glimpse of you. Claire remembered one old dear calling out 'don't you look lovely, dear', to her as she walked down the path, holding her dress up so that it didn't brush against the lollopy gravestones lining her route. Her Auntie Suzy had made the dress. It had been polyester satin, with a lace overlay, made from material meant for curtains. It had cost next to nothing, compared to the dresses in the shops, but she'd done a beautiful job. She'd loved that dress. Loved herself in that dress. Loved walking towards Simon with the wedding march playing and her whole life lying before her at the end of the aisle, in that dress.

Claire knew that Fleur would feel that too. She hoped, at least. That Fleur couldn't imagine a life without Mike in it. That Fleur had woken up that morning thinking she might levitate with happiness, because today, finally, was the day. Every single detail about their two weddings might be different, but that needed to be true.

It couldn't be quite the same, of course. Fleur and Mike had been living in their flat for two years. She and Simon had never spent the night together before that first night. Never seen each other naked. She might have loved the dress, but she'd loved taking it off, too. God, they'd been so excited about that part. That would be different. She'd always been old-fashioned. Lots of girls slept with their fiancés in

1974. And more men besides, quite often. Even in the country, where she lived. The pill had been available to unmarried women for years by then, and she knew girls who were making the most of the freedom it offered. But she hadn't wanted to. Her wedding fantasy included a wedding night. And Simon hadn't pushed her. At the time it had been one of the things she'd loved most about him – his being willing to wait for her. Fleur had slept with Mike the night before, for God's sake, so he was hardly going to be peeling the Swarovski crystals and seed pearls off a mystery gift, was he? She didn't mind, not that it was her place to mind. It made sense, she supposed: they'd know what they were doing. She and Simon hadn't, not really. Not that first night, at least.

Claire had never made it to her silver wedding, of course. Seventeen years, she and Simon had lasted. Almost half of her life up until that point. Fleur had been thirteen in 1991, the year they divorced. Claire had worried about that almost more than anything else. Had they damaged her? Had they stopped her believing in true love? Fleur slammed doors and wouldn't speak, and sometimes cried in her bed at night when she thought Claire couldn't hear her, although she did, and the sound made her wretched. It was such a tough age. She'd wanted to hang on. She'd wanted to make it until Fleur was, maybe, eighteen. She could have done, too. He left her, in the end. It might have been either one of them, because they were both dying inside, but she'd have waited. Until Fleur was grown up.

It was too soon to get dressed. Claire wandered in the gardens. The hotel had built a small, white wedding chapel in the grounds, with stained-glass windows and a steeple. It was pretty, but it looked not quite real. Stray rose petals from an earlier ceremony clung on to the shrubbery. Fleur and Mike had written some of their own vows. Another difference. In a couple of hours they would be speaking them to each other, right here. They would make promises each believed they could keep. They would mean every word. Their voices would break when they spoke, straining with how much they meant what they said.

But they couldn't promise not to change. They couldn't promise that if one of them did change, the other person would still love them. They couldn't promise to continue to want the same things from life and from each other. They couldn't promise that in seventeen years from now they wouldn't wake up and look at each other across on the pillows and suddenly not be able to remember a morning when they looked with joy and not with disdain. They couldn't promise to love each other forever, or that neither of them would ever fall in love with anyone else.

They could only promise to try. They could only believe.

Claire had believed, in 1974, in her curtain-fabric dress. Believed with her whole heart. Thought that the love between a man and a woman was unconditional, because she hadn't yet had Fleur, and understood, in an instant, the difference.

Simon would be there, across from her in the church. And that was OK. That was how it should be. He was Fleur's father. They'd been divorced for seventeen years now, as long as they'd been married. The wounds were scars, and the terrible, awful words they had said to each other were ancient whispers now. He was somewhere in this hotel, now, getting ready to walk his only child down an aisle towards her own future. Maybe he was thinking about 1974, and about what he had promised, and believed. It didn't matter any more.

It was time to get dressed.

Fleur had had lots of boyfriends. She'd never seemed to be without one for long. She had easy good looks, and she was fun. The boys were that way, too. Some she brought home, some were just names mentioned on the telephone, and pictures brought out over Sunday lunches. It had seemed to Claire like Fleur held herself back from them. They were for fun, and for holidays, and for sex, but not for promises. She was glad, through Fleur's teens and twenties. More anxious as she turned thirty, haunted by the notion that she and Simon had spoiled something for her. Mike had been different from the start, and Claire's relief had made her laugh, the first time she'd seen them together. Fleur's whole demeanour had changed. She was lit up. They needed to be touching each other the whole time – holding hands, or his hand on her cheek.

Claire walked behind them, somewhere, she didn't remember where, and their legs moved in perfect time, their hips brushing together.

She'd forgotten, somehow. It was this wedding. It was all the differences, and all the tiny details – the miniature roast beef and Yorkshire pudding crudités and the save-the-date cards and the imported lily of the valley. Claire had felt alienated by it all. She'd lost her way in it all. She'd forgotten how Fleur lit up and how their hips brushed together when they walked.

She was dressed now. Co-ordinating. It was going to be too hot. She needed to see her daughter.

'Mum! Where've you been?' Fleur was grinning at her. She looked about five years old. 'I'm about to put the dress on, but I wanted you to be here.'

'I'm here now, darling.'

'Good.'

'I'm sorry I didn't come to the spa. I should have come.'

'Don't be. I'm sorry I've been such a bridezilla.'

'Don't be. You haven't.'

'I have. But you know what? I woke up this morning, and all that stuff just doesn't seem important any more, you know? I just want to see Mike, standing there, waiting for me. I just want to marry him. I'm so happy I could burst.'

Claire hugged her. Clive snapped away, like a paparazzi, and Claire tried not to mind. 'Do you remember when I was a little girl, how I wanted to wear your wedding dress when I got married?'

Claire laughed. 'You did.'

'In a way, I wish I was.'

'Nonsense. It was polyester. You'd melt!' Claire made a joke of it, because she was suddenly afraid that she was going to cry, and it was too soon to cry. 'No, love, this one is much nicer . . .' She stroked the dress. 'I bought you something, though. Just something silly . . .'

'I remember the something old, something borrowed routine, but I don't remember the something silly . . .'

'Well, then, call this the something old, and the something borrowed.' Claire opened her hand, and, pulling her daughter's open hand towards her heart, dropped something very small and very light into Fleur's palm. A peach rose petal. Nearly forty years old. Pressed flat, and brown with age. Fleur's eyes filled with tears. 'Mum.' Claire held both Fleur's hands tightly at her chest, and stared at her beautiful, familiar face. She needed to say it. 'Now you go out there, walk up the aisle to him, and you promise me you'll promise, and you promise me you'll believe . . .'

At the door of the chapel, as the swimming, sun-screening families stopped to watch, Claire passed a beaming Fleur's hand to Simon's, though for a moment she thought she might never be able to let go, and kissed both of them lightly on the cheek.

And then walked inside, past the guests, and slipped into the front pew, next to Tom, who took her hand, and squeezed. Tall, slim, Tom, greying at the temples.

Tom, who she had met at the golf club where she'd started taking lessons about ten years ago when Fleur – bold and knowing everything because she was twenty-five, and twenty-five-year-olds do indeed know everything – told her she needed a hobby. Tom, whose own 1974 wife had left him, and who thought he would always be alone.

Tom, who she had married, in a quiet civil ceremony with no photographer and no dress and no ice sculptures, on Millennium Eve, when everything was about to be brand new, and making promises seemed possible again.

Topiary

BY FREYA NORTH

Summer always put Lady Lott in a bad mood. Which wasn't to say that she was particularly affable during the other seasons. Her temper increased exponentially with the temperature. If she was grumpy in early June, by late August she could be quite unbearable. This was no quirk of her advancing years, no foible attributable to having outlived two husbands, one child, most of her friends and a few lovers too. Nor could it be pinned on her colourful past or her wheelchair-bound present. She'd never liked summer, like she'd never liked courgettes – it wasn't something that one grew out of or in to. It was as simple as that.

Every year, the first cuckoo would wind back the clock of her memory to childhood summers replete with hornet stings and sweet peas and aged aunts whose aroma of pee really wasn't very nice at all. Then there were the summers of her adolescence; the wall-flower and the louche friends of her father gallivanting about wearing not nearly enough whilst drinking far too much. Next came wisteria and hysteria: the bloody war, which did not incorporate a summer recess into its strategy, and no one could decide whether one was safer indoors or out. Peacetime brought with it sweet-william and love-in-a-mist: the summers of her young adulthood reverberated to the monotonous sound of tennis and the courtship contests played out on court. Wretched game – even if an apparent trophy was her first husband. Interminable summers followed with whining children wound round her legs – a definite downside of two husbands in quick succession, both of whom were potent in the fiscal and physical sense.

The little Lotts have long since grown and moved away. If Lady Lott finds them enough of an imposition when they descend at Christmas, she shudders to imagine them during the summer with their overheated offspring.

Here she is now, mid-June of her eighty-second year. Being immobile doesn't really add to the frustration – it is not as if she was ever one for roaming summer meadows feeling all Thomas Hardy about the land. And she has a great deal of land. It is just more difficult to turn her back on the weather now, because she is rather dependent on assistance to physically move. But Elena, her private nurse, has exercised her contractual rights to take a summer-long sabbatical in Cyprus. And Mrs Meacher, the housekeeper, is no substitute. Over the decades, Lady Lott has observed with some awe but also alarm the way Mrs Meacher mishandles the broom and manhandles the potatoes. Lady Lott has no doubt that the woman can cook and clean – but those calloused hands and those stout forearms and those purposefully pursed lips will not be invited anywhere near her.

Lady Lott swats imaginary flies and despairs at the idleness of the breeze. Surveying her estate, she watches Si tweak the topiary. He's been at it for hours, for days in fact. His selection of shears and secateurs and even kitchen scissors are laid out on a hessian sack, selected and replaced with the caution and dexterity of a surgeon.

'Fool!' she suddenly barks. 'You're making a pig's ear out of that cockerel's tail.'

Si, however, has worked here long enough and is naturally temperate enough simply to feign not to hear her. She can holler and chide him all she likes but he always strolls over, pleasant and courteous. 'Lady L, were you calling me?' he'll ask. 'Can I move you into the shade? Would you like me to take you to the lavender? Is it time to feed the fish?'

Every summer it's the same. The kinder he is to her, the hotter she feels. Today is no different.

'Si! Si! You cack-handed oaf – if you hack off any more, that unicorn will be a common old nag. Si!'

Oaf is her new word for him this summer. Now that he's forty, she just can't justify using 'boy' any longer.

Si walks over with a wave as if to say, Oh! Lady Lott! Didn't see you sitting up there on the terrace! He wheels her over to the shade, where a pitcher of iced water stands. He pours for her and then helps himself, paying no attention to her witheringly raised eyebrow.

While she sips demurely, he downs the water in long, appreciative gulps and, though Lady Lott thinks the sight of his undulating throat vulgar, the leather neck-lace around his neck ridiculous, his tanned skin rather uncouth, she can't quite look away.

'Perfect,' he says, putting the glass down gently, 'lovely day.'

'It's too hot for this time of year.'

'It's a pleasure to work in this weather, Lady Lott.'

'You're too snip-happy with the topiary.'

'Shorter horns are all the rage amongst fashionable unicorns this summer,' he says, 'and all topiary cock-erels are wearing their tails short. It's the new black.'

'What are you talking about?'

Si himself isn't quite sure, so he changes the subject. 'The new girl will be arriving soon. That'll be nice for you – company during the summer.'

'Girl?' Lady Lott snaps, 'Girl?'

'Carer?'

'Carer?' She bellows, 'I'm not an invalid, I'm not incapacitated, I'm not an imbecile. I just have legs that are eighty-two years old. And no girl is looking after me. I have paid an agency to send a woman to help with – chores. I don't require company. I am simply purchasing practical assistance.'

'I see,' Si says, 'and is the woman arriving soon?'

Lady Lott straightens her upper body and pretends not to notice that Si has his hand at her elbow to help her. 'Tomorrow, actually. The woman arrives tomorrow.'

Si looks thoughtful. 'What we are today comes from our thoughts of yesterday, and our present thoughts build our life of tomorrow.'

'What are you talking about?' Lady Lott sighs.

'It's a Buddhist saying.'

'Dear God,' Lady Lott mutters irritably, trying to fan herself with a paper napkin.

Si shrugs and returns to sculpting the box hedging, eliciting a certain stately charm from the lion. He's rather proud of his work and sneaks a glance to see if Lady Lott is watching. She is. Even from this distance he can detect her glower, but he gives her an expansive wave anyway.

'What are the odds on the woman who's arriving tomorrow being a fearsome old battleaxe who'll give this old girl a run for her money?' he asks the lion. He scratches his head and laughs. 'What am I doing, talking to you, hedge face?'

Jenny's friends had commented that it was rather an odd way to spend the summer. You should be in your bikini on a gorgeous Greek beach, they had said. You should be pampering yourself at some heavenly spa! It's your first summer of freedom – you should be enjoying yourself! Take the summer off work at the very least, they'd said. But the truth was, Jenny couldn't really afford to. Few people get rich from divorce – and she certainly wasn't one of them. She didn't feel particularly young pushing forty, nor had her newly single status brought with it the sense of freedom and adventure that her friends presumed. Relief, yes, but tinged with sadness too. No regrets, though. None at all. But still she felt a little reflective – a state of mind she was sure was healthier than being brazen and bronzed and on the rebound on some far-flung shore.

'The pay is amazing,' she had justified, 'looking after a little old lady who owns some kind of stately home. I'll be afforded the same salubrious surroundings of any top spa. In fact, I'll probably have the guest wing and dedicated staff all to myself.'

And now she is looking out of the minicab window. She doesn't know this part of the world and the Lincolnshire landscape appears to be flat and rather uninspiring. She manufactures a smile to fend off the creeping sense of disappointment. The driver is indicating, turning left.

'She's a character, that Lady Lott,' he tells her.

But Jenny doesn't pick up on the tone of his voice. The grounds of Lott Hall, rolling and verdant and vast, distract her. And look at all that topiary! What eccentricity! She wears her smile easily now. A man waves as they drive past. He appears to be holding kitchen scissors in one hand and huge shears in the other. He resembles a fiddler crab – and a rather handsome one at that. The drive sweeps up towards the house – grander, more beautiful than she'd imagined. 'I'll walk the last few yards,' she tells the driver.

Before she ventures to the front door, she takes a moment to stand still and just breathe; the summer-soft air, the fragrant jasmine, so sweet she can almost taste it. It is an idyllic day; the weather is beautiful and the Lott estate is spread before her, the stuff of day-dreams. Summer stretches ahead and Jenny welcomes it.

The housekeeper could have come straight from the cast of a BBC costume drama, all doughy arms and floury hands; but when Jenny finally meets Lady Lott, she thinks Dickens himself would have been hard-pressed to have created such a character. Thin without being bony; twisted feet encased in old-fashioned satin shoes; rings too large for skinny fingers whose joints are too swollen to prise the gold off; eyes as beady and dark as a blackbird's; a mouth ready to peck.

'You're a girl!' are Lady Lott's first words to Jenny.

If the timbre of her voice is surprisingly deep for such a slight lady, the tone of contempt is alarming.

'I'm Jenny.'

'And I asked for someone experienced. And strong. You're just a girl.'

'I'll take that as a compliment,' Jenny says lightly, 'and I'm pretty strong and experienced.'

'Push me through to the drawing room!' Lady Lott barks and she doesn't have to add that she does not expect her staff to answer her back.

'Of course,' Jenny says convivially, 'but you'll have to direct me. I don't have a drawing room – I live in a one-bedroom top-floor flat.'

Lady Lott huffs in the direction of the grand double doors some way off to the left and Jenny's job begins.

*

For the first two days, Jenny managed to smile through
Lady Lott's asperity, rationalising it as a small price to
pay for such a well-paid job.

'I'm just finding my feet,' Jenny had said gently, on
being reprimanded for something trivial before they'd
even taken breakfast.

'You'd find them far quicker if you wore sensible
shoes rather than those frivolous pumps,' Lady Lott
had said while Jenny struggled not to comment on
hers.

All day long, Lady Lott hissed orders, snapped
instructions and snarled about the right way to do the
things she considered Jenny to have done incorrectly.
The effect on Jenny's self-esteem was insidious – as if
woodworm were mining the very fabric of her morale.
Apart from lifting Lady Lott in and out of the chair, or
bed, or facilitating her in the toilet or bath, the other
side of her skills as a private nurse were being pointedly
ignored. When Jenny tried to actually care, she was
shot down. When she attempted to greet the day, she
was snubbed. Suggestions of fresh air were dismissed, a
game of cards was rejected and any attempt at conversation was obviously considered impertinent. In
fact, for the first few days, Jenny barely ventured out
of the house, confined to its surprisingly cluttered
interior until gone supper time. Before the week was
out, her cups of tea taken in solitude on the terrace as
the night sky seeped in, became the time when she
most doubted that she'd made the right decision for

her summer. Her mind wandered to Greece. She'd never been to Greece. Was there still time to change her plans?

Little did Jenny know that it was far more than a fine cotton handkerchief edged in exquisite Nottingham lace which Lady Lott kept up her sleeve.

At the end of her first week, when Jenny is insulted to the point of tears so that she runs from the house mid-morning, it doesn't cross her mind that Lady Lott has planned the precise timing and direction of her flee.

Jenny bolts across the terrace and down the long sweep of the first lawn to the gravel promenade and takes refuge behind the topiary lion. She tries every trick she knows to keep tears at bay – skills she'd honed the previous year to deny her ex the satisfaction of seeing her pain. But she can't dig her nails into the palms of her hands because Lady Lott has insisted she file them down. And she can't threaten herself with streaky mascara because Lady Lott has told her not to come down to breakfast 'painted like a tart'. And she is hyperventilating too much to remember about long, deep breaths. And she's spitting with rage so she can't count to ten.

'She's a crotchety old witch,' the topiary lion suddenly says, 'and you're allowed to say so.'

'I bloody well will, then,' Jenny replies before leaping up in alarm. She must be going mad. She is imagining that a lion made from hedge is talking to her. Worse, she's actually answered back.

'Go on – say it: crotchety old witch.'

And Jenny now sees that it isn't the lion speaking. It's the fiddler crab man – but he has no shears, no scissors to hand today. So it is just him – the handsome him who waved to her as she was driven to the house a week ago.

'I wondered what had become of you,' he says, wiping his right hand on the knee of his jeans and extending it. 'Hello, I'm Si.'

'Jenny.'

'You haven't said it yet,' he smiles.

'Said what?'

'That Lady Lott is a crotchety old hag who thinks her wealth is the wherewithal to treat us underlings like dirt.'

Jenny nods gratefully.

'Say it,' Si laughs, 'it'll make you feel so much better.'

'It's madness!' she declares instead. 'How can I have made it through the ugliness of divorce with my dignity relatively unscathed and yet feel so completely crushed by an octogenarian old bat?'

'Octogenarian old bat,' Si muses, 'I like that better than crotchety old witch. May I borrow it? When I next need it?'

Jenny smiles. 'You may.' She feels calmer. She turns to him.

'How long have you worked here?'

'Over a decade.'

'Why have you stayed so long? Hasn't she driven you mad?'

'Look around you, Jenny. Look at this place. So she gives me an earful every now and then – look around you, there are acres and acres where I can't hear her.'

'What do you do here?'

'Much as I'd like to be called Estate Manager, I suppose I'm just the skivvy. General dogsbody for the grounds.'

'Do you do the topiary?'

'Yes.'

'It's amazing. You're not a skivvy, you're an artist.'

'Why, thank you.'

Si and Jenny look around and regard the tight-leaved, glossy-green menagerie. 'Lady Lott, though, would say I'm more of a butcher,' says Si.

And then they pause and they don't want there to be a pause because they don't want the other to think they've run out of things to say. Just then, both Si and Jenny consider how they could quite happily while away the day together.

There is something about him.

There is something about her.

And the shared shy smile that lingers tells them so.

But they aren't here to chat and flirt, much as they suddenly think how they'd gladly snatch any spare moments to do just that. They are at work. They have jobs to do.

'I'd better go,' Jenny says, 'she'll roast me alive. Or sack me.'

'If it's to be the lesser of two evils, then I suppose I'd

rather it was the former,' Si says and he touches her wrist. 'I wouldn't want you to go just yet.'

Jenny feels herself redden. She casts her eyes down and stares at her pale blue ballet pumps.

'I bet she had a field day with your shoes,' Si says and he edges his work boot to the tip of her toes.

'I must go,' Jenny says. She starts to walk away but stops midway up the lawn and turns back. Si is gently patting the rump of the lion. He raises his hand and Jenny mirrors the gesture. She stands still a moment longer before turning towards the house. But soon enough she stops again and faces the lion and the unicorn and Si now standing in between.

'She'll roast you alive,' Si warns under his breath as Jenny walks back to him.

She stops a little way off, just out of reach but within earshot. 'I – well, I usually have a cup of tea on the terrace at nine-ish.'

'Milk and two sugars.'

'Yes! How did you know that?'

'I didn't. I'm telling you that's how I take it.'

'Will you join me?'

'Digestives? Hobnobs?'

'How about Mrs Meacher's home-made short-bread?'

'It's a date. I mean deal. It's a deal.'

They grin at their shoes. They both know it's a date.

Jenny walks up the lawn towards the house. She's beaming at the flowers, she's saluting the topiary cockerel, she turns her face to the sun and closes her eyes as she welcomes its warmth and brightness.

'Silly old trout,' she says under her breath as she looks towards the house, the drawing-room windows. 'I'll take you out for fresh air this afternoon whatever you say. It'll do you good. It's a beautiful day.'

Out of sight in the drawing room, Lady Lott takes a long look down to the promenade. She can see Si, still standing between the lion and unicorn, gazing after Jenny. It needed to be done this morning – if she'd driven Jenny from the house this afternoon, they'd never have found each other. Wednesday afternoons Si checks the pond. And the pond is just beyond both running and spying distance from the drawing room. She watches Jenny cross the lawn. Lady Lott has already noted the spring in her step. In fact, the girl is now practically dancing the last few yards. Those silly, silly shoes.

Lady Lott observes Si watching Jenny, his head cocked to one side. She senses he is smiling, she knows his smile – how his eyes crinkle at the corners and dimples settle deep in his cheeks. She had previously noticed how he doesn't smile so much these days, not since the business with that awful girl in the village last year.

Something is happening to Lady Lott's mouth. A private, slightly mischievous satisfaction is pulling the corners of her lips upwards. This particular summer might not be so bad, after all. So what if there's only tennis on the television – she's never cared much for the game. It seems there's to be far greater entertainment played out against the stunning backdrop of her very own garden this summer. Jenny. Si. Lady Lott is smiling broadly now. And they will think their sole audience is the topiary menagerie. What fun.

One Careful Owner

BY HAZEL OSMOND

I don't know how long I stood there looking down at her body, the sledge-hammer held high over my head. Long enough for the muscles in my arms to start telling me to either damn well do something or put it down. I do know that.

I remember more than once determining to go through with it and making that little movement backwards with my hands that would start the swing downwards.

And really it was only the newspaper that stopped me. There, stacked in the recycling box catching my eye, was our over-excitable local rag. I saw myself in a week's time pigeon-holed in a punning headline and unflattering photograph.

'Jealous wife's revenge!', 'Years of neglect led to moment of madness.'

I thought of staring up at a legion of rabbits' and cats' behinds; being wrapped around Lord knows what; sniggered at by those half-wits at the book club.

And after all, was it really fair to take it out on this particular model? Why should she suffer because she was the most recent in a long, long line? At least this one had class, even I could see that. I lowered the sledge-hammer with difficulty, laid it down on the floor and then walked swiftly back into the house. Away from the nauseating smell of oil and petrol.

Two large glasses of Bordeaux later and the tremors in my arms and hands have stopped. Holding something heavy over your head will do that to your muscles. Or perhaps it was the thought of what I could have done, the malevolent violence, that had made me shake.

When really, not all of it was his fault.

After all, I had married a man whom I had imagined was Heathcliff, only to find that underneath all that granite, there was simply more granite. Not a seam of poetry or passion anywhere. Not even a fossilised footprint.

Except, of course, when it came to his beloved, his soul mate, his car.

Not just one car, of course. Fifteen years of cars; a newer, sleeker model taking the place each time of the one that only months before had fulfilled all his heart's desire. A new rictus grin from me to greet each arrival on the drive.

A fresh mistress to get used to, to work around. More demanding little ways.

Of course, if I'm honest (and after two glasses of red, who isn't?), the signs were there at the start. Screeching to the kerb, his arm along the passenger seat and the top down, telling me how it handled, how it performed. Erotic in its way; his enthusiasm hinting at underlying depths of passion that surely would be transferred to me. I even found the engine oil under his nails exciting. I had bagged an engineer and a northern one at that. Well, that was practically double points and a thumbed nose at Grace, my sister, with her accountant from Swanage.

Even sweeter so many years after they had all put me neatly in the spinster box.

Finally, the sky was blue above me, the air was warm. We would travel through a new life together.

Except we stalled.

I up-end the Bordeaux bottle into my glass again and hunt down a jar of olives in the fridge, skirmishing about among the packets of ham and ready-meals.

I know, I know. But if you're planning a fast exit, cooking a casserole from scratch isn't uppermost in your mind. And cramming the fridge with easy-cook stuff means he won't starve when I'm gone. Old habits and all that.

So, at the start, at the offset, I took all this car love in my stride. Normal manly behaviour. And it has to be said, I had previous form.

A father in love with steam. Years of him being half there, half in the loft with his train track. Holidays planned around the last outposts of the steam engine.

So how was I to know what was 'normal' and what was not? Although to be fair to my father, he did find time to sire five children and put a large smile on my mother's face. Even when he asked her to help with his train layouts and make those awful, fiddly little trees from that sponge stuff.

How was I to know that this was a step further than my father's obsession?

That my husband would spend more time lying under cars than on top of me?

It took me about four years of marriage to really understand what I was up against. In fact, I can remember the date exactly. January 12th. It was my thirty-ninth birthday and we'd been out for lunch. A long drive there, a quick meal and then a long drive home. We came back here and I made us a cup of tea. By the time the tea was in the cups, he was out in the garage. Again. He must have positively raced up the stairs to strip off his clothes and get safely into those nasty snot-green overalls of his. Everything neatly zipped up out of harm's way.

Out of my way, more like.

I carried his tea out to discover him already elbow deep in that hideous Jag he had at the time.

'Oh,' I said, 'so you're here then?'

He looked at the cup of tea. 'Just put it down over there.' He nodded at a space on his workbench. Well, I hadn't spent all those years as a primary school teacher not to be able to recognise when somebody was avoiding answering a sticky question.

I put the tea down and went and stood by his side. I remember leaning against him, for once not really caring if the oil from his overalls rubbed off on my clothes.

'Only I was thinking we could just waste the rest of the day in bed. You know. As it's my birthday.'

He gave me a look as though I had suggested having sex in front of his mother. Or even with his damned mother. Then he dipped his head under the bonnet. Not, I believe, because he wanted to see something close up.

'There's no call for all that,' I heard his muffled voice say. 'It's not a special birthday.'

In anybody else's mouth it would have sounded like a very funny joke. But it was his mouth, and I was not laughing. That was all he said. Just that. End of discussion. I had suggested spending the entire afternoon in bed with him as we had once done, right at the start, and that was his response.

I almost hit him with a wrench. Was I going to have to wait a year for the next time he might want to go to bed with me? Until the big four-oh? I mean, it was my birthday, you would have thought, wouldn't you, that he might have wanted to please me; even if he found the whole thing distasteful. Sorry, even though he found the whole thing distasteful. You would have thought that he could just have made the effort.

Like I always did with his birthdays; steeling myself to attend some damned car rally or another. Sitting there in a fold-up chair with a paperback while he preened and buffed the latest ruddy lump of metal to within an inch of its life and showed her off like some eager pimp. I would often look around at the other wives all sitting in their little fold-up chairs and think I should run screaming from the place. But you don't, do you? All those ideas about 'give and take', about accommodating your loved one's interests.

Anyway, I digress (and who doesn't after three glasses of red?). So, that was the first sign, having my offer of an afternoon of sex turned down. Or was it the culmination of a lot of little first signs? Him staying downstairs long after I had gone to bed with his filthy, much pawed car magazines. The way he wouldn't let me drive 'his' cars. That time he made me walk back from a hospital appointment as it was raining and he'd just given the car a special wax? It was as though he was absenting himself from more and more of our marriage, as if he had just slipped into the garage and was never really, fully, coming back.

I haul myself up from the kitchen table, open the fridge again and dig out a block of cheese. I know there are oatcakes somewhere.

Well after that, things got steadily worse. Children might have helped, but they were not to be. It would have been something of a miracle after all.

Perhaps if we had produced a herd of boys who loved cars our lives would have been different. Then again, perhaps it would have made it worse.

The car seats and the crumbs; the bikes scraping along his paintwork. I cannot imagine how he could have coped with that. Or with the bigger questions: 'Daddy, Daddy, can I pretend to drive?', 'I need some practice for my test, can we go in yours?', 'I've got a date, mind if I borrow your car?'

At least they were arguments I never had to watch or referee.

I don't really know what I was staying for. Some sign that it was over, perhaps? And I am a sticker not a bolter. He wasn't a bad husband. There were no bruises and some kindness. You could take him anywhere and he would blend in. Perhaps a different woman would have ignited his passion and kept it lit. I watched it splutter and spit and finally die.

Sometimes I would get in from work and just yearn, positively yearn for someone to scoop me up and give me a long cuddle. I wasn't demanding 'swinging from the chandelier' passion. Just a bit of warmth, a bit of skin against my skin. But you can't pick an orange and then be disappointed it's not an apple, can you?

Then there came the day.

I walked into the garage and saw him with yet another car and stood transfixed. Later, when I registered that I was feeling dizzy, I knew that what I saw must have made me hold my breath, too.

There he was, making love to his car. This man who, as far as I was concerned, might as well be dead from the waist down.

It was not the literal act of course, thank the Lord. I never actually caught him doing that. There was no horrible scene involving an open petrol tank and a guilty, hasty withdrawal. No, he was caressing the bitch. He was running his hand along her sides, down her bonnet, around the edge of her wheel arches and the look on his face was one of ecstasy. Well, I supposed it was, not that I had ever seen it anywhere near our dull bed. He looked overcome by something huge, completely swept away in it. The warmth in his eyes as his hand moved over her stabbed me right in the heart. She was speaking to him in a language I had never mastered and he was listening intently.

I could see his lips moving; I could almost hear the sighs and whispered endearments.

The overwhelming smell of sweat and oil caught in the back of my throat.

I should have left him then, realised it wasn't ever going to get any better for me.

I look down at the packet of oatcakes in my hand and see they are now no more than crumbs. I put the packet down and refill my glass with wine.

Not long after that incident, I joined our local walking club.

Yes, I do understand irony.

And there I managed to walk right into John. A walker and a talker, thank goodness.

At first I only saw him as a bulky man in a kagool. Then one day, after a particularly long walk, I got cramp in the calf of my right leg. He stayed back to help me, and the way his hands felt, smoothing out the pain, caressing it away; well, it was soft rain on my drought.

John and I walked rapidly through companionship and friendship and then arrived at the outskirts of lust. John was keen to go further, but I was a good girl.

Always a good girl. I told him everything, but I could not take that final step.

A vow is a vow, after all.

I turned my back on John and reapplied myself to my marriage.

Determination could be the glue that kept us together. I borrowed money, suggested a holiday, a second honeymoon. We discussed where we should go and I was firm. Not Le Mans, not the Nuremburg Ring, or Monaco or Detroit, but Venice.

'Why?' he asked.

'No roads,' I said.

He gave me his look. He knew it was a test, I knew it was a test.

He nodded his head and I felt such relief. Everything was going to be all right.

But as ever it was what he had not said that I should have listened to.

I get up and throw the broken oatcakes into the bin along with the remainder of the jar of olives. I put the cheese back into the fridge. I wash up the plate and leave it to dry in the rack.

Of course, it was not a new start. Two weeks ago I went to pay the deposit for the holiday, only to be informed that there were not enough funds in our account. I knew before I got home what I would find.

There she was in the garage. Shiny, svelte, expensive-looking.

He was already fiddling under her bonnet. I watched the infinitesimal adjustments he made to her. He fumbled and swore and could never locate anything with any precision where I was concerned.

I stood there for quite a while. He knew I was there, I could tell. And then I left the house and did not stop walking until I reached John.

I have walked over to his house quite a few times since then, while my husband tinkered and fine-tuned another. And during those visits I learned that John was passionate about many things. India, wine, Mozart, but mainly, me. Not me after Mozart, or second to Mumbai, but me up front, in front, first, first, first.

I learned that there are many ways to die, too. Like John's wife, quickly and unexpectedly, or like me, over time, unnecessarily.

Today I will not walk to John's. I have too much to carry.

I take the empty wine bottle out into the garage and drop it in the box marked 'glass'. Then I say goodbye to his latest; the one he finally left me for.

She is quite, quite beautiful. And completely heartless.

He would do well to remember that.

Judging a Book by its Cover

BY ADELE PARKS

*H*elena sank back into her couch, balancing a floral china teacup and saucer and two plain biscuits; she took a moment to admire the neat and tidy environment she had re-established. She loved the children coming home from university for the weekend. She liked to hear their news and see them eat properly; she didn't mind that they brought a huge bag of laundry each. She was their mother and as such would do anything to care and help. That's what mothers were for.

Besides, Amanda and Michael never took her for granted; they were both truly grateful for her attention and concern. They showered her with brief pecks on the cheek as they garbled, 'Thank you' and 'You're the best, Mum'. Helena admitted that at nineteen and twenty-one her offspring were 'on paper, adults' but they still seemed very young to her. Life was so tough, stressful and expensive nowadays, much harder than when she and Eddie started out; the children often appeared to be just as vulnerable as they were on their very first day of school. She encouraged them to visit home as regularly as possible. She didn't mind the extra work.

That said, they were incredibly messy. After they returned back to university the house always had the appearance of a flustered maiden aunt who has had one too many sherries at a wedding reception; everything was a little askew and nothing made sense. White towels were bruised with smudges of mascara, plates of cold, half-finished food took refuge under Michael's bed, jars and bottles repelled their lids, bins spat out litter and coffee tables were tattooed with coffee-cup rings.

Mrs Cooper, Helena's cleaner, came in every Wednesday for three hours and had been doing so for eighteen years. Helena decided she would not wait for Wednesday to re-establish calm and order in the house, so she tidied it herself.

For one thing, Mrs Cooper was asthmatic and older than Helena by a generation, therefore not an especially effective cleaner. Anything beyond light dusting was a stretch. Helena didn't actually need a cleaner as she was the only one at home nowadays, but she kept Mrs Cooper because she appreciated continuity. She couldn't very well just fire the woman after so many years of devotion (as Eddie had done to Helena). Besides there were certain things a woman of Helena's standing was supposed to have – a detached property, a cleaner, a window cleaner, a husband who worked in the City. She hadn't been able to hold on to her husband but she was determined to cling to the rest.

Their divorce had been relatively amicable. Eddie moved to Hong Kong with his younger, prettier, blonder (sillier!) PA and left Helena with the family home and enough cash to get by. Guilt, she supposed, motivated him to find his way to a squabble-free divorce. Helena didn't miss Eddie any more. He was absent long before they divorced. Helena found she'd been able to fill the gap he left with nothing more than a tasteful flower arrangement. Helena sipped her tea and surveyed the now dust-free surfaces, the neatly stacked magazines and the polished floorboards with the same pleasure as other women ogled George Clooney in a surgeon's outfit. A tap at the front door awoke her from her domestic fantasy.

'Afternoon, Helena.'

Helena sighed quietly. She'd really prefer it if David, the window cleaner, would call her Mrs Jackson but he insisted on being familiar. If ever she tried to call him Mr Simmons (which was the name on his van), he would make a joke about his dad being retired and insist that she call him Dave; they compromised with David.

'Would you be so good as to refill my bucket?' David asked with a polite smile. He always asked for fresh water but Helena didn't mind. It was an unequivocal joy to her when the sunlight bounced through her streak-free windows and splattered into the immaculate front room.

'Have you been spring-cleaning?' he asked, craning his neck into the spotless hallway. David was always cheerful and made pleasant small talk. On cold, blowy days he commented how fresh everything was; on a hot day he didn't grumble but said it was lovely weather to be outside in.

Eddie had always been dour; he didn't 'do' chat. Not that it was fair to compare; one was a window cleaner and therefore carefree and with little responsibility. Eddie had an important job with a great deal of stress, so of course he was too busy to chat. Or to be kind. He never noticed Helena's polished surfaces. 'Would you like a cold drink? I've some delicious home-made lemonade, I hasten to add it wasn't made in this home. I bought it from a farm. The children were here, we had a jaunt out.'

David followed her through to the kitchen. 'How are the kids? Working hard?'

'Fine, I think. The only thing they worry about is me. This month Amanda suggested I consider placing an ad in the lonely hearts column in *The Times*. That suggestion came hot on the heels of suggesting internet dating last month.' Helena rolled her eyes. 'She thinks I'm short on company.'

'Are you?'

'Not at all.'

David had been cleaning Helena's windows for five years. For four of those five years they barely spoke to one another. Sometimes she'd sit inside a room as he cleaned the windows outside that same room and she wouldn't acknowledge him, instead she'd keep her nose buried in her novel.

Helena found it a strangely uncomfortable situation. She didn't want to be rude; it was more that she didn't really know what to say to him. What could they possibly have in common? Then, about a year ago, David asked for some clean water and she obliged. Naturally, they shared a few words. Now they had a cup of tea or a juice together almost every week. Helena was surprised to discover that she found David extremely easy to talk to.

He knew all about the trials of her children's exams, he understood about her anxiety as to whether she ought to move her fiercely independent father into an assisted living flat. How far must a good daughter go?

David knew a lot about Helena's life.

She knew nothing of his.

He wore a wedding ring. So she thought any enquiry she might make would seem inappropriate. She also thought it would be inappropriate to admit that yes, sometimes she was short of a certain type of company. The company she couldn't get from chatting to her cleaner, or window cleaner, or even her friends at the book group.

She nervously searched around for a new topic of conversation. Suddenly David seemed very big and very male, stood in her neat and gleaming kitchen. David must have been having the same thought; his eyes flicked around the room and then settled – with some relief – on Helena's novel.

'What are you reading?'

'It's the book group's choice.'

'Any good?'

David picked up the book and started to read the blurb on the back. Irrationally, Helena felt embarrassed. She wasn't sure it was the sort of book a window cleaner would enjoy. It was very deep and complex. It was a novel split into two parts; half set in nineteenth-century India, the other part twenty years in the future.

'I'm enjoying it.'

'Why?'

Helena always had a book on the go, sometimes two. She loved diving into stories and living other people's lives for a short time. She enjoyed being challenged, exploring the world and growing her vocabulary – all from the comfort of her front room. But when anyone ever asked her about why she enjoyed reading she found it impossible to articulate.

'Oh, it's erm, unexpected,' she mumbled. 'Fancy a biscuit?'

'I think he sounds interesting,' said Cath, with a cheeky, wink-wink grin that Helena knew so well and dreaded so much.

'Who sounds interesting?' asked Liz.

'Helena's window cleaner.'

'Oughtn't we to talk about the book?' asked Helena.

It frustrated her that every month the book group followed the same chaotic course. Wine would be poured, nibbles handed around and the chatter and gossip would flow. The book would be forgotten.

'We can't start yet, everyone's not here,' said Julie. 'We're expecting a new member.'

The worst thing about the gossip, as far as Helena was concerned, was that the women tended to focus on her situation. They all had partners and were either blissfully happy or horribly miserable in their relationships; it seemed neither state was as fascinating as her single status. Since Eddie left her the book group's *raison d'être* was not to discuss analogy, imagery or even plot, it was to find Helena a new man. Helena was reluctant.

It was difficult to imagine meeting anyone new. When asked what she wanted in a man she'd say she wanted someone steady, financially secure, diligent.

'Dull, you mean,' objected Cath the first time she heard the list of prosaic expectations.

'I mean someone like Eddie.'

'But Eddie had an affair and left you,' Cath resisted adding that Eddie was dull.

'Like Eddie but without the affair,' admitted Helena.

'I think you should try something totally different,' insisted Cath.

Helena had found herself dragged to salsa classes, life drawing classes and even a bowling club, as Cath wanted Helena to meet someone with hobbies; Eddie had no interests outside work (he even chose his mistress from the selection offered at the office). Helena had yet to meet a man she liked at any of these places. Now Cath was becoming fascinated by Helena's window cleaner; the thought terrified Helena. Cath was a force to be reckoned with when she latched on to an idea, she was like a starving dog with a juicy meat cut. Helena was certain she did not want to date her window cleaner. She had to nip the idea in the bud instantly.

'He's not my type.'

'You don't have a type, there's only ever been Eddie,' said Liz.

'Window cleaners earn good money nowadays, you know,' added Julie.

Helena blushed. 'It's not the money. I don't need money, it's . . .' She didn't know how to phrase it without sounding snobby.

'I don't think we'll have that much to talk about.'

'But you said that you find him easy to talk to. You tell him all about your kids and dad.'

'Yes, but I'm not sure he'll have any interest in art, or literature, or even politics.'

Cath hooted with laughter. 'He might be a perfect bit of rough.'

'That's what you think I need, is it?' said Helena, trying not to become flustered.

'Who is to say he's rough just because he works with his hands?' demanded Karen. She was trying to make a sensible point but Cath just shrieked with laughter again and made a joke about the importance of finding a man who is good with his hands. The token male group member, Mike, wiggled uncomfortably on his chair.

The doorbell rang, saving Helena.

'Can I introduce Dave Simmons,' said Julie with a beam.

For a nano-second Helena didn't recognise David. She knew his face as well as the back of her hand but seeing him out of context and in smarter clothes startled her. He startled all the other female members of the group too. They sat with their backs straight and chests out, grinning and wide-eyed.

'Take a seat next to Helena,' said Cath, pointing to the free chair. Helena smiled at David but before they got the chance to tell the rest of the group that they knew one another Mike seized the moment to talk about the book.

'I don't suppose you've had a chance to read it yet, have you, Dave?'

'I just picked it up this week but managed to finish it this morning.'

'Good going. It's chunky, isn't it?'

'Yes, but fascinating.'

'What did you like about it, Dave?' asked Cath.

'I was transported. The descriptions were lyrical. The characters were so complex and believable, even though their dilemmas were very removed from my own experience.'

Helena couldn't agree more. She nodded enthusiastically but somehow couldn't find her tongue. For the rest of the evening Helena listened as David enthused about books. He was familiar with many classics and most of the recent prize-winners. He'd read lots of the books Helena had bought and knew she ought to read but had never got round to. He had an opinion on them all.

Helena was enthralled by each well-observed point he made and mesmerised by his perception and confidence. He was nothing like she thought him to be.

How had she known him for five years and not known him at all? The extent of her prejudice shamed her. Shivers of terror ran up her spine; she had to find a way of ensuring none of the others would inadvertently expose her by resuming the conversation about her window cleaner. If he was mentioned she was sure her snobbery and prejudice would be uncovered. She waited for a pause in the discussion and an appropriate moment to mention her relationship with David. None came.

Helena remained tense all evening; she wanted to get home. She'd call the group members tomorrow and explain the situation. Then she'd leave the group. As wonderful as the book club was, she wouldn't be able to face the members after she confessed that she had a thing for the window cleaner – who she'd previously dismissed. Helena struggled to find the arm of her coat. Over and over again she jabbed at her sleeve but somehow couldn't twist in the correct way to put it on.

David helped her.

'Thanks.' A blush flared up on her neck and crept up to the roots of her hair.

'You were very quiet this evening. I thought you liked the book.'

'I did. It's just that . . .'

Helena didn't get time to finish the sentence as Cath appeared at their side.

'She's shy.'

Cath lived just five minutes' walk from Julie's and so had seen off almost a bottle of wine; thus fortified she asked, 'Are you married?'

'Widowed, actually.'

'Oh,' said Helena. 'Sorry.'

'Nine years ago now. Look, maybe we could go for a coffee and you can tell me your thoughts on the book without a crowd,' said David to Helena.

'Don't waste your time, Dave. You're not her type,' grinned Cath.

Helena froze.

'She has a type?' asked David, with a curious and friendly grin.

Helen thought she might be ill on Julie's hall carpet.

'Yes, she's after a bit of rough. She fancies her window cleaner. You, sir, are far too educated,' joked Cath.

'That's very interesting,' said David. Helena wouldn't meet his eye but she could feel his boring into her. 'Do you think it's fair to have such pre-conceptions? Couldn't you give me a chance?'

Helena forced herself to look up.

'You're right. Just because you are well read it doesn't necessarily mean that you won't know what to do with your hands. I'd love a coffee.'

Space of my Own

BY ANNA RALPH

*I*t was a bad-tempered, blustery autumn day, but too late for Peggy to cancel. Her daughter, Eve, would already be on her way from Newcastle, hunched over the steering wheel of her Nissan Micra, inching along the A1 towards Durham. If she'd decided to come.

Time to set off. Peggy dug out her late husband's long raincoat from the cupboard under the stairs, still stiff with damp from the last time he'd worn it. She wanted to be early in any case, have a few minutes alone with her plot.

Her plot. She'd never had a garden before, never wanted one, but in the last few months before Tom had gone into the hospice she'd found herself planting window boxes. Primulas, for colour, and because they seemed to survive even when she forgot to water them. Then, later, geraniums, pansies, violas and even a miniature herb garden planted in an old bucket. Those first few nights they'd spent apart, when it was impossible to lie in the bed without him, she'd gone and sat beside the open window with her face among the flowers, breathing in their scent, while the full moon hid its face behind rags of cloud.

The allotments were only a few minutes' walk from the flat. Over the years she must have passed them hundreds of times, but she never took much notice of them. A balding hawthorn hedge divided them from the road and on the far side they were bordered by St Jude's churchyard. Several rooks circled around the tallest spire before settling to roost.

Peggy pushed on, her collar pulled up high around her neck. A knob of sun slid like melting butter towards the horizon and her shadow had begun to lengthen in front of her as if impatient to arrive. Once inside the allotments she stood for a moment and marvelled at the wild landscape. The plots were criss-crossed with narrow grass paths trodden almost bare, and dotted around there were sheds, some made of timber, others of corrugated iron and plastic, milky with age. There was no one to be seen, though there were signs of habitation; a coil of blue smoke rose from a fire, a bicycle propped against the side of a shed.

The paths were the only way to move through the plots, though the network had no logic; several led nowhere, one ended at a compost heap. She liked that, the haphazard paths mixed with the disciplined rows within the plots themselves, perfect quarters and halves, regimented columns of freshly dug earth and lines of green leafy plants she couldn't name.

The site representative had given her a map and from this she was able to work out which was her plot.

It would be obvious anyway she'd been told, it hadn't been touched in over a year. She stood in front of it. A thick matt of yellow couch grass covered the earth, broken pots scattered here and there, and a pile of what looked like rotting turnips. Well positioned though, beside the hedge, sheltered, and arranged beside the shed there was a line of sunflowers, their stalks drooping with age like a dowager's humps.

She bent down, scraped aside the rotting leaves, and dug into the earth. It was damp and warm, unexpectedly responsive to her probing fingers. When had they last held hands? Consciously, knowingly? At home? Before he'd gone into the hospice? Or the last night of his life? She swallowed, dismayed because she couldn't remember. Lately she often thought it was as though a whole chunk of her brain had gone into the grave with him.

'Goldfinches love the seeds.'

The voice startled Peggy. She spun around, pricking her hand on a thistle. She hadn't been aware of anyone else, but now there was this woman, a woollen hat pulled low over her forehead, helping her to her feet.

'Sorry, I didn't mean to startle you.'

'No, no, it's OK. I was just visiting, I'm the new . . . person for this plot.'

She raised her eyebrows and glanced over Peggy's shoulder at the plot. 'You've got your work cut out.'

'Not sure I know where to start.'

'Mine's the one in the far left corner. I'm Alice

Springs. The Ozzies named them after me,' she added with a wink.

She was thick set, broad across the shoulders and tall. Together they walked between the plots, occasionally pausing to look at one, Alice chatting away, delighted, it seemed, to have the opportunity to introduce Peggy to the other allotmenteers by way of their plots.

'That one is Mike's.'

It was a fruit garden and bordered Peggy's plot on the north side, rather beautiful and wild with several odd-looking boxes that seemed as though they might be intended to house something, hedgehogs perhaps. Peggy bent down to peer inside one of the entrances.

'And over there's Harry. His knowledge of the *Nicotania tobacum* is nothing short of encyclopaedic.'

Peggy nodded, smiled. They were people she'd know soon, have to know. There were marrow showmen, fruiterers, vegetable growers, a beekeeper and permaculturalist, whatever one of those was. What was she going to do with her plot? She didn't know anything.

'And I'm the only woman,' Alice added. 'Or I was. Would you like some coffee? I've brought a flask.'

'Actually I'm supposed to be meeting my daughter here.' Peggy looked back over the allotments to where the hedge met the road. No sign of Eve. 'Though it doesn't look as if she's coming.'

Once inside her shed, Alice took a box of brown cigarettes from her coat pocket and lit one, her face illuminated momentarily in the flame. Age had scored lines around her eyes and mouth, and her eyebrows were bushier than a man's. She didn't seem to care and she was attractive despite it, brilliant white hair, striking, tufts of which could be seen sprouting from the edges of her hat.

After a moment's awkwardness Peggy sat down on one of two deckchairs. Next to her was an old dresser that held trays full of seeds and, in a line against the small plastic window, there were cardboard inner tubes from toilet rolls, each housing a column of dark, damp soil. Right at the back, in the shadows, a cage containing a mynah bird hung from the ceiling.

'That's Roger. Or Erogenous as I sometimes call him. He likes to tease the pigeons.'

She gave a gravelly smoker's laugh. She had the trace of an American accent, which ought to have been the first thing Peggy noticed, but it had been a long time since she'd met anybody new. Before Tom died her only contact had been the home help and, towards the end, the staff at the hospice. She couldn't remember much about any of them.

'My daughter's probably got stuck in traffic, she works in Newcastle. A solicitor.'

'Oh, right. My son's a policeman.'

'Really? That's . . .' Peggy skidded to a halt, embarrassed suddenly, though she didn't know why.

Alice smiled and, after a moment, went on, talking quickly. She had a granddaughter called Annabel, used to go through on the train to see her every week, but not often now because her son had started night shifts.

339

Listening to her, Peggy felt herself relax. Here, in the confines of the shed with its warm air and earthy smells, she seemed to have crossed some kind of frontier. In one direction, behind her, row upon row of suburbia, schools and offices, and then here, the quiet, a smell of wood smoke, of damp soil, of the life growing underneath it.

'I like your plot,' she said.

'Thanks.' Alice drew hard on her cigarette and exhaled out of the door.

'Things have finished for this year, but in spring it's a gem. The start of a new season is a bit like a new lover. You forget all the disappointments that went before.'

Peggy wondered if Alice was divorced. It seemed like an odd thing to say. She looked again at the plot. There were no straight lines or angular beds here. Some areas were edged with wine bottles, bottoms up, and in the centre of one bed there appeared to be a shop mannequin's arm emerging from the ground.

'My husband died,' she heard herself say. She shifted, ashamed of how abruptly she'd blurted out the words. 'Vic. In June.'

'Oh.' Alice nodded and blew out another plume of smoke that hung in the air around her head before drifting away. 'That's tough. What did he die of?'

No one had asked her that before. They just said sorry, or sometimes they didn't say anything at all. 'Lung cancer. It took a while.'

Alice looked at her cigarette, then back at Peggy.

'Mine's dead too. His heart. Said he was going out to buy us something for dinner and dropped down dead in the pub round the corner. Poor bugger.'

'How long ago?'

'Five years.'

Peggy hesitated. 'Has it got any easier?'

'Honestly?' She stared at the burning ember of her cigarette. 'No. I live around it.'

Peggy crossed her arms, surprised by how easy it was with Alice. There was something almost illicit about the two of them sat in the shed, alive.

'Is that your daughter?'

A dark figure was walking along the path towards them, confident, as though she knew where she was going, but then she stopped. Peggy caught sight of Eve's face. Tight, nipped with tension. She was looking towards the door of the shed.

'Mum?'

'Over here.' Peggy turned to Alice. 'This is my daughter, Eve.'

The two of them shook hands. Eve was looking at Alice in such a way as to appear not to be taking her in at all. A glazed look, not really paying her attention, the way some were around old people. It made Peggy think Eve might well look at her in the same way, were she not her mother. She was surprised by this and felt a stab of resentment on Alice's behalf.

'You'll have to put your wellies on next time,' Alice was saying.

341

'Yes.' Eve tried a smile and stared at her shoes, the heels sucked into the mud.

'Well, I better be making a move,' Alice said. She put a hand on Peggy's arm.

'I'll see you around.'

'You will.' Peggy watched her leave.

'What's this about, Mum? Your message said it was important.'

'It is.' She turned back to Eve and they moved together for a brief embrace. 'I wanted you to see my plot.'

'Mum, do you know what I had to do to get out of work this afternoon?'

'It won't take long.'

'I know what an allotment looks like, just can't fathom why you'd want one.'

'To grow vegetables.' She took a deep breath. 'It's wonderful you came.'

'If I'd known why I was coming I mightn't have bothered.' Eve sighed and brushed her hair back from her face. 'What are you going to do with an allotment? They're for old men.'

Peggy strode up the path ahead of her, making for her own plot, partly to get away from the sharpness of Eve's face, partly because she needed reminding why she'd wanted it so much.

She pointed at the decaying rectangle of land. 'I'm going to grow things. I'm not going to sit around any more feeling sorry for myself, I'm going to come here.'

'Like the sculpture classes you didn't go to? Like Italy? You were going to go to Italy, remember?'

'I didn't feel ready then.'

Eve jangled her car keys. It was a Mercedes with a computer that beeped until you'd put your seatbelt on. She was doing all right, she'd got the promotion she'd been working for, though Peggy didn't have any real sense of what it meant to her.

'Are you happy, Eve?'

'Please, Mum. Don't start that.'

Perhaps too much had gone unsaid. But there had to be some point of contact between them. Sometimes it was painful just to look at her, her father's hands and eyes. They'd shared more than that though, a humour that had always put Peggy on the outside. Not so that it hurt; she'd loved watching them together, but they'd shared a bond that she and Eve didn't have.

'I wish you could forgive me.'

'What for?'

'I know we swore he'd never go into a hospice, Eve, but you weren't living with it, day in, day out. I'd reached the end of the line.'

'That's what the home help was for, they'd have come three times a day if you'd wanted.'

'What about the nights? You could go home, to work, to a life. I didn't have one. For the best part of six months I didn't go out.'

'Look, Mum, it's over now. What's the sense in going over it? I'm not blaming you.'

And she hadn't, not anything she'd said, but every

look, every gesture in those last few weeks had felt like a silent condemnation. Peggy looked behind her to Alice's shed, but the door was closed. 'My God, Eve, I deserve some respect for the job I did.'

'I do respect you. I know how hard it was. I know . . .' She trailed off and broke into sobs.

It was the first time Peggy had seen her cry over the death, she'd been stone-faced even at the funeral. She took Eve by the shoulders and pulled her close, gripping her tightly around the back with both arms.

'I won't let you go. I love you, Eve. Do you hear?'

'I'm sorry. I miss him so much. I'm sorry.'

Gradually her sobs lightened, but Peggy didn't let go, not until Eve pushed her back and looked at her. It had started to rain.

Eve wiped away her tears on the back of her hand.

'You know, the best way to get rid of slugs is to have ducks,' Peggy said, glancing up the full length of the plot.

'What?' Eve laughed, incredulously. 'You're going to turn into a real weirdo, aren't you?'

'There's a good chance.' She took Eve's hand and for a minute or two they just stood and looked at each other. 'Your Dad loved sunflowers.'

'I remember.'

'I'll plant them every year.'

'Come on,' Eve said. 'I thought we might try that new restaurant in town if you like?'

'Sure. I just want to do one thing.' Peggy walked across to the shed where a spade was resting against the door. It looked worn, half the handle missing, but after a few attempts she was able to dig down into the soil. She dug part of one row and then stood at one end and looked at the line of new earth. 'Yes, that's it.'

The Handyman

BY JENNY STEEL

Stella was, is, my first-born and now only child. Since her father's death, she has chosen to monitor my well-being via weekly phone calls, a chore made easier by the knowledge that I am, as I have always been, 'fine'. Any suggestion of inadequacy would threaten our mutual independence.

For my part, I choose to answer her calls and her questions while in the security of my sitting room, a space pleasing to my eye, made comfortable by my own hand, echoing as it does the colours and patterns of the garden.

It was from here that I chose to let her know of the small change I had made to my circumstances.

'Oh, by the way, dear, I've found a handyman at last.'

Silence.

'What do you mean "found"?'

'Usual channels – you know, word of mouth.' I lied, thinking of him standing on my doorstep, holding the postcard that had long been pinned on the post office board.

347

'What about references?'

I had named her Stella in the hope of liberating her from the conventional family mould, but at forty she was still, as she had always been, a disappointingly pedantic child.

'Immaculate.' For this was how I assessed my own judgement of the man who had presented himself.

Dressed in the colours of the earth and seasons, his tweed jacket, moleskin trousers and working shirt were of stiff material, grown comfortable with age, as indeed had he.

Ash-handled tools, patinated with use and care, arranged in a roughened leather pannier were eloquent in their recommendation of this working man.

'Where does he come from?'

I suppressed the desire to shock with a literal truth.

'He's local. I've seen him around. He rides a bicycle. Oh, and another thing – it could be an advantage . . .' I had thought about attempting a light laugh, '. . . he doesn't speak . . . or hear.'

With my free hand, I twisted a wilting blossom from the pale pink cyclamen on my writing table. Responding mechanically to the expected, blustering cautions, I recalled to mind the few fluttering and cupping movements of his huge hands with which he had conveyed his silent world.

'I promise you that it is not a problem. We can communicate very well.'

And so it was that Joseph Jones came into my life.

348

Our contract was set in accordance with the few terms I had suggested on the postcard.

Each Tuesday and Thursday he would arrive promptly at 9.30 a.m. and work as needed in the house or garden for three hours. He was to be paid by cheque each week. Extra expenses to be covered in cash.

Having myself a distaste for either receiving or handing out payment, I decided it would be mutually most comfortable to carry out our commercial transactions as indirectly as possible. The due amount was to be placed in an envelope and left in a small tray in the greenhouse. Any requirements that either of us had were to be noted on a pad hung by the door.

I came to enjoy writing 'Mr J. Jones' on the fibrous brown envelope I had selected as appropriate. Although I checked each day, several weeks passed before I finally received a request – for raffia, 'which I can supply if you wish. Price £2.39.'

He wrote using a gardener's pencil, soft and dark. The letters were each clearly formed and flowing with a regular angularity. I found myself tracing their path.

'Thank you, Mr Jones. Please supply.' Then I added, 'I too prefer raffia.'

He was, as I expected, a most competent and reliable worker. I rarely had to indicate a job that needed attention. Peeling paintwork, loose screws, dripping taps were spotted and remedied without comment. He seemed able to gentle the earth into a soft tilth, easing the path of tender plants so that they flowered earlier and with greater vigour than I remembered. I knew that this was fanciful, but the notion pleased me. I soon began to feel a comfort in his regular coming and going and in watching him work at each task with quiet persistence.

There was about him an independence of attitude, an assuredness of manner, with nothing of the subservient. He was clearly unimpressed by machines, the aids to my self-sufficiency, acquired on well-meaning advice. I could not resent that, without reference to me, he consigned the expensive motor mower, the strimmer, the leaf blower and shredder to the shed and hauled out equipment and machines long forgotten.

He must have worked on these in his own time, cleaning and sharpening, oiling and setting, until they were fitting companions for his own cherished tools.

I am not such a fool that I did not recognise that I was becoming mesmerised by my enigmatic handyman, but, truthfully, it was not imagination that the cut grass smelt sweeter when mown by a clicking, purring cylinder. There were no more angry sounds of demented disciplining. Mr Jones, Joseph, had brought something of his own silence to my garden.

Of course there were problems.

In the early days, I made an effort to learn the hand shapes of the alphabet, trying to grasp the basics of signing. I hoped to surprise him as I began to combine my fingers and hands to form G . . . O . . . O . . . D . . . The effect was as if I had slapped him. Very gently he placed one large hand over mine and held it still, then stepping back, almost in apology, he raised his hand, palm tilted towards me, long, loosely jointed fingers outspread. In exaggerated slow motion, he nodded his head to the right, and gave me the accustomed smile of greeting that he and I both understood.

I recall one particular day. It had been raining – big coins of rain that seemed to kick up the smell of earth. Joseph – I had started to call him Joseph by then – was working in the greenhouse. He loved the build-up of warmth in there and used it almost as a workshop. Although his back was towards me and the door was closed, as clear as the song of the blackbird, I heard whistling, and in the sweet, squeezed notes, I recognised the distinctive pattern of tunes and rhythms from my youth.

The beaker of coffee I had brought for him was almost too hot for my hands, but I cupped it against me, and moving like a predatory cat, sought to prolong the moment and savour the sound. Sweet tendrils of honeysuckle curved over the glass, obscuring the corner, but as I inched on to the shingle surround, the slightest shift of movement was enough to make him aware of my presence.

The whistling stopped. He stood and half turned, as straight as the low-angled panes would allow, looked straight at me, gave a broad, all-embracing smile and the exaggerated bow of a performer. The coffee became an accepted tribute and I mimed my applause, and the moment to question had passed.

There was, too, a misunderstanding over my beloved

black elder. Its untrammelled, searching growth had lifted the fragrant pink blossoms beyond my reach, threatening my summer wine production. I wanted him to tidy it, to take the long growth and use the withes as a frame for sweet peas. By chance, I first heard and then saw him lopping through old, twisted, varicose branches, exposing the heartwood.

'Stop! Joseph! MISTER Jones, what the hell are you doing?' I knew that I was shrieking.

He spun round, losing his balance on the old apple ladder. The lopper fell forward and he attempted to catch the open blade. Across the pink palm of his hand, a deep gash opened. We watched in horror as crimson blood began to surge from the wound. Instinctively, I tore a towel from the washing line, ripped it into strips and pressed a pad to the flow. His fingers closed over mine increasing the pressure until the flow had been staunched, but not before his blood had seeped between my fingers. Overwhelmed by relief and moved by tenderness, I raised the stains to my lips, and he touched my shoulder, understanding.

I drove to the hospital. The twenty-odd miles – penalty of country living – had never threatened to be longer. It was the first time that we had shared so intimate a space and I became intensely aware of his presence. We could each breathe the other, aware of the smoke of a bonfire, smells of cooking and creosote, leather, wax polish and rosemary . . . skin . . . hair. Neither of us looked at the other, but the contact, the comfort, was palpable.

He wanted to go in alone. There was no doubt of his need for Accident and Emergency treatment, and I had no qualms about his ability to communicate. With the same protective obsession of a mother at the school gate, I watched him walk towards the white doors. Anxious that others should not rush to wrong judgement, I tried to see him with objective eyes, noticing for the first time the slight bandiness of his long legs. A tall man, loose-limbed, I liked the suggestion of awareness in the way he inclined his back, or perhaps – I tried to be realistic – it was a stoop of age. If I tried to recapture the first impression I had formed, I would say that he was functionally kempt – his close-cropped grey hair, neat like an astrakhan cap. I felt almost proudly possessive as, with his usual gentleness of manner, he stood aside and held the door to aid another patient. For this is what he was – a patient man.

But I am not a patient woman. I tensed to move each time the exit doors slid open, ready to claim him. Unable to sit any longer, I got out of the car at the same time as he came out.

My concentration had been so total that I did not notice the Gaylord sisters approaching. They had grown more like twin walruses than ever, wrapped in shiny black, pendulous-bodied, bullet-headed and, I swear, with visible moustaches.

'Betty. Betty Preston!' they honked in unison, swaying towards me.

I hurried Joseph towards the car.

'We heard you'd got a man. But nobody told us . . .' Their beady eyes flashed, exchanging arch looks, jowls wobbling, raising wide nostrils to sniff the air, heads weaving together, apart, in choreographed movement. Then they looked in wonder directly at Joseph and extravagantly mouthed the unspeakable words . . .

'HE'S . . . BLACK!'

I took Joseph's arm and opened the passenger door, controlling my venom.

'Oh really. How wonderful. I hadn't noticed. And you may be interested to know that Mr Jones is in fact deaf. But he is not blind.'

I knew that Joseph must have seen their reaction, and I was incensed, furious on his behalf. He felt my anger but did not seem to share it. Instead, he cupped his uninjured hand first across his mouth, then against his eyes and then against his ear and I recognised his mimed philosophy of speak no evil, see no evil, hear no evil. But I knew only too well what pleasure would be taken by those who lived by a more vitriolic code.

Stella's phone call came that evening, even more promptly than I had expected.

'I'm coming to see you.'

Could I possibly guess why? Usually she said, 'I'll come and see you some time. Or you must come to us, when we are less busy.'

'I'm coming on Thursday morning.'

Surprise, surprise. Any contribution from me was obviously superfluous. My compliance was assumed.

In spite of his injured hand, Joseph was working in

the garden when she arrived, tapping vine eyes into the wall, preparing to train the old clematis into better ways. I wished he could have had the same influence on my daughter.

I watched him through the kitchen window while Stella clattered dishes and nosed into cupboards, her high heels irritating on the tiled floor. All the time she was talking, hectoring. It was the brittle tone of exasperation that she assumed to indicate to me, to the world, that she cared.

'I will have my say. You may have forgotten that this was my father's house.'

My home.

'What would he say?'

Very little to me – he never did.

'What about the neighbours?'

What neighbours? Old friends had all moved, were dead, or in care homes. Incomers, weekenders led different lives.

She was generating her own steaming resentment. Her words were such bitter anathema to me that I shut them out, and focused only on what I found pleasing, gentle. I looked at Joseph.

'What do you pay him?'

Not enough, not nearly enough. Her very presence was making me adhere ever more strongly to Joseph. I would pay him more. Ask him to work longer hours . . . more days.

'And what is all this rubbish about him being deaf?'

I'm listening.

'The Gaylords spoke to Lizzie Frame. Her daughter works in casualty and she said categorically, CATE-GORICALLY, that he spoke just like everyone else. He was able to tell the doctor what happened, AND he heard his name called and could understand everything they said to him.' She chose to emphasise her words by banging a metal spoon on the old wooden table, careless of dents, inflicting her damage.

My lack of response was no longer stubborn wilful-ness. I was stunned. The pain that flared in my stomach ripped into my heart, and took all breath from my body.

'Now will you get rid of him? He has lied to you.' The final blow.

She and I both recognised her victory.

My eyes could no longer focus. Like my brain, they had become bleary. Joseph had become the prop to my world and he was to be taken away. I was again to be bereft.

I responded with the words and the voice of a stranger.

'I will speak to him. You are right. If he has . . . misled . . . me . . . But not today.'

As Stella perceived me, I felt myself to be – a vulnerable, silly old woman, prey to any self-seeker, victim of my own foolishness.

The next time that Joseph was working in the greenhouse, his territory, concentrating on pricking out seedlings, I stood a little away from the door.

'Mr Jones, please will you come into the house. I

wish to speak to you,' and I turned away, steeling myself to composure.

I chose to see him in my sitting room. He was conscious of his working clothes, unwilling to sully the pale colours. My insistence overrode the awkwardness and he sat. The truth was that, even in my hurt, I could not allow him a cap-in-hand demeanour.

'Why, Joseph? Why should you deceive me?'

Was I expecting shame, explanations, apologies?

He looked at me steadily. And then he spoke: 'When I came to you, we agreed a contract.' His voice was soft, the consonants blurred, the vowels elongated into a rhythm that lulled. He pulled my old postcard from his pocket.

'These were your terms, and these . . .' He again simulated a world of silence with his cupped hands . . . 'were mine.'

I was stunned by the ingenuousness of the man. He forestalled my response.

'I came to you, as I have come to many ladies, to help with odd jobs. This is my contract. What is it that makes these ladies think that because they have paid for my time, they have bought my mind? Mrs Preston, have you any idea of how some of these ladies can talk? Forgive me, Mrs Preston, but a man has to protect himself from the prattling of women.'

I thought of the Gaylords. I thought of Stella in full flow, and I remembered, to my shame, my own strident command. I knew his thoughts matched mine, but there was humour in his eyes as he said, 'You, my dear Mrs Preston, are not a prattling woman.'

I took the postcard from him, picked up a soft pencil, 3B as I remember, and added: 'Good Sense of Humour absolutely essential. Must be able to whistle "Stardust"'.

So Joseph stayed, splashing my muted garden with the vibrance of canna lilies, and we drank the elderflower wine, and my world felt good again, listening to the garden, and speaking volumes.

My, how that man can talk!

The Last Joan

BY ROSIE THOMAS

I think I might have been the last baby girl in the world to be named Joan.

No, I'm not going to tell you the exact date. I don't need to, really.

You can take it as falling somewhere in the span of history between Joan of Arc and 1963, in which year – according to those over-familiar lines of Philip Larkin's – sexual intercourse began. After which significant date, could anyone imagine one of the sweat-slippery protagonists engrossed in those exciting bedroom discoveries, supposedly unknown before the sixties, being called Joan? Or, following the Beatles' first LP, do you suppose that a single one of those petal-painted girls in loon pants and velvet waistcoats, dancing with their elbows in the air and their fingers twining imaginary vine tendrils, went by my name?

Of course not. Sky or Saffron or Layla, that would be more like it.

But I am Joan. Not old enough to be an Ethel or an Evangeline and, on the evidence of my name, not young either. *D'un certain age*, then.

(I hate the archness of that phrase, don't you?)

I read recently in a Sunday newspaper – I'm quoting now – that 'the central issue for older women is invisibility'.

The lines jumped out at me from a mass of newsprint, because I am aware of the approach of absence. My extremities are already fading away; you could probably read the newspaper through the palms of my hands or the soles of my feet and my calves and thighs and upper arms, which were once so nicely curved and satiny, only later becoming pale and doughy, are now quite insubstantial. I have lost a bit of weight, you see.

Before too long, all that will be left of me will be a dim blur where my centre once was, a sketchy suggestion of some appendages and a face hovering in the air. I imagine that even this much will finally melt away, leaving only a disembodied frown, the opposite of the Cheshire Cat.

No, of course I'm not being serious.

I'm only playing with this idea of fading from view because of what seems to be going on in my body. On the other hand, when I found my glasses and read the rest of the article, I learned that the Sunday newspaper's expert was actually writing about how we're so bombarded with images of youth and sexiness these days that we older women feel robbed of our very identities because men no longer desire us.

Can this really be true?

I can hardly believe such a proposition, but then this is a Joan speaking.

Maybe as a Zoë I would be out at this very moment, getting botulinum toxin shot into my forehead in the hope that men on scaffolding might start whistling at me again. I would probably be trawling the internet for a younger lover.

I'm laughing now but my daughter tells me I do frown a lot. She wouldn't say that I have no identity though. She'd laugh too and then there would be that comical puckering up of her mouth that she's been doing since she was a baby. I can hear her voice right now, even though she's such a long way away.

'God, Mum. No identity? You? Ha. Do you re-member the time when you stood up in the middle of Planky Carpenter's speech at the parents' assembly and said that the school should have an open admissions policy? Matt and I wished we were invisible.'

There you are. My daughter. I may pre-date 1963 and I may not be called Tigerlily but I fell in love, married and had children, two of them.

And therefore I know that sex didn't begin when Larkin claims it did. It just began to get talked about, which might be the same thing as far as he was con-cerned, but not for me. I know for sure that passion pre-dates the Beatles (and Joan of Arc as well, I'm prepared to bet). I'm not talking about just marrying and quietly doing your procreative duty between the sheets either but about the real thing.

My husband's name was Raymond, which falls into the same category as Joan, doesn't it? He died suddenly at the age of fifty-eight on a fishing trip with his friend

Harry. Acute cardiac infarction. He worked all his life as a market gardener and he was an ordinary decent husband and father.

In bed, though, for the thirty-four years of our marriage, Ray and I discovered something the newspapers never consider. It was simple satisfaction with each other. I don't mean just having orgasms, a topic which I now understand to be acceptable at almost any gathering, but a completeness that had its centre in our bedroom and then reached far beyond those four walls.

Yes, if you want to know, the earth did move for us.

That line (Hemingway, I believe) is also over-used.

We were very, very happy together.

Enough. I'm only talking to myself while I search for my other shoe but even so I'm not going to say any more. I remember what I remember and I know what I know. And with all this knowledge, with a life behind me and two children to show for it, why should I feel stricken by invisibility?

There now, I've been so absorbed in my one-sided conversation and the shoe hunt that I've forgotten why I'm going out and needed two matching shoes in the first place. But that hooting will be the minicab and it's the doctor's appointment. One left, one right, that will have to do.

I'm coming, what's the matter with the man?

By the time I reach the front gate he's backing up, ready to drive away again. I step off the kerb right in front of his bumper so he sticks his head out of the driver's window.

'Look out! Thought you'd decided not to bother, love.'

He's putting aside his newspaper, cocking one eyebrow to the rear-view mirror and listening to the noise and static booming out of his radio, all at the same time. I climb into the back seat.

'Summerhill Surgery, right?'

'That is correct.'

We are already hurtling down the road.

Outside the surgery he takes my money and continues a conversation with an unseen third party, presumably via some form of mobile phone. 'Ta love,' he says in my general direction.

The doctor's receptionist is the young impatient one and the waiting room is crowded.

'Mrs Ambler,' I announce myself. She stares into her computer screen and taps at the keyboard.

'Hello there, Joan. I'm afraid Dr Harris is running a few minutes behind. D'you mind helping us with our customer survey while you're waiting, dear?'

I'm rather unevenly balanced, because of the shoes. When I turn to see where she's pointing, I catch my heel and almost tip over. There's another woman coming towards me and the first thing I notice is the flash of concern in her face. She hurries past people's legs and shopping bags and pushchairs and takes hold of my arm. Her sari is pink with a gold-patterned border and the folds sweetly rustle as she guides me into her office cubicle.

'Are you all right?' she murmurs, helping me to a

chair. I'm glad to sit down but I'm not sure that I want to be surveyed.

'What's this about?'

'We want to find out whether you are satisfied with the service we provide here at the surgery, Mrs Ambler.' She looks imploringly at me and her gentleness makes me regret being irritable. She has a broad, smooth, young face with a red bindi and is very plump. At her waist a thick roll of satiny brown flesh swells between her tight, shocking-pink top and the paler folds of her sari. The colours are so bright that they seem to set the air vibrating. But I can see that her eyelids are swollen and there are traces of tears on her cheeks.

'What's your name?' I ask.

She looks surprised. 'Sunayana. Shall we begin? I could fill in the answers for you, if you'd rather.'

'No, thank you.'

I read the printed form (a choice of several languages). You can tick a box to indicate whether you are pleased, very pleased or insanely delighted with the appointments system at Summerhill Surgery and so on for half a dozen further questions to which a response of indifference or even dissatisfaction does not appear to be an option. There follows a much longer section devoted to establishing my ethnicity and sexuality.

What business is it of theirs, may I ask?

Lies, damned lies and statistics, I can hear Ray growl. He hated all kinds of form-filling, bureaucracy and public intrusion into private lives and Matthew and Kate are the same. Their father's legacy.

I scrawl a line through the questions, let the pen drop and Sunayana and I look at each other.

'Do you . . . do you know that you are wearing odd shoes, Mrs Ambler?'

'Yes, I do. What does Sunayana mean?'

'It means "one with beautiful eyes".'

'Then why have you been making them red and swollen with crying?'

Shoes or tears, it's one personal question in response to another I think.

She bites her lip, which is the colour of a fig's ripe heart. She doesn't want to seem unprofessional but the urge to tell is too much for her. Sometimes it is easier to talk to a stranger.

'It is my son. He has been making trouble in school. You know I am working because I must, but Viru is angry with me and so disobedient. I think if I was at home for more time in the day, I could make a difference but then I would not be earning money.'

She tries to shrug but now the tears are rolling down her face.

'I am sorry,' she sniffs.

A box of tissues stands on the desk between us. I twitch one loose and Sunayana uses it to mop her eyes. I reach out, rather stiffly, and put my hand over her free one. Hers is warm and smooth as chocolate, dimpled at the knuckles, and the only resemblance to my own is that we both have four fingers and a thumb.

'I am sure you are doing your best. Children do grow up, you know. You think they never will and you believe that every mistake they make on the way is yours, but that's maternal guilt. Guilt goes with mothering like salt goes with the sea. You should tell your Viru that he's lucky. Ask him to imagine what his life would be like if he didn't have your love to play with.'

I can tell how much she loves him. It's written in her tear-stained face and I can hear the sigh of it in her voice.

Can you love or be loved too much, I wonder? Thinking of Raymond, I don't believe so.

Sunayana glances at my spoiled form. She withdraws her hand from beneath mine and squares the paper on the desktop.

'Do you have children, Mrs Ambler?'

'Two. They're in their thirties now. My daughter emigrated, she runs a successful travel business in Australia and my son is married and lives down in London. He's got a daughter of his own.'

They named her Page. You might as well call a child Table or Carrot but I wouldn't say as much to them. And under any name my granddaughter would be the most exquisite creature in the world.

'Viru is not yet thirteen.'

'In that case, believe me that the worst is still to come.'

I meant it but Sunayana's dark eyebrows shoot up and she starts to giggle.

'Poor me,' she groans, but suddenly she is laughing so much that her shoulders shake and a fold of her sari slides down her upper arm. She secures it again and covers her mouth with her hand, trying to collect herself. Her amusement is infectious and now I find that I am laughing too. They can probably hear us out in the waiting room, even over the hacking coughs and the crying babies.

'Much better,' I tell her. 'That suits you more than crying.'

When we have command of ourselves again she says, 'Mrs Ambler, maybe you will tell me now why you are wearing odd shoes?'

I look down at our feet. Hers in flat slippers, round-toed and defenceless. And mine, one brown suede, laced, and one slip-on with garden mud crusted on the toe and heel.

I'm trying to frame a reason but the words come out anyhow.

'Because I miss my husband.'

She nods, and I know she won't try to force any more questions on me.

Nor do I try to give her any more advice.

Of course, I can't tell what will happen to her boy. Maybe he will end up hot-wiring cars or buying over-the-counter medications and cooking them up into crystal meth. Or maybe he will study for his accountancy exams and marry a suitable girl, just like in her dreams. Having met his mother, I know which outcome I would bet my diminished pension on.

Sunayana and I just look at each other.

'What about the survey, Mrs Ambler?'

I sigh. 'Go on then. You can fill it in for me. Tick all the insanely delighted boxes if you like. And underneath that ridiculous and intrusive "sexuality" section you can write, "I am not invisible and I never shall be".'

She looks confused, but I can hear the receptionist calling my name. The doctor is standing in his doorway, scanning the rows of seats. I stand up, careful with my feet.

'Thank you,' I tell Sunayana and I mean it. I walk lopsided back through the waiting room, past the pushchairs, the young mothers and the phlegmy old men.

Once I am safely inside the doctor's office, he tells me to take a seat.

'Well, Joan . . .' he says.

His broad, scrubbed hands are resting on a buff folder. Sun is shining on the leaves outside the window and a poster on the wall behind him shows a circle of laughing babies. There is one of every conceivable colour, of course.

I look my doctor straight in the eye.

'Go on,' I say.

Forty Wonderful

BY ADRIANA TRIGIANI

I've lost myself. It doesn't help one bit that my husband, after nineteen years of marriage, put the following in my birthday card:

'My darling: you are not forty-one. You are . . .

forty wonderful.'

This is all well and good, if you are a vintage 1968 Maserati or a bottle of platinum Parisian bubbly champagne, but for me, a semi-sensible woman, this message is a gong, a gong of a giant bell, ringing the chimes of death. It's not that the number itself is so high, but rather, the realisation that it will go higher and higher still, and as the number rises, so will go my highest dreams, up and out, through the clouds like a pink balloon on its way to some faraway place, like, say, Australia. You see, I've reached most of my dreams, and now, at forty-one, am in crisis. I have to find new dreams, set new goals, devise a new way of being, and the truth is: I've never been one for the reinvention business.

I am one of those women who thought that survival was thriving. I married Alex at twenty-two, had our twins Emma and Charlotte at twenty-three, and now, eighteen years later, I look down at what I just wrote, and my life is reduced to years and numbers, markers and set points, instead of faces and places. I'm a master of the slog, of the details of life. I married young, had the children, kept the house and got a job as soon as the girls were in school. It's out of a textbook, really, but what book? And who wrote it?

I've been the assistant accountant at The John Belding Firm for twelve years, and I'm so apt, that it looks as though I could be there another forty – easily. I've carried the same lunch to work for twelve years: a turkey on white with tomato and mustard, a small bag of raw carrots and a thermos of ice water. Some days, I surprise myself with a cup of yogurt or a red twizzler licorice whip, but only when I think I should shake things up.

The train platform in Chatham, New Jersey, is packed with commuters on their way to New York City. The June sun hangs over the smoky skies like an orange button. Men in suits have loosened their ties in the heat. The women sling their suit jackets over their arms, while planting their feet to read the newspaper, or scroll through the latest novel on Kindle.

The scent of freshly applied cologne, a mix of patchouli and freesia, provides a fresh jolt and reminds me that the working class still enjoys some extras – in a bad economy, at least we can put on our lipstick and give ourselves a spritz of something exotic. The faces on the commuters tell a different story. There's a slight tension, perhaps it's the tardy 7.40 a.m. train, or the first blast of summer heat, but this is far from a peppy bunch on this Monday morning. Somber would describe the group as a whole. And me? The most somber of all.

'Can you believe this heat?'

I look up from my notebook. 'It's hot all right.'

'Global warming,' the man says definitively.

I shove the pen into the spiral binding. 'Have you noticed that everything that goes wrong, or is uncomfortable or unpleasant is now blamed on global warming?'

The man throws his head back and laughs. He's about my age. He has black hair with the first flecks of white – but it's good hair. He's about six feet tall, though I'm in heels, he's still a head taller than me. He has a strong profile, and what looks like a wash of sunburn across the bridge of his nose and cheeks. He's what my mum would call 'the picture of health itself'.

'You're right,' he says. 'If there was a blizzard in June, it would be blamed on global warming.' He checks his watch. 'Is this train always late?'

'Hardly ever.'

'It's my first day at my new job, and I don't want to be late.'

'We won't be.'

'You sound so sure.' He smiles. He has beautiful teeth.

'What do you do?'

'Internet set-ups.'

'You picked the right field. The internet is here to stay.' I sound like an idiot – of course the internet is here to stay – what would replace it?

'I hope so.' He smiles again and shifts his polished black leather briefcase from his right hand to his left. He extends his hand to me. 'I'm Alex,' he says.

'Dear God, that's my husband's name,' I blurt.

'Is that a problem?'

'Never has been,' I tell him. Maybe he will think the red flush across my cheeks is the heat. I doubt it. I'm embarrassed. Well, not embarrassed exactly, attracted. I'm attracted and he knows it. And I know he knows it. This makes the sudden rash worse. 'Where are you from?' I want to get the subject off of me and on to him as quickly as possible.

'Florida. The past six years in Florida.'

'You're used to the heat.'

'Not really. I'm from Pennsylvania originally, and I'm actually a fan of the four seasons.'

'Not me. I'd move to the Bahamas if I could,' I tell him.

'Why don't you?' he smiles.

This is interesting. I just admitted that I'd like to live somewhere warm, and I've never said those words aloud to anyone – not even my own Alex, my Alex without the good hair. 'Maybe I will some day,' I tell him.

'It's good to have a dream,' he says.

'What are you thinking?' My cubicle mate Ruth wants to know. Ruth is micro-petite. A tiny brunette with

372

small hands and perfect bow-shaped lips. She just turned forty so we call our cubicle '—40 south' because of our ages, and the fact that we face the Statue of Liberty in the harbor of the Hudson River.

'Do you really want to know?'

She sits. 'It was something nice.'

'A man,' I shrug.

'Really?' Ruth moves her rolling desk chair closer to mine and leans in.

'I met a man at the train this morning. Alex Phillips. He's forty-four, divorced. One son. The son is in college. He works on the internet. He just moved to Chatham from Florida.'

'Cute?'

'Very.'

'Annie . . .' Ruth's voice has a warning tone.

'Don't even say it.'

'I know I don't have to – but you know, you want to shake your life up, but that's not a good way to shake it up.'

'Oh, I wouldn't have an affair,' I tell her.

'You have a lot of information about him.'

'Casual conversation.'

'That's how it starts,' Ruth says.

'How what starts?'

'New chapters.'

'I need more than a new chapter. And a new man is, let's face it, a whole new story entirely. I'm not throwing out my old Alex for a new one.'

'How do you know for sure?' Ruth lowers her voice to a whisper as the secretary to the CFO walks by.

'Because of my lunch.'

'What does your lunch have to do with anything?'

'I've eaten the same lunch every day for twelve years. I'm hardly a risk taker. Even when the man is adorable and available and has the bluest eyes I've ever seen.'

'I think you need to take a different train.'

'I've been thinking the same thing,' I tell her.

The 5.47 for Chatham is packed. There's not a seat, but the train car's air conditioning is working. I lean against the door and pull out a magazine.

'Ask me about my first day,' Alex says.

'How was your first day?' I ask him. I smile at him, happy to see him again. I don't like that I'm happy to see him again. And I was hoping to see him, and I don't like admitting that to myself either. So, I smile.

'You have a beautiful smile,' he says.

'I floss,' I tell him.

He laughs. 'You're funny,' he says.

'So I'm told.'

'All the good ones are taken,' Alex flirts.

I like that he flirts. 'Why do people always say that?'

'Say what?'

'That the good ones are taken? I mean, it can't be true. And maybe it's just the unavailability that's attractive – and not the person herself.'

'What are you saying?'

'If I wasn't wearing this ring for nineteen years, if I

wasn't married and I was looking, we would never meet. You see, that's the law of supply and demand – I learned that in twelve years of accounting.'

'Not very sexy,' he says.

'I'm not trying to be,' I tell him.

'You can't help it,' he smiles.

What is going on here? When my husband said forty wonderful on my birthday card, I'm sure he didn't mean this. What is it about me that new Alex likes? I'm wearing a trim linen suit and black patent leather high heels – but my eyebrows need shaping and my hair needs highlights. OK, I went for the tomato-red lipstick this morning – but it's suppertime and I've chewed it off. So, what is it that he sees?

'. . . some women . . .' he continues, 'just have that thing. And you have that thing, Annie.'

'I do?' I swear I'm not fishing, but I'm forty-one and don't I deserve a little unsolicited male attention? I'd never do anything – and maybe that's my problem – I never do anything.

'You run, don't you?' he says.

I almost laugh out loud – loudly. 'Run?'

'You have runner's legs.'

'They're not from running. They're from sitting in a cubicle.'

'Really?'

'Do you run?' I ask him.

'Every morning.'

'Why?'

He smiles again. 'It's my gift to myself. I'm out

there, alone – thinking and moving my body – the results are pretty great physically but it's the emotional part of it that helps the most.'

'How so?' Now, I'm intrigued.

'I race myself. It sounds silly, I guess. But it's a way for me to set a goal and meet it – without the influence or input of anyone else or anything. You know – we all need to push ourselves.'

'We do?'

'Oh yeah. And once you push yourself, you set a pattern in motion – a pattern that brings you excellence in all things.'

'You're serious.'

'When my wife left me, I wanted to die. She got tired of being married – and I guess tired of me. So one morning, I got up early and put on my tennis shoes and took off. I ran a long time – and only when I got so far from my house did I realise what I was doing. I was running from myself, I thought. But as I did it morning after morning – I began to realise that I was running towards something.'

'And what was that?'

'You have to run to find out,' he grins.

'What are you doing?' my husband says groggily from his side of the bed.

'I'm going for a run.'

He rolls over. 'It's five thirty in the morning.'

'I have a 7.40 train.'

'I know what train you take, Annie. Why are you running?'

'To get in shape.'

'I like your shape.'

'Be supportive.'

'How is that unsupportive?'

'I don't know.' I yank the laces tight on my sneakers. 'Encourage me to be better – don't expect less.'

'You're fine.'

'Maybe I want to be more than fine. Maybe I want to be the best I can be.'

Alex rolls over. 'Go run.' He gives up.

I walk past the girls' bedroom – it's neat and clean with stuffed animals along the headboards. I stop and smile. They're off to college and the house is empty, but it's a good empty. I miss them of course, but I did my time, and so I have no regrets. Besides, they're forever my girls, so they'll be back – and then that new chapter will begin – when they have their own families. I grab the keys and pull on my windbreaker. I unlock the door and push through the screen door, out on to our porch.

The sun is pulling up over our neighborhood on a swirling pattern of violet and peach. I haven't seen the sun come up since summer camp when I was ten years old. It's even more beautiful now than it was back then.

I close my eyes and inhale. I bend deeply from the waist as I learned in yoga class, then raise myself up slowly, vertebra by vertebra, aware of every bone in my long, sleek back (I imagine the long and sleek, as my instructor taught me). I raise my hands high over my head, and swish them in the air overhead, like a ballerina before she jumps. I exhale and open my eyes, listening to the stillness. I skip down the steps.

I run.

At first, I smile because I'm actually doing it. I'm running. I'm a runner! I set the alarm, woke early and actually did the thing I thought I'd never do. As my feet hit the pavement, I remember my form and lift my shoulders up and back, and loosen my arms and hands so they swing naturally and freely by my side. I looked up everything I needed to know about running, beginning a routine on the internet. I printed out the diagrams and hung them in my cubicle at work. Now, I'm off!

I feel the tug of my glutes through to my thighs as I press forward and connect with the ground below. I lift my abs high and pull them toward the small of my back, as I breathe rhythmically into the movement. Soon, I'm on the path to the park, and before me, I see other runners, who remind me of those runners I often passed on my way to work, feeling sorry for them, that they were running. I'm ashamed of myself. I am learning the lesson, thank you Alex Phillips. I am learning how to challenge myself when I believed there was nothing new for me to learn.

My heart beats faster and my breathing becomes a good pant as I speed up. When the challenge proves too great for my first run, the first of my life, I slow down and savor the form of my body as I move gracefully, slowly and surely. I have nothing to prove. I'm doing it.

'Hi gorgeous,' he says to me.

'Hi.' I look up at my husband.

'Didn't know it was you from behind,' he says.

'Oh, it's me.'

My husband puts his arms around me. 'I think I like the results of this running thing.'

'I think I do, too,' I tell him as he slides his hands over my hips.

'You're dedicated,' he says.

'My eight-month anniversary,' I tell him proudly.

'Every morning.'

'Every single morning, rain or shine.'

'Even winter.'

'Especially winter.'

My husband kisses me, and I pour all of myself into it. I'm in the moment. I remember when I wasn't in the moment − when I thought forty wonderful meant less than wonderful. What a difference a year makes.

'Annie?'

I look up from my newspaper as I wait at the Chatham station. The 7.40 a.m. train is late.

'Alex Phillips! Where have you been?'

'I joined a car pool.'

'Why?'

'I met a nice woman.'

'Good for you.'

379

'But now we have unmet,' he says.

'There will be more,' I promise him.

'How are you?' he asks.

'I'm running.'

He looks confused. 'You are?'

'Thanks to you. I just got up and put on my sneakers and took off.'

'I encouraged that?'

'Totally.'

'You're kidding.' Now, months later, he blushes.

'I thought there wasn't anything new left to learn – I don't know, to experience. And something you said months ago just clicked.'

'I thought I was flirting.'

'You were. And it worked,' I smile.

'You're happy.'

'I can't even tell you how happy I am,' I tell him.

'Good for you,' Alex Phillips says and means it.

We stand on the platform for a long time.

'Thank you,' I tell him. 'You shook me up.'

'I never had this effect on a woman,' he says.

This time, I laugh. 'You do, and you just didn't know it.'

The 7.40 a.m. pulls into the station, I climb into the second car, crowded and full, while Alex Phillips splinters off and goes into the third car.

I don't wish he'd have followed me, and I don't feel sad that he didn't – I have a moment of complete and utter peace instead. I remember asking him, why he runs, and what he was running to – and he told me that

I would find the answer when I ran myself. And I found the answer, every morning, with every run.

I was running towards home. Home.

Tokyo Girl Power

BY JOANNA TROLLOPE

*W*hen he was twenty-six, my brother fell in love with a male impersonator. Yes, you heard me. A male impersonator. A woman dressed as a man, performing as a man, for a living. And what is more, she was Japanese.

I don't think our parents are particularly narrow-minded but they're easily thrown off balance with something unfamiliar, something they don't know. So when she heard about the Japanese male impersonator, my mother began, at once, to fret about how would she ever see her Japanese grandchildren and would they speak English? And Dad said after a pause, 'Is she a lesbian?'

'Ignore him,' I told my brother.

'I am,' Matt said, 'and she's not. She's an otokoyaku.'

'A what?'

'An otokoyaku. She plays the male roles. She isn't the star of her troupe but . . .' proudly, '. . . she's the next best thing.'

My brother worked in an international bank's head

office, in the City of London, travelling every day from Slough, where we grew up. Not particularly exciting. He had his job, a flat he shared with two guys from school, the rugby club, and Sophie, his girlfriend since they were both fifteen. When I got married, Matt was our best man, and Sophie caught my bouquet (apricot and cream roses), and everyone said ah, bless, like they do, that'll be the next wedding, won't it?

But it wasn't. Matt went on just the same and Sophie began to look a bit tense and gaunt. So I said to Matt, using my usual bossy elder sister licence, 'What are you going to do about Sophie, Matt? Aren't you going to ask her to marry you?'

And he looked out of my kitchen window, as I was spooning apple purée into the baby – and said, 'I can't. I'm going to Japan.'

He'd asked his manager, it seemed, saying that he felt stuck in a rut, but that he didn't want to leave. And after a few weeks, his manager called him in and said there was a vacancy going, to assist in managing expatriate accounts, in Tokyo.

'Tokyo!' Matt said. He couldn't even picture Tokyo, at that moment, on his mental globe. 'Japan, you mean?'

His manager looked at him.

'That's the one,' he said.

We couldn't believe it, none of us. We were stunned. Mum cried buckets, but Sophie didn't. She just went very pale, and very quiet, and then she took herself off to a friend in Edinburgh.

'You're a fool,' I told Matt.

He was packing. Throwing things into a case in no order.

'You've always thought that,' he said. 'What's new?'

He had a service flat in Marunouchi, the business district of Tokyo. I expected sliding screens and tatami mats, but he said it was actually very Western, only barer and the lavatory had an electrically heated seat and a button you pressed for a hygienic water spray. He said Tokyo and the Japanese were very clean and there was almost no litter, the taxis had white lace seat covers and the older drivers wore white cotton gloves. He said the subway was efficient, and safe – girls could travel late, dressed in hot pants and thigh boots, without being bothered. He said there was no tipping – the Japanese expected to give and receive good service, and that the younger, bolder people stared openly at his blue eyes.

I know, especially at the beginning, that he was lonely, quietly and acutely so. There were two other Englishmen in his section, but older, with Japanese families, and the younger men went drinking and clubbing in a dedicated way Matt didn't feel quite comfortable with. Whatever happened after six in the evening, whatever was said, was never referred to again, and this left him with a hangover from too much saké, and no real friends. It was hard.

He did his best; I'll say that for him. With a guide book, he set off to explore Tokyo, to look at the wacky teenagers parading in Harajuku on Sunday mornings, to Shibuya on Friday nights. He took the monorail across to Odaiba and watched neat couples and families, sitting on the man-made beach below Rainbow Bridge watching the flying fish, flipping in the sunset. He went to the Shinto shrines in Akasaka and Zojo-ji, he climbed the Tokyo Tower, he stood under the giant TV screen beside Shinjuku Station, apparently Tokyo's favourite meeting place; he went window shopping in Ginza. And then returning to his bare flat, via a cheap noodle bar, he'd e-mail me.

I said, 'Why don't you tell Sophie all this?'

'Can't,' Matt said.

I think, despite all this, he was getting pretty low. He couldn't say so, and he sent lovely things back at Christmas, the kind of things that would never have occurred to him before, like embroidered slippers and a padded coat for the baby, with a dragon on the back, and red piping. He spent Christmas Day alone, watching a DVD of great football goals, drinking Sapporo beer, and he said I wasn't to tell anyone.

I didn't. But I was really relieved when Mr Nori began to appear in the e-mails. He was a senior assistant manager in Matt's section, and he spoke some English. He was older than the others, Matt said, and a great smiler. When he smiled, or laughed, his eyes disappeared into the other lines in his face, so he was just a big mouth of laughing teeth.

Mr Nori was not just unusual in that he was so genial, but because he asked Matt to come out to his house, and have a meal. Matt had been told that he wouldn't be asked to a Japanese house, because of the commuting distance problem, and because Japanese houses were considered too small to welcome big Westerners. But Mr Nori's wife wanted to see Matt, at their home, so he was to take a train out to the suburbs – one and a half hours – on Saturday.

He was quite nervous, he said. He remembered to wear clean socks, and he bought Mrs Nori some English tea in a heritage tin, wrapped up like a present, and whisky for Mr Nori – Chivas Regal seemed to be the thing – also wrapped, in red paper, with ribbons. He expected their house to be made of light timber, or even paper, to be in a pretty street of similar houses with ornamental ponds in front, and willow and cherry trees, and little lacquered bridges. But it was a small grey-beige house, in a narrow grey-beige street, and the only tree in sight was a plastic one, in the Noris' front garden, under which crouched a plastic rabbit. He felt, he said, the size of an elephant.

Mrs Nori was small, and also smiling. She wore a kimono and white toe-split socks. She took away his jacket and his shoes, and ushered him into a long, narrow room, with a smooth wooden floor and almost no furniture beyond a huge, cream leather Western-style sofa in front of a vast plasma TV screen. Around the sofa was a scattering of wooden tables on which were prominently displayed over a dozen photographs, in silver frames and bamboo frames and frames of fancy gilding. They struck Matt because they were all of the same person, a young woman, and they were all posed and formal and the girl was made up to the nines.

Mrs Nori made Matt sit on the sofa. He gestured at the photographs.

'Your daughter?'

The Japanese, apparently, don't like saying no. So Mr Nori laughed uproariously and said that he and his wife were just two people.

'No children?'

Both Noris laughed again. Mrs Nori gestured towards the nearest photograph – the girl was very strangely dressed in a red sequinned waistcoat and a ludicrously ruffled shirt – and said something in Japanese, beaming at my brother. He looked at Mr Nori.

'My wife is in fan club,' Mr Nori said.

'Fan club?'

'Takarazuka,' Mr Nori said. 'She is big fan. Her mother is big fan. Her sister is big fan. This girl is big star. Not top top star, but big star. My wife takes her lunch box sometimes. Fish, pickled vegetables, rice, cake. You like cake?'

The girl, it transpired, was called Shakiko, known to her adorers as Kiko. She was a member of the Takarazuka Revue, Western-style musical shows using only unmarried women, with audiences – mostly women – of over two and a half million a year. The most important, and popular, stars of this revue were the otokoyaku, who took the male roles, and Kiko was one of those. She had been selected – from thousands of applicants – when she was sixteen, and she was now twenty-four and in her golden period. She had had big roles in *Manon*, and *Guys and Dolls*, and a version of *Aïda* called *Song of the Kingdom*. Her greatest role was in *The Rose of Versailles*, an adaptation from Japanese manga. Her fan club was official, devoted, and responsible for her comforts and her reputation.

'Is whole life!' said Mr Nori, smiling broadly. 'When she is not here, in house, she is doing fan club for Kiko!' He clapped his hands together. He had thought of a joke. 'In Japan, men have geisha! In Japan, women have Takarazuka!'

Matt looked at the photographs. The girl, despite the mask-like make-up, was very, very pretty.

'Could I meet her?'

Mr Nori laughed tremendously. 'No boyfriend allowed! Not permitted boyfriend!'

Matt looked at Mrs Nori.

'Could I come with you? To the Revue? To see her on stage?'

The Takarazuka Theatre in Tokyo was enormous, with a special revolving stage and a walkway, called the Silver Bridge, which took the girls right out into the audience. There must have been thousands and thousands of women there, Matt said, and almost no men, and only one Westerner. Him. He said the atmosphere was as reverent as in a church and he felt really, really privileged to be there. He said he didn't mind the sentimentality, or the melodrama, or the over-lavish feathered outfits, because the whole thing was just fantastic. Kiko, dressed as a matador, stamping her glossy booted feet, was the most fantastic thing of all.

Mrs Nori let him wait with her at the stage door, because he was a blue-eyed Westerner, and that gave him status. Kiko's fan club had to wait below the top star's fan club, and the front row of fans had to kneel, to give the back row a good view of the star. There was no pushing, or screaming, or jostling. The star's glory would be diminished if her fans behaved badly. When Kiko came out, dressed in a man's tuxedo, with her short, bronzed hair tucked behind her ears, and a mannish swagger, Matt said he was ready to faint.

He could think, after that, of nothing else. He badgered Mr Nori to badger Mrs Nori until he was allowed to come in the car once or twice when Mrs Nori drove Kiko to rehearsals. Kiko spoke English. Without looking at him, she told him that English conversation was part of a Takarasienne's training, along with ballet, modern and traditional dance, tap, music, theatre history, singing, tea ceremony and etiquette. She told him that the Takarazuka motto – Be pure, be proper, be beautiful – was very strictly observed. She told him that the first-year girls have to clean the dormitories for everyone else, with mops and brushes, to teach them humility. She told him she had never had a boyfriend, but that there was a rich industrialist who wanted to marry her when she was twenty-five, the classic Japanese age for marriage.

'And will you?' Matt said. He said his knuckles were white with clenching.

'I don't want to be married,' Kiko said. Then she flicked a glance at him, the first time she had ever looked his way. 'I am an artist,' she said.

His e-mails were obsessed. He could only write about Kiko. Because he was a Westerner, because he was being promoted, because he had blue eyes, Matt was allowed to see Kiko sometimes, in Mrs Nori's house, discreetly, away from any possibility of being seen. He couldn't kiss her, he couldn't even hold her hand, but they could talk and he could gaze and gaze. He said he loved it that she had trained herself to be a man, because she was so much a girl and the contrast was electrifying. She gave him a signed photograph of herself in a white spangled suit and a silver top hat, and one, which he cherished, of her when she first went to the Takarazuka Music School, one of the most competitive schools in the world, dressed in the school uniform of white blouse, grey flannel skirt and jacket, and red tie, with her then black hair in pigtails.

It went on for a whole year, and by the end of that year, Matt's Japanese was good, his manners were better, and he was almost dead with frustration. He decided to take the plunge. Kiko had shown herself more than happy to be in his company, more than ready with the favours that the rules permitted, so, one afternoon when Mrs Nori was brewing yet more green tea, he went down on one knee beside the cream sofa, and asked Kiko to marry him.

'Get up,' she said.

'Not until—'

'Get up,' she said, 'in Japan, it is women who kneel.'

'Did you hear me?'

'Perhaps,' she said.

'Will you marry me? I am absolutely mad about you and I'll do anything and everything to make you happy.'

Kiko looked at her lap.

'I don't want to marry.'

'Don't you love me?'

She looked at him. She said, 'I love you.'

'Well then—'

'But I can't marry. I love you but I won't marry you.'

'Why on earth not?'

'Because,' she said, 'I love what I do more.'

He said he got angry then. He accused her of being addicted to adoration, like some silly pop star, he told her that her best days in the Takarazuka were over, that she was trying to live a fantasy, that she was afraid of reality.

'This is reality,' Kiko said. 'For hundreds and thousands of women, this is reality. They need this idealisation of men. I belong in the life that helps them to bear what they bear. In Japan, they have much to bear.'

'You'll be too old, soon,' Matt said angrily, cruelly.

Kiko wasn't in the least upset.

'I shall join the Special Troupe. I'll have parts for decades. I'll get other acting work.'

'Don't you need me?'

She sighed. She was wearing a girl version of English cricketing clothes, cream flannel and wool, with a blazer. He said she looked adorable.

'I love you,' she said, 'but I don't need you. Not like I need this. This is a calling for me. Nothing will ever satisfy me like this does.'

He shuffled over so that he was kneeling close to her. He took her hands. For the first time. And she didn't pull away.

'Are you sure?' Matt said.

She looked at him. She smiled. She said, 'Completely,' and then she leaned forwards and kissed him quietly on the mouth.

He was in an awful state when he came home. The bank acted very generously really, and gave him an even better position than before, and he took a room in a colleague's house in Battersea and we didn't see him properly for months.

I think he went a bit wild. He certainly looked as if he had and I got quite angry with him because Mum and Dad were worrying about him all the time and I had two children by then so I didn't have the time or energy to prop them up as well as everything else.

'Grow up,' I said to Matt. 'Grow up and accept

what's happened and stop behaving like a stroppy teenager.'

And he did stop. Not then, of course, but just after his twenty-eighth birthday, he appeared at Mum and Dad's, with Sophie, and she'd had her hair cut, and she looked much better, and she was wearing a ring on her engagement finger. She's a lovely person, Sophie, but you couldn't really call her pretty. But she looked pretty that day, in Mum's kitchen, not able to help fiddling with her ring.

They've got a baby now, Matt and Sophie, and live the other side of Newbury, so we don't see all that much of them, but I think they're happy. The baby is lovely and Matt's a great father, and if he thinks about Tokyo and Kiko now – I wouldn't know about it. Sometimes, I wonder if he's got those photographs of her, hidden somewhere to remind him of all those hopes and dreams. Or perhaps he has trained himself never to think of her again.

The odd thing is, that I haven't. I think about Kiko quite regularly, and I never met her. I'll be forty next birthday, one of those birthdays that makes you take stuff out of your mental cupboards and have a look at it. And I'm looking at my own hopes and dreams, and realising that I never had enough of them, I was never ambitious enough, never sufficiently curious or adventurous or – or certain. But Kiko was. Kiko knew what she wanted and what would make her happy, and it wasn't the conventional things that society and up-bringing and magazines tell you will make you happy.

It was something else, something to do, very much, with romance and with love, but not in the conventional way, not the way featuring a man, and wedding bells. Kiko understood it, and she understood that it would serve her better in the long run, than even Matt's love would. So she made her choice. She was serenely certain of it, and I envy her that. I really do.

A Charitable Woman

BY JANE ELIZABETH VARLEY

I do not hate my sister-in-law. Hate is not a nice word. Miss Harrison told me so, and even though her powdered, whiskered face last looked down on me some forty years ago, her instruction remains with me to this day. 'You may dislike someone, Anne. But it is not nice to hate them.' Caroline Cresswell had refused to let me into the play kitchen. I still hated her, but I learned not to say so.

In less than an hour we are due to leave but Martin is in the kitchen reading the Sunday newspapers. He likes to keep up and get new ideas for assembly. I step out of the shower and dry myself, then check the spot that the doctors identify as four o'clock. Nothing. I dry my hair and apply a new brand of mousse spray, which is my latest weapon in the war against my hair. I remember that I must plug in my electric rollers.

When Tessa is going to be there I always make an effort. She is, after all, a hairdresser and the owner of two salons. We are going to Martin's parents for Sunday lunch. It is my mother-in-law's birthday. More often than not, Tessa and Ed are absent from family get-togethers now that they have the flat in Spain. Ed is Martin's younger brother. Ed, the brother who didn't go to university, has done very well for himself.

When I was about ten, Miss Harrison stood up in assembly and said goodbye. The teachers presented her with a watercolour of the school. She told us God had a plan for her and his plan was for her to go to South America to help the children there. I wondered then when you got given your plan.

I look at myself in the steamy mirror. My scar is pale now, longer than I had imagined it would be, a crescent. But officially I am a survivor. My five- and ten-year prognosis is not merely good but very good. I am testament to the wisdom of self-examination and early treatment. Except I didn't find it myself. Martin did, one evening when we were lying on the sofa and he slipped his hand inside my bra. That's the advantage of being married to a science teacher, he has an enquiring hand. I never told the hospital staff though, just lapped up the compliments for finding it. I think Miss Harrison would have had something to say about that.

I open the bathroom door and shout down the stairs for Martin to get ready.

A few years ago, Martin's school started sending shoeboxes filled with Christmas gifts to children in poor countries. It was Mrs Baxter's idea, naturally, which she then asked Martin to implement. You should know that in recent years Mrs Baxter's partiality to a tipple got a little out of hand. Martin was already doing the Christmas concert so I took on the shoe-boxes. The dining room was filled floor to ceiling with them. Mrs Baxter had set an arbitrary target of 200. By the end, I was trekking round McDonald's, begging for toys. Martin's mother, Stella, did three. I even called Tessa to ask if she would do one. There was a pause. Then, 'No. I don't think so. I mean, you never know if they're going to reach the right people, do you?'

No. You don't. And frankly, I feel the same way about cancer. Not that anyone actually deserves it. But aged forty-two I was classified as a young patient. In the days after my diagnosis I would look around at all the old women in the food department in Marks & Spencer and I would think, why me? How come this crabby-looking bunch get to see their grandchildren grow up and I don't?

I should be accurate here and say I don't actually have any grandchildren. I have two sons. Richard is twenty-two and at university in Edinburgh. Chris will be eighteen in a couple of months' time. Richard sailed through but Chris's grades are iffy and he's going to wait until he gets his A-level results before he makes any decisions. Chris was fifteen when I was diagnosed. It's a difficult age anyway.

I apply body lotion in the cramped and humid bath-room. I am heavier now but I can't honestly blame that on the cancer. My waist effectively disappeared after Chris was born and now I am barrel-shaped I look back on my old pear-shape with fond memories. I think about my sister-in-law, Tessa, who is probably alone in her bathroom now, too. A couple of years ago they extended their house to add an en-suite. It is this bathroom, carpeted in pale pink and tiled in marble, that Tessa uses. Ed has been banished to the old bathroom on the landing. Of course, it was cheaper for them because Ed is a builder. And they have no children, only a dog to support, Sherlock, who is a Scottie with a wardrobe of tartan coats and collars.

I looked through each of the donated shoeboxes. Some people were generous. They gave little toys with their labels still attached, brand-new face flannels and miniature bars of soap. Others filled them with tat. So I tried to even them up so that everyone got something nice. Chris was going through an anarchist phase at the time – why are you bothering, Mum? It's not your responsibility. But I think Miss Harrison would have approved.

When the boys were little, we had a pale blue paddling pool which I would fill with six inches of water from the hose-pipe, feeling guilty because of water shortages. The boys loved it. Life was simpler back then, people didn't seem to shop so much, they didn't have so much stuff. Ed and Tessa's house in Spain has a pool. We haven't been. Ed posts the photographs on the internet.

Our house is a 1930s semi, the type estate agents say would benefit from updating. The bathroom is an unfashionable shade of pale blue. As for the kitchen, the kindest thing one can say is that it is lived-in. I work part-time, doing admin for a firm of insurance brokers. I work with Judith and Liz and we've all been there for years. I joined as a temp planning to stay for six weeks to earn some extra money for Christmas.

I am, according to the local newspaper, a brave cancer mum. It's true that I'm a mum but I'm not sure I was brave. I didn't have any choice, did I? Last year, Judith and Liz signed up for a five-kilometre walk for cancer research. Well, I couldn't not join in. We raised a total of £5,345 and the local newspaper sent a photographer. I would have preferred not to have the publicity but it's good for the charity. I admire women with breast cancer who get photographed. The celebrities. But that is not my style. I want to be normal or at least anonymous. Sometimes, in the cycle of disbelief, anger and acceptance, I think I may still be in disbelief. But nearly three years on that can't be possible?

After the shoebox incident I didn't ask Tessa to sponsor me.

A few years ago, I saw Ed coming out of a pub with a young girl. I was in the car, stopped by the lights. They were laughing and he had his hand on her shoulder but that's not to say she couldn't have been a business colleague. He didn't see me and I never mentioned it.

By the time Martin has showered, I am half-dressed with my scalp burning from the scorching rollers. I think the thermostat is broken. Chris is still in his pyjamas. He says, 'Mum, I've got coursework . . .' but this is rubbish. There is an Arsenal match on and he wants to stay at home to watch it. I tell him he has to go and he stalks off moaning to himself.

I hate that I am losing my boys and I mean it, Miss Harrison or not. The old days are gone and I miss them like hell. I ache for my little boys and the days of sunshine and the six inches of water in the paddling pool. The days were longer then. How did it go by so quickly? I want to stop women with small children when I see them in Sainsbury's and tell them to live every sweet, precious, perfect day. Don't do what I did, I will urge them, trailing behind them like a lunatic. I took it all for granted.

Martin does not understand this. 'It's natural. They're young men. They want to go out into the world.' Sometimes it seemed to me that he was pushing them away and we argued about it.

'Anne, they need to break out. They need to see the world.'

'Do they?' I spat back once. 'Or do you?'

It was Martin's idea that Richard apply to Edinburgh. The department there is apparently one of the best. Chris wants to stay close to home and I can't say I'm sorry. The anarchist phase appears to be at an end now that he has his driving licence.

When I was first diagnosed, I got a bit ahead of myself and started making a guest list for the funeral. When you start thinking about it, there's a lot to plan. As well as the guests, there are the readings and the hymns and, if like me you are the type who pays attention to detail, the flowers and typeface for the order of service. Martin found my list. He was furious. He was so angry he was almost crying. 'If you want to think about the future,' he shouted, 'go to a travel agent and get some brochures.' Once Chris finishes his A-levels, we're going to China.

We arrive at Martin's parents' house and pull on to the driveway. There is no sign of Tessa's car, a BMW two-seater that they use at the weekend. Ed has a van for work. Tessa has two salons now, which have been renamed 'Teddy's Spa and Salon'. She asks me from time to time to go in for a free hairdo or, worse still, a spa day. I say that I'll call but I never do. I didn't lose my hair, by the way. No chemo deemed necessary. Out with the pesky lump, in with several bursts of radiation and off you go with a prescription for tamoxifen. My cancer, it turned out, was small and contained and obedient. Not radical or invasive. If my cancer had been a person it would have shopped somewhere safe and voted Conservative.

Tessa shops at 'Collection', a designer boutique, and goes to the gym five times a week. Ed likes to tell us that, twelve years after the event, she can still fit into her wedding dress.

We go in and I present my mother-in-law with a Marks & Spencer's basket arrangement with an African violet and a small chrysanthemum and her present, a set of placemats. Chris kisses her and asks if he can go and watch the match. Martin hands his father a bottle of red wine. It will play out as it always does. Sherry in the lounge, two wooden bowls of dry-roasted peanuts on the G-Plan coffee table, then into the dining room, which will be bloody freezing because his father always forgets to turn on the radiator. Frankly, the whole house is on the chilly side.

Miss Harrison's death in Guatemala was reported in the local newspaper. The headline said 'A charitable woman'. She had died suddenly from a heart attack. It said that Miss Harrison was a woman who had devoted her life to helping others.

I think Martin has done that and I bloody well hope he gets his reward in heaven because there's been precious little down here lately. When Mrs Baxter retired, or was pushed, depending on whether you believe the education department rumours, Martin was the obvious choice for Head. And then I was diagnosed. Of course, you hope for the best and plan for the worst. A headship would have meant longer hours, training weekends, summer courses away from home. The new Head's younger than Martin, can you credit it? He's got a Masters in Early Childhood Education. Youth and qualifications, that's what they seem to look for nowadays.

I join my mother-in-law in the kitchen. I am dismayed, but not surprised, to see that she has already boiled the Brussels sprouts and carrots to death and decanted them into her hostess trolley, presumably to kill off any lingering vitamins. I should not complain. My mother-in-law cooked and cleaned and ran Chris into school. She is someone who means it when she asks can I help? Martin is her favourite. She will, just occasionally, let slip some sharp aside about 'Ed's toys', meaning the hot tub or the boat they sold after a year. 'That's what happens when people don't have children. It's not as if there's a problem. They would have said . . .' Stella was a teacher. She would have liked Miss Harrison.

When I was in hospital, Tessa and Ed sent flowers and visited once when I got home. They brought Sherlock, which was a blessing because it gave us something to talk about. There was talk of getting a Holmes and a discussion of the psychological effect of this on Sherlock. Some people, when they hear that you have got cancer they do a double take, first at your boobs and then your hair, checking if you're real or fake. Ed did that.

Tessa and Ed arrive. My sister-in-law is tanned and glossy, heavily made-up and dressed up in a pale beige suede trouser suit. Ed is in Pringle. Sherlock is in Black Watch tartan. We are crowded into the kitchen.

Tessa hands Stella an enormous cellophane-wrapped bouquet crammed with lilies and roses and Ed says that her present will be delivered tomorrow. It's a thirty-seven-inch plasma television, he announces. I can think of nothing nice to say about this. Ed puts his arm around his mother. 'Next year, we'll take you to the Ritz.' He is referring to Stella's seventieth. Do they sit around thinking of new ways to spend even more money? Tessa turns to me. 'How's the job, Anne?' It is boring and undemanding. 'Very busy,' I reply. 'It's our year end.'

I look at Tessa's manicured hands. She has beautiful rings. Next to her wedding ring is a diamond the size of a peanut.

We sit down to lunch and soon all conversation is impossible because Martin's father brings out the electric carving knife. Stella likes everything well-done and power is needed to slice through the beef. When we are able to start talking again, Ed tells us about a house he is refurbishing. It is, he tells us, a seven-figure job. In the early days, I took it all at face value but now I wonder how much of it is true? Ed is a boastful little boy. Miss Harrison would instruct him not to tell fibs. Chris is eating at breakneck speed to get back to the television and I glare at him but he ignores me.

Then Ed puts his knife and fork down. 'Tessa's got some news to tell you.' His tone is portentous. I look up at her across the table.

Another salon? Car? House? Diamond? Dog? I am shocked at how hostile I feel towards her.

'I haven't,' she says, clearly caught off guard. She looks at me, then down at her plate.

'It's nothing to be ashamed of,' Ed protests.

And I can see that Tessa is embarrassed and whatever it is that Ed is about to say she is desperate to detach herself.

'Not now, Ed.'

He ignores her. 'Tessa's having her boobs done. Aug-ment-a-tion,' he pronounces heavily. 'And I say why not?'

'Ed,' Tessa hisses.

He looks at her, his expression one of stupid incomprehension, the same one I have seen a few times before. 'What? They're a woman's best asset, aren't they?'

There is a silence. And as I turn, I see that Martin's colour has risen. Chris is eating doggedly.

So Tessa will be even more perfect.

And at that moment, I hate my sister-in-law. I hate her for her body, her money and her looks. I hate her for every clean and pure cell in her body.

Years of festering anger and injustice rise up inside me. And I am about to tell Tessa and Ed exactly what I feel. 'Do you ever think about anyone except yourselves?'

And then two totally unexpected things happen.

Martin's voice rings out. 'Shut up, Ed.'

And Tessa silently mouths to me, 'I'm sorry.'

I am caught off guard. I am stunned by the pain and vulnerability in her eyes. I hold her gaze even though I don't want to. For the first time in thirteen years, we make a connection with each other. And all at once I understand everything that I have known and yet failed to comprehend in all the years that have gone before.

I understand that Tessa could not have children. I know that she is lonely. I see that Ed – insensitive, philandering, lying Ed – is all that she has. I realise why she loves that pampered dog so much.

I see her and not myself.

I understand that I do not hate Tessa. I hate the

407

parts of my life she holds up to me. I hate my thickened body, my ageing bones, my scar.

And I mouth back, 'So am I.'

And I know that next time she invites me to the salon for the day I must say yes.

Miss Harrison wouldn't have wanted to go either. But it's what Miss Harrison would have done.

The Book Lovers' Appreciation Society

breast
cancer
care

Breast Cancer Care is here for anyone affected by breast cancer. We bring people together, provide information and support, and campaign for improved standards of care. We use our understanding of people's experience of breast cancer and our clinical expertise in everything we do.

Every year more and more people need our support. By buying this book, you are helping us to be there for every one of them. We are also enormously grateful to Orion Books and *woman&home* for their generous support in bringing this book to you.

If you would like more information about our work, you can visit www.breastcancercare.org.uk or call our free helpline on 0808 800 6000.